Praise for #1 *New York Times* and *USA TODAY* bestselling author

NORA ROBERTS

"Roberts nails her characters and settings with awesome precision, drawing readers into a vividly rendered world of family-centered warmth."
—*Library Journal*

"Roberts has a warm feel for her characters and an eye for the evocative detail."
—*Chicago Tribune*

"Some estimates have [Nora Roberts] selling 12 books an hour, 24 hours a day, 7 days a week, 52 weeks a year."
—*New York Times Magazine*

"The publishing world might be hard-pressed to find an author with a more diverse style or fertile imagination than Roberts."
—*Publishers Weekly*

"Nora Roberts' gift…is her ability to pull the reader into the lives of her characters—we live, love, anguish and triumph with them."
—*Rendezvous*

"Romance will never die as long as the megaselling Roberts keeps writing."
—*Kirkus Reviews*

Dear Reader,

When there's a storm coming, you can feel it in the air. There's a sense of anticipation and excitement, a feeling that it will blow away what's old, and sweep in something new.

In *Second Nature,* Lee Radcliffe is definitely dealing with a force of nature, and its name is Hunter Brown. Dark, mysterious and untamed, he shakes the foundations of her neat and orderly world. Hunter refuses to settle for anything but all of Lee, including the pieces she's kept hidden, even from herself. But when Lee turns the tables and digs into Hunter's secrets, will he be as open with her as he demands she be with him?

Carlo Franconi has no secrets in *Lessons Learned*. As a celebrity, he's out there for everyone to see—and they can't get enough of him, especially his female fans. He enters publicist Juliet Trent's world like a tornado, eliminating her carefully built defenses. But as a successful and independent businesswoman, Juliet can't afford to be swept up by Carlo, and she refuses to be just another one of his conquests. Still, she doesn't count on Carlo's determination...or her own desire to give in and enjoy the ride.

In these two classic stories, Nora Roberts evokes a potent combination of emotion and passion that you won't soon forget.

The Editors,

Silhouette Books

NORA ROBERTS

Sweet Rains

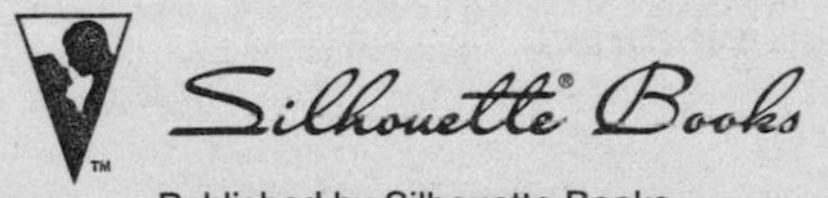

Published by Silhouette Books
America's Publisher of Contemporary Romance

Recycling programs for this product may not exist in your area.

SWEET RAINS

ISBN-13: 978-0-373-28590-7

This edition published by arrangement with Harlequin Books S.A.

For questions and comments about the quality of this book please contact us at Customer_eCare@Harlequin.ca.

Visit Silhouette Books at www.eHarlequin.com

Printed in U.S.A.

CONTENTS

Also available from Silhouette Books and Harlequin Books by

NORA ROBERTS

WORTH THE RISK
Putting it all on the line for love

DUETS
Two timeless stories about love's power and endurance

NIGHT TALES: NIGHT SHIFT & NIGHT SHADOW
Containing the first two books in the thrilling Night Tales series

NIGHT TALES: NIGHTSHADE & NIGHT SMOKE
The fabulous Night Tales series continues with books three and four

NIGHT TALES: NIGHT SHIELD & NIGHT MOVES
The final book in our Night Tales series, plus a riveting bonus story

SUMMER DREAMS
Two classic stories of believing in the impossible

And coming soon
SECRETS & SUNSETS

SECOND NATURE

To Deb Horm, for the mutual memories.

Prologue

...with the moon full and white and cold. He saw the shadows shift and shiver like living things over the ice-crusted snow. Black on white. Black sky, white moon, black shadows, white snow. As far as he could see there was nothing else. There was such emptiness, an absence of color, the only sound the whistling moan of wind through naked trees. But he knew he wasn't alone, that there was no safety in the black or the white. Through his frozen heart moved a trickle of hot fear. His breath, labored, almost spent, puffed out in small white clouds. Over the frosted ground fell a black shadow. There was no place left to run.

Hunter drew on his cigarette, then stared at the words on the terminal through a haze of smoke. Michael Trent was dead. Hunter had created him, molded him exclusively for that cold, pitiful death under a full moon. He felt a sense of accomplishment rather than remorse for destroying the man he knew more intimately than he knew himself.

He'd end the chapter there, however, leaving the details of Michael's murder to the reader's imagination. The mood was set, secrets hinted at, doom tangible but unexplained. He knew his habit of doing just that both frustrated and fascinated his following. Since that was precisely his purpose, he was pleased. He often wasn't.

He created the terrifying, the breathtaking, the unspeakable. Hunter explored the darkest nightmares of the human mind and, with cool precision, made them tangible. He made the impossible plausible and the uncanny commonplace. The commonplace he would often turn into something chilling. He used words the way an artist used a palette and he fabricated stories of such color and simplicity a reader was drawn in from the first page.

His business was horror, and he was phenomenally successful.

For five years he'd been considered the master of his particular game. He'd had six runaway bestsellers, four of which he'd transposed into screenplays for feature films. The critics raved, sales soared, letters poured in from fans all over the world. Hunter couldn't have cared less. He wrote for himself first, because the telling of a story was what he did best. If he entertained with his writing, he was satisfied. But whatever reaction the critics and the readers had, he'd still have written. He had his work; he had his privacy. These were the two vital things in his life.

He didn't consider himself a recluse; he didn't consider himself unsociable. He simply lived his life exactly as he chose. He'd done the same thing six years before...before the fame, success and large advances.

If someone had asked him if having a string of bestsellers had changed his life, he'd have answered, why should it? He'd been a writer before *The Devil's Due* had shot to number one on the *New York Times* list. He was a writer now. If he'd wanted his life to change, he'd have become a plumber.

Some said his lifestyle was calculated—that he created the image of an eccentric for effect. Good promotion. Some said he raised wolves. Some said he didn't exist at all but was a clever product of a publisher's imagination. But Hunter Brown had a fine disregard for what anyone said. Invariably, he listened only to what he wanted to hear, saw only what he chose to see and remembered everything.

After pressing a series of buttons on his word processor, he set up for the next chapter. The next chapter, the next word, the next book, was of much more importance to him than any speculative article he might read.

He'd worked for six hours that day, and he thought he was good for at least two more. The story was flowing out of him like ice water: cold and clear.

The hands that played the keys of the machine were beautiful—tanned, lean, long-fingered and wide-palmed. One might have looked at them and thought they would compose concertos or epic poems. What they composed were dark dreams and monsters—not the dripping-fanged, scaly-skinned variety, but monsters real enough to make the flesh crawl. He always included enough realism, enough of the everyday, in his stories to make the horror commonplace and all too plausible. There was a creature lurking in the dark closet of his work, and that creature was the private fear of every man. He found it, always. Then, inch by inch, he opened the closet door.

Half-forgotten, the cigarette smoldered in the overflowing ashtray at his elbow. He smoked too much. It was perhaps the only outward sign of the pressure he put on himself, a pressure he'd have tolerated from no one else. He wanted this book finished by the end of the month, his self-imposed deadline. In one of his rare impulses, he'd agreed to speak at a writers' conference in Flagstaff the first week of June.

It wasn't often he agreed to public appearances, and when he did it was never at a large, publicized event. This particular conference would boast no more than two hundred published and aspiring writers. He'd give his workshop, answer questions, then go home. There would be no speaker's fee.

That year alone, Hunter had summarily turned down offers from some of the most prestigious organizations in the publishing business. Prestige didn't interest him, but he considered, in his odd way, the contribution to the Central Arizona Writers' Guild a matter of paying his dues. Hunter had always understood that nothing was free.

It was late afternoon when the dog lying at his feet lifted his head. The dog was lean, with a shining gray coat and the narrow, intelligent look of a wolf.

"Is it time, Santanas?" With a gentleness the hand appeared made for, Hunter reached down to stroke the dog's head. Satisfied, but already deciding that he'd work late that evening, he turned off his word processor.

Hunter stepped out of the chaos of his office into the tidy living room with its tall, many-paned windows and lofted ceiling. It smelled of vanilla and daisies. Large and sleek, the dog padded alongside him.

After pushing open the doors that led to a terra-cotta patio, he looked into the thick surrounding woods. They shut him in, shut others out. Hunter had never considered which, only knew that he needed them. He needed the peace, the mystery and the beauty, just as he needed the rich red walls of the canyon that rose up around him. Through the quiet he could hear the trickle of water from the creek and smell the heady freshness of the air. These he never took for granted; he hadn't had them forever.

Then he saw her, walking leisurely down the winding path toward the house. The dog's tail began to swish back and forth.

Sometimes, when he watched her like this, Hunter would think it impossible that anything so lovely belonged to him. She was dark and delicately formed, moving with a careless confidence that made him grin even as it made him ache. She was Sarah. His work and his privacy were the two vital things in his life. Sarah was his life. She'd been worth the struggles, the frustration, the fears and the pain. She was worth everything.

Looking over, she broke into a smile that flashed with braces. *"Hi, Dad!"*

Chapter 1

The week a magazine like *Celebrity* went to bed was utter chaos. Every department head was in a frenzy. Desks were littered, phones were tied up and lunches were skipped. The air was tinged with a sense of panic that built with every hour. Tempers grew short, demands outrageous. In most offices the lights burned late into the night. The rich scent of coffee and the sting of tobacco smoke were never absent. Rolls of antacids were consumed and bottles of eye drops constantly changed hands. After five years on staff, Lee took the monthly panic as a matter of course.

Celebrity was a slick, respected publication whose sales generated millions of dollars a year. In addition to stories on the rich and famous, it ran articles by eminent psychologists and journalists, interviews with both statesmen and rock stars. Its photography was first-class, just as its text was thoroughly researched and concisely written. Some of its detractors might have termed it quality gossip, but the word *quality* wasn't forgotten.

An ad in *Celebrity* was a sure bet for generating sales and interest and was priced accordingly. *Celebrity* was, in a tough, competitive business, one of the leading monthly publications in the country. Lee Radcliffe wouldn't have settled for less.

"How'd the piece on the sculptures turn out?"

Lee glanced up at Bryan Mitchell, one of the top photographers on the West Coast. Grateful, she accepted the cup of coffee Bryan passed her. In the past four days, she'd had a total of twenty hours' sleep. "Good," she said simply.

"I've seen better art scrawled in alleys."

Though she privately agreed, Lee only shrugged. "Some people like the clunky and obscure."

With a laugh, Bryan shook her head. "When they told me to photograph that red and black tangle of wire to its best advantage, I nearly asked them to shut off the lights."

"You made it look almost mystical."

"I can make a junkyard look mystical with the right lighting." She shot Lee a grin. "The same way you can make it sound fascinating."

A smile touched Lee's mouth but her mind was veering off in a dozen other directions. "All in a day's work, right?"

"Speaking of which—" Bryan rested one slim jean-clad hip on Lee's organized desk, drinking her own coffee black. "Still trying to dig something up on Hunter Brown?"

A frown drew Lee's elegant brows together. Hunter

Brown was becoming her personal quest and almost an obsession. Perhaps because he was so completely inaccessible, she'd become determined to be the first to break through the cloud of mystery. It had taken her nearly five years to earn her title as staff reporter, and she had a reputation for being tenacious, thorough and cool. Lee knew she'd earned those adjectives. Three months of hitting blank walls in researching Hunter Brown didn't deter her. One way or the other, she was going to get the story.

"So far I haven't gotten beyond his agent's name and his editor's phone number." There might've been a hint of frustration in her tone, but her expression was determined. "I've never known people so close-mouthed."

"His latest book hit the stands last week." Absently, Bryan picked up the top sheet from one of the tidy piles of papers Lee was systematically dealing with. "Have you read it?"

"I picked it up, but I haven't had a chance to start it yet."

Bryan tossed back the long honey-colored braid that fell over her shoulder. "Don't start it on a dark night." She sipped at her coffee, then gave a laugh. "God, I ended up sleeping with every light in the apartment burning. I don't know how he does it."

Lee glanced up again, her eyes calm and confident. "That's one of the things I'm going to find out."

Bryan nodded. She'd known Lee for three years, and she didn't doubt Lee would. "Why?" Her frank, almond-shaped eyes rested on Lee's.

"Because—" Lee finished off her coffee and tossed the empty cup into her overflowing wastebasket "—no one else has."

"The Mount Everest syndrome," Bryan commented, and earned a rare, spontaneous grin.

A quick glance would have shown two attractive women in casual conversation in a modern, attractively decorated office. A closer look would have uncovered the contrasts. Bryan, in jeans and a snug T-shirt, was completely relaxed. Everything about her was casual and not quite tidy, from her smudged sneakers to the loose braid. Her sharp-featured, arresting face was touched only with a hasty dab of mascara. She'd probably meant to add lipstick or blusher and then forgotten.

Lee, on the other hand, wore a very elegant ice-blue suit, and the nerves that gave her her drive were evident in the hands that were never quite still. Her hair was expertly cut in a short swinging style that took very little care—which was every bit as important to her as having it look good. Its shade fell somewhere between copper and gold. Her skin was the delicate, milky white some redheads bless and others curse. Her makeup had been meticulously applied that morning, down to the dusky blue shadow that matched her eyes. She had delicate, elegant features offset by a full and obviously stubborn mouth.

The two women had entirely different styles and entirely different tastes but oddly enough, their friendship had begun the moment they'd met. Though Bryan didn't always like Lee's aggressive tactics and Lee didn't always approve of Bryan's laid-back approach, their closeness hadn't wavered in three years.

"So." Bryan found the candy bar she'd stuck in her jeans pocket and proceeded to unwrap it. "What's your master plan?"

"To keep digging," Lee returned almost grimly. "I do

have a couple of connections at Horizon, his publishing house. Maybe one of them'll come through with something." Without being fully aware of it, she drummed her fingers on the desk. "Damn it, Bryan, he's like the man who wasn't there. I can't even find out what state he lives in."

"I'm half-inclined to believe some of the rumors," Bryan said thoughtfully. Outside Lee's office someone was having hysterics over the final editing of an article. "I'd say the guy lives in a cave somewhere, full of bats with a couple of stray wolves thrown in. He probably writes the original manuscript in sheep's blood."

"And sacrifices virgins every new moon."

"I wouldn't be surprised." Bryan swung her feet lazily while she munched on her chocolate bar. "I tell you the man's weird."

"*Silent Scream*'s already on the bestseller list."

"I didn't say he wasn't brilliant," Bryan countered, "I said he was weird. What kind of a mind does he have?" She shook her head with a half-sheepish smile. "I can tell you I wished I'd never heard of Hunter Brown last night while I was trying to sleep with my eyes open."

"That's just it." Impatient, Lee rose and paced to the tiny window on the east wall. She wasn't looking out; the view of Los Angeles didn't interest her. She just had to move around. "What kind of mind *does* he have? What kind of life does he live? Is he married? Is he sixty-five or twenty-five? Why does he write novels about the supernatural?" She turned, her impatience and her annoyance showing beneath the surface of the sophisticated grooming. "Why did you read his book?"

"Because it was fascinating," Bryan answered immediately. "Because by the time I was on page three, I was so into it you couldn't have gotten the book away from me with a crowbar."

"And you're an intelligent woman."

"Damn right," Bryan agreed and grinned. "So?"

"Why do intelligent people buy and read something that's going to terrify them?" Lee demanded. "When you pick up a Hunter Brown, you know what it's going to do to you, yet his books consistently spring to the top of the bestseller list and stay there. Why does an obviously intelligent man write books like that?" She began, in a habit Bryan recognized, to fiddle with whatever was at hand—the leaves of a philodendron, the stub of a pencil, the left earring she'd removed during a phone conversation.

"Do I hear a hint of disapproval?"

"Yeah, maybe." Frowning, Lee looked up again. "The man is probably the best colorist in the country. If he's describing a room in an old house, you can smell the dust. His characterizations are so real you'd swear you'd met the people in his books. And he uses that talent to write about things that go bump in the night. I want to find out why."

Bryan crumpled her candy wrapper into a ball. "I know a woman who has one of the sharpest, most analytical minds I've ever come across. She has a talent for digging up obscure facts, some of them impossibly dry, and turning them into intriguing stories. She's ambitious, has a remarkable talent for words, but works on a magazine and lets a half-finished novel sit abandoned in a drawer. She's lovely, but she rarely dates for any purpose other than business. And she has a habit of twisting paper clips into ungodly shapes while she's talking."

Lee glanced down at the small mangled piece of metal in her hands, then met Bryan's eyes coolly. "Do you know why?"

There was a hint of humor in Bryan's eyes, but her tone was serious enough. "I've tried to figure it out for three years, but I can't precisely put my finger on it."

With a smile, Lee tossed the bent paper clip into the trash. "But then, you're not a reporter."

Because she wasn't very good at taking advice, Lee switched on her bedside lamp, stretched out and opened Hunter Brown's latest novel. She would read a chapter or two, she decided, then make it an early night. An early night was an almost sinful luxury after the week she'd put in at *Celebrity*.

Her bedroom was done in creamy ivories and shades of blue from the palest aqua to indigo. She'd indulged herself here, with dozens of plump throw pillows, a huge Turkish rug and a Queen Anne stand that held an urn filled with peacock feathers and eucalyptus. Her latest acquisition, a large ficus tree, sat by the window and thrived.

She considered this room the only truly private spot in her life. As a reporter, Lee accepted that she was public property as much as the people she sought out. Privacy wasn't something she could cling to when she constantly dug into other people's lives. But in this little corner of the world, she could relax completely, forget there was work to do, ladders to climb. She could pretend L.A. wasn't bustling outside, as long as she had this oasis of peace. Without it, without the hours she spent sleeping and unwinding there, she knew she'd overload.

Knowing herself well, Lee understood that she had

a tendency to push too hard, run too fast. In the quiet of her bedroom she could recharge herself each night so that she'd be ready for the race again the following day.

Relaxed, she opened Hunter Brown's latest effort.

Within a half hour, Lee was disturbed, uncomfortable and completely engrossed. She'd have been angry with the author for drawing her in if she hadn't been so busy turning pages. He'd put an ordinary man in an extraordinary situation and done it with such skill that Lee was already relating to the teacher who'd found himself caught up in a small town with a dark secret.

The prose flowed and the dialogue was so natural she could hear the voices. He filled the town with so many recognizable things, she could have sworn she'd been there herself. She knew the story was going to give her more than one bad moment in the dark, but she had to go on. That was the magic of a major storyteller. Cursing him, she read on, so tense that when the phone rang beside her, the book flew out of her hands. Lee swore again, at herself, and lifted the receiver.

Her annoyance at being disturbed didn't last. Grabbing a pencil, she began to scrawl on the pad beside the phone. With her tongue caught between her teeth, she set down the pencil and smiled. She owed the contact in New York an enormous favor, but she'd pay off when the time came, as she always did. For now, Lee thought, running her hand over Hunter's book, she had to make arrangements to attend a small writers' conference in Flagstaff, Arizona.

She had to admit the country was impressive. As was her habit, Lee had spent the time during the flight from L.A. to Phoenix working, but once she'd changed to the small commuter plane for the trip to Flagstaff, her work had been forgotten. She'd flown through thin clouds over a vastness almost impossible to conceive after the skyscrapers and traffic of Los Angeles. She'd looked down on the peaks and dips and castlelike rocks of Oak Creek Canyon, feeling a drumming excitement that was rare in a woman who wasn't easily impressed. If she'd had more time…

Lee sighed as she stepped off the plane. There was never time enough.

The tiny airport boasted a one-room lobby with a choice of concession stand or soda and candy machines. No loudspeaker announced incoming and outgoing flights. No skycap bustled up to her to relieve her of her bags. There wasn't a line of cabs waiting outside to compete for the handful of people who'd disembarked. With her garment bag slung over her shoulder, she frowned at the inconvenience. Patience wasn't one of her virtues.

Tired, hungry and inwardly a little frazzled by the shaky commuter flight, she stepped up to one of the counters. "I need to arrange for a car to take me to town."

The man in shirtsleeves and loosened tie stopped pushing buttons on his computer. His first polite glance sharpened when he saw her face. She reminded him of a cameo his grandmother had worn at her neck on special occasions. Automatically he straightened his shoulders. "Did you want to rent a car?"

Lee considered that a moment, then rejected it. She hadn't come to do any sightseeing, so a car would hardly be worthwhile. "No, just transportation into

Flagstaff." Shifting her bag, she gave him the name of her hotel. "Do they have a courtesy car?"

"Sure do. You go on over to that phone by the wall there. Number's listed. Just give 'em a call and they'll send someone out."

"Thank you."

He watched her walk to the phone and thought he was the one who should have said thank-you.

Lee caught the scent of grilling hot dogs as she crossed the room. Since she'd turned down the dubious tray offered on the flight, the scent had her stomach juices swimming. Quickly and efficiently, she dialed the hotel, gave her name and was assured a car would be there within twenty minutes. Satisfied, she bought a hot dog and settled in one of the black plastic chairs to wait.

She was going to get what she'd come for, Lee told herself almost fiercely as she looked out at the distant mountains. The time wasn't going to be wasted. After three months of frustration, she was finally going to get a firsthand look at Hunter Brown.

It had taken skill and determination to persuade her editor-in-chief to spring for the trip, but it would pay off. It had to. Leaning back, she reviewed the questions she'd ask Hunter Brown once she'd cornered him.

All she needed, Lee decided, was an hour with him. Sixty minutes. In that time, she could pull out enough information for a concise, and very exclusive, article. She'd done precisely that with this year's Oscar winner, though he'd been reluctant, and a presidential candidate, though he'd been hostile. Hunter Brown would probably be both, she decided with a half smile. It would only add spice. If she'd wanted a bland, simple life, she'd have bent under the pressure and married Jonathan. Right now she'd be planning her next garden party rather than calculating how to ambush an award-winning writer.

Lee nearly laughed aloud. Garden parties, bridge parties and the yacht club. That might have been perfect for her family, but she'd wanted more. More what? her mother had demanded, and Lee could only reply, Just more.

Checking her watch, she left her luggage neatly stacked by the chair and went into the ladies' room. The door had hardly closed behind her when the object of all her planning strolled into the lobby.

He didn't often do good deeds, and then only for people he had a genuine affection for. Because he'd gotten into town with time to spare, Hunter had driven to the airport with the intention of picking up his editor. With barely a glance around, he walked over to the same counter Lee had approached ten minutes before.

"Flight 471 on time?"

"Yes, sir, got in ten minutes ago."

"Did a woman get off?" Hunter glanced at the nearly empty lobby again. "Attractive, midtwenties—"

"Yes, sir," the clerk interrupted. "She just stepped into the restroom. That's her luggage over there."

"Thanks." Satisfied, Hunter walked over to Lee's neat stack of luggage. Doesn't believe in traveling light, he noticed, scanning the garment bag, small Pullman and briefcase. Then, what woman did? Hadn't his Sarah taken two suitcases for the brief three-day stay with his sister in Phoenix? Strange that his little girl should be two parts woman already. Perhaps not so strange, Hunter reflected. Females were born two parts woman, while males took years to grow out of boyhood—if they ever did. Perhaps that's why he trusted men a great deal more.

Lee saw him when she came back into the lobby. His back was to her, so that she had only the impression of a tall, leanly built man with black hair curling carelessly down to the neck of his T-shirt. Right on time, she thought with satisfaction, and approached him.

"I'm Lee Radcliffe."

When he turned, she went stone-still, the impersonal smile freezing on her face. In the first instant, she couldn't have said why. He was attractive—perhaps too attractive. His face was narrow but not scholarly, raw-boned but not rugged. It was too much a combination of both to be either. His nose was straight and aristocratic, while his mouth was sculpted like a poet's. His hair was dark and full and unruly, as though he'd been driving fast for hours with the wind blowing free. But it wasn't these things that caused her to lose her voice. It was his eyes.

She'd never seen eyes darker than his, more direct, more...disturbing. It was as though they looked through her. No, not through, Lee corrected numbly. Into. In ten seconds, they had looked into her and seen everything.

He saw a stunning, milk-pale face with dusky eyes gone wide in astonishment. He saw a soft, feminine mouth, lightly tinted. He saw nerves. He saw a stubborn chin and molten copper hair that would feel like silk between the fingers. What he saw was an outwardly poised, inwardly tense woman who smelled like spring evenings and looked like a *Vogue* cover. If it hadn't been for that inner tension, he might have dismissed her, but what lay beneath people's surfaces always intrigued him.

He skimmed her neat traveling suit so quickly his eyes might never have left hers. "Yes?"

"Well, I..." Forced to swallow, she trailed off. That alone infuriated her. She wasn't about to be set off into stammers by a driver for the hotel. "If you've come to pick me up," Lee said curtly, "you'll need to get my bags."

Lifting a brow, he said nothing. Her mistake was simple and obvious. It would have taken only a sentence from him to correct it. Then again, it was her mistake, not his. Hunter had always believed more in impulses than explanations. Bending down, he picked up the Pullman, then slung the strap of the garment bag over his shoulder. "The car's out here."

She felt a great deal more secure with the briefcase in her hand and his back to her. The oddness, Lee told herself, had come from excitement and a long flight. Men never surprised her; they certainly never made her stare and stammer. What she needed was a bath and something a bit more substantial to eat than that hot dog.

The car he'd referred to wasn't a car, she noted, but a Jeep. Supposing this made sense, with the steep roads and hard winters, Lee climbed in.

Moves well, he thought, and dresses flawlessly. He noted, too, that she bit her nails. "Are you from the area?" Hunter asked conversationally when he'd stowed her bags in the back.

"No. I'm here for the writers' conference."

Hunter climbed in beside her and shut the door. Now he knew where to take her. "You're a writer?"

She thought of the two chapters of her manuscript she'd brought along in case she needed a cover. "Yes."

Hunter swung through the parking lot, taking the back road that led to the highway. "What do you write?"

Settling back, Lee decided she might as well try her routine out on him before she was in the middle of two hundred published and aspiring writers. "I've done articles and some short stories," she told him truthfully enough. Then she added what she'd rarely told anyone. "I've started a novel."

With a speed that surprised but didn't unsettle her, he burst onto the highway. "Are you going to finish it?" he asked, showing an insight that disturbed her.

"I suppose that depends on a lot of things."

He took another careful look at her profile. "Such as?"

She wanted to shift in her seat but forced herself to be still. This was just the sort of question she might have to answer over the weekend. "Such as if what I've done so far is any good."

He found both her answer and her discomfort reasonable. "Do you go to many of these conferences?"

"No, this is my first."

Which might account for the nerves, Hunter mused, but he didn't think he'd found the entire answer.

"I'm hoping to learn something," Lee said with a small smile. "I registered at the last minute, but when I learned Hunter Brown would be here, I couldn't resist."

The frown in his eyes came and went too quickly to be noticed. He'd agreed to do the workshop only because it wouldn't be publicized. Even the registrants wouldn't know he'd be there, until the following morning. Just how, he wondered, had the little redhead with the Italian shoes and midnight eyes found out? He passed a truck. "Who?"

"Hunter Brown," Lee repeated. "The novelist."

Impulse took over again. "Is he any good?"

Surprised, Lee turned to study his profile. It was infinitely easier to look at him, she discovered, when those eyes weren't focused on her. "You've never read any of his work?"

"Should I have?"

"I suppose that depends on whether you like to read with all the lights on and the doors locked. He writes horror fiction."

If she'd looked more closely, she wouldn't have missed the quick humor in his eyes. "Ghouls and fangs?"

"Not exactly," she said after a moment. "Not that simple. If there's something you're afraid of, he'll put it into words and make you wish him to the devil."

Hunter laughed, greatly pleased. "So, you like to be scared?"

"No," Lee said definitely.

"Then why do you read him?"

"I've asked myself that when I'm up at 3:00 a.m. finishing one of his books." Lee shrugged as the Jeep slowed for the turn-off. "It's irresistible. I think he must be a very odd man," she murmured, half to herself. "Not quite, well, not quite like the rest of us."

"Do you?" After a quick, sharp turn, he pulled up in front of the hotel, more interested in her than he'd planned to be. "But isn't writing just words and imagination?"

"And sweat and blood," she added, moving her shoulders again. "I just don't see how it could be very comfortable to live with an imagination like Brown's. I'd like to know how he feels about it."

Amused, Hunter jumped out of the Jeep to retrieve her bags. "You're going to ask him."

"Yes." Lee stepped down. "I am."

For a moment, they stood on the sidewalk, silently.

He looked at her with what might have been mild interest, but she sensed something more—something she shouldn't have felt from a hotel driver after a ten-minute acquaintance. For the second time she wanted to shift and made herself stand still. Wasting no more words, Hunter turned toward the hotel, her bags in hand.

It didn't occur to Lee until she was following him inside that she'd had a nonstop conversation with a hotel driver, a conversation that hadn't dwelt on the usual pleasantries or tourist plugs. As she watched him walk to the desk, she felt an aura of cool confidence from him and traces, very subtle traces, of arrogance. Why was a man like this driving back and forth and getting nowhere? she wondered. Stepping up to the desk, she told herself it wasn't her concern. She had bigger fish to fry.

"Lenore Radcliffe," she told the clerk.

"Yes, Ms. Radcliffe." He handed her a form and imprinted her credit card before he passed her a key. Before she could take it, Hunter slipped it into his own hand. It was then she noticed the odd ring on his pinky, four thin bands of gold and silver twisted into one.

"I'll take you around," he said simply, then crossed through the lobby with her again in his wake. He wound through a corridor, turned left, then stopped. Lee waited while he unlocked the door and gestured her inside.

The room was on the garden level with its own patio, she was pleased to note. As she scanned the room, Hunter carelessly switched on the TV and flipped through the channels before he checked the air conditioner. "Just call the desk if you need anything else," he advised, stowing her garment bag in the closet.

"Yes, I will." Lee hunted through her purse and came up with a five. "Thank you," she said, holding it out.

His eyes met hers again, giving her that same frozen jolt they had in the airport. She felt something stir deep within but wasn't sure if it was trying to reach out to him or struggling to hide. The fingers holding the bill nearly trembled. Then he smiled, so quickly, so charmingly, she was speechless.

"Thank you, Ms. Radcliffe." Without a blink, Hunter pocketed the five dollars and strolled out.

Chapter 2

If writers were often considered odd, writers' conferences, Lee was to discover, were oddities in themselves. They certainly couldn't be considered quiet or organized or stuffy.

Like nearly every other of the two hundred or so participants, she stood in one of the dozen lines at 8:00 a.m. for registration. From the laughing and calling and embracing, it was obvious that many of the writers and would-be writers knew one another. There was an air of congeniality, shared knowledge and camaraderie. Overlaying it all was excitement.

Still, more than one member stood in the noisy lobby like a child lost in a shipwreck, clinging to a folder or briefcase as though it were a life preserver and staring about with awe or simple confusion. Lee could appreciate the feeling, though she looked calm and poised as she accepted her packet and pinned her badge to the mint-green lapel of her blazer.

Concentrating on the business at hand, she found a chair in a corner and skimmed the schedule for Hunter Brown's workshop. With a dawning smile, she took out a pen and underlined.

CREATING HORROR THROUGH
ATMOSPHERE AND EMOTION
Speaker to be announced.

Bingo, Lee thought, capping her pen. She'd make certain she had a front-row seat. A glance at her watch showed her that she had three hours before Brown began to speak. Never one to take chances, she took out her notebook to skim over the questions she'd listed, while people filed by her or merely loitered, chatting.

"If I get rejected again, I'm going to put my head in the oven."

"Your oven's electric, Judy."

"It's the thought that counts."

Amused, Lee began to listen to the passing comments with half an ear while she added a few more questions.

"And when they brought in my breakfast this morning, there was a five-hundred-page manuscript under my plate. I completely lost my appetite."

"That's nothing. I got one in my office last week written in calligraphy. One hundred and fifty thousand words of flowing script."

Editors, she mused. She could tell them a few stories about some of the submissions that found their way to *Celebrity*.

"He said his editor hacked his first chapter to pieces so he's going into mourning before the rewrites."

"I always go into mourning before rewrites. It's after a rejection that I seriously consider taking up basket weaving as a profession."

"Did you hear Jeffries is here again trying to peddle that manuscript about the virgin with acrophobia and telekinesis? I can't believe he won't let it die a quiet death. When's your next murder coming out?"

"In August. It's poison."

"Darling, that's no way to talk about your work."

As they passed by her, Lee caught the variety of tones, some muted, some sophisticated, some flamboyant. Gestures and conversations followed the same wide range. Amazed, she watched one man swoop by in a long, dramatic black cape.

Definitely an odd group, Lee thought, but she warmed to them. It was true she confined her skill to articles and profiles, but at heart she was a storyteller. Her position on the magazine had been hard-earned, and she'd built her world around it. For all her ambition, she had a firm fear of rejection that kept her own manuscript unfinished, buried in a drawer for weeks and sometimes months at a time. At the magazine, she had prestige, security and room for advancement. The weekly paycheck put the roof over her head, the clothes on her back and the food on her table.

If it hadn't been so important that she prove she could do all this for herself, she might have taken the chance of sending those first hundred pages to a publishing house. But then… Shaking her head, Lee watched the people mill through the registration area, all types, all sizes, all ages. Clothes varied from trim professional suits to jeans to flamboyant caftans and smocks. Apparently style was a matter of taste and taste a matter of individuality. She wondered if she'd see quite the same variety anywhere else. Absently, she glanced at the partial manuscript she'd tucked into her briefcase. Just for cover, she reminded herself. That was all.

No, she didn't believe she had it in her to be a great writer, but she knew she had the skill for great reporting. She'd never, never settle for being second-rate at anything.

Still, while she was here, it wouldn't hurt to sit in on one or two of the seminars. She might pick up some pointers. More importantly, she told herself as she rose, she might be able to stretch this trip into another story on the ins and outs of a writers' conference. Who attended, why, what they did, what they hoped for. Yes, it could make quite an interesting little piece. The job, after all, came first.

An hour later, a bit more enthusiastic than she wanted to be after her first workshop, she wandered into the coffee shop. She'd take a short break, assimilate the notes she'd written, then go back and make certain she had the best seat in the house for Hunter Brown's lecture.

Hunter glanced up from his paper and watched her enter the coffee shop. Lee Radcliffe, he mused, finding her of more interest than the local news he'd been scanning. He'd enjoyed his conversation with her the day before, and as often as not, he found conversations tedious. She had a quality about her—an innate frankness glossed with sophistication—that he found intriguing enough to hold his interest. An obsessive writer who believed that the characters themselves were the plot of any book, Hunter always looked for the unique and the individual. Instinct told him Lee Radcliffe was quite an individual.

Unobserved, he watched her. From the way she looked absently around the room it was obvious she was preoccupied. The suit she wore was very simple but showed both style and taste in the color and cut. She was a woman who could wear the simple, he decided, because she was a woman who'd been born with style. If he wasn't very much mistaken, she'd been born into wealth as well. There was always a subtle difference between those who were accustomed to money and those who'd spent years earning it.

So where did the nerves come from? he wondered. Curious, he decided it would be worth an hour of his time to try to find out.

Setting his paper aside, Hunter lit a cigarette and continued to stare at her, knowing there was no quicker way to catch someone's eye.

Lee, thinking more about the story she was going to write than the coffee she'd come for, felt an odd tingle run up her spine. It was real enough to give her an urge to turn around and walk out again when she glanced over and found herself staring back at the man she'd met at the airport.

It was his eyes, she decided, at first not thinking of him as a man or the hotel driver from the previous day. It was his eyes. Dark, almost the color of jet, they'd draw you in and draw you in until you were caught, and every secret you'd ever had would be secret no longer. It was frightening. It was…irresistible.

Amazed that such a fanciful thought had crept into

her own practical, organized mind, Lee approached him. He was just a man, she told herself, a man who worked for his living like any other man. There was certainly nothing to be frightened of.

"Ms. Radcliffe." With the same unsmiling stare, he gestured to the chair across from him. "Buy you a cup of coffee?"

Normally she would've refused, politely enough. But now, for some intangible reason, Lee felt as though she had a point to prove. For the same intangible reason, she felt she had to prove it to him as much as to herself. "Thank you." The moment she sat down, a waitress was there, pouring coffee.

"Enjoying the conference?"

"Yes." Lee poured cream into the cup, stirring it around and around until a tiny whirlpool formed in the center. "As disorganized as everything seems to be, there was an amazing amount of information generated at the workshop I went to this morning."

A smile touched his lips, so lightly that it was barely there at all. "You prefer organization?"

"It's more productive." Though he was dressed more formally than he'd been the day before, the pleated slacks and open-necked shirt were still casual. She wondered why he wasn't required to wear a uniform. But then, she thought, you could put him in one of those nifty white jackets and neat ties and his eyes would simply defy them.

"A lot of fascinating things can come out of chaos, don't you think?"

"Perhaps." She frowned down at the whirlpool in her cup. Why did she feel as though she was being sucked in, in just that way? And why, she thought with a sudden flash of impatience, was she sitting here having a philosophical discussion with a stranger when she should be outlining the two stories she planned to write?

"Did you find Hunter Brown?" he asked her as he studied her over the rim of his cup. Annoyed with herself, he guessed accurately, and anxious to be off doing.

"What?" Distracted, Lee looked back up to find those strange eyes still on her.

"I asked if you'd run into Hunter Brown." The whisper of a smile was on his lips again, and this time it touched his eyes as well. It didn't make them any less intense.

"No." Defensive without knowing why, Lee sipped at her cooling coffee. "Why?"

"After the things you said yesterday, I was curious what you'd think of him once you met him." He took a drag from his cigarette and blew smoke out in a haze. "People usually have a preconceived image of someone but it rarely holds up in the flesh."

"It's difficult to have any kind of an image of someone who hides away from the world."

His brow went up, but his voice remained mild. "Hides?"

"It's the word that comes to my mind," Lee returned, again finding that she was speaking her thoughts aloud to him. "There's no picture of him on the back of any of his books, no bio. He never grants interviews, never denies or substantiates anything written about him. Any awards he's received have been accepted by his agent or his editor." She ran her fingers up and down the handle of her spoon. "I've heard he occasionally attends affairs like this, but only if it's a very small conference and there's no publicity about his appearance."

All during her speech, Hunter kept his eyes on her, watching every nuance of expression. There were traces of frustration, he was certain, and of eagerness. The lovely cameo face was calm while her fingers moved restlessly. She'd be in his next book, he decided on the spot. He'd never met anyone with more potential for being a central character.

Because his direct, unblinking stare made her want to stammer, Lee gave him back the hard, uncompromising look. "Why do you stare at me like that?"

He continued to do so without any show of discomfort. "Because you're an interesting woman."

Another man might have said beautiful, still another might have said fascinating. Lee could have tossed off either one with light scorn. She picked up her spoon again, then set it down. "Why?"

"You have a tidy mind, innate style, and you're a bundle of nerves." He liked the way the faint line appeared between her brows when she frowned. It meant stubbornness to him, and tenacity. He respected both. "I've always been intrigued by pockets," Hunter went on. "The deeper the better. I find myself wondering just what's in your pockets, Ms. Radcliffe."

She felt the tremor again, up her spine, then down. It wasn't comfortable to sit near a man who could do that. She had a moment's sympathy for every person she'd ever interviewed. "You have an odd way of putting things," she muttered.

"So I've been told."

She instructed herself to get up and leave. It didn't make sense to sit there being disturbed by a man she could dismiss with a five-dollar tip. "What are you doing in Flagstaff?" she demanded. "You don't strike me as someone who'd be content to drive back and forth to an airport day after day, shuttling passengers and hauling luggage."

"Impressions make fascinating little paintings, don't they?" He smiled at her fully, as he had the day before when she'd tipped him. Lee wasn't sure why she'd felt he'd been laughing at her then, any more than why she felt he was laughing at her now. Despite herself, her lips curved in response. He found the smile a pleasant and very alluring surprise.

"You're a very odd man."

"I've been told that, too." His smile faded and his eyes became intense again. "Have dinner with me tonight."

The question didn't surprise her as much as the fact that she wanted to accept, and nearly had. "No," she said, cautiously retreating. "I don't think so."

"Let me know if you change your mind."

She was surprised again. Most men would've pressed a bit. It was, well, expected, Lee reflected, wishing she could figure him out. "I have to get back." She reached for her briefcase. "Do you know where the Canyon Room is?"

With an inward chuckle, he dropped bills on the table. "Yes, I'll show you."

"That's not necessary," Lee began, rising.

"I've got time." He walked with her out of the coffee shop and into the wide, carpeted lobby. "Do you plan to do any sightseeing while you're here?"

"There won't be time." She glanced out one of the wide windows at the towering peak of Humphrey Peak. "As soon as the conference is over I have to get back."

"To where?"

"Los Angeles."

"Too many people," Hunter said automatically. "Don't you ever feel as though they're using up your air?"

She wouldn't have put it that way, would never have thought of it, but there were times she felt a twinge of what might be called claustrophobia. Still, her home was there, and more importantly, her work. "No. There's enough air, such as it is, for everyone."

"You've never stood at the south rim of the canyon and looked out, and breathed in."

Again, Lee shot him a look. He had a way of saying things that gave you an immediate picture. For the second time, she regretted that she wouldn't be able to take a day or two to explore some of the vastness of Arizona. "Maybe some other time." Shrugging, she turned with him as he headed down a corridor to the right.

"Time's fickle," he commented. "When you need it, there's too little of it. Then you wake up at three o'clock in the morning, and there's too much of it. It's usually better to take it than to anticipate it. You might try that," he said, looking down at her again. "It might help your nerves."

Her brows drew together. "There's nothing wrong with my nerves."

"Some people can thrive on nervous energy for weeks at a time, then they have to find that little valve that lets the steam escape." For the first time, he touched her, just fingertips to the ends of her hair. But she felt it, experienced it, as hard and strong as if his hand had closed firmly over hers. "What do you do to let the steam escape, Lenore?"

She didn't stiffen, or casually nudge his hand away as she would have done at any other time. Instead, she stood still, toying with a sensation she couldn't remember ever experiencing before. Thunder and lightning, she thought. There was thunder and lightning in this man, deep under the strangely aloof, oddly open exterior. She wasn't about to be caught in the storm.

"I work," she said easily, but her fingers had tightened on the handle of her briefcase. "I don't need any other escape valve." She didn't step back, but let the haughtiness that had always protected her enter her tone. "No one calls me Lenore."

"No?" He nearly smiled. It was this look, she realized, the secret amusement the onlooker could only guess at rather than see, that most intrigued. She thought he probably knew that. "But it suits you. Feminine, elegant, a little distant. *And the only word there spoken was the whispered word, 'Lenore!'* Yes." He let his fingertips linger a moment longer on her hair. "I think Poe would've found you very apt."

Before she could prevent it, before she could anticipate it, her knees were weak. She'd felt the sound of her own name feather over her skin. "Who are you?" Lee found herself demanding. Was it possible to be so deeply affected by someone without even knowing his name? She stepped forward in what seemed to be a challenge. "Just who are you?"

He smiled again, with the oddly gentle charm that shouldn't have suited his eyes yet somehow did. "Strange, you never asked before. You'd better go in," he told her as people began to gravitate toward the open doors of the Canyon Room. "You'll want a good seat."

"Yes." She drew back, a bit shaken by the ferocity of the desire she felt to learn more about him. With a last look over her shoulder, Lee walked in and settled in the front row. It was time to get her mind back on the business she'd come for, and the business was Hunter Brown. Distractions like incomprehensible men who drove Jeeps for a living would have to be put aside.

From her briefcase, Lee took a fresh notebook and two pencils, slipping one behind her ear. Within a few moments, she'd be able to see and study the mysterious Hunter Brown. She'd be able to listen and take notes with perfect freedom. After his lecture, she'd be able to question him, and if she had her way, she'd arrange some kind of one-on-one for later.

Lee had given the ethics of the situation careful thought. She didn't feel it would be necessary to tell Brown she was a reporter. She was there as an aspiring writer and had the fledgling manuscript to prove it. Anyone there was free to try to write and sell an article on the conference and its participants. Only if Brown used the words *off the record* would she be bound to silence. Without that, anything he said was public property.

This story could be her next step up the ladder. Would be, Lee corrected. The first documented, authentically researched story on Hunter Brown could push her beyond *Celebrity*'s scope. It would be controversial, colorful and, most importantly, exclusive. With this under her belt, even her quietly critical family would be impressed. With this under her belt, Lee thought, she'd be that much closer to the top rung, where her sights were always set.

Once she was there, all the hard work, the long hours, the obsessive dedication would be worth it. Because once she was there, she was there to stay. At the top, Lee thought almost fiercely. As high as she could reach.

On the other side of the doors, on the other side of

the corridor, Hunter stood with his editor, half listening to her comments on an interview she'd had with an aspiring writer. He caught the gist, that she was excited about the writer's potential. It was a talent of his to be able to conduct a perfectly lucid conversation when his mind was on something entirely different. It was something he roused himself to do only when the mood was on him. So he spoke to his editor and thought of Lee Radcliffe.

Yes, he was definitely going to use her in his next book. True, the plot was only a vague notion in his head, but he already knew she'd be the core of it. He needed to dig a bit deeper before he'd be satisfied, but he didn't foresee any problem there. If he'd gauged her correctly, she'd be confused when he walked to the podium, then stunned, then furious. If she wanted to talk to him as badly as she'd indicated, she'd swallow her temper.

A strong woman, Hunter decided. A will of iron and skin like cream. Vulnerable eyes and a damn-the-devil chin. A character was nothing without contrasts, strengths and weaknesses. And secrets, he thought, already certain he'd discover hers. He had another day and a half to explore Lenore Radcliffe. Hunter figured that was enough.

The corridor was full of laughter and complaints and enthusiasm as people loitered or filed through into the adjoining room. He knew what it was to feel enthusiastic about being a writer. If the pleasure went out of it, he'd still write. He was compelled to. But it would show in his work. Emotions always showed. He never *allowed* his feelings and thoughts to pour into his work—they would have done so regardless of his permission.

Hunter considered it a fair trade-off. His emotions, his thoughts, were there for anyone who cared to read them. His life was completely and without exception his own.

The woman beside him had his affection and his respect. He'd argued with her over motivation and sentence structure, losing as often as winning. He'd shouted at her, laughed with her and given her emotional support through her recent divorce. He knew her age, her favorite drink and her weakness for cashews. She'd been his editor for three years, which was as close to a marriage as many people come. Yet she had no idea he had a ten-year-old daughter named Sarah who liked to bake cookies and play soccer.

Hunter took a last drag on his cigarette as the president of the small writers' group approached. The man was a slick, imaginative science fiction writer whom Hunter had read and enjoyed. Otherwise, he wouldn't be there, about to make one of his rare appearances in the writing community.

"Mr. Brown, I don't need to tell you again how honored we are to have you here."

"No—" Hunter gave him the easy half smile "—you don't."

"There's liable to be quite a commotion when I announce you. After your lecture, I'll do everything I can to keep the thundering horde back."

"Don't worry about it. I'll manage."

The man nodded, never doubting it. "I'm having a small reception in my suite this evening, if you'd like to join us."

"I appreciate it, but I have a dinner engagement."

Though he didn't know quite what to make of the smile, the organization's president was too intelligent to press his luck when he was about to pull off a coup. "If you're ready, then, I'll announce you."

"Any time."

Hunter followed him into the Canyon Room, then loitered just inside the doors. The room was already buzzing with anticipation and curiosity. The podium was set on a small stage in front of two hundred chairs that were nearly all filled. Talk died down when the president approached the stage, but continued in pockets of murmurs even after he'd begun to speak. Hunter heard one of the men nearest him whisper to a companion that he had three publishing houses competing for his manuscript. Hunter skimmed over the crowd, barely listening to the beginning of his introduction. Then his gaze rested again on Lee.

She was watching the speaker with a small, polite smile on her lips, but her eyes gave her away. They were dark and eager. Hunter let his gaze roam down until it rested on her lap. There, her hand opened and closed on the pencil. A bundle of nerves and energy wrapped in a very thin layer of confidence, he thought.

For the second time Lee felt his eyes on her, and for the second time she turned so that their gazes locked. The faint line marred her brow again as she wondered what he was doing inside the conference room. Unperturbed, leaning easily against the wall, Hunter stared back at her.

"His career's risen steadily since the publication of his first book, only five years ago. Since the first, *The Devil's Due,* he's given us the pleasure of being scared out of our socks every time we pick up his work." At the mention of the title, the murmurs increased and heads began to swivel. Hunter continued to stare at Lee, and she back at him, frowning. "His latest, *Silent Scream,* is already solid in the number-one spot on the bestseller list. We're honored and privileged to welcome to Flagstaff—Hunter Brown."

The effusive applause competed with the growing murmurs of two hundred people in a closed room. Casually, Hunter straightened from the wall and walked to the stage. He saw the pencil fall out of Lee's hand and roll to the floor. Without breaking rhythm, he stooped and picked it up.

"Better hold on to this," he advised, looking into her astonished eyes. As he handed it back, he watched astonishment flare into fury.

"You're a—"

"Yes, but you'd better tell me later." Walking the rest of the way to the stage, Hunter stepped behind the podium and waited for the applause to fade. Again he skimmed the crowd, but this time with such a quiet intensity that all sound died. For ten seconds there wasn't even the sound of breathing. "Terror," Hunter said into the microphone.

From the first word he had them spellbound, and held them captive for forty minutes. No one moved, no one yawned, no one slipped out for a cigarette. With her teeth clenched tight, Lee knew she despised him.

Simmering, struggling against the urge to spring up and stalk out, Lee sat stiffly and took meticulous notes. In the margin of the book she drew a perfectly recognizable caricature of Hunter with a dagger through his heart. It gave her enormous satisfaction.

When he agreed to field questions for ten minutes, Lee's was the first hand up. Hunter looked directly at her, smiled and called on someone three rows back.

He answered professional questions professionally and evaded any personal references. She had to admire his skill, particularly since she was well aware he so seldom spoke in public. He showed no nerves, no hesitation and absolutely no inclination to call on her, though her hand was up and her eyes shot fiery little darts at him. But she was a reporter, Lee reminded herself. Reporters got nowhere if they stood on ceremony.

"Mr. Brown," Lee began, and rose.

"Sorry." With his slow smile, he held up a hand. "I'm afraid we're already overtime. Best of luck to all of you." He left the podium and the room, under a hail of applause. By the time Lee could work her way to the doors, she'd heard enough praise of Hunter Brown to turn her simmering temper to boil.

The nerve, she thought as she finally made it into the corridor. The unspeakable nerve. She didn't mind being bested in a game of chess; she could handle having her work criticized and her opinion questioned. All in all, Lee considered herself a reasonable, low-key person with no more than her fair share of conceit. The one thing she couldn't, wouldn't, tolerate was being made a fool of.

Revenge sprang into her mind, nasty, petty revenge. Oh, yes, she thought as she tried to work her way through the thick crowd of Hunter Brown fans, she'd have her revenge, somehow, some way. And when she did, it would be perfect.

She turned off at the elevators, knowing she was too full of fury to deal successfully with Hunter at that moment. She needed an hour to cool off and to plan. The pencil she still held snapped between her fingers.

If it was the last thing she did, she was going to make Hunter Brown squirm.

Just as she started to push the button for her floor, Hunter slipped inside the elevator. "Going up?" he asked easily, and pushed the number himself.

Lee felt the fury rise to her throat and burn. With an effort, she clamped her lips tight on the venom and stared straight ahead.

"Broke your pencil," Hunter observed, finding himself more amused than he'd been in days. He glanced at her open notebook, spotting the meticulously drawn caricature. An appreciative grin appeared. "Well done," he told her. "How'd you enjoy the workshop?"

Lee gave him one scathing look as the elevator doors opened. "You're a font of trivial information, Mr. Brown."

"You've got murder in your eyes, Lenore." He stepped into the hall with her. "It suits your hair. Your drawing makes it clear enough what you'd like to do. Why don't you stab me while you have the chance?"

As she continued to walk, Lee told herself she wouldn't give him the satisfaction of speaking to him. She wouldn't speak to him at all. Her head jerked up. "You've had a good laugh at my expense," she grated, and dug in her briefcase for her room key.

"A quiet chuckle or two," he corrected while she continued to simmer and search. "Lose your key?"

"No, I haven't lost my key." Frustrated, Lee looked up until fury met amusement. "Why don't you go away and sit on your laurels?"

"I've always found that uncomfortable. Why don't you vent your spleen, Lenore. You'd feel better."

"Don't call me Lenore!" she exploded as her

control slipped. "You had no right to use me as the brunt of a joke. You had no right to pretend you worked for the hotel."

"You assumed," he corrected. "As I recall, I never pretended anything. You asked for a ride yesterday. I simply gave you one."

"You knew I thought you were the hotel driver. You were standing there beside my luggage—"

"A classic case of mistaken identity." He noted that her skin tinted with pale rose when she was angry. An attractive side effect, Hunter decided. "I'd come to pick up my editor, who'd missed her Phoenix connection, as it turned out. I thought the luggage was hers."

"All you had to do was say that at the time."

"You never asked," he pointed out. "And you did tell me to get the luggage."

"Oh, you're infuriating." Clamping her teeth shut, she began to fumble in her briefcase again.

"But brilliant. You mentioned that yourself."

"Being able to string words together is an admirable talent, Mr. Brown." Hauteur was one of her most practiced skills. Lee used it to the fullest. "It doesn't make you an admirable person."

"No, I wouldn't say I was, particularly." While he waited for her to find her key, Hunter leaned comfortably against the wall.

"You carried my luggage to my room," she continued, infuriated. "I gave you a five-dollar tip."

"Very generous."

She let out a huff of breath, grateful that her hands were busy. She didn't know how else she could have prevented herself from slapping his calm, self-satisfied face. "You've had your joke," she said, finding her key at last. "Now I'd like you to do me the courtesy of never speaking to me again."

"I don't know where you got the impression I was courteous." Before she could unlock the door, he'd put his hand over hers on the key. She felt the little tingle of power and cursed him for it even as she met his calmly amused look. "You did mention, however, that you'd like to speak to me. We can talk over dinner tonight."

She stared at him. Why should she have thought he wouldn't be able to surprise her again? "You have the most incredible nerve."

"You mentioned that already. Seven o'clock?"

She wanted to tell him she wouldn't have dinner with him even if he groveled. She wanted to tell him that and all manner of other unpleasant things. Temper fought with practicality. There was a job she'd come to do, one she'd been working on unsuccessfully for three months. Success was more important than pride. He was offering her the perfect way to do what she'd come to do, and to do it more extensively than she could've hoped for. And perhaps, just perhaps, he was opening the door himself for her revenge. It would make it all the sweeter.

Though it was a large lump, Lee swallowed her pride.

"That's fine," she agreed, but he noticed she didn't look too pleased. "Where should I meet you?"

He never trusted easy agreement. But then Hunter trusted very little. She was going to be a challenge, he felt. "I'll pick you up here." His fingers ran casually up to her wrist before he released her. "You might bring your manuscript along. I'm curious to see your work."

She smiled and thought of the article she was going to write. "I very much want you to see my work." Lee stepped into her room and gave herself the small satisfaction of slamming the door in his face.

Chapter 3

Midnight-blue silk. Lee took a great deal of time and gave a great deal of thought to choosing the right dress for her evening with Hunter. It was business.

The deep blue silk shot through with thin silver threads appealed to her because of its clean, elegant lines and lack of ornamentation. Lee would, on the occasions when she shopped, spend as much time choosing the right scarf as she would researching a subject. It was all business.

Now, after a thorough debate, she slipped into the silk. It coolly skimmed her skin; it draped subtly over curves. Her own reflection satisfied her. The unsmiling woman who looked back at her presented precisely the sort of image she wanted to project—elegant, sophisticated and a bit remote. If nothing else, this soothed her bruised ego.

As Lee looked back over her life, concentrating on her career, she could remember no incident where she'd found herself bested. Her mouth became grim as she ran a brush through her hair. It wasn't going to happen now.

Hunter Brown was going to get back some of his own, if for no other reason than that half-amused smile of his. No one laughed at her and got away with it, Lee told herself as she slapped the brush back on the dresser smartly enough to make the bottles jump. Whatever game she had to play to get what she wanted, she'd play. When the article on Hunter Brown hit the stands, she'd have won. She'd have the satisfaction of knowing he'd helped her. In the final analysis, Lee mused, there was no substitute for winning.

When the knock sounded at her door, she glanced at her watch. Prompt. She'd have to make a note of it. Her mood was smug as, after picking up her slim evening bag, she went to answer.

Inherently casual in dress, but not sloppy, she noted, filing the information away as she glanced at the open-collared shirt under his dark jacket. Some men could wear black tie and not look as elegant as Hunter Brown looked in jeans. That was something that might interest her readers. By the end of the evening, Lee reminded herself, she'd know all she possibly could about him.

"Good evening." She started to step across the threshold, but he took her hand, holding her motionless as he studied her.

"Very lovely," Hunter declared. Her hand was very soft and very cool, though her eyes were still hot with annoyance. He liked the contrast. "You wear silk and a very alluring scent but manage to maintain that aura of untouchability. It's quite a talent."

"I'm not interested in being analyzed."

"The curse or blessing of the writer," he countered. "Depending on your viewpoint. Being one yourself, you should understand. Where's your manuscript?"

She'd thought he'd forget—she'd hoped he would. Now, she was back to the disadvantage of stammering. "It, ah, it isn't..."

"Bring it along," Hunter ordered. "I want to take a look at it."

"I don't see why."

"Every writer wants his words read."

She didn't. It wasn't polished. It wasn't perfect. Without a doubt, the last person she wanted to allow a glimpse of her inner thoughts was Hunter. But he was standing, watching, with those dark eyes already seeing beyond the outer layers. Trapped, Lee turned back into the room and slipped the folder from her briefcase. If she could keep him busy enough, she thought, there wouldn't be time for him to look at it anyway.

"It'll be difficult for you to read anything in a restaurant," she pointed out as she closed the door behind her.

"That's why we're having dinner in my suite."

When she stopped, he simply took her hand and continued on to the elevators as if he hadn't noticed. "Perhaps I've given you the wrong impression," she began coldly.

"I don't think so." He turned, still holding her hand. His palm wasn't as smooth as she'd expected a writer's to be. The palm was as wide as a concert pianist's, but it was ridged with calluses. It made, Lee discovered, a very intriguing and uncomfortable combination. "My imagination hasn't gone very deeply into the prospect of seducing you, Lenore." Though he felt her stiffen in outrage, he drew her into the elevator. "The point is, I don't care for restaurants and I care less for crowds and interruptions." The elevator hummed quietly on the short ascent. "Have you found the conference worthwhile?"

"I'm going to get what I came for." She stepped through the doors as they slid open.

"And what's that?"

"What did you come for?" she countered. "You don't exactly make it a habit to attend conferences, and this one is certainly small and off the beaten path."

"Occasionally I enjoy the contact with other writers." Unlocking the door, he gestured her inside.

"This conference certainly isn't bulging with authors who've attained your degree of success."

"Success has nothing to do with writing."

She set her purse and folder aside and faced him straight on. "Easy to say when you have it."

"Is it?" As if amused, he shrugged, then gestured toward the window. "You should drink in as much of the view as you can. You won't see anything like this through any window in Los Angeles."

"You don't care for L.A." If she was careful and clever, she should be able to pin him down on where he lived and why he lived there.

"L.A. has its points. Would you like some wine?"

"Yes." She wandered over to the window. The vastness still had the power to stun her and almost… almost frighten. Once you were beyond the city limits, you might wander for miles without seeing another face, hearing another voice. The isolation, she thought, or perhaps just the space itself, would overwhelm.

"Have you been there often?" she asked, deliberately turning her back to the window.

"Hmm?"

"To Los Angeles?"

"No." He crossed to her and offered a glass of pale gold wine.

"You prefer the East to the West?"

He smiled and lifted his glass. "I make it a point to prefer where I am."

He was very adept at evasions, she thought, and turned away to wander the room. It seemed he was also very adept at making her uneasy. Unless she missed her guess, he did both on purpose. "Do you travel often?"

"Only when it's necessary."

Tipping back her glass, Lee decided to try a more direct approach. "Why are you so secretive about yourself? Most people in your position would make the most of the promotion and publicity that's available."

"I don't consider myself secretive, nor do I consider myself most people."

"You don't even have a bio or a photo on your book covers."

"My face and my background have nothing to do with the stories I tell. Does the wine suit you?"

"It's very good." Though she'd barely tasted it. "Don't you feel it's part of your profession to satisfy the readers' curiosity when it comes to the person who creates a story that interests them?"

"No. My profession is words—putting words together so that someone who reads them is entertained, intrigued and satisfied with a tale. And tales spring from imagination rather than hard fact." He sipped wine himself and approved it. "The teller of the tale is nothing compared to the tale itself."

"Modesty?" Lee asked with a trace of scorn she couldn't prevent.

The scorn seemed to amuse him. "Not at all. It's a matter of priorities, not humility. If you knew me better, you'd understand I have very few virtues." He smiled, but Lee told herself she'd imagined that brief predatory flash in his eyes. Imagined, she told herself again and shuddered. Annoyed at her own reaction, she held out her wineglass for a refill.

"Have you any virtues?"

He liked the fact that she struck back even when her nerves were racing. "Some say vices are more interesting and certainly more entertaining than virtues." He filled her glass to just under the rim. "Would you agree?"

"More interesting, perhaps more entertaining." She refused to let her eyes falter from his as she drank. "Certainly more demanding."

He mulled this over, enjoying her quick response and her clean, direct thought patterns. "You have an interesting mind, Lenore. You keep it exercised."

"A woman who doesn't finds herself watching other people climb to the top while she fills water glasses and makes the coffee." She could have cursed in frustration the moment she'd spoken. It wasn't her habit to speak that freely. The point was, she was here to interview him, Lee reminded herself, not the other way around.

"An interesting analogy," Hunter murmured. Ambition. Yes, he'd sensed that about her from the beginning. But what was it she wanted to achieve? Whatever it was, he mused, she wouldn't be above stepping over a few people to get it. He found he could respect that, could almost admire it. "Tell me, do you ever relax?"

"I beg your pardon?"

"Your hands are rarely still, though you appear to have a great deal of control otherwise." He noted that at his words her fingers stopped toying with the stem of her glass. "Since you've come into this room, you haven't stayed in one spot more than a few seconds. Do I make you nervous?"

Sending him a cool look, she sat on the plush sofa and crossed her legs. "No." But her pulse thudded a bit when he sat down beside her.

"What does?"

"Small, loud dogs."

He laughed, pleased with the moment and with her. "You're a very entertaining woman." He took her hand lightly in his. "I should tell you that's my highest compliment."

"You set a great store by entertainment."

"The world's a grim place—worse, often tedious." Her hand was delicate, and delicacy drew him. Her eyes held secrets, and there was little that intrigued him more. "If we can't be entertained, there're only two places to go. Back to the cave, or on to oblivion."

"So you entertain with terror." She wanted to shift farther away from him, but his fingers had tightened almost imperceptibly on her hand. And his eyes were searching for her thoughts.

"If you're worried about the unspeakable terror lurking outside your bedroom window, would you worry about your next dentist appointment or the fact that your washer overflowed?"

"Escape?"

He reached up to touch her hair. It seemed a very casual, very natural gesture to him. Lee's eyes flew open as if she'd been pinched. "I don't care for the word *escape.*"

She was a difficult combination to resist, Hunter thought, as he let his fingertips skim down the side of her throat. The fiery hair, the vulnerable eyes, the cool gloss of breeding, the bubbling nerves. She'd make a fascinating character and, he realized, a fascinating lover. He'd already decided to have her for the first; now, as he toyed with the ends of her hair, he decided to have her for the second.

She sensed something when his gaze locked on hers again. Decision, determination, desire. Her mouth went dry. It wasn't often that she felt she could be outmatched by another. It was rarer still when anyone or anything truly frightened her. Though he said nothing, though he moved no closer, she found herself fighting back fear—and the knowledge that whatever game she challenged him to, she would lose because he would look into her eyes and know each move before she made it.

A knock sounded at the door, but he continued to look at her for long silent seconds before he rose. "I took the liberty of ordering dinner," he said, so calmly that Lee wondered if she'd imagined the flare of passion she'd seen in his eyes. While he went to the door, she sat where she was, struggling to sort her own thoughts. She was imagining things, Lee told herself. He couldn't see into her and read her thoughts. He was just a man. Since the game was hers, and only she knew the rules, she wouldn't lose. Settled again, she rose to walk to the table.

The salmon was tender and pink. Pleased with the

choice, Lee sat down at the table as the waiter closed the door behind him. So far, Lee reflected, she'd answered more questions than Hunter. It was time to change that.

"The advice you gave earlier to struggling writers about blocking out time to write every day no matter how discouraged they get—did that come from personal experience?"

Hunter sampled the salmon. "All writers face discouragement from time to time. Just as they face criticism and rejection."

"Did you face many rejections before the sale of *The Devil's Due?*"

"I suspect anything that comes too easily." He lifted the wine bottle to fill her glass again. She had a face made for candlelight, he mused as he watched the shadow and light flicker over the cream-soft skin and delicate features. He was determined to find out what lay beneath, before the evening ended.

He never considered he was using her, though he fully intended to pick her brain for everything he could learn about her. It was a writer's privilege.

"What made you become a writer?"

He lifted a brow as he continued to eat. "I was born a writer."

Lee ate slowly, planning her next line of questions. She had to move carefully, avoid putting him on the defensive, maneuver around any suspicions. She never considered she was using him, though she fully intended to pick his brain for everything she could learn about him. It was a reporter's privilege.

"Born a writer," she repeated, flaking off another bite of salmon. "Do you think it's that simple? Weren't there elements in your background, circumstances, early experiences, that led you toward your career?"

"I didn't say it was simple," Hunter corrected. "We're all born with a certain set of choices to make. The matter of making the right ones is anything but simple. Every novel written has to do with choices. Writing novels is what I was meant to do."

He interested her enough that she forgot the unofficial interview and asked for herself, "So you always wanted to be a writer?"

"You're very literal-minded," Hunter observed. Comfortable, he leaned back and swirled the wine in his glass. "No, I didn't. I wanted to play professional soccer."

"Soccer?"

Her astonished disbelief made him smile. "Soccer," he repeated. "I wanted to make a career of it and might have been successful at it, but I had to write."

Lee was silent a moment, then decided he was telling her precisely the truth. "So you became a writer without really wanting to."

"I made a choice," Hunter corrected, intrigued by the orderly logic of her mind. "I believe a great many people are born writer or artist, and die without ever realizing it. Books go unwritten, paintings unpainted. The fortunate ones are those who discover what they were meant to do. I might have been an excellent soccer player. I might have been an excellent writer. If I'd tried to do both, I'd have been no more than mediocre. I chose not to be mediocre."

"There're several million readers who'd agree you made the right choice." Forgetting the cool facade, she propped her elbows on the table and leaned forward. "Why horror fiction, Hunter? Someone with your skill and your imagination could write anything. Why did you turn your talents toward that particular genre?"

He lit a cigarette so that the scent of tobacco stung the air. "Why do you read it?"

She frowned; he hadn't turned one of her questions back on her for some time. "I don't as a rule, except yours."

"I'm flattered. Why mine?"

"Your first was recommended to me, and then..." She hesitated, not wanting to say she'd been hooked from the first page. Instead, she ran her fingertip around the rim of her glass and sorted through her answer. "You have a way of creating atmosphere and drawing characters that make the impossibility of your stories perfectly believable."

He blew out a stream of smoke. "Do you think they're impossible?"

She gave a quick laugh, a laugh he recognized as genuine from the humor that lit her eyes. It did something very special to her beauty. It made it accessible. "I hardly believe in people being possessed by demons or a house being inherently evil."

"No?" He smiled. "No superstitions, Lenore?"

She met his gaze levelly. "None."

"Strange, most of us have a few."

"Do you?"

"Of course, and even the ones I don't have fascinate me." He took her hand, linking fingers firmly. "It's said some people are able to sense another's aura, or personality if the word suits you better, by a simple clasp of hands." His palm was warm and hard as he kept his eyes fixed on hers. She could feel, cool against her hand, the twisted metal of his ring.

"I don't believe that." But she wasn't so sure, not with him.

"You believe only in what you see or feel. Only in what can be touched with one of the five senses that you understand." He rose, drawing her to her feet. "Everything that is can't be understood. Everything that's understood can't be explained."

"Everything has an explanation." But she found the words, like her pulse, a bit unsteady.

She might have drawn her hand away, and he might have let her, but her statement seemed to be a direct challenge. "Can you explain why your heart beats faster when I step closer?" His face looked mysterious, his eyes like jet in the candlelight. "You said you weren't afraid of me."

"I'm not."

"But your pulse throbs." His fingertip lightly touched the hollow of her throat. "Can you explain why when we've yet to spend even one full day together, I want to touch you, like this?" Gently, incredibly gently, he ran the back of his hand up the side of her face.

"Don't." It was only a whisper.

"Can you explain this kind of attraction between two strangers?" He traced a finger over her lips, felt them tremble, wondered about their taste.

Something soft, something flowing, moved through her. "Physical attraction's no more than chemistry."

"Science?" He brought her hand up, pressing his lips to the center of her palm. She felt the muscles in her thighs turn to liquid. "Is there an equation for this?" Still watching her, he brushed his lips over her wrist. Her skin chilled, then heated. Her pulse jolted and scrambled. He smiled. "Does this—" he whispered a kiss at the corner of her mouth "—have to do with logic?"

"I don't want you to touch me like this."

"You want me to touch you," Hunter corrected. "But you can't explain it." In an expected move, he thrust his hands into her hair. "Try the unexplainable," he challenged before his lips closed over hers.

Power. It sped through her. Desire was a rush of heat. She could feel need sing through her as she stood motionless in his arms. She should have refused him. Lee was experienced in the art of refusals. There was suddenly no wit to evade, no strength to refuse.

For all his intensity, for all the force of his personality, the kiss was meltingly soft. Though his fingers were strong and firm in her hair, so firm if she'd tried to move away she'd have found herself trapped, his lips were as gentle and warm as the light that flickered on the table beside them. She didn't know when she reached for him, but her arms were around him, bodies merging, silk rustling. The quiet, intoxicating taste of wine was on his tongue. Lee drank it in. She could smell the candle wax and her own perfume. Her ordered, disciplined mind swam first with confusion, then with sensation after alluring sensation.

Her lips were cool but warmed quickly. Her body was tense but slowly relaxed. He enjoyed both changes. She wasn't a woman who gave herself freely or easily. He knew that just as he knew she wasn't a woman often taken by surprise.

She seemed very small against him, very fragile. He'd always treated fragility with great care. Even as the kiss grew deeper, even as his own need grew surprisingly greater, his mouth remained gentle on hers, teasing, requesting. He believed that lovemaking, from first touch to fulfillment, was an art. He believed that art could never be rushed. So, slowly, patiently, he showed her what might be, while his hands stayed only in her hair and his mouth stayed softly on her.

He was draining her. Lee could feel her will, her strength, her thoughts, seeping out of her. And as they drained away, a flood of sensation replenished what she lost. There was no dealing with it, no…explaining. It could only be experienced.

Pleasure this fluid couldn't be contained. Desire this strong couldn't be guided. It was the lack of control more than the flood of feeling that frightened her most. If she lost her control, she'd lose her purpose. Then she would flounder. With a murmured protest, she pulled away but found that while he freed her lips, he still held her.

Later, he thought, at some lonely, dark hour, he'd explore his own reaction. Now he was much more interested in hers. She looked at him as though she'd been struck—face pale, eyes dark. Though her lips parted, she said nothing. Under his fingers he could feel the light tremor that coursed through her—once, then twice.

"Some things can't be explained, even when they're understood." He said it softly, so softly she might have thought it a threat.

"I don't understand you at all." She put her hands on his forearms as if to draw him away. "I don't think I want to anymore."

He didn't smile as he let his hands slide down to her shoulders. "Perhaps not. You'll have a choice to make."

"No." Shaken, she stepped away and snatched up her purse. "The conference ends tomorrow and I go back to L.A." Suddenly angry, she turned to face him. "You'll go back to whatever hole it is you hide in."

He inclined his head. "Perhaps." It was best she'd put

some distance between them. Very abruptly, he realized that if he'd held her a moment longer, he wouldn't have let her go. "We'll talk tomorrow."

She didn't question her own illogic, but shook her head. "No, we won't talk anymore."

He didn't correct her when she walked to the door, and he stood where he was when the door closed behind her. There was no need to contradict her; he knew they'd talk again. Lifting his glass of wine, Hunter gathered up the manuscript she'd forgotten and settled himself in a chair.

Chapter 4

Anger. Perhaps what Lee felt was simple anger, without other eddies and currents of emotion, but she wasn't certain whom she felt angry with.

What had happened the evening before could have been avoided—should have been, she corrected as she stepped out of the shower. Because she'd allowed Hunter to set the pace and the tone, she'd put herself in a vulnerable position *and* she'd wasted a valuable opportunity. If Lee had learned anything in her years as a reporter, it was that a wasted opportunity was the most destructive mistake in the business.

How much did she know of Hunter Brown that could be used in a concise, informative article? Enough for a paragraph, Lee thought in disgust. A very short paragraph.

She might have only one chance to make up for lost time. Time lost because she'd let herself feel like a woman instead of thinking like a reporter. He'd led her along on a leash, she admitted bitterly, rubbing a towel over her dripping hair while the heat lamp in the ceiling warmed her skin. Instead of balking, she'd gone obediently where he'd taken her. And had missed the most important interview of her career. Lee tossed down the towel and stalked out of the steamy bathroom.

Telling herself she felt nothing but annoyance for him and for herself, Lee pulled on a robe before she sat down at the small writing desk. She still had some time before room service would deliver her first cup of coffee, but there wasn't any more time to waste. Business first…and last. She pulled out a pad and pencil.

HUNTER BROWN. Lee headed the top of the pad in bold letters and underlined the name. The problem had been, she admitted, that she hadn't approached Hunter—the assignment—logically, systematically. She could correct that now with a basic outline. She had, after all, seen him, spoken to him, asked him a few elementary questions. As far as she knew, no other reporter could make such a claim. It was time to stop berating herself for not tying everything up neatly in a matter of hours and make the slim advantage she still had work for her. She began to write in a decisive hand.

APPEARANCE. Not typical. Now there was a positive statement, she thought with a frown. In three bold strokes, she crossed out the words. Dark; lean, rangy build, she wrote. Like a long-distance runner, a cross-country skier. Her eyes narrowed as she brought his face to the foreground of her memory. Rugged face, offset by an air of intelligence. Most outstanding feature—eyes. Very dark, very direct, very…unnerving.

Was that editorializing? she asked herself. Would those long, quiet stares disturb everyone? Shrugging the question away, Lee continued to write. Tall, perhaps six-one, approximately a hundred sixty pounds. Very confident. Musician's hands, poet's mouth.

A bit surprised by her own description, Lee went on to her next category.

PERSONALITY. Enigmatic. Not enough, she decided, huffing slightly. Arrogant, self-absorbed, rude. Definitely editorializing. She set down her pen and took a deep breath, then picked it up again. A skilled, mesmerizing speaker, she admitted in print. Perceptive, cool, taciturn and open by turns, physical.

The last word had been a mistake, Lee discovered, as it brought back the memory of that long, soft, draining kiss, the gentleness of the mouth, the firmness of his hands. No, that wasn't for publication, nor would she need notes to bring back all the details, all the sensations. She would, however, be wise to remember that he was a man who moved quickly when he chose, a man who apparently took precisely what he wanted.

Humor? Yes, under the intensity there was humor in him. She didn't like recalling how he'd laughed at her, but when she had such a dearth of material, she needed every detail, uncomfortable or not.

She remembered every word he'd said on his philosophy of writing. But how could she translate something so intangible into a few clean, pragmatic sentences? She could say he thought of his work as an obligation. A vocation. It just wasn't enough, she thought in frustration. She needed his own words here, not a translation of his meaning. The simple truth was, she had to speak to him again.

Dragging a hand through her hair, she read over her orderly notes. She should have held the reins of the conversation from the very beginning. If she was an expert on anything, it was on channeling and steering talk along the lines she wanted. She'd interviewed subjects more closemouthed than Hunter, more hostile, but she couldn't remember any more frustrating.

Absently, she began to tap the end of her pencil against the table. It wasn't her job to be frustrated, but to be productive. It wasn't her job, she added, to allow herself to be so utterly seduced by an assignment.

She could have prevented the kiss. It still wasn't clear to Lee why she hadn't. She could have controlled her response to it. She didn't want to dwell on why she hadn't. It was much too easy to remember that long, strangely intense moment and in remembering, to feel it all again. If she was going to prevent herself from doing that, and remember instead all the reasons she'd come to Flagstaff, she had to put Hunter Brown firmly in the category of assignment and keep him there. For now, her biggest problem was how she was going to manage to see him again.

Professionally, she warned herself. But she couldn't sit still thinking of it, or him. Pacing, she tried to block out the incredibly gentle feel of his mouth on hers. And failed.

A flood of feeling; she'd never experienced anything like it. The weakness, the power—it was beyond her to understand it. The longing, the need—how could she know the way to control it?

If she understood him better perhaps… No. Lee lifted her hairbrush, then set it down again. No, understanding Hunter would have nothing to do with fighting her desire for him. She'd wanted to be touched by him, and though she had no logical reason for it, she'd wanted to be touched more than she'd wanted to do her job. It was unprecedented, Lee admitted as she absently pushed bottles and jars around on her dresser. When something was unprecedented, you had to make up your own guidelines.

Uneasy, she glanced up and saw a pale woman with sleepy eyes and unruly hair reflected in the glass. She looked too young, too…fragile. No one ever saw her without the defensive shield of grooming, but she knew what was beneath the fastidiousness and gloss. Fear. Fear of failure.

She'd built her confidence stone by meticulous stone, until most of the time she believed in it herself. But at moments like this, when she was alone, a little weary, a little discouraged, the woman inside crept out, and with her, all the tiny doubts and fears behind that laboriously built wall.

She'd been trained from birth to be little more than an intelligent, attractive ornament. Well-spoken, well-groomed, well-disciplined. It was all her family expected of her. No, Lee corrected. It was *what* had been expected of her. In that respect, she'd already failed.

What trick of fate had made it so impossible for her to fit the mold she'd been fashioned for? Since childhood she'd known she needed more, yet it had taken her until after college to store up enough courage to break away from the road that would have led her from proper debutante to proper matron.

When she'd told her parents she wasn't going to be Mrs. Jonathan T. Willoby, but was leaving Palm Springs to live and work in Los Angeles, she'd been quaking inside. Not until later did she realize it had been their training that had seen her through the very difficult meeting. She'd been taught to remain cool and composed, never to raise her voice, never to show any vulgar signs of temper. When she'd spoken to them, she'd seemed perfectly sure of her own mind, while in truth she'd been terrified of leaving that comfortable gilt cage they'd been fashioning for her since before she was born.

Five years later, the fear had dulled, but it remained. Part of her drive to reach the top in her profession came from the very basic need to prove herself to her parents.

Foolish, she told herself, turning away from the vulnerability of the woman in the glass. She had nothing to prove to anyone, unless it was to herself. She'd come for a story, and that was her first, her only priority. The story was going to gel for her if she had to dog Hunter Brown's footsteps like a bloodhound.

Lee looked down at her notebook again, and at the notes that filled less than a page. She'd have more before the day was over, she promised herself. Much more. He wouldn't get the upper hand again, nor would he distract her from her purpose. As soon as she'd dressed and had her morning coffee, she'd look for Hunter. This time, she'd stay firmly behind the wheel.

When she heard the knock, Lee glanced at the clock beside her bed and gave a little sigh of frustration. She was running behind schedule, something she never permitted herself to do. She'd deliberately requested coffee and rolls for nine o'clock so that she could be dressed and ready to go when they were delivered. Now she'd have to rush to make certain she had a couple of solid hours with Hunter before check-out time. She wasn't going to miss an opportunity twice.

Impatient with herself, she went to the door, drew off the chain and pulled it open.

"You might as well eat nothing if you think you can subsist on a couple of pieces of bread and some jam." Before she could recover, Hunter swooped by her, carrying her breakfast tray. "And an intelligent woman never answers the door without asking who's on the other side." Setting the tray on the table, he turned to pin her with one of his long, intrusive stares.

She looked younger without the gloss of makeup and careful style. The traces of fragility he'd already sensed had no patina of sophistication over them now, though her robe was silk and the sapphire color flattering. He felt a flare of desire and a simultaneous protective twinge. Neither could completely deaden his anger.

She wasn't about to let him know how stunned she was to see him, or how disturbed she was that he was here alone with her when she was all but naked. "First a chauffeur, now a waiter," she said coolly, unsmiling. "You're a man of many talents, Hunter."

"I could return the compliment." Because he knew just how volatile his temper could be, he poured a cup of coffee. "Since one of the first requirements of a fiction writer is that he be a good liar, you're well on your way." He gestured to a chair, putting Lee uncomfortably in the position of visitor. As though she weren't the least concerned, she crossed the room and seated herself at the table.

"I'd ask you to join me, but there's only one cup." She broke a croissant in two and nibbled on it, unbuttered. "You're welcome to a roll." With a steady hand, she added cream to the coffee. "Perhaps you'd like to explain what you mean about my being a good liar."

"I suppose it's a requirement of a reporter as well." Hunter saw her fingers tense on the flaky bit of bread then relax, one by one.

"No." Lee took another bite of her roll as if her stomach hadn't just sunk to her knees. "Reporters deal in fact, not fiction." He said nothing, but the silent look demanded more of her than a dozen words would have. Taking her time, determined not to fumble again, she sipped at her coffee. "I don't remember mentioning that I was a reporter."

"No, you didn't mention it." He caught her wrist as she set down the cup. The grip of his fingers told her immediately just how angry he was. "You quite deliberately didn't mention it."

With a jerk of her head, she tossed the hair out of her eyes. If she'd lost, she wouldn't go down groveling. "It wasn't required that I tell you." Ignoring the fact that he held one of her hands prisoner, Lee picked up her croissant with the other and took a bite. "I paid my registration fee."

"And pretended to be something you're not."

She met his gaze without flinching. "Apparently, we both pretended to be something we weren't, right from the start."

He tilted his head at her reference to their initial meeting. "I didn't want anything from you. You, on the other hand, went beyond the harmless in your deception."

She didn't like the way it sounded when he said it—so petty, so dirty. And so true. If his fingers hadn't been biting into her wrist, she might have found herself apologizing. Instead, Lee held her ground. "I have a perfect right to be here and a perfect right to try to sell an article on any facet of this conference."

"And I," he said, so mildly her flesh chilled, "have a perfect right to my privacy, to the choice of speaking to a reporter or refusing to speak to one."

"If I'd told you that I was on staff at *Celebrity,*" she threw back, making her first attempt to free her arm, "would you have spoken to me at all?"

He still held her wrist; he still held her eyes. For several long seconds, he said nothing. "That's something neither of us will ever know now." He released her wrist so abruptly, her arm dropped to the table, clattering the cup. Lee found that she'd squeezed the flaky pastry into an unpalatable ball.

He frightened her. There was no use denying it even to herself. The force of his anger, so finely restrained, had tiny shocks of cold moving up and down her back. She didn't know him or understand him, nor did she have any way of being certain of what he might do. There was violence in his books; therefore, there was violence in his mind. Clinging to her composure, she lifted her coffee again, drank and tasted absolutely nothing.

"I'm curious to know how you found out." Good, her voice was calm, unhurried. She took the cup in both hands to cover the one quick tremor she couldn't control.

She looked like a kitten backed into a corner, Hunter observed. Ready to spit and scratch, even though her heart was pounding hard enough to be almost audible. He didn't want to respect her for it when he'd rather strangle her. He didn't want to feel a strong urge to touch the pale skin of her cheek. Being deceived by a woman was perhaps the only thing that still had the power to bring him to this degree of rage.

"Oddly enough, I took an interest in you, Lenore.

Last night—" He saw her stiffen and felt a certain satisfaction. No, he wasn't going to let her forget that, any more than he could forget it himself. "Last night," he repeated slowly, waiting until her gaze lifted to his again, "I wanted to make love with you. I wanted to get beneath the careful layer of polish and discover you. When I had, you'd have looked as you do now. Soft, fragile, with your mouth naked and your eyes clouded."

Her bones were already melting, her skin already heating, and it was only words. He didn't touch her, didn't attempt to, but the sound of his voice flowed over her skin like the gentlest of caresses. "I don't— I had no intention of letting you make love to me."

"I don't believe in making love to a woman, only with." His eyes never left hers. She could feel her head begin to swim with passion, her breath tremble with it. "Only with," Hunter repeated. "When you left, I turned to the next best way of discovering you."

Lee gripped her hands together in her lap, knowing she had to control the shudders. How could a man have such power? And how could she fight it? Why did she feel as though they were already lovers? Was it just the sense of inevitability that they would be, no matter what her choice? "I don't know what you mean." Her voice was no longer calm.

"Your manuscript."

Uncomprehending, she stared. She'd completely forgotten it the night before in her fear of him, and of herself. Anger and frustration had prevented her from remembering it that morning. Now, on top of a dazed desire, she felt the helplessness of a novice confronted by the master. "I never intended for you to read it," she began. Without thinking, she was shredding her napkin in her lap. "I don't have any aspirations toward being a novelist."

"Then you're a fool as well as a liar."

All sense of helplessness fled. No one, no one in all of her memory, had ever spoken to her like that. "I'm neither a fool nor a liar, Hunter. What I am is an excellent reporter. I want to write an exclusive, in-depth and accurate article on you for our readers."

"Why do you waste your time writing gossip when you've got a novel to finish?"

She went rigid. The eyes that had been clouded with confused desire became frosty. "I don't write gossip."

"You can gloss over it, you can write it with style and intelligence, but it's still gossip." Before Lee could retort, he rose up so quickly, so furiously, her own words were swallowed. "You've no right working forty hours a week on anything but the novel you have inside you. Talent's a two-headed coin, Lenore, and the other side's obligation."

"I don't know what you're talking about." She rose, too, and found she could shout just as effectively as he. "I know my obligations, and one of them's to write a story on you for my magazine."

"And what about the novel?"

Flinging up her hands, she whirled away from him. "What about it?"

"When do you intend to finish it?"

Finish it? She should never have started it. Hadn't she told herself that a dozen times? "Damn it, Hunter, it's a pipe dream."

"It's good."

She turned back, her brows still drawn together with anger but the eyes beneath them suddenly wary. "What?"

"If it hadn't been, your camouflage would have worked very well." He drew out a cigarette while she stared at him. How could he be so patient, move so slowly, when she was ready to jump at every word? "I nearly called you last night to see if you had any more with you, but decided it would keep. I called my editor instead." Still calm, he blew out smoke. "When I gave the chapters to her to read, she recognized your name. Apparently she's quite a fan of *Celebrity*."

"You gave her…" Astonished, Lee dropped into the chair again. "You had no right to show anyone."

"At the time, I fully believed you were precisely what you'd led me to believe you were."

She stood again, then gripped the back of her chair. "I'm a reporter, not a novelist. I'd like you to get the manuscript from her and return it to me."

He tapped his cigarette in an ashtray, only then noticing her neatly written notes. As he skimmed them, Hunter felt twin surges of amusement and annoyance. So, she was trying to put him into a few tidy little slots. She'd find it more difficult than she'd imagined. "Why should I do that?"

"Because it belongs to me. You had no right to give it to anyone else."

"What are you afraid of?" he demanded.

Of failure. The words were almost out before Lee managed to bite them back. "I'm not afraid of anything. I do what I'm best at, and I intend to continue doing it. What are you afraid of?" she retorted. "What are you hiding from?"

She didn't like the look in his eyes when he turned his head toward her again. It wasn't anger she saw there, nor was it arrogance, but something beyond both. "I do what I do best, Lenore." When he'd come into the room, he hadn't planned to do any more than rake her to the bone for her deception and berate her for wasting her talent. Now, as he watched her, Hunter began to think there was a better way to do that and at the same time learn more about her for his own purposes. He was a long way from finished with Lenore Radcliffe. "Just how important is doing a story on me to you?"

Alerted by the change in tone, Lee studied him cautiously. She'd tried everything else, she decided abruptly, perhaps she could appeal to his ego. "It's very important. I've been trying to learn something about you for over three months. You're one of the most popular and critically acclaimed writers of the decade. If you—"

He cut her off by merely lifting a hand. "If I decided to give you an interview, we'd have to spend a great deal of time together, and under my terms."

Lee heard the little warning bell, but ignored it. She could almost taste success. "We can hash out the terms beforehand. I keep my word, Hunter."

"I don't doubt that, once it's given." Crushing out his cigarette, Hunter considered the angles. Perhaps he was asking for trouble. Then again, he hadn't asked for any in quite some time. He was due. "How much more of the manuscript do you have completed?"

"That has nothing to do with this." When he merely lifted a brow and stared, she clenched her teeth. Humor him, Lee told herself. You're too close now. "About two hundred pages."

"Send the rest to my editor." He gave her a mild look. "I'm sure you have her name by now."

"What does that have to do with the interview?"

"It's one of the terms," Hunter told her easily. "I've

plans for the week after next," he continued. "You can join me—with another copy of your manuscript."

"Join you? Where?"

"For two weeks I'll be camping in Oak Creek Canyon. You'd better buy some sturdy shoes."

"Camping?" She had visions of tents and mosquitoes. "If you're not leaving for your vacation right away, why can't we set up the interview a day or two before?"

"Terms," he reminded her. "My terms."

"You're trying to make this difficult."

"Yes." He smiled then, just a hint of amusement around his sculpted mouth. "You'll work for your exclusive, Lenore."

"All right." Her chin came up. "Where should I meet you and when?"

Now he smiled fully, appreciating determination when he saw it. "In Sedona. I'll contact you when I'm certain of the date—and when my editor's let me know she's received the rest of your manuscript."

"I hardly see why you're using that to blackmail me."

He crossed to her then, unexpectedly combing his fingers through her hair. It was casual, friendly and uncannily intimate. "Perhaps one of the first things you should know about me is I'm eccentric. If people accept their own eccentricities, they can justify anything they do. Anything at all." He ended the words by closing his mouth over hers.

He heard her suck in her breath, felt her stiffen. But she didn't struggle away. Perhaps she was testing herself, though he didn't think she could know she tested him, too. He wanted to carry her to the rumpled bed, slip off that thin swirl of silk and fit his body to hers. It would fit; somehow he already knew. She'd move with him, for him, as if they'd always been lovers. He knew, though he couldn't explain.

He could feel her melting into him, her lips growing warm and moist from his. They were alone and the need was like iron. Yet he knew, without understanding, that if they made love now, sated that need, he'd never see her again. They both had fears to face before they became lovers, and after.

Hunter gave himself the pleasure of one long, last kiss, drawing her taste into him, allowing himself to be overwhelmed, just for a moment, by the feel of her against him. Then he forced himself to level, forced himself to remember that they each wanted something from the other—secrets and an intimacy both would put into words in their own ways.

Drawing back, he let his hands linger only a moment on the curve of her cheek, the softness of her hair, while she said nothing. "If you can get through two weeks in the canyon, you'll have your story."

Leaving her with that, he turned and strolled out the door.

"If I can make it through two weeks," Lee muttered, pulling a heavy sweater out of her drawer. "I tell you, Bryan, I've never met anyone who says as little who can irritate me as much." Ten days back in L.A. hadn't dulled her fury.

Bryan fingered the soft wool of the sweater. "Lee, don't you have *any* grub-around clothes?"

"I bought some sweatshirts," she said under her breath. "I haven't spent a great deal of my time in a tent."

"Advice." Before another pair of the trim slacks

could be packed into the knapsack Lee had borrowed from her, Bryan took her hand.

Lee lifted one thin coppery brow. "You know I detest advice."

Grinning, Bryan dropped down on the bed. "I know. That's why I can never resist dishing it out. Lee, really, I know you have a pair of jeans. I've *seen* you wear them." She brushed at the hair that escaped her braid. "Designer or not, take jeans, not seventy-five-dollar slacks. Invest in another pair or two," she went on while Lee frowned down at the clothes still in her free hand. "Put that gorgeous wool sweater back in your drawer and pick up a couple of flannel shirts. That'll take care of the nights if it turns cool. Now…"

Because Lee was listening with a frown of concentration, she continued. "Put in some T-shirts—blouses are for the office, not for hiking. Take at least one pair of shorts and invest in some good thick socks. If you had more time, I'd tell you to break in those new hiking boots, because they're going to make you suffer."

"The salesman said—"

"There's nothing wrong with them, Lee, except they've never been out of the box. Face it." She stretched back among Lee's collection of pillows. "You've been too concerned about packing enough paper and pencils to worry about gear. If you don't want to make an ass of yourself, listen to momma."

With a quick hiss of breath, Lee replaced the sweater. "I've already made an ass of myself, several times." She slammed one of her dresser drawers. "He's not going to get the best of me during these next two weeks, Bryan. If I have to sleep out in a tent and climb rocks to get this story, then I'll do it."

"If you tried real hard, you could have fun at the same time."

"I'm not looking for fun. I'm looking for an exclusive."

"We're friends."

Though it was a statement, not a question, Lee glanced over. "Yes." For the first time since she'd begun packing, she smiled. "We're friends."

"Then tell me what it is that bothers you about this guy. You've been ready to chew your nails for over a week." Though she spoke lightly, the concern leaked through. "You wanted to interview Hunter Brown, and you're going to interview Hunter Brown. How come you look like you're preparing for war?"

"Because that's how I feel." With anyone else, Lee would have evaded the question or turned cold. Because it was Bryan, she sat on the edge of the bed, twisting a newly purchased sweatshirt in her hands. "He makes me want what I don't want to want, feel what I don't want to feel. Bryan, I don't have room in my life for complications."

"Who does?"

"I know exactly where I'm going," Lee insisted, a bit too vehemently. "I know exactly how to get there. Somehow I have a feeling that Hunter's a detour."

"Sometimes a detour is more interesting than a planned route, and you get to the same place eventually."

"He looks at me as though he knows what I'm thinking. More, as if he knows what I thought yesterday, or last year. It's not comfortable."

"You've never looked for the comfortable," Bryan stated, pillowing her head on her folded arms. "You've always looked for a challenge. You've just never found one in a man before."

"I don't want one in a man." Violently, Lee stuffed the sweatshirt into the knapsack. "I want them in my work."

"You don't have to go."

Lee lifted her head. "I'm going."

"Then don't go with your teeth gritted." Crossing her legs under her, Bryan sat up. She was as rumpled as Lee was tidy but seemed oddly suited to the luxurious pile of pillows around her. "This is a tremendous opportunity for you, professionally and personally. Oak Creek's one of the most beautiful canyons in the country. You'll have two weeks to be part of it. There's a man who doesn't bore or cater to you." She grinned at Lee's arch look. "You know damn well they do one or the other and you can't abide it. Enjoy the change of scene."

"I'm going to work," Lee reminded her. "Not to pick wildflowers."

"Pick a few anyway. You'll still get your story."

"And make Hunter Brown squirm."

Bryan gave her throaty laugh, tossing a pillow into the air. "If that's what you're set on doing, you'll do it. I'd feel sorry for the guy if he hadn't given me nightmares." After a quick grimace, her look softened into one of affection. "And, Lee..." She laid her hand over her friend's. "If he makes you want something, take it. Life isn't crowded with offers. Give yourself a present."

Lee sat silently for a moment, then sighed. "I'm not sure if I'd be giving myself a present or a curse." Rising, she went to her dresser. "How many pairs of socks?"

"But is she pretty?" Sarah sat in the middle of the rug, one leg bent toward her while she tried valiantly to hook the other behind her neck. "*Really* pretty?"

Hunter dug into the basket of laundry. Sarah had

scrupulously reminded him it was his turn to sort and fold. "I wouldn't use the word *pretty.* A carefully arranged basket of fruit's pretty."

Sarah giggled, then rolled and arched into a back bend. She liked nothing better than talking with her father, because no one else talked like him. "What word would you use, then?"

Hunter folded a T-shirt with the name of a popular rock band glittered across it. "She has a rare, classic beauty that a lot of women wouldn't know precisely what to do with."

"But she does?"

He remembered. He wanted. "She does."

Sarah lay down on her back to snuggle with the dog that stretched out beside her. She liked the soft, warm feel of Santanas's fur, in much the same way she liked to close her eyes and listen to her father's voice. "She tried to fool you," Sarah reminded him. "You don't like it when people try to fool you."

"To her way of thinking, she was doing her job."

With one hand on the dog's neck, Sarah looked up at her father with big, dark eyes so much like his own. "You never talk to reporters."

"They don't interest me." Hunter came upon a pair of jeans with a widening hole in the knee. "Aren't these new?"

"Sort of. So why are you taking her camping with you?"

"Sort of new shouldn't have holes already, and I'm not taking her, she's coming with me."

Digging in her pocket, she came up with a stick of gum. She wasn't supposed to chew any because of her braces, so she fondled the wrapped piece instead. In six months, Sarah thought, she was going to chew a dozen pieces, all at once. "Because she's a reporter or because she has a rare, classic beauty?"

Hunter glanced down to see his daughter's eyes laughing at him. She was entirely too clever, he decided, and threw a pair of rolled socks at her. "Both, but mostly because I find her interesting and talented. I want to see how much I can find out about her, while she's trying to find out about me."

"You'll find out more," Sarah declared, idly tossing the socks up in the air. "You always do. I think it's a good idea," she added after a moment. "Aunt Bonnie says you don't see enough women, especially women who challenge your mind."

"Aunt Bonnie thinks in couples."

"Maybe she'll incite your simmering passion."

Hunter's hand paused on its way to the basket. "What?"

"I read it in a book." Expertly, she rolled so that her feet touched the floor behind her head. "This man met this woman, and they didn't like each other at first, but there was this strong physical attraction and this growing desire, and—"

"I get the picture." Hunter looked down at the slim, dark-haired girl on the floor. She was his daughter, he thought. She was ten. How in God's name had they gotten involved in the subject of passion? "You of all people should know that things don't often happen in real life the way they do in books."

"Fiction's based on reality." Sarah grinned, pleased to throw one of his own quotes back at him. "But before you do fall in love with her, or have too much simmering passion, I want to meet her."

"I'll keep that in mind." Still watching her, Hunter

held up three unmatched socks. “Just how does this happen every week?”

Sarah considered the socks a moment, then sat up. “I think there’s a parallel universe in the dryer. On the other side of the door, at this very minute, someone else is holding up three unmatched socks.”

“An interesting theory.” Reaching down, Hunter grabbed her. As Sarah’s laughter bounced off the lofted ceiling, he dropped her, bottom first, into the basket.

Chapter 5

It was like every Western she'd ever seen. With the sun bright in her eyes, Lee could almost see outlaws out-running posses and Indians hiding in wait behind rocks and buttes. If she let her imagination go, she could almost hear the hoofbeats ring against the rock-hard ground. Because she was alone in the car, she could let her imagination go.

The rich red mountains rose up into a painfully blue sky. There was a vastness that was almost outrageous in scope, with no lushness, with no need for any, with no patience for any. It made her throat dry and her heart thud.

There was green—the silvery-green of sage clinging to the red, rocky soil and the deeper hue of junipers, which would give way to a sudden, seemingly planned sparseness. Yet the sparseness was rich in itself. The space, the overwhelming space, left her stunned and humble and oddly hungry for more. Everywhere there were more rocky ridges, more color, more... Lee shook her head. Just more.

Even when she came closer to town, the houses and buildings couldn't compete with the openness. Stop signs, streetlights, flower gardens were inconsequential. Her car joined more cars, but five times the number would still have been insignificant. It was a view you drank in, she thought, but its taste was hot and packed a punch.

She liked Sedona immediately. Its tidy Western flavor suited the fabulous backdrop instead of marring it. She hadn't been sure anything could.

The main street was lined with shops with neat signs and clean plate glass. She noticed lots of wood, lots of bargains and absolutely no sense of urgency. Sedona clung to the aura of town rather than city. It seemed comfortable with itself and with the spectacular spread of sky. Perhaps, Lee mused as she followed the directions to the rental-car drop-off, just perhaps, she'd enjoy the next two weeks after all.

Since she was early for her arranged meeting time with Hunter even after dealing with the paperwork on her rental car, Lee decided she could afford to indulge herself playing tourist. She had nearly an hour to vacation before work began again.

The liquid silver necklaces and turquoise earrings in the shop windows tempted her, but she moved past them. There'd be plenty of opportunities after this little adventure for something frivolous—as a reward for success. For now, she was only passing time.

But the scent of fudge drew her. Slipping inside the little shop that claimed to sell the world's best, Lee bought a half pound. For energy, she told herself as the sample melted in her mouth. There was no telling what kind of food she'd get over the next two weeks. Hunter had very specifically told her when he contacted her by phone that he'd handle the supplies. The fudge, Lee told herself, would be emergency rations.

Besides, some of Bryan's advice had been valid enough. There was no use going into this thing thinking she'd be miserable and uncomfortable. There wasn't any harm getting into the spirit a bit, Lee decided as she strolled into a Western-wear shop. If she viewed the next two weeks as a working vacation, she'd be much better off.

Though she toyed with conch belts for a few minutes, Lee rejected them. They wouldn't suit her, any more than the fringed or sequined shirts would. Perhaps she'd pick one up for Bryan before heading back to L.A. Anything Bryan put on suited her, Lee mused with something closer to a sigh than to envy. Bryan never had to feel restricted to the tailored, the simple or the proper.

Was it a matter of suitability, Lee wondered, or a matter of image? With a shrug, she ran a fingertip down the shoulder of a short suede jacket. Image or not, she'd locked herself into it for too long to change now. She didn't want to change, in any case, Lee reminded herself as she wandered through rows and rows of hats. She understood Lee Radcliffe just as she was.

Telling herself she'd stay only another minute, she set her knapsack at her feet. She wasn't particularly athletic. Lee tried on a dung-colored Stetson with a curved brim. She wasn't flighty. She exchanged the first hat for a smaller one with a spray of feathers in the band. What she was, was businesslike and down-to-earth. She dropped a black flat-brimmed hat on her head and studied the result. Sedate, she decided, smiling a little. Practical. Yes, if she were in the market for—

"You're wearing it all wrong."

Before Lee could react, two strong hands were tilting the hat farther down on her head. Critically, Hunter angled it slightly, then stepped away. "Yes, it's the perfect choice for you. The contrast with your hair and skin, that practical sort of dash." Taking her shoulders, her turned her toward the mirror, where both his image and hers looked back at her.

She saw the way his fingers held her shoulders, long and confident. She could see how small she looked pressing against him. In no more than an instant, Lee could feel the pleasure she wanted to ignore and the annoyance she had to concentrate on.

"I've no intention of buying it." Embarrassed, she drew the hat off and returned it to the shelf.

"Why not?"

"I've no need for it."

"A woman who buys only what she needs?" Amusement crossed his face even as anger crossed hers. "A sexist remark if I've ever heard one," Hunter continued before she could speak. "Still, it's a pity you won't buy it. It gives you a breezy air of confidence."

Ignoring that, Lee bent down and picked up her knapsack again. "I hope I haven't kept you waiting long. I got into town early and decided to kill some time."

"I saw you wander in here when I drove in. Even in jeans you walk as though you were wearing a three-piece suit." While she tried to work out if that had been a compliment, he smiled. "What kind did you buy?"

"What?" She was still frowning over his comment.

"Fudge." He glanced down at the bag. "What kind did you buy?"

Caught again, Lee thought, nearly resigned to it. "Some milk chocolate and some rocky road."

"Good choice." Taking her arm, he led her through the shop. "If you're determined to resist the hat, we may as well get started."

She noted the Jeep parked at the curb and narrowed her eyes. This was certainly the same one he'd had in Flagstaff. "Have you been staying in Arizona?"

He circled the hood, leaving her to climb in on her own. "I've had some business to take care of."

Her reporter's sense sharpened. "Research?"

He gave her that odd ghost of a smile. "A writer's always researching." He wouldn't tell her—yet—that his research on Lenore Radcliffe had led him to some intriguing conclusions. "You brought a copy of the rest of your manuscript?"

Unable to prevent herself, Lee shot him a look of intense dislike. "That was one of the conditions."

"So it was." Easily he backed up, then pulled into the thin stream of traffic. "What's your impression of Sedona?"

"I can see that the weather and the atmosphere would draw the tourist trade." She found it necessary to sit very erect and to look straight ahead.

"The same might be said of Maui or the South of France."

She couldn't stop her lips from curving, but turned to look out the side window. "It has the air of having been here forever, with very little change. The sense of space is fierce, not at all soothing, but it pulls you in. I suppose it makes me think of the people who first saw it from horseback or the seat of a wagon. I imagine some of them would have been compelled to build right away, to set up a community so that the vastness didn't overwhelm them."

"And others would have been drawn to the desert or the mountains so that the buildings wouldn't close them in."

As she nodded, it occurred to her that she might fit into the first group, and he into the second.

The road he took narrowed and twisted down. He didn't drive sedately, but with the air of a man who knew he could negotiate whatever curve was thrown at him. Lee gripped the door handle, determined not to comment on his speed. It was like taking the downhill rush of a roller coaster without having had the preparatory uphill climb. They whooshed down, a rock wall on one side, a spiraling drop on the other.

"Do you camp often?" Her knuckles were whitening on the handle, but though she had to shout to be heard she was satisfied that her voice was calm enough.

"Now and again."

"I'm curious..." She stopped and cleared her throat as Hunter whipped around a snaking turn. "Why camping?" Did the rocks in the sheer wall beside them ever loosen and tumble onto the road? She decided it was best not to think about it. "A man in your position could go anywhere and do anything he chose."

"This is what I chose," he pointed out.

"All right. Why?"

"There are times when everyone needs simplicity."

Her foot pressed down on the floorboard as if it were a brake pedal. "Isn't this just one more way you have of avoiding people?"

"Yes." His easy agreement had her turning her head

to stare at him. He was amused to note that her hand loosened on the handle and that her concentration was on him now rather than the road. "It's also a way of getting away from my work. You never get away from writing, but there are times you need to get away from the trappings of writing."

Her gaze sharpened. Though her fingers itched for her notebook, Lee had faith in her own powers of retention. "You don't like trappings."

"We don't always like what's necessary."

Oblivious to the speed and the curves now, Lee tucked one leg under her and turned toward him. That attracted him, Hunter reflected. The way she'd unconsciously drop that careful shield whenever something challenged her mind. That attracted him every bit as much as her cool, nineteenth-century beauty.

"What do you consider trappings as regards your profession?"

"The confinement of an office, the hum of a machine, the paperwork that's unavoidable but interferes with the story flow."

Odd, but that was precisely what she needed in order to maintain discipline. "If you could change it, what would you do?"

He smiled again. Hunter had never known anyone who thought in more basic terms or straighter lines. "I'd go back a few centuries to when I could simply travel and tell the story."

She believed him. Though he had wealth and fame and critical acclaim, Lee believed him. "None of the rest means anything to you, does it? The glory, the admiration?"

"Whose admiration?"

"Your readers and the critics."

He pulled off the road next to a small wooden building that served as a trading post. "I'm not indifferent to my readership, Lenore."

"But to the critics."

"I admire the orderliness of your mind," he said and stepped from the Jeep.

It was a good beginning, Lee thought, pleased, as she climbed out the passenger side. He'd already told her more than anyone else knew, and the two weeks had barely begun. If she could just keep him talking, learn enough generalities, then she could pin him down on specifics. But she'd have to pace herself. When you were dealing with a master of evasion, you had to tread carefully. She couldn't afford to relax.

"Do we have to check in?"

From behind her back Hunter grinned, while Lee struggled to pull out her knapsack. "I've already taken care of the paperwork."

"I see." Her pack was heavy, but she told herself she'd refuse any offer of assistance and carry it herself. A moment later, she saw it wouldn't be an issue. Hunter merely stood aside, watching as she wriggled into the shoulder straps. So much for chivalry, she thought, annoyed that he hadn't given her the opportunity to assert her independence. She caught the gleam in his eye. He read her mind much too easily.

"Want me to carry the fudge?"

She closed her fingers firmly over the bag. "I'll manage."

With his own gear on his back, Hunter started down a path, leaving her no choice but to follow. He moved as though he'd been walking dirt paths all his life—as if perhaps he'd cut a few of his own. Though she felt out of place in her hiking boots, Lee was determined to keep up and to make it look easy.

"You've camped here before?"

"Mmm-hmm."

"Why?"

He stopped, turning to fix her with that dark, intense stare that always took her breath away. "You only have to look."

She did and saw that the walls and peaks of the canyon rose up as if they'd never stop. They were a color and texture unique to themselves, enhanced by the snatches of green from rough, hardy trees and shrubs that seemed to grow out of the rock. As she had from the air, Lee thought of castles and fortresses, but without the distance the plane had given her, she couldn't be sure whether she was storming the walls or being enveloped by them.

She was warm. The sun was strong, even with the shade of trees that grew thickly at this elevation. Though she saw other people—children, adults, babies carried papoose-style—she felt no sense of crowding.

It's like a painting, she realized all at once. It's as though we're walking into a canvas. The feeling it gave her was both eerie and irresistible. She shifted the pack on her back as she kept pace with Hunter.

"I noticed some houses," she began. "I didn't realize people actually lived in the canyon."

"Apparently."

Sensing his mind was elsewhere, Lee lapsed into silence. She'd done too well to start pushing. For now, she'd follow Hunter, since he obviously knew where he was going.

It surprised her that she found the walk pleasant. For

years her life had been directed by deadlines, rush and self-imposed demands. If someone had asked her where she'd choose to spend two weeks relaxing, her mind would have gone blank. But when ideas had begun to come, roughing it in a canyon in Arizona wouldn't have made the top ten. She'd never have considered that the purity of air and the unimpeded arch of sky would be so appealing to her.

She heard a quiet, musical tinkle that took her several moments to identify. The creek, Lee realized. She could smell the water. The new sensation gave her a quick thrill. Her guide, and her project, continued to move at a steady pace in front of her. Lee banked down the urge to share her discovery with him. He'd only think her foolish.

Did she realize how totally out of her element she looked? Hunter wondered. It had taken him only one glance to see that the jeans and the boots she wore were straight out of the box. Even the T-shirt that fit softly over her torso was obviously boutiqueware rather than a department-store purchase. She looked like a model posing as a camper. She smelled expensive, exclusive. Wonderful. What kind of woman carried a worn knap-sack and wore sapphire studs in her ears?

As her scent wafted toward him again, carried on the breeze, Hunter reminded himself that he had two weeks to find out. Whatever notes she would make on him, he'd be making an equal number on her. Perhaps both of them would have what they wanted before the time was up. Perhaps both of them would have cause to regret it.

He wanted her. It had been a long time since he'd wanted anything, anyone, that he didn't already have. Over the past days he'd thought often of her response to that long, lingering kiss. He'd thought of his own response. They'd learn about each other over the next two weeks, though they each had their own purposes. But nothing was free. They'd both pay for it.

The quiet soothed him. The towering walls of the canyon soothed him. Lee saw their ferocity, he their tranquillity. Perhaps they both saw what they needed to see.

"For a woman, and a reporter, you have an amazing capacity for silence."

The weight of her pack was beginning to take precedence over the novelty of the scenery. Not once had he asked if she wanted to stop and rest, not once had he even bothered to look back to see if she was still behind him. She wondered why he didn't feel the hole her eyes were boring into his back.

"You have an amazing capacity for the insulting compliment."

Hunter turned to look at her for the first time since they'd started out. There was a thin sheen of perspiration on her brow and her breath came quickly. It didn't detract an iota from her cool, innate beauty. "Sorry," he said, but didn't appear to be. "Have I been walking too fast? You don't look out of shape."

Despite the ache that ran down the length of her back, Lee straightened. "I'm *not* out of shape." Her feet were killing her.

"The site's not much farther." Reaching down to his hip, he lifted the canteen and unscrewed the top. "It's perfect weather for hiking," he said mildly. "Mid-seventies, and there's a breeze."

Lee managed to suppress a scowl as she eyed the canteen. "Don't you have a cup?"

It took Hunter a moment to realize she was perfectly

serious. Wisely, he decided to swallow the chuckle. "Packed away with the china," he told her soberly enough.

"I'll wait." She hooked her hands in the front straps of her knapsack to ease some of the weight.

"Suit yourself." While Lee looked on, Hunter drank deeply. If he sensed her resentment, he gave no sign as he capped the canteen again and resumed the walk.

Her throat was all the drier at the thought of water. He'd done it on purpose, she thought while she gritted her teeth. Did he think she'd missed that quick flash of humor in his eyes? It was just one more thing to pay him back for when the time came. Oh, she couldn't wait to write the article and expose Hunter Brown for the arrogant, coldhearted demigod he'd set himself up to be.

She wouldn't be surprised if he was walking her in circles, just to make her suffer. Bryan had been all too right about the boots. Lee had lost count of the number of campsites they'd passed, some occupied and some empty. If this was his way of punishing her for not revealing from the start that she worked for *Celebrity,* he was certainly doing an elaborate job.

Disgusted, exhausted, with her legs feeling less like flesh and more like rubber, she reached out and grabbed his arm. "Just why, when you obviously have a dislike for women and for reporters, did you agree to spend two weeks with me?"

"Dislike women?" His brows arched. "My likes and dislikes aren't as generalized as that, Lenore." Her skin was warm and slightly damp when he curled his fingers around the back of her neck. "Have I given you the impression I dislike you?"

She had to fight the urge to stretch like a cat under

his hand. "I don't care what your personal feelings are toward me. This is business."

"For you." His fingers squeezed gently, bringing her an inch closer. "I'm on vacation. Do you know, your mouth's every bit as appealing now as it was the first time I saw it."

"I don't want to appeal to you." But her voice was breathy. "I want you to think of me only as a reporter."

The smile hovered at the edges of his mouth, around the corners of his eyes. "All right," he agreed. "In a minute."

Then he touched his lips to hers, as gently as he had the first time, and as devastatingly. She stood still, amazed to feel as intense a swirl of sensation as she had before. When he touched her, hardly touching her, it was as if she'd never been kissed before. A new discovery, a fresh beginning—how could it be?

The weight on her back seemed to vanish. The ache in her muscles turned into a deeper, richer ache that penetrated to the bone. Her lips parted, though she knew what she invited. Then his tongue joined with hers, slipping into the moistness, drinking up her flavor.

Lee felt the urgency scream through her body, but he was patient. So patient, she couldn't know what the patience cost him. He hadn't expected pain. No woman had ever brought him pain with desire. He hadn't expected the need to flame through him like brushfire, fast and out of control. Hunter had a vision, with perfect clarity, of what it would be like to take her there, on the ground, under the blazing sun with the canyon circling like castle walls around them and the sky like a cathedral dome.

But there was too much fear in her. He could sense

it. Perhaps there was too much fear in him. When they came together, it might have the power to topple both their worlds.

"Your lips melt against mine, Lenore," he whispered. "It's all but impossible to resist."

She drew back, aroused, alarmed and all too aware of how helpless she'd been. "I don't want to repeat myself, Hunter," she managed. "And I don't want to amuse you with clichés, but this is business. I'm a reporter on assignment. If we're to make it through the next two weeks peacefully, it'd be wise to remember that."

"I don't know about the peace," he countered, "but we'll try your rules first."

Suspicious, but finding no room to argue, Lee followed him again. They walked out of the sunlight into the dim coolness of a stand of trees. The creek was distant but still audible. From somewhere to the left came the tinny sound of music from a portable radio. Closer at hand was the rustling of small animals. With a nervous look around, Lee convinced herself they were nothing more than squirrels and rabbits.

With the trees closing around them, they might have been anywhere. The sun filtered through, but softly, on the rough, uneven ground. There was a clearing, small and snug, with a circle of stones surrounding a long-dead campfire. Lee glanced around, fighting off the uneasiness. Somehow, she hadn't thought it would be this remote, this quiet, this…alone.

"There're shower and bathroom facilities a few hundred yards east," Hunter began as he slipped off his pack. "Primitive but adequate. The metal can's for trash. Be sure the lid's tightly closed or it'll attract animals. How's your sense of direction?"

Gratefully, she slipped out of her own pack and let it drop. "It's fine." Now, if she could just take off the boots and rest her feet.

"Good. Then you can gather some firewood while I set up the tent."

Annoyed with the order, she opened her mouth, then firmly shut it again with only a slight hiss. He wouldn't have any cause to complain about her. But as she started to stalk off, the rest of his sentence hit home.

"What do you mean *the* tent?"

He was already unfastening the straps of his pack. "I prefer sleeping in something in case it rains."

"*The* tent," Lee repeated, closing in on him. "As in singular?"

He didn't even spare her a look. "One tent, two sleeping bags."

She wasn't going to explode; she wasn't going to make a scene. After taking a deep breath, she spoke precisely. "I don't consider those adequate arrangements."

He didn't speak for a minute, not because he was choosing his words but because the unpacking occupied him more than the conversation. "If you want to sleep in the open, it's up to you." Hunter drew out a slim, folded piece of material that looked more like a bedsheet than a tent. "But when we decide to become lovers, the arrangements won't make any difference."

"We didn't come here to be lovers," Lee snapped back furiously.

"A reporter and an assignment," Hunter replied mildly. "Two sexless terms. They shouldn't have any problem sharing a tent."

Caught in her own logic, Lee turned and stalked

away. She wouldn't give him the satisfaction of seeing her behave like a woman.

Hunter lifted his head and watched her storm off through the trees. She'd make the first move, he promised himself, suddenly angry. By God, he wouldn't touch her until she came to him.

While he set up camp, he tried to convince himself it was as easy as it sounded.

Chapter 6

Two sexless terms, Lee repeated silently as she scooped up some twigs. *Bastard,* she thought with grim satisfaction, was also a sexless term. It suited Hunter Brown to perfection. He had no business treating her like a fool just because she'd made a fool of herself already.

She wasn't going to give an inch. She'd sleep in the damn sleeping bag in the damn tent for the next thirteen nights without saying another word about it.

Thirteen, she thought, sending a malicious look over her shoulder. He'd probably planned that, too. If he thought she was going to make a scene, or curl up outside the tent to sleep in the open to spite him, he'd be disappointed. She'd be scrupulously professional, unspeakably cooperative and utterly sexless. Before it was over, he'd think he'd been sharing his tent with a robot.

But she'd know better. Lee let out one long, frustrated breath as she scouted for more sticks. She'd know there was a man beside her in the night. A powerfully sexy, impossibly attractive man who could make her blood swim with no more than a look.

It wouldn't be easy to forget she was a woman over the next two weeks, when she'd be spending every night with a man who already had her nerves jumping.

Her job wasn't to make herself forget, Lee reminded herself, but to make certain *he* forgot. A challenge. That was the best way to look at it. It was a challenge she promised herself she'd succeed at.

With her arms full of sticks and twigs, Lee lifted her chin. She felt hot, dirty and tired. It wasn't an auspicious way to begin a war. Ignoring the ache, she squared her shoulders. She might have to sacrifice a round or two, but she'd win the battle. With a dangerous light in her eyes, she headed toward camp.

She had to be grateful his back was to her when she walked into the clearing. The tent was smaller, much, much smaller, than she'd imagined. It was fashioned from tough, lightweight material that looked nearly transparent. It arched, rounded rather than pointed at the peak, and low to the ground. So low, Lee noted, that she'd have to crawl to get inside. Once in, they'd be forced to sleep nearly elbow to elbow. Then and there, she determined to sleep like a rock. Unmoving.

The size of the tent preoccupied her, so that she didn't notice what Hunter was doing until she was almost beside him. Fresh rage broke out as she dropped her load of wood on the ground. "Just what the hell do you think you're doing?"

Unperturbed by the fury in her voice, Hunter glanced

up. In one hand he held a large clear-plastic bag filled with makeup, in the other a flimsy piece of peach-colored material trimmed with ivory lace. "You did know we were going camping," he said mildly, "not to the Beverly Wilshire?"

The color she considered the curse of fair skin flooded her cheeks. "You have no right to go digging around in my things." She snatched the teddy out of his hand, then balled it in her fist.

"I was unpacking." Idly, he turned the makeup bag over to study it from both sides. "I thought you knew to bring only necessities. While I'll admit you have a very subtle, experienced way with this sort of thing—" he gestured with the bag "—eye shadow and lip gloss are excess baggage around a campfire." His voice was infuriatingly friendly, his eyes were only lightly amused. "I've seen you without any of it and had no cause to complain. You certainly don't have to bother with this on my account."

"You conceited jerk." Lee snatched the bag out of his hand. "I don't care if I look like a hag on your account." Taking the knapsack, she stuffed her belongings back inside. "It's *my* baggage, and I'll carry it."

"You certainly will."

"You officious sonofa—" She broke off, barely. "Just don't tell me how to run my life."

"Now, now, name-calling's no way to promote goodwill." Rising, Hunter held out a friendly hand. "Truce?"

Lee eyed him warily. "On what terms?"

He grinned. "That's what I like about you, Lenore, no easy capitulations. A truce with as little interference as possible on both sides. An amiable business arrangement." He saw her relax slightly and couldn't resist the temptation to ruffle her feathers again. "You won't complain about my coffee, and I won't complain when you wear that little scrap of lace to bed."

She gave him a cool smile as she took his hand. "I'm sleeping in my clothes."

"Fair enough." He gave her hand a quick squeeze. "I'm not. Let's see about that coffee."

As he often did, he left her torn between frustration and amusement.

When he put his mind to it, Lee was to discover, Hunter could make things easier. Without fuss, he had the campfire burning and the coffee brewing. Its scent alone was enough to soothe her temper. The economical way he went about it made her think more kindly of him.

There was no point in being at each other's throats for the next two weeks, she decided as she found a convenient rock to sit on. Relaxing might be out of the question, she mused, watching him take clever, compact cooking utensils out of the pack, but animosity wouldn't help, not with a man like Hunter. He was playing games with her. As long as she knew that and avoided the pitfalls, she'd get what she'd come for. So far, she'd allowed him to set the rules and change them at his whim. That would have to change. Lee hooked her hands around a raised knee.

"Do you go camping to get away from the pressure?"

Hunter didn't look back at her, but checked the lantern. So, they were going to start playing word games already. "What pressure?"

Lee might have sighed if she weren't so determined to be pleasantly professional. "There must be pressures from all sides in your line of work. Demands from your publisher, disagreements with your editor, a story that just won't gel the way you want it to, deadlines."

"I don't believe in deadlines."

There was something, Lee thought, and reached for her notepad. "But doesn't every writer face deadlines from time to time? And can't they be an enormous pressure when the story isn't flowing or you're blocked?"

"Writer's block?" Hunter poured coffee into a metal cup. "There's no such thing."

She glanced over for only a second, brow raised. "Oh, come on, Hunter, some very successful writers have suffered from it, even sought professional help. There must have been a time in your career when you found yourself up against a wall."

"You push the wall out of the way."

Frowning, she accepted the cup he handed her. "How?"

"By working through it." He had a jar of powdered milk, which she refused. "If you don't believe in something, refuse to believe it exists, it doesn't, not for you."

"But you write about things that couldn't possibly exist."

"Why not?"

She stared at him, a dark, attractive man sitting on the ground drinking coffee from a metal cup. He looked so at ease with himself, so relaxed, that for a moment she found it difficult to connect him to the man who created stark terror out of words. "Because there aren't monsters under the bed or demons in the closet."

"There's demons in every closet," he disagreed mildly, "some better hidden than others."

"You're saying you believe in what you write about."

"Every writer believes in what he writes. There'd be no purpose in it otherwise."

"You think some—" She didn't want to use the word *demon* again, and her hand moved in frustration as she sought the right phrase. "Some evil force," Lee chose, "can actually manipulate people?"

"It's more accurate to say I don't believe in anything. Possibilities." Did his eyes become darker, or was it her imagination? "There's no limit to possibilities, Lenore."

His eyes were too dark to read. If he was playing with her, baiting her, she couldn't tell. Uncomfortable, she shifted the topic. "When you sit down to write a story, you craft it, spending hours, days, on the angles and the edges, the same way a carpenter builds a cabinet."

He liked her analogy. Hunter sipped at the strong black coffee, enjoying the taste, enjoying the mingled scents of burning wood, summer and Lee's quiet perfume. "Telling a story's an art, writing's a craft."

Lee felt a quick kick of excitement. That was exactly what she was after, those concise little quotes that gave an insight into his character. "Do you consider yourself an artist, then, or a craftsman?"

He drank without hurry, noting that Lee had barely touched her coffee. The eagerness was with her again, her pen poised, her eyes fixed on his. He found he wanted her more when she was like this. He wanted to see that eager look on her face for him, for the man, not the writer. He wanted to sense the ripe anticipation, lover to lover, arms reaching, mouth softening.

If he were writing the script, he'd keep these two people from fulfilling each other's needs for some time yet. It was necessary to flesh them out a bit first, but the ache told him what he needed. Carefully he arranged another piece of wood on the fire.

"An artist by birth," he said at length, "a craftsman by choice."

"I know it's a standard question," she began, with a brisk professionalism that made him smile, "but where do you get your ideas?"

"From life."

She looked over again as he lit a cigarette. "Hunter, you can't convince me that the plot for *Devil's Due* came out of the everyday."

"If you take the everyday, twist it, add a few maybes, you can come up with anything."

"So you take the ordinary, twist it and come up with the extraordinary." Understanding this a bit better, she nodded, satisfied. "How much of yourself goes into your characters?"

"As much as they need."

Again it was so simply, so easily said, she knew he meant it exactly. "Do you ever base one of your characters on someone you know?"

"From time to time." He smiled at her, a smile she neither trusted nor understood. "When I find someone intriguing enough. Do you ever get tired of writing about other people when you've got a world of characters in your own head?"

"It's my job."

"That's not an answer."

"I'm not here to answer questions."

"Why are you here?"

He was closer. Lee hadn't realized he'd moved. He was sitting just below her, obviously relaxed, slightly curious, in charge. "To do an interview with a successful, award-winning author."

"An award-winning author wouldn't make you nervous."

The pencil was growing damp in her hand. She could have cursed in frustration. "You don't."

"You lie too quickly, and not easily at all." His hands rested loosely on his knees as he watched her. The odd ring he wore glinted dully, gold and silver. "If I were to touch you, just touch you, right now, you'd tremble."

"You think too much of yourself," she told him, but rose.

"I think of you," he said, so quietly the pad slipped out of her hand, unnoticed. "You make me want, I make you nervous." He was looking into her again; she could almost feel it. "It should be an interesting combination over the next couple of weeks."

He wasn't going to intimidate her. He *wasn't* going to make her tremble. "The sooner you remember I'm going to be working for the next two weeks, the simpler things will be." Trying to sound haughty nearly worked. Lee wondered if he heard the slight catch in her voice.

"Since you're resigned to working," he said easily, "you can give me a hand starting dinner. After tonight, we'll take turns making meals."

She wasn't going to give him the satisfaction of telling him she knew nothing about cooking over a fire. He already knew. Neither would she give the satisfaction of being confused by his mercurial mood changes. Instead, Lee brushed at her bangs. "I'm going to wash up first."

Hunter watched her start off in the wrong direction, but said nothing. She'd find the shower facilities sooner or later, he figured. Things would be more interesting if neither of them gave the other an inch.

He wasn't sure, but Hunter thought he heard Lee swear from somewhere behind him. Smiling a little, he leaned back against the rock and finished his cigarette.

Groggy, stiff and sniffing the scent of coffee in the air, Lee woke. She knew exactly where she was—as far over on her side of the tent as she could get, deep into the sleeping bag Hunter had provided for her. And alone. It took her only seconds to sense that Hunter no longer shared the tent with her. Just as it had taken her hours the night before to convince herself it didn't matter that he was only inches away.

Dinner had been surprisingly easy. Easy, Lee realized as she stared at the ceiling of the tent, because Hunter's mood had shifted again when she'd returned to help him fix it. Amiable? No, she decided, cautiously stretching her cramped muscles. *Amiable* was too free a word when applied to Hunter. *Moderately friendly* was more suitable. Cooperative he hadn't been at all. He'd spent the evening hours reading by the light of his lamp, while she'd taken out a fresh notepad and begun what would be a journal on her two weeks in Oak Creek Canyon.

She found it helpful to write down her feelings. Lee had often used her manuscript in much the same fashion. She could say what she wanted, feel what she wanted, without ever taking the risk that anyone would read her words. Perhaps it hadn't worked out precisely that way with her book, since Hunter had read more of her neat double-spaced typing under the steady lamplight, but the journal would be for no one's eyes but her own.

In any case, she thought, it was to her advantage that he'd been occupied with her manuscript. She hadn't had to talk to him as the night had grown later, the darkness deeper. While he'd still been reading, she'd been able to crawl into the tent and squeeze herself into a corner. When he'd joined her, much later, it hadn't been necessary to exchange words in the intimacy of the tent. She'd made certain he'd thought her asleep—though sleep hadn't come for hours.

In the quiet, she'd listened to him breathe beside her. Quiet, steady. That was the kind of man he was. Lee had lain still, telling herself the closeness meant nothing. But this morning, she saw that her nails, which had begun to grow again, had been gnawed down.

The first night was bound to be the hardest, she told herself and sat up, dragging a hand through her hair. She'd survived it. Her problem now was how to get by him and to the showers, where she could change out of the clothes she'd slept in and fix her hair and face. Cautiously, she crept forward to peek through the tent flap.

He knew she was awake. Hunter had sensed it almost the moment she'd opened her eyes. He'd gotten up early to start coffee, knowing that if he'd had trouble sleeping beside her, he'd never have been able to handle waking with her.

He'd seen little more than the coppery mass of hair above the sleeping bag in the dim morning light of the tent. Because he'd wanted to touch it, draw her to him, wake her, he'd given himself some distance. Today he'd walk for miles and fish for hours. Lee could stick to her role of reporter, and by answering her questions he'd learn as much about her as she believed she was learning about him. That was his plan, Hunter reminded himself, and poured a second cup of coffee. He was better off remembering it.

"Coffee's hot," Hunter commented without turning around. Though she'd taken great care to be quiet, he'd heard Lee push the tent flap aside.

Biting back an oath, Lee scooped up her pack. The man had ears like a wolf. "I want to shower first," she mumbled.

"I told you that you didn't have to fix up your face for me." He began to arrange strips of bacon in a skillet. "I like it fine the way it is."

Infuriated, Lee scrambled to her feet. "I'm not fixing anything for you. Sleeping all night in my clothes tends to make me feel dirty."

"Probably sleep better without them," Hunter agreed mildly. "Breakfast's in fifteen minutes, so I'd move along if I wanted to eat."

Clutching her bag and her dignity, Lee strode off through the trees.

He wouldn't get to her so easily if she wasn't stiff and grubby and half-starved, she thought, making her way along the path to the showers. God knows how he could be so cheerful after spending the night sleeping on the ground. Maybe Bryan had been right all along. The man was weird. Lee took her shampoo and her plastic case of French-milled soap and stepped into a shower stall.

The spot he'd chosen might be magnificent, the air might smell clean and pure, but a sleeping bag wasn't a feather bed. Lee stripped and hung her clothes over the door. She heard the water running in the stall next to hers and sighed. For the next two weeks she'd be sharing bathroom facilities. She might as well get used to it.

The water came out in a steady gush, lukewarm. Gritting her teeth, she stepped under. Today, she was going to begin to dig out a few more personal facts on Hunter Brown.

Was he married? She frowned, then deliberately relaxed her features. The question was for the article, not for herself. His marital status meant nothing to her.

He probably wasn't. She soaped her hair vigorously. What woman would put up with him? Besides, wouldn't a wife come along on camping trips even if she detested them? Would that kind of man marry anyone who didn't like precisely what he did?

What did he do for relaxation? Besides playing Daniel Boone in the woods, she added with a grim smile. Where did he live? Where had he grown up? What sort of childhood had he had?

The water streamed over her, sluicing away soap and shampoo. The curiosity she felt was purely professional. Lee found she had to remind herself of that a bit too often. She needed the whole man to do an incisive article. She needed the whole man…

Alarmed at her own thoughts, she opened her eyes wide, then swore when shampoo stung them. Damn the whole man! she thought fiercely. She'd take whatever pieces of him she could get and write an article that would pay him back, in spades, for all the trouble he'd caused her.

Clean, fragrant and shivering, she turned off the water. It wasn't until that moment that Lee remembered she hadn't brought a towel. Campground showers didn't lay in their own linen supply. Damn it, how was she supposed to remember everything?

Dripping, her chilled skin covered with gooseflesh,

she stood in the middle of the stall and swore silently and pungently. For as long as she could stand it, Lee let the air dry her while she squeezed water out of her hair. Revenge, she thought, placing the blame squarely on Hunter's shoulders. Sooner or later, she'd have it.

She reached under the stall door for her pack and pulled out a fresh sweatshirt. Resigned, she dabbed at her wet face with the soft outside. Once she'd dragged it over her damp shoulders, she hunted up underwear. Though her clothes clung to her, her skin warmed. In front of the line of sinks and mirrors, she plugged in her blow-dryer and set to work on her hair.

In spite of him, Lee thought, not because of him, she spent more than her usual time perfecting her makeup. Satisfied, she repacked her portable hairdryer and left the showers, smelling lightly of jasmine.

Her scent was the first thing he sensed when she stepped back into the clearing. Hunter's stomach muscles tightened. As if he were unaffected, he finished off another cup of coffee, but he didn't taste it.

Calmer and much more at ease now, Lee stowed her pack before she walked toward the low-burning campfire. On a small shelf of rocks beside it sat the skillet with the remainder of the bacon and eggs. She didn't have to taste them to know they were cold.

"Feel better?" Hunter asked conversationally.

"I feel fine." She wouldn't say one word about the food being cold and, Lee told herself as she scooped her breakfast onto a plate, she'd eat every bite. She'd give him no more cause to smirk at her.

While she nibbled on the bacon, Lee glanced over at him. He'd obviously showered earlier. His hair glinted in the sun and he smelled cleanly of soap without the interference of cologne or aftershave. A man didn't use aftershave if he didn't bother with a razor, Lee concluded, studying the shadow of stubble over his chin. It should've made him look unkempt, but somehow he managed to look oddly dashing. She concentrated on her cold eggs.

"Sleep well?"

"I slept fine," she lied, and gratefully washed down her breakfast with strong, hot coffee. "You?"

"Very well," he lied, and lit a cigarette. She was getting on nerves he hadn't known he had.

"Have you been up long?"

Since dawn, Hunter thought. "Long enough." He glanced down at her barely scuffed hiking boots and wondered how long it would take before her feet just gave out. "I plan to do some hiking today."

She wanted to groan but put on a bright smile. "Fine, I'd like to see some of the canyon while I'm here." Preferably in a Jeep, she thought, swallowing the last crumb of bacon. If there was one cliché she could now attest to, it was that the open air increased the appetite.

It took Lee perhaps half again as long to wash up the breakfast dishes with the plastic water container as it would've taken Hunter, but she already understood the unstated rule. One cooks, the other cleans.

By the time she was finished, he was standing impatiently, binocular and canteen straps crisscrossed over his chest and a light pack in one hand. This he shoved at her. Lee resisted the urge to shove it back at him.

"I want my camera." Without giving him a chance to complain, she dug it out of her own gear and slipped the small rectangle in the back pocket of her jeans.

"What's in here?" she asked, adjusting the strap of the pack over her shoulder.

"Lunch."

Lee lengthened her stride to keep up with Hunter as he headed out of the clearing. If he'd packed a lunch, she'd have to resign herself to a very long day on her feet. "How do you know where you're going and how to get back?"

For the first time since she'd returned to camp smelling like fragility and flowers, Hunter smiled. "Landmarks, the sun."

"Do you mean moss growing on one side of a tree?" She looked around, hoping to find some point of reference for herself. "I've never trusted that sort of thing."

She wouldn't know east from west, either, he mused, unless they were discussing L.A. and New York. "I've got a compass, if that makes you feel better."

It did—a little. When you hadn't the faintest idea how something worked, you had to take it on faith. Lee was far from comfortable putting her faith in Hunter.

But as they walked, she forgot to worry about losing her way. The sun was a white flash of light, and though it was still shy of 9:00 a.m., the air was warm. She liked the way the light hit the red walls of the canyon and deepened the colors. The path inclined upward, narrow, pebbled with loose stones. She heard people laugh, and the sound carried so cleanly over the air, they might have been standing beside her.

Green became sparser as they climbed. What she saw now was scrubby bushes, dusty and faded, that forced their way out of thin ribbons of dirt in the rock. Curious, she broke off a spray of leaves. Their scent was strong, tangy and fresh. Then she found she had to dash to catch up with Hunter. It had been his idea to hike, but he didn't appear to be enjoying it. More, he looked like a man who had some urgent, unpleasant appointment to keep.

It might be a good time, Lee considered, to start a casual conversation that could lead to the kind of personal information she was shooting for. As the path became steadily steeper, she decided she'd better talk while she had the breath to do it. The sweatshirt had been a mistake, too. Her back was damp again, this time from sweat.

"Have you always preferred the outdoors?"

"For hiking."

Undaunted, she scowled at his back. "I suppose you were a Boy Scout."

"No."

"Your interest in camping and hiking is fairly new, then."

"No."

She had to grit her teeth to hold back a groan. "Did you go off and pitch a tent in the woods with your father when you were a boy?"

She'd have been interested in the amused expression on his face if she could have seen it. "No."

"You lived in the city, then."

She was clever, Hunter reflected. And persistent. He shrugged. "Yes."

At last, Lee thought. "What city?"

"L.A."

She tripped over a rock and nearly stumbled headlong into his back. Hunter never slackened his pace. "L.A.?" she repeated. "You live in Los Angeles and still manage to bury yourself so that no one knows you're there?"

"I grew up in L.A.," he said mildly. "In a part of the city you'd have little occasion for visiting. Socially, Lenore Radcliffe, formerly of Palm Springs, wouldn't even know such neighborhoods existed."

That pulled her up short. Again, she had to dash to catch him, but this time she grabbed his arm and made him stop. "How do you know I came from Palm Springs?"

He watched her with the tolerant amusement she found both infuriating and irresistible. "I did my research. You graduated from U.C.L.A. with honors, after three years in a very classy Swiss boarding school. Your engagement to Jonathan Willoby, up-and-coming plastic surgeon, was broken when you accepted a position in *Celebrity*'s Los Angeles office."

"I was never engaged to Jonathan," she began furiously, then decisively bit her tongue. "You have no business probing into my life, Hunter. I'm doing the article, not you."

"I make it a habit to find out everything I can about anyone I do business with. We do have a business arrangement, don't we, Lenore?"

He was clever with words, she thought grimly. But so was she. "Yes, and it consists of my interviewing you, not the other way around."

"On my terms," Hunter reminded her. "I don't talk to anyone unless I know who they are." He reached out, touching the ends of her hair as he'd done once before. "I think I know who you are."

"You don't," she corrected, struggling against the need to back away from a touch that was barely a touch. "And you don't have to. But the more honest and open you are with me, the more honest the article I write will be."

He uncapped the canteen. When she refused his offer with a shake of her head, Hunter drank. "I am being honest with you." He secured the cap. "If I made it easier for you, you wouldn't get a true picture of who I am." His eyes were suddenly dark, intense and piercing. Without warning, he reached out. The power in his eyes made her believe he could quite easily sweep her off the path. Yet his hand skimmed down her cheek, light as rain. "You wouldn't understand what I am," he said quietly. "Perhaps, for my own reasons, I want you to."

She'd have been less frightened if he'd shouted at her, raged at her, grabbed at her. The sound of her own heartbeat vibrated in her head. Instinctively, she stepped back, escape her first and only thought. Her foot met empty space.

In an instant, she was caught against him, pressed body to body, so that the warmth from his seeped right into hers. The fear tripled so that she arched back, raising both hands to his chest.

"Idiot," he said, with an edge to his voice that made her head snap up. "Take a look behind you before you tell me to let you go."

Automatically, she turned her head to look over her shoulder. Her stomach rose up to her throat, then plummeted. The hands that had been poised to push him away grabbed his shoulders until the fingers dug into his flesh. The view behind her was magnificent, sweeping and straight down.

"We—we walked farther up than I'd thought," she managed. And if she didn't sit down, very, very soon, she was going to disgrace herself.

"The trick is to watch where you're going." Hunter

didn't move her away from the edge, but took her chin in his hand until their eyes met and held. "Always watch exactly where you're going, then you'll know how to fall."

He kissed her, just as unexpectedly as before, but not so gently. Not nearly so gently. This time, she felt the full force of the strength that had been only an undercurrent each other time his mouth had touched hers. If she'd pitched back and taken that dizzying fall, she'd have been no more helpless than she was at this moment, molded to him, supported by him, wrapped around him. The edge was close—inside her, behind her. Lee couldn't tell which would be more fatal. But she knew, helplessly, that either could break her.

He hadn't meant to touch her just then, but the demanding climb up the path hadn't deadened the need he'd woken with. He'd take this much, her taste, her softness, and make it last until she willingly turned to him. He wanted the sweetness she tried to gloss over, the fragility she tried to deny. And he wanted the strength that kept her pushing for more. Yes, he thought he knew her and was very close to understanding her. He knew he wanted her.

Slowly, very slowly, for lingering mouth-to-mouth both soothed and excited him, Hunter drew her away. Her eyes were as clouded as his thoughts, her pulse as rapid as his. He shifted her until she was close to the cliff wall and away from the drop.

"Never step back unless you've looked over your shoulder first," he said quietly. "And don't step forward until you've tested the ground."

Turning, he continued up the path, leaving her to wonder if he'd been speaking of hiking or something entirely different.

Chapter 7

Lee wrote in her journal:

On the eighth day of this odd on-again, off-again interview, I know more about Hunter and understand less. By turns, he's friendly, then distant. There's an aloof streak in him, bound so tightly around his private life that I've found no way through it. When I ask about his preference in books, he can go on indefinitely—apparently he has no real preference except for the written word itself. When I ask about his family, he just smiles and changes the subject or gives me one of those intense stares and says nothing. In either case, he keeps a cloak of mystery around his privacy.

He's possibly the most efficient man I've ever met. There's no waste of time, no extra movements and, infuriating to me, never a mistake, when it comes to starting a campfire or cooking a meal—such as they are.

Yet, he's content to do absolutely nothing for hours at a time.

He's fastidious—the camp looks as if we've been here no more than a half hour rather than a week—yet he hasn't shaved in that amount of time. The beard should look scruffy, but somehow it looks so natural I find myself wondering if he didn't always have one.

Always, I've been able to find a category to slip an assignment into. An acquaintance into. Not with Hunter. In all this time, I've found no easy file for him.

Last night we had a heated discussion on Sylvia Plath, and this morning I found him paging through a comic book over coffee. When I questioned him on it, his answer was that he respected all forms of literature. I believed him. One of the problems I'm having on this assignment is that I find myself believing everything he says, no matter how contradictory the statement might be to another he makes. Can a total lack of consistency make someone consistent?

He's the most complex, frustrating, fascinating man I've ever known. I've yet to find a way of controlling the attraction he holds for me, or even the proper label for it. Is it physical? Hunter's very compelling physically. Is it intellectual? His mind has such odd twists and turns, it takes all my effort to follow them.

Either of these I believe I could handle successfully enough. Over the years, I've had to deal professionally with attractive, intelligent, charismatic men. It's a challenge, certainly, but here I have the uncomfortable feeling that I'm caught in the middle of a silent chess game and have already lost my queen.

My greatest fear at this moment is that I'm going to find myself emotionally involved.

Since the first day we walked up the canyon, he

hasn't touched me. I can still remember exactly how I felt, exactly what the air smelled like at that moment. It's foolish, overly romantic and absolutely true.

Each night we sleep together in the same tent, so close I can feel his breath. Each morning I wake alone. I should be grateful that he isn't making this assignment any more difficult than it already is, and yet I find myself waiting to be held by him.

For over a week I've thought of little else but him. The more I learn, the more I want to know—for myself. Too much for myself.

Twice, I've woken in the middle of the night, aching, and nearly turned to him. Now, I wonder what would happen if I did. If I believed in the spells and forces Hunter writes of, I'd think one was on me. No one's ever made me want so much, feel so much. Fear so much. Every night, I wonder.

Sometimes Lee wrote of the scenery and her feelings about it. Sometimes, she wrote a play-by-play description of the day. But most of the time, more of the time, she wrote of Hunter. What she put down in her journal had nothing to do with her organized, precisely written notes for the article. She wouldn't permit it. What she didn't understand, and what she wouldn't write down in either space, was that she was losing sleep. And she was having fun.

Though he was cannily evasive on personal details, she was gathering information. Even now, barely halfway through the allotted time, Lee had enough for a solid, successful article—more, she knew, than she'd expected to gather. But she wanted even more, for her readers and, undeniably, for herself.

"I don't see how any self-respecting fish could be fooled by something like this." Lee fiddled with the small rubbery fly Hunter attached to her line.

"Myopic," Hunter countered, bending to choose his own lure. "Fish are notoriously nearsighted."

"I don't believe you." Clumsily, she cast off. "But this time *I'm* going to catch one."

"You'll need to get your fly in the water first." He glanced down at the line tangled on the bank of the creek before expertly casting his own.

He wouldn't even offer to help. After a week in his company, Lee had learned not to expect it. She'd also learned that if she wanted to compete with him in this, or in a discussion of eighteenth-century English literature, she had to get into the spirit of things.

It wasn't simple and it wasn't quick, but kneeling, Lee worked on the tangles until she was back to square one. She shot a look at Hunter, who appeared much too engrossed with the surface of the creek to notice her progress. By now, Lee knew better. He saw everything that went on around him, whether he looked or not.

Standing a few feet away, Lee tried again. This time, her lure landed with a quiet plop.

Hunter saw the rare, quick grin break out, but said nothing. She was, he'd learned, a woman who generally took herself too seriously. Yet he saw the sweetness beneath, and the warmth Lee tried to be so frugal with.

She had a low, smoky laugh she didn't use often enough. It only made him want to urge it out of her.

The past week hadn't been easy for her. Hunter hadn't intended it to be. You learned more about people by observing them in difficult situations than at a catered cocktail party. He was adding to the layers of the first impression he'd had, at the airport in Flagstaff. But he had layers still to go.

She could, unlike most people he knew, be comfortable with long spells of silence. It appealed to him. The more careless he became in his attire and appearance, the more meticulous she became in hers. It amused him to see her go off every morning and return with her makeup perfected and her hair carefully groomed. Hunter made sure they'd been mussed a bit by the end of the day.

Hiking, fishing. Hunter had seen to it that her jeans and boots were thoroughly broken in. Often, in the evening, he'd caught her rubbing her tired feet. When she was back in Los Angeles, sitting in her cozy office, she wouldn't forget the two weeks she'd spent in Oak Creek Canyon.

Now, Lee stood near the edge of the creek, a fishing rod held in both hands, a look of smug concentration on her face. He liked her for it—for her innate need to compete and for the vulnerability beneath the confidence. She'd stand there, holding the rod, until he called a halt to the venture. Back in camp, he knew she'd rub her hands with cream and they would smell lightly of jasmine and stay temptingly soft.

Since it was her turn to cook, she'd do it, though she still fumbled a bit with the utensils and managed to singe almost anything she put on the fire. He liked her for that, too—for the fact that she never gave up on anything.

Her curiosity remained unflagging. She'd question him, and he'd evade or answer as he chose. Then she'd grant him silence to read, while she wrote. Comfortable. Hunter found that she was an unusually comfortable woman in the quiet light of a campfire. Whether she knew it or not, she relaxed then, writing in the journal, which intrigued him, or going over her daily notes for the article, which didn't.

He'd expected to learn about her during the two weeks together, knowing he'd have to give some information on himself in return. That, he considered, was an even enough exchange. But he hadn't expected to enjoy her companionship.

The sun was strong, the air almost still, with an early-morning taste to it. But the sky wasn't clear. Hunter wondered if she'd noticed the bank of clouds to the east and if she realized there'd be a storm by nightfall. The clouds held lightning. He simply sat cross-legged on the ground. It'd be more interesting if Lee found out for herself.

The morning passed in silence, but for the occasional voice from around them or the rustle of leaves. Twice Hunter pulled a trout out of the creek, throwing the second back because of size. He said nothing. Lee said nothing, but barely prevented herself from grinding her teeth. On every jaunt, he'd gone back to camp with fish. She'd gone back with a sore neck.

"I begin to wonder," she said, at length, "if you've put something on that lure that chases fish away."

He'd been smoking lazily and now he stirred himself to crush out the cigarette. "Want to change rods?"

She slanted him a look, taking in the slight amusement in his arresting face. When her muscles quivered, Lee stiffened them. Would she never become completely accustomed to the way her body reacted when they looked at each other? "No," she said coolly. "I'll keep this one. You're rather good at this sort of thing, for a boy who didn't go fishing."

"I've always been a quick study."

"What did your father do in L.A.?" Lee asked, knowing he would either answer in the most offhand way or evade completely.

"He sold shoes."

It took a moment, as she'd been expecting the latter. "Sold shoes?"

"That's right. In the shoe department of a moderately successful department store downtown. My mother sold stationery on the third floor." He didn't have to look at her to know she was frowning, her brows drawn together. "Surprised?"

"Yes," she admitted. "A bit. I suppose I imagined you'd been influenced by your parents to some extent and that they'd had some unusual career or interests."

Hunter cast off again with an agile flick of his wrist. "Before my father sold shoes, he sold tickets at the local theater. Before that, it was linoleum, I think." His shoulders moved slightly before he turned to her. "He was a man trapped by financial circumstances into working, when he'd been born to dream. If he'd been born into affluence, he might've been a painter or a poet. As it was, he sold things and regularly lost his job because he wasn't suited to selling anything, not even himself."

Though he spoke casually, Lee had to struggle to distance herself emotionally. "You speak as though he's not living."

"I've always believed my mother died from overwork, and my father from lack of interest in life without her."

Sympathy welled up in her throat. She couldn't swallow at all. "When did you lose them?"

"I was eighteen. They died within six months of each other."

"Too old for the state to care for you," she murmured, "too young to be alone."

Touched, Hunter studied her profile. "Don't feel sorry for me, Lenore. I managed very well."

"But you weren't a man yet." No, she mused, perhaps he had been. "You had college to face."

"I had some help, and I waited tables for a while."

Lee remembered the wallet full of credit cards she'd carried through college. Anything she'd wanted had always been at her fingertips. "It couldn't have been easy."

"It didn't have to be." He lit a cigarette, watching the clouds move slowly closer. "By the time I was finished with college, I knew I was a writer."

"What happened from the time you graduated from college to when your first book was published?"

He smiled through the smoke that drifted between them. "I lived, I wrote, I went fishing when I could."

She wasn't about to be put off so easily. Hardly realizing she did it, Lee sat down on the ground beside him. "You must've worked."

"Writing, though many disagree, is work." He had a talent for making the sharpest sarcasm sound mildly droll.

Another time, she might have smiled. "You know that's not what I mean. You had to have an income, and your first book wasn't published until nearly six years ago."

"I wasn't starving in a garret, Lenore." He ran a finger down the hand she held on the rod and felt a flash of pleasure at the quick skip of her pulse. "You'd just have been starting at *Celebrity* when *The Devil's Due* hit the stands. One might say our stars were on the rise at the same time."

"I suppose." She turned from him to look back at the surface of the creek again.

"You're happy there?"

Unconsciously, she lifted her chin. "I've worked my way up from gofer to staff reporter in five years."

"That's not an answer."

"Neither are most of yours," she mumbled.

"True enough. What're you looking for there?"

"Success," she said immediately. "Security."

"One doesn't always equal the other."

Her voice was as defiant as the look she aimed at him. "You have both."

"A writer's never secure," Hunter disagreed. "Only a foolish one expects to be. I've read all of the manuscript you brought."

Lee said nothing. She'd known he'd bring it up before the two weeks were over, but she'd hoped to put it off a bit longer. The faintest of breezes played with the ends of her hair while she sat, staring at the moving waters of the creek. Some of the pebbles looked like gems. Such were illusions.

"You know you have to finish it," he told her calmly. "You can't make me believe you're content to leave your characters in limbo, when you've drawn them so carefully. Your story's two-thirds told, Lenore."

"I don't have time," she began.

"Not good enough."

Frustrated, she turned to him again. "Easy for you to say from your little pinnacle of fame. I have a demanding full-time job. If I give it my time and my talent, there's no place I can go but up at *Celebrity*."

"Your novel needs your time and talent."

She didn't like the way he said it—as if she had no

real choice. "Hunter, I didn't come here to discuss my work, but you and yours. I'm flattered that you think my novel has some merit, but I have a job to do."

"Flattered?" he countered. The deep, black gaze pinned her again, and his hand closed over hers. "No, you're not. You wish I'd never seen your novel and you don't want to discuss it. Even if you were convinced it was worthwhile, you'd still be afraid to put it all on the line."

The truth grated on her nerves and on her temper. "My job is my first priority. Whether that suits you or not doesn't matter. It's none of your business."

"No, perhaps not," he said slowly, watching her. "You've got a fish on your line."

"I don't want you to—" Eyes narrowing, she broke off. "What?"

"There's a fish on your line," he repeated. "You'd better reel it in."

"I've got one?" Stunned, Lee felt the rod jerk in her hands. "I've got one! Oh, God." She gripped the rod in both hands again and watched the line jiggle. "I've really caught one. What do I do now?"

"Reel it in," Hunter suggested again, leaning back on the grass.

"Aren't you going to help?" Her hands felt foolishly clumsy as she started to crank the reel. Hoping leverage would give her some advantage, she scrambled to her feet. "Hunter, I don't know what I'm doing. I might lose it."

"Your fish," he pointed out. Grinning, he watched her. Would she look any more exuberant if she'd been given an interview with the president? Somehow, Hunter didn't think so, though he was sure Lee would disagree. But then, she couldn't see herself at that moment, hair mussed, cheeks glowing, eyes wide and her tongue caught firmly between her teeth. The late-morning sunlight did exquisite things to her skin, and the quick laugh she gave when she pulled the struggling fish from the water ran over the back of his neck like soft fingers.

Desire moved lazily through him as he took his gaze up the long length of leg flattered by brief shorts, then over the subtle curves accented by the shifting of muscle under her shirt as she continued to fight with the fish, to her face, still flushed with surprise.

"Hunter!" She laughed as she held the still-wriggling fish high over the grass. "I did it."

It was nearly as big as the largest one he'd caught that week. He pursed his lips as he sized it up. It was tempting to compliment her, but he decided she looked smug enough already. "Gotta get it off the hook," he reminded her, shifting only slightly on his elbows.

"Off the hook?" Lee shot him an astonished look. "I don't want to touch it."

"You have to touch it to take it off the hook."

Lee lifted a brow. "I'll just toss it back in."

With a shrug, Hunter shut his eyes and enjoyed the faint breeze. The hell she would. "Your fish, not mine."

Torn between an abhorrence of touching the still-flopping fish and pride at having caught it, Lee stared down at Hunter. He wasn't going to help; that was painfully obvious. If she threw the fish back into the water, he'd smirk at her for the rest of the evening. Intolerable. And, she reasoned logically, wouldn't she still have to touch it to get rid of it? Setting her teeth, Lee reached out a hand for the catch of the day.

It was wet, slippery and cold. She pulled her hand back. Then, out of the corner of her eye, she saw Hunter grinning up at her. Holding her breath, Lee took the trout firmly in one hand and wiggled the hook out with the other. If he hadn't been looking at her, challenging her, she never would've managed it. With the haughtiest air at her disposal, she dropped the trout into the small cooler Hunter brought along on fishing trips.

"Very good." He closed the lid on the cooler before he reeled in his line. "That looks like enough for tonight's dinner. You caught a good-sized one, Lenore."

"Thank you." The words were icily polite and self-satisfied.

"It'll nearly be enough for both of us, even after you've cleaned it."

"It's as big as…" He was already walking back toward camp, so that she had to run to catch up with him and his statement. "*I* clean it?"

"Rule is, you catch, you clean."

She planted her feet, but he wasn't paying attention. "I'm not cleaning any fish."

"Then you don't eat any fish." His words were as offhand and careless as a shrug.

Abandoning pride, Lee caught at his arm. "Hunter, you'll have to change the rule." She sighed, but convinced herself she wouldn't choke on the word. At least not very much. "Please."

He stopped, considering. "If I clean it, you've got to balance the scales—" the smile flickered over his face "—no pun intended, by doing me a favor."

"I can cook two nights in a row."

"I said a favor."

Her head turned sharply, but one look at his face had her laughing. “All right, what’s the deal?”

“Why don’t we leave it open-ended?” he suggested. “I don’t have anything in mind at the moment.”

This time, she considered. “It’ll be negotiable?”

“Naturally.”

“Deal.” Turning her palms up, Lee wrinkled her nose. “Now I’m going to wash my hands.”

She hadn’t realized she could get such a kick out of catching a fish or out of cooking it herself over an open fire. There were other things Lee hadn’t realized. She hadn’t looked at the trim gold watch on her wrist in days. If she hadn’t kept a journal, she probably wouldn’t know what day it was. It was true that her muscles still revolted after a night in the tent and the shower facilities were an inconvenience at best, purgatory at worst, but despite herself she was relaxing.

For the first time in her memory, her day wasn’t regimented, by herself or by anyone else. She got up when she woke, slept when she was tired and ate when she was hungry. For the moment, the word *deadline* didn’t exist. That was something she hadn’t allowed herself since the day she’d walked out of her parents’ home in Palm Springs.

No matter how rapid Hunter could make her pulse by one of those unexpected looks, or how much desire for him simmered under the surface, she found him comfortable to be with. Because it was so unlikely, Lee didn’t try to find the reasons. On this late afternoon, in the hour before dusk, she was content to sit by the fire and tend supper.

“I never knew anything could smell so good.”

Hunter continued to pour a cup of coffee before he glanced over at her. "We cooked fish two days ago."

"Your fish," Lee pointed out, carefully turning the trout. "This one's mine."

He grinned, wondering if she remembered just how horrified she'd been the first time he'd suggested she pick up a rod and reel. "Beginner's luck."

Lee opened her mouth, ready with a biting retort, then saw the way he smiled at her. Not only did her retort vanish, but so did much of her defensive wall. She let out a long, quiet breath as she turned back to the skillet. The man became only more dangerous with familiarity. "If fishing depends on luck," she managed, "you've had more than your share."

"Everything depends on luck." He held out two plates. Lee slipped the sizzling trout onto them, then sat back to enjoy.

"If you believe that, what about fate? You've said more than once that we can fight against our fate, but we can't win."

He lifted a brow. That consistently sharp, consistently logical mind of hers never failed to impress him. "One works with the other." He tasted a bit of trout, noting that she'd been careful enough not to singe her own catch. "It's your fate to be here, with me. You were lucky enough to catch a fish for dinner."

"It sounds to me as though you twist things to your own point of view."

"Yes. Doesn't everyone?"

"I suppose." Lee ate, thoughtfully studying the view over his shoulder. Had anything ever tasted this wonderful? Would anything ever again? "But not everyone makes it work as well as you." Reluctantly, she accepted some of the dried fruit he offered. He seemed to have an unending supply, but Lee had yet to grow used to the taste or texture.

"If you could change one thing about your life, what would it be?"

Perhaps because he'd asked without preamble, perhaps because she was so unexpectedly relaxed, Lee answered without thinking. "I'd have more."

He didn't, as her parents had done, ask more what. Hunter only nodded. "We could say it's your fate to want it, and your luck to have it or not."

Nibbling on an apricot, she studied him. The lowering light and flickering fire cast his face in shadows. They suited him. The short, rough beard surrounded the poet's mouth, making it all the more compelling. He was a man a woman would never be able to ignore, never be able to forget. Lee wondered if he knew it. Then she nearly laughed. Of course he did. He knew entirely too much.

"What about you?" She leaned forward a bit, as she did whenever the answer was important. "What would you change?"

He smiled in the way that made her blood heat. "I'd take more," he said quietly.

She felt the shiver race up her spine, was all but certain Hunter could see it. Lee found she was compelled to remind herself of her job. "You know," she began easily enough, "you've told me quite a bit over this week, more in some ways than I'd expected, but much less in others." Steady again, she took another bite of trout. "I might understand you quite a bit better if you'd give me a run-through of a typical day."

He ate, enjoying the tender, open-air flavor. The

clouds were rolling in, the breeze picking up. He wondered if she noticed. "There's no such thing as a typical day."

"You're evading again."

"Yeah."

"It's my job to pin you down."

He watched her over the rim of his coffee cup. "I like watching you do your job."

She laughed. It seemed he could always frustrate and amuse her at the same time. "Hunter, why do I have the feeling you're doing your best to make this difficult for me?"

"You're very perceptive." Setting his plate aside, he began to toy with the ends of her hair in a habit she could never take casually. "I have an image of a woman with a romantic kind of beauty and an orderly, logical mind."

"Hunter—"

"Wait, I'm just fleshing her out. She's ambitious, full of nerves, highly sensuous without being fully aware of it." He could see her eyes change, growing as dark as the sky above them. "She's caught in the middle of something she can't explain or understand. Things happen around her and she's finding it more and more difficult to distance herself from it. And there's a man, a man she desires but can't quite trust. He doesn't offer her the logical explanations she wants, but the illogic he offers seems terrifyingly close to the truth. If she puts her trust in him, she has to turn her back on most of what she believes is fact. If she doesn't, she'll be alone."

He was talking to her, about her, for her. Lee knew her throat was dry and her palms were damp, but she didn't know if it was from his words or the light touch on the ends of her hair. "You're trying to frighten me by weaving a plot around me."

"I'm weaving a plot around you," Hunter agreed. "Whether I frighten you or not depends on how successful I am with that plot. Shadows and storms are my business." As if on cue, lightning snaked out in the sky overhead. "But all writers need a foil. Smooth, pale skin—" He stroked the back of his hand up her cheek. "Soft hair with touches of gold and fire. Against that I have darkness, wind, voices that speak from shadows. Logic against the impossible. The unspeakable against cool, polished beauty."

She swallowed to relieve the dryness in her throat and tried to speak casually. "I suppose I should be flattered, but I'm not sure I want to see myself molded into a character in a horror story."

"That comes back to fate again, doesn't it?" Lightning ripped through the early dusk as their eyes met again. "I need you, Lenore," he murmured. "For the tale I have to tell—and more."

Nerves prickled along her skin, all the more frantically because of the relaxed hours. "It's going to rain." But her voice wasn't calm and even. Her senses were already swimming. When she started to rise, she found that her hand was caught in his and that he stood with her. The wind blew around her, stirring leaves, stirring desire. The light dimmed to shadow. Thunder rumbled.

What she saw in his eyes chilled her, then heated her blood so quickly she had no way to keep up with the change. The grip on her hand was light. Lee could've broken the hold if she'd had the will to do so. It was his look that drained the will from her. They stood there, hands touching, eyes locked, while the storm swirled like madness around them.

Perhaps life was made up of the choices Hunter had once spoken of. Perhaps luck swayed the balance. But at that moment, for hardly more than a heartbeat, Lee believed that fate ruled everything. She was meant to go to him, to give to him, with no more choice than one of the characters his imagination formed.

Then the sky opened. The rain poured out. The shock of the sudden drenching had Lee jolting back, breaking contact. Yet for several long seconds she stood still while water ran over her and lightning flashed in wicked bolts.

"Damn it!" But he knew she spoke to him, not the storm. "Now what am I supposed to do?"

Hunter smiled, barely resisting the urge to cup her face in his hands and kiss her until her legs gave way. "Head for drier land." He continued to smile despite the rain, the wind, the lightning.

Wet, edgy and angry, Lee crawled inside the tent. He's enjoying this, she thought, tugging on the sodden laces of her boots. There's nothing he likes better than to see me at my worst. It would probably take a week for the boots to dry out, she thought grimly as she managed to pry the first one off.

When Hunter slipped into the tent beside her, she said nothing. Concentrating on anger seemed the best solution. The pounding of the rain on the sides of the tent made the space inside seem to shrink. She'd never been more aware of him, or of herself. Water dripped uncomfortably down her neck as she leaned forward to pull off her socks.

"I don't suppose this'll last long."

Hunter pulled the sodden shirt over his head. "I wouldn't count on it stopping much before morning."

"Terrific." She shivered and wondered how the hell she was supposed to get out of the wet clothes and into dry ones.

Hunter turned the lantern he'd carried in with him down to a dim glow. "Relax and listen to it. It's different from rain in the city. There's no swish of tires on wet asphalt, no horns, no feet running on the sidewalk." He took a towel out of his pack and began to dry her hair.

"I can do it." She reached up, but his hands continued to massage.

"I like to do it. Wet fire," he murmured. "That's what your hair looks like now."

He was so close she could smell the rain on him. The heat from his body called subtly, temptingly, to hers. Was the rain suddenly louder, or were her senses more acute? For a moment, she thought she could hear each individual drop as it hit the tent. The light was dim, a smoky gray that held touches of unreality. Lee felt as though she'd been running away from this one isolated spot all her life. Or perhaps she'd been running toward it.

"You need to shave," she murmured, and found that her hand was already reaching out to touch the untrimmed growth of beard on his face. "This hides too much. You're already difficult to know."

"Am I?" He moved the towel over her hair, soothing and arousing by turns.

"You know you are." She didn't want to turn away now, from the look that could infuse such warmth through her chilled, damp skin. Lightning flashed, illuminating the tent brilliantly before plunging it back into gloom. Yet, through the gloom she could see all she needed to, perhaps more than she wanted to. "It's my job to find out more, to find out everything."

"And my right to tell you only what I want to."

"We just don't look at things the same way."

"No."

She took the towel and, half dreaming, began to dry his hair. "We have no business being together like this."

He hadn't known desire with claws. If he didn't touch her soon, he'd be ripped through. "Why?"

"We're too different. You look for the unexplainable, I look for the logical." But his mouth was so near hers, and his eyes held such power. "Hunter..." She knew what was going to happen, recognized the impossibility of it and the pain that was bound to follow. "I don't want this to happen."

He didn't touch her, though he was certain he'd soon be mad from the lack of it. "You have a choice."

"No." It was said quietly, almost on a sigh. "I don't think I do." She let the towel fall. She saw the flicker of lightning and waited, six long heartbeats, for the answering thunder. "Maybe neither one of us has a choice."

Her breath was already unsteady as she let her hands curl over his bare shoulders. There was strength there. She wanted to feel it, but had been afraid to. His eyes never left hers as she touched him. Though the force of need curled tight in his stomach, he'd let her set the pace this first time, this most important time.

Her fingers were long and smooth on his skin, cool, not so much hesitant as cautious. They ran down his arms, moving slowly over his chest and back until desire was taut as a bow poised for firing. The sound of the rain drummed in his head. Her face was pale and elegant in the gloomy light. The tent was suddenly too big. He wanted her in a space that was too small to move in unless they moved together.

She could hardly believe she could touch him this way, freely, openly, so that his skin quivered under the trace of her fingers. All the while, he watched her with a passion so fierce it would have terrified her if she hadn't been so dazed with her own need. Carefully, afraid to make the wrong move and break the mood for both of them, she touched her mouth to his.

The rough brush of beard was a stunning contrast to the softness of his lips. He gave back to her such feelings, such warmth, with no pressure. She'd never known anyone who could give without taking. This generosity was, to her, the ultimate seduction. In that moment, any reserve she'd clung to was washed away. Her arms went around his neck, her cheek pressed to his.

"Make love to me, Hunter."

He drew her away, only far enough so that they could see each other again. Wet hair curled around her face. Her eyes were as the sky had been an hour before. Dusky and clouded. "With."

Her lips curved. Her heart opened. He poured inside. "Make love with me."

Then his hands were framing her face, and the kiss was so gentle it drugged every cell of her body. She felt him tug the wet shirt from her, and shivered once before he warmed her. His body felt so strong against hers, so solid, yet his hands played over her with the care of a jeweler polishing a rare gem. He sighed when she touched him, so she touched once again, wanting to give pleasure as it was given to her.

She'd thought the panic would return, or at least the need to rush. But they'd been given all the time in the world. The rain could fall, the thunder bellow. It didn't involve them. She tasted hunger on his lips, but he held it in check. He'd sup slowly. Pleasure bubbled up inside her and came softly through her lips.

His mouth on her breast had the need leaping up to the next plane. Yet he didn't hurry, even when she arched against him. His tongue flicked, his teeth nibbled, until he could feel the crazed desire vibrating through her. She thought only of him now, Hunter knew it even as he struggled to hold the reins of his own passion. She'd have more. She'd take all. And so, by God, would he.

When she struggled with the snap of his jeans, he let her have her way. He wanted to be flesh-to-flesh with her, body-to-body, without barriers. In his mind, he'd already had her bare, like this, a dozen times. Her hair was cool and wet, her skin smooth and fragrant. Spring flowers and summer rain. The scents raced through him as her hands became more urgent.

Her breathing was ragged as she tugged the wet denim down his legs. She recognized strength, power and control. It was only the last she needed to break so that she could have what she ached for.

Wherever she could reach, she touched, she tasted, wallowing in pleasure each time she heard his breath tremble. Her shorts were drawn slowly down her body by strong, clever hands, until she wore nothing but the lacy triangle riding low on her hips. With his lips, he journeyed down, down her body, slowly, so that the bristle of beard awakened every pore. His tongue slid under the lace, making her gasp. Then, as abruptly as the storm had broken, Lee was lost in a morass of sensation too dark, too deep, to understand.

He felt her explode, and the power sang through him. He heard her call his name, and the greed to hear it again almost overwhelmed him. Bracing himself over her, Hunter held back that final, desperate need until she opened her eyes. She'd look at him when they came together. He'd promised himself that.

Dazed, trembling, frenzied, Lee stared at him. He looked invincible. "What do you want from me?"

His mouth swooped down on hers, and for the first time the kiss was hard, urgent, almost brutal with the force of passion finally unleashed. "Everything." He plunged into her, catapulting them both closer to the crest. "Everything."

Chapter 8

Dawn was clear as glass. Lee woke to it slowly, naked, warm and, for the first time in over a week, comfortable. And for the first time in over a week, she woke not precisely sure where she was.

Her head was pillowed in the curve of Hunter's shoulder, her body turned toward his of its own volition and by the weight of the arm held firmly around her. There was a drowsy feeling that was a mix of security and excitement. In all of her memory, she couldn't recall experiencing anything quite like it.

Before she was fully awake, she smelled the lingering fragrance of rain on his skin and remembered. In remembering, she took a deep, drinking breath of the scent.

It was like a dream, like something in some subliminal fantasy, or a scene that had come straight from the imagination. She'd never offered herself to anyone so freely before, or so completely. Never. Lee knew there'd never been anyone who'd tempted her to.

She could still remember the sensation of her lips touching his, and all doubt, all fear, melting away with the gentle contact.

Should she feel so content now that the rain had stopped and dawn was breaking? Fantasies were for that private hour of the night, not for the daylight. After all, it hadn't been a dream, and there'd be no pretending it had been. Perhaps she should be appalled that she'd given him exactly what he'd demanded: everything.

She couldn't. No, it was more than that, she realized. She wouldn't. Nothing, no one, would spoil what had happened, not even she herself.

Still, it might be best if he didn't realize quite yet how completely victorious he'd been. Lee let her eyes close and wrapped the sensation of closeness around her. For the next few days, there was no desk, no typewriter, no phone ringing with more demands. There'd be no self-imposed schedule. For the next few days, she was alone with her lover. Maybe the time had come to pick those wildflowers.

She tilted her head, wanting to look at him, trying not to wake him. Over the week they'd spent in such intimate quarters, she'd never seen him sleep. Every other morning he'd been up, already making coffee. She wanted the luxury of absorbing him when he was unaware.

Lee knew that most people looked more vulnerable in sleep, more innocent, perhaps. Hunter looked just as dangerous, just as compelling, as ever. True, those dark, intense eyes were hidden, but knowing the lids could lift at any moment, and the eyes spear you with that peculiar power, didn't add innocence to his face, only more mystery.

Lee discovered she didn't want it to. She was glad he was more dangerous than the other men she'd known. In an odd way, she was glad he was more difficult. She hadn't fallen in love with the ordinary, the everyday, but with the unique.

Fallen in love. She ran the phrase around in her head, taking it apart and putting it back together again with the caution she was prone to. It triggered a trickle of unease. The phrase itself connoted bruises. Hadn't Hunter himself warned her to test the ground before she started forward? Even warned, she hadn't. Even seeing the pit, she hadn't checked her step. The tumble she'd taken had a soft fall. This time. Lee knew it was all too possible to stumble and be destroyed.

She wasn't going to think about it. Lee allowed herself the luxury of cuddling closer. She was going to find those wildflowers and enjoy each individual petal. The dream would end soon enough, and she'd be back to the reality of her life. It was, of course, what she wanted. For a while, she lay still, just listening to the silence.

The clever thing to do, she thought lazily, would be to hang their wet clothes out in the sun. Her boots certainly needed drying out, but in the meantime, she had her sneakers. She yawned, thinking she wanted a few moments to write in her journal as well. Hunter's breathing was slow and even. A smile curved her lips. She could do all that, then come back and wake him. Waking him, in whatever way she chose, was a lover's privilege.

Lover. Skimming her gaze over his face again, she wondered why she didn't feel any particular surprise at the word. Was it possible she'd recognized it from the beginning? Foolish, she told herself, and shook her head.

Slowly, she shifted away from him, then crawled to the front of the tent to peek out. Even as she reached for the flap, a hand closed around her ankle. Hunter pillowed his other hand under his head as he watched her.

"If you're going out like that, we won't keep everyone away from the campsite for long."

As she was naked, the haughty look she sent him lost something. "I was just looking out. I thought you were asleep."

He smiled, thinking she was the only woman who could make a viable stab at dignity while on her hands and knees in a tent, without a stitch on. The finger around her ankle stroked absently. "You're up early."

"I thought I'd hang these clothes out to dry."

"Very practical." Because he sensed she was feeling awkward, Hunter sat up and grabbed her arm, tugging until she tumbled back, sprawled over him. Content, he held her against him and sighed. "We'll do it later."

Unsure whether to laugh or complain, Lee blew the hair out of her eyes as she propped herself on one elbow. "I'm not tired."

"You don't have to be tired to lie down." Then he rolled on top of her. "It's called relaxing."

As the planes of his body fit against the curves of hers, Lee felt the warmth seep in. A hundred tiny pulse points began to drum. "I don't think this has a lot to do with relaxing."

"No?" He'd wanted to see her like this, in the thin light of dawn with her hair mussed from his hands, her skin flushed from sleep, her limbs heavy from a night of loving and alert for more. He ran a hand down her with a surge of possession that wasn't quite comfortable, wasn't quite expected. "Then we'll relax later, too." He saw her lips form a gentle smile just before he brushed his over them.

Hunter didn't question that he wanted her just as urgently now as he had all the days and nights before. He rarely questioned feelings, because he trusted them. Her arms went around him, her lips parted. The completeness of her giving shot a shaft of heat through him that turned to a unified warmth. Lifting his head, Hunter looked down at her.

Milkmaid skin over a duchess's cheekbones, eyes like the sky at dusk and hair like copper shot with gold. Hunter gave himself the pleasure of looking at all of her, slowly.

She was small and sleek and smooth. He ran a fingertip along the curve of her shoulder and studied the contrast of his skin against hers. Fragile, delicate—but he remembered how much strength there was inside her.

"You always look at me as if you know everything there is to know about me."

The intensity in his eyes remained, as he caught her hand in his. "Not enough. Not nearly enough." With the lightest of touches, he kissed her shoulder, her temple, then her lips.

"Hunter…" She wanted to tell him that no one had ever made her feel this way before. She wanted to tell him that no one had ever made her want so badly to believe in magic and fairy tales and the simplicity of love. But as she started to speak, courage deserted her. She was afraid to risk, afraid to fail. Instead she touched a hand to his cheek. "Kiss me again."

He understood there was something more, something he needed to know. But he understood, too, that when something fragile was handled clumsily, it broke. He did as she asked and savored the warm, dark taste of her mouth.

Soft…sweet…silky. It was how he could make her feel with only a kiss. The ground was hard and unyielding under the thin tent mattress, but it might have been a luxurious pile of feathers. It was so easy to forget where she was, when he was with her this way, to forget a world existed outside that small space two bodies required. He could make her float, and she'd never known she'd wanted to. He could make her ache, and she'd never known there could be pleasure from it. He spoke against her mouth words she didn't need to understand. She wanted and was wanted, needed and was needed. She loved…

With an inarticulate murmur of acceptance for whatever he could give, Lee drew him closer. Closer. The moment was all that mattered.

Deep, intoxicating, tender, the kiss went on and on and on.

Even an imagination as fluid as his hadn't fantasized anything so sweet, anything so soft. It was as though she melted into him, giving everything before he could ask. Once, only once, only briefly, it sped through his mind that he was as vulnerable as she. The unease came, flicking at the corner of his mind. Then her hands ran over him, stroking, and he accepted the weakness.

Only one other person had ever had the power to reach inside him and hold his heart. Now there were two. The time to deal with it was tomorrow. Today was for them alone.

Without hurry, he whispered kisses over her face.

Perhaps it was an homage to beauty, perhaps it was much, much more. He didn't question his motives as he traced the slope of her cheek. There was an immediacy he'd never experienced before, but it didn't carry the urgency he'd expected. She was there for him as long as he needed. He understood that, without words.

"You smell of spring and rain," he murmured against her ear. "Why should that drive me mad?"

The words vibrated through her, as arousing as the most intimate caress. Heavy-lidded, clouded, her eyes met his. "Just show me. Show me again."

He loved her with such generosity. Each touch was a separate pleasure, each kiss a luxurious taste. Patience—there was more patience in him than in her. Her body was tossed between utter contentment and urgency, until reason was something too vague to grasp.

"Here—" He nibbled lightly at her breast, listening to and allured by her unsteady breaths. "You're small and soft. Here—" He took his hand over her hip to her thigh. "You're taut and lean. I can't seem to touch enough, taste enough." He drew the peak of her breast into his mouth, so that she arched against him, center to center.

"Hunter." His name was barely audible, but the sound of it was enough to bring him to desperation. "I need you."

God, had he wanted to hear that so badly? Struggling to understand what those three simple words had triggered, he buried his mouth against her skin. But he couldn't think, only feel. Only want. "You have me."

With his hands and lips alone, he took her spiraling over the first peak.

Her movements beneath him grew wild, her murmurs frenzied, but she was unaware. All Lee knew was that they were flesh-to-flesh. This was the storm he'd gentled the night before, the power unleashed, the demands unsoftened. The tenderness became passion so quickly, she could only ride with it, blind to her own power and her own demands. She was spinning too fast in the world they'd created to know how hungrily her mouth sought him, how sure were her own hands. She drew from him everything he drew from her. Again and again she took him to the edge, and again and again he clung, wanting more. And still more.

Greed. He'd never known this degree of greed. With the blood pounding in his head, singing in his veins, he molded his open mouth to hers. With his hands gripping her hips, he rolled until she lay over him. They were still mouth-to-mouth when they joined, and her gasp of pleasure rocketed through him.

Strength seemed to build, impossibly. She thought she could feel each individual muscle of her body coil and release as they moved together. Power called to power. Lee remembered the lightning, remembered the thunder, and lived it again. When the storm broke, she was clasped against him, as if the heat had fused them.

Minutes, hours, days. Lee couldn't have measured the time. Slowly, her body settled. Gradually, her heartbeat leveled. With her body pressed close to his, she could feel each breath he took and found a foolish satisfaction that the rhythm matched her own.

"A pity we wasted a week." Finding the effort to open his eyes too great, Hunter kept them closed as he combed his fingers through her hair.

She smiled a little, because he couldn't see. "Wasted?"

"If we'd started out this way, I'd've slept a lot better."

"Really?" Schooling her features, Lee lifted her head. "Have you had trouble sleeping?"

His eyelids opened lazily. "I've rarely found it necessary to get up at dawn, unless it's to write."

The surge of pleasure made her voice smug. She traced a fingertip over his shoulder. "Is that so?"

"You insisted on wearing that perfume to make me crazy."

"To make you crazy?" Folding her arms on his chest, she arched a brow. "It's a very subtle scent."

"Subtle." He ran a casual hand over her bottom. "Like a hammer in the solar plexus."

The laugh nearly escaped. "You were the one who insisted we share a tent."

"Insisted?" He gave her a mildly amused glance. "I told you I had no objection if you chose to sleep outside."

"Knowing I wouldn't."

"True, but I didn't expect you to resist me for so long."

Her head came up off her folded arms. "Resist you?" she repeated. "Are you saying you plotted this out like a scene in a book?"

Grinning, he pillowed his arms behind his head. God, he couldn't remember a time he'd felt so clean, so... complete. "It worked."

"Typical," she said, wishing she were insulted and trying her best to act as though she were. "I'm surprised there was room in here for the two of us and your inflated ego."

"And your stubbornness."

She sat up at the word, both brows disappearing under her tousled bangs. "I suppose you thought I'd just—" her hand gestured in a quick circle "—fall at your feet."

Hunter considered this a moment, while he gave

himself the pleasure of memorizing every curve of her body. "It might've been nice, but I'd figured a few detours into the scenario."

"Oh, had you?" She wondered if he realized he was steadily digging himself into a hole. "I bet we can come up with a great many more." Searching in her pack, Lee found a fresh T-shirt. "Starting now."

As she started to drag the shirt over her head, Hunter grabbed the hem and yanked. Lee tumbled down on top of him again, to find her mouth captured. When he let her surface, she narrowed her eyes. "You think you're pretty clever, don't you?"

"Yeah." He caught her chin in his hand and kissed her again. "Let's have breakfast."

She swallowed a laugh, but her eyes gave her away. "Bastard."

"Okay, but I'm still hungry." He tugged her shirt down her torso before he started to dress.

Lying back, Lee strugggled into a pair of jeans. "I don't suppose, now that the point's been made, we could finish out this week at a nice resort?"

Hunter dug out a fresh pair of socks. "A resort? Don't tell me you're having problems roughing it, Lenore."

"I wouldn't say problems." She stuck a hand in one boot and found the inside damp. Resigned, she hunted for her sneakers. "But there is the matter of having fantasies about a hot tub and a soft bed." She pressed a hand to her lower back. "Wonderful fantasies."

"Camping does take a certain amount of strength and endurance," he said easily. "I suppose if you've reached your limit and want to quit—"

"I didn't say anything about quitting," she retorted. She set her teeth, knowing whichever way she went, she lost. "We'll finish out the damn two weeks," she mumbled, and crawled out of the tent.

Lee couldn't deny that the quality of the air was exquisite and the clarity of the sky more perfect than any she'd ever seen. Nor, if he'd asked, would she have told Hunter that she wanted to be back in Los Angeles. It was a matter of basic creature comforts, she thought. Like soaking in hot, fragrant water and stretching out on a firm, linen-covered mattress. Certainly, it wasn't more than most people wanted in their day-to-day lives. But then, she reflected, Hunter Brown wasn't most people.

"Fabulous, isn't it?" His arms came around her waist, drawing her back to his chest. He wanted her to see what he saw, feel what he felt. Perhaps he wanted it too much.

"It's a beautiful spot. It hardly seems real." Then she sighed, not entirely sure why. Would Los Angeles seem more real to her when this final week was up? At the very least, she understood the tall buildings and crowded streets. Here—here she seemed so small, and that top rung of the ladder seemed so vague and unimportant.

Abruptly, she turned and clung to him. "I hate to admit it, but I'm glad you brought me." She found she wanted to continue clinging, continue holding, so that there wouldn't be a time when she had to let go. Pushing away all thoughts of tomorrow, Lee told herself to remember the wildflowers. "I'm starving," she said, able to smile when she drew away. "It's your turn to cook."

"A small blessing."

Lee gave him a quick jab before they cleaned up the dishes they'd left out in the rain.

In his quick, efficient manner, Hunter had the

campfire burning and bacon sizzling. Lee sat back, absorbing the scents while she watched him break eggs into the pan.

"We've been through a lot of eggs," she commented idly. "How do you manage to keep them fresh out here?"

Because she was watching his hands, she missed the quick smile. "Just one of the many mysteries of life. You'd better pass me a plate."

"Yes, but— Oh, look." The movement that had caught her eye turned out to be two rabbits, curious enough to bound to the edge of the clearing and watch. The mystery of the eggs was forgotten in the simple fascination of something she'd just begun to appreciate. "Every time I see one, I want to touch."

"If you managed to get close enough to touch, they'd show you they have very sharp teeth."

Shrugging, she dropped her chin to her knees and continued to stare back at the visitors. "The bunnies I think about don't bite."

Hunter reached for a plate himself. "Bunnies, fuzzy little squirrels and cute raccoons are nice to look at but foolish to handle. I remember having a long, heated argument with Sarah on the subject a couple of years ago."

"Sarah?" Lee accepted the plate he offered, but her attention was fully on him.

Until that moment, Hunter hadn't realized how completely he'd forgotten who she was and why she was there. To have mentioned Sarah so casually showed him he needed to keep personal feelings separate from professional agreements. "Someone very special," he told her as he scooped the remaining eggs onto his plate. He remembered his daughter's comment about simmering passion and falling in love. The smile couldn't be prevented. "I imagine she'd like to meet you."

Lee felt something cold squeeze her heart and fought to ignore it. They'd said nothing about commitment, nothing about exclusivity. They were adults. She was responsible for her own emotions and their consequences. "Would she?" Taking the first bite of eggs, she tasted nothing. Her eyes were drawn to the ring on his finger. It wasn't a wedding band, but... She had to ask, she had to know before things went any further.

"The ring you wear," she began, satisfied her voice was even. "It's very unusual. I've never seen another quite like it."

"You shouldn't." He ate with the ease of a man completely content. "My sister made it."

"Sister?" If her name was Sarah...

"Bonnie raises children and makes jewelry," Hunter went on. "I'm not sure which comes first."

"Bonnie." Nodding, she forced herself to continue eating. "Is she your only sister?"

"There were just the two of us. For some odd reason, we got along very well." He remembered those early years when he was struggling to learn how to be both father and mother to Sarah. He smiled. "We still do."

"How does she feel about what you do?"

"Bonnie's a firm believer that everyone should do exactly what suits them. As long as they're married, with a half-dozen children." He grinned, recognizing the unspoken question in Lee's eyes. "In that area, I've disappointed her." He paused for a moment, the grin fading. "Do you think I could make love with you if I had a wife waiting for me at home?"

She dropped her gaze to her plate. Why could he always read her when she couldn't read him? "I still don't know very much about you."

He didn't know if he consciously made the decision at that moment or if he'd been ready to make it all along. "Ask," he said simply.

Lee looked up at him. It no longer mattered if she needed to know for herself or for her job. She just needed to know. "You've never been married?"

"No."

"Is that an outgrowth of your need for privacy?"

"No, it's an outgrowth of not finding anyone who could deal with the way I live and my obligations."

Lee mulled this over, thinking it a rather odd way to phrase it. "Your writing?"

"Yes, there's that."

She started to press further, then decided to change directions. Personal questions could be reciprocated with personal questions. "You said you hadn't always wanted to be a writer, but were born to be one. What made you realize it?"

"I don't think it was a matter of realizing, but of accepting." Understanding that she wanted something specific, he drew out a cigarette, studying the tip. He was no more certain why he was answering than Lee was why she was asking. "It must've been in my first year of college. I'd written stories ever since I could remember, but I was dead set on a career as an athlete. Then I wrote something that seemed to trigger it. It was nothing fabulous," he added thoughtfully. "A very basic plot, simple background, but the characters pulled me in. I knew them as well as I knew anyone. There was nothing else for me to do."

"It must've been difficult. Publishing isn't an easy field. Even when you break in, it isn't particularly lucrative unless you write bestsellers. With your parents gone, you had to support yourself."

"I had experience waiting tables." He smiled, a bit more easily now. "And detested it. Sometimes you have to put it all on the line, Lenore. So I did."

"How did you support yourself from the time you graduated from college until you broke through with *The Devil's Due?*"

"I wrote."

Lee shook her head, forgetting the half-full plate on her lap. "The articles and short stories couldn't have brought in very much. And that was your first book."

"No, I'd had a dozen others before it." Blowing out a stream of smoke, he reached for the coffeepot. "Want some?"

She leaned forward a bit, her brows drawing together. "Look, Hunter, I've been researching you for months. I might not have gotten much, but I know every book, every article and every short story you've written, including the majority of your college work. There's no way I'd've missed a dozen books."

"You know everything Hunter Brown's written," he corrected and poured himself coffee.

"That's precisely what I said."

"You didn't research Laura Miles."

"Who?"

He sipped, enjoying the coffee and the conversation more than he'd anticipated. "A great many writers use pseudonyms. Laura Miles was mine."

"A woman's name?" Confused on one level, reporter's instincts humming on another, she frowned at him. "You wrote a dozen books before *The Devil's Due* under a woman's name?"

"Yeah. One of the problems with writing is that the name alone can project a certain perception of the author." He offered her the last piece of bacon. "Hunter Brown wasn't right for what I was doing at the time."

Lee let out a frustrated breath. "What were you doing?"

"Writing romance novels." He flicked his cigarette into the fire.

"Writing… *You?*"

He studied her incredulous face before he leaned back. He was used to criticism of genre fiction and, more often than not, amused by it. "Do you object to the genre in general, or to my writing in it?"

"I don't—" Confused, she broke off to try to gather her thoughts. "I just can't picture you writing happy-ever-after love stories. Hunter, I just finished *Silent Scream.* I kept my bedroom door locked for a week." She dragged a hand through her hair as he quietly watched her. "Romances?"

"Most novels have some kind of relationship with them. A romance simply focuses on it, rather than using it as a subplot or a device."

"But didn't you feel you were wasting your talent?" Lee knew his skill in drawing the reader in from the first page, from the first sentence. "I understand there being a matter of putting food on the table, but—"

"No." He cut her off. "I never wrote for the money, Lenore, any more than the novel you're writing is done for financial gain. As far as wasting my talent, you shouldn't look down your nose at something you don't understand."

"I'm sorry, I don't mean to be condescending. I'm just—" Helplessly, she shrugged. "I'm just surprised. No, I'm astonished. I see those colorful little paperbacks everywhere, but—"

"You never considered reading one," he finished. "You should, they're good for you."

"I suppose, for simple entertainment."

He liked the way she said it, as though it were something to be enjoyed in secret, like a child's lollipop. "If a novel doesn't entertain, it isn't a novel and it's wasted your time. I imagine you've read *Jane Eyre, Rebecca, Gone with the Wind, Ivanhoe.*"

"Yes, of course."

"Romances. A lot of the same ingredients are in those colorful little paperbacks."

He was perfectly serious. At that moment, Lee would've given up half the books in her personal library for the chance to read one Laura Miles story. "Hunter, I want to print this."

"Go ahead."

Her mouth was already open for the argument she'd expected. "Go ahead?" she repeated. "You don't care?"

"Why should I? I'm not ashamed of the work I did as Laura Miles. In fact…" He smiled, thinking back. "I'm rather pleased with most of it."

"Then why—" She shook her head as she began to absently nibble on cold bacon. "Damn it, Hunter, why haven't you ever said so before? Laura Miles is as much a deep, dark secret as everything else about you."

"I never met a reporter I chose to tell before." He rose, stretching, and enjoyed the wide blue expanse of sky. Just as he'd never met a woman he'd have chosen to live with before. Hunter was beginning to wonder if one had very much to do with the other. "Don't complicate the simple, Lenore," he told her, thinking aloud. "It usually manages to complicate itself."

Setting her plate aside, she stood in front of him. "One more question, then."

He brought his gaze back down to hers. She hadn't bothered to fuss with her hair or makeup that morning, as she had from the first morning of the trip. For a moment, he wondered if the reporter was too anxious for the story or the woman was too involved with the man. He wished he knew. "All right," he agreed. "One more question."

"Why me?"

How did he answer what he didn't know? How did he answer what he was hesitant to ask himself? Framing her face, he brought his lips to hers. Long, lingering and very, very new. "I see something in you," Hunter murmured, holding her face still so that he could study it. "I want something from you. I don't know what either one is yet, and maybe I never will. Is that answer enough?"

She put her hands on his wrists and felt his life pump through them. It was almost possible to believe hers pumped through them, too. "It has to be."

Chapter 9

Standing high on the bluff, Lee could see down the canyon, over the peaks and pinnacles, beyond the rich red buttes to the sheer-faced walls. There were pictures in them. People, creatures, stories. They pleased her all the more because she hadn't realized she could find them.

She hadn't known land could be so demanding, or so compelling. Not knowing that, how could she have known she would feel at home so far away from the world she knew or the life she'd made?

Perhaps it was the mystery, the awesomeness—the centuries of work nature had done to form beauty out of rock, the centuries it had yet to work. Weather had landscaped, carved and created without pampering. It might have been the quiet she'd learned to listen to, the quiet she'd learned to hear more than she'd ever heard sound before. Or it might have been the man she'd discovered in the canyon, who was slowly, inevitably dominating every aspect of her life in much the same way wind, water and sun dominated the shape of everything around her. He wouldn't pamper, either.

They'd been lovers only a matter of days, yet he seemed to know just where her strengths lay, and her weaknesses. She learned about him, step by gradual step, always amazed that each new discovery came so naturally, as though she'd always known. Perhaps the intensity came from the briefness. Lee could almost accept that theory, but for the timelessness of the hours they spent together.

In two days, she'd leave the canyon, and the man, and go back to being the Lee Radcliffe she'd molded herself into over the years. She'd step back into the rhythm, write her article and go on to the next stage of her career.

What choice was there? Lee asked herself as she stood with the afternoon sun beating down on her. In L.A., her life had direction, it had purpose. There, she had one goal: to succeed. That goal didn't seem so important here and now, where just being, just breathing, was enough, but this world wasn't the one she would live in day after day. Even if Hunter had asked, even if she'd wanted to, Lee couldn't go on indefinitely in this unscheduled, unplanned existence. Purpose, she wondered. What would her purpose be here? She couldn't dream by the campfire forever.

But two days. She closed her eyes, telling herself that everything she'd done and everything she'd seen would be forever implanted in her memory. Did the time left have to be so short? And the time ahead of her loomed so long.

"Here." Hunter came up alongside her, holding out a pair of binoculars. "You should always see as far as you can."

She took them, with a smile for the way he had of putting things. The canyon zoomed closer, abruptly becoming more personal. She could see the water rushing by in the creek, rushing with a sound too distant to be heard. Why had she never noticed how unique each leaf on a tree could be? She could see other campers loitering near their sites or mingling with the day tourists on paths. Lee let the binoculars drop. They brought intrusion too close.

"Will you come back next year?" She wanted to be able to picture him there, looking out over the endless space, remembering.

"If I can."

"It won't have changed," she murmured. If she came back, five, ten years from then, the creek would still snake by, the buttes would still stand. But she couldn't come back. With an effort, she shook off the mood and smiled at him. "It must be nearly lunchtime."

"It's too hot to eat up here." Hunter wiped at the sweat on his brow. "We'll go down and find some shade."

"All right." She could see the dust plume up from his boots as he walked. "Someplace near the creek." She glanced to the right. "Let's go this way, Hunter. We haven't walked down there yet."

He hesitated only a moment. "Fine." Holding her hand, he took the path she'd chosen.

The walk down was always easier than the walk up. That was another invaluable fact Lee had filed away during the last couple of weeks. And Hunter, though he held her hand, didn't guide or lead. He simply walked his own way. Just as he'd walk his own way in forty-eight hours, she mused, and stretched her stride to keep pace with him.

"Will you start on your next book as soon as you get back?"

Questions, he thought. He'd never known anyone with such an endless supply of questions. "Yes."

"Are you ever afraid you'll, well, dry up?"

"Always."

Interested, she stopped a moment. "Really?" She'd considered him a man without any fear at all. "I'd have thought that the more success you achieved, the more confident you'd become."

"Success is a deity that's never satisfied." She frowned, a bit uncomfortable with his description. "Every time I face that first blank page, I wonder how I'll ever get through a beginning, middle and end."

"How do you?"

He began to walk again, so that she had to keep up or be left behind. "I tell the story. It's as simple and as miserably complex as that."

So was he, she reflected, that simple, that complex. Lee thought over his words as she felt the temperature gradually change with the decrease in elevation.

It seemed tidier in this section of the canyon. Once she thought she heard the purr of a car's engine, a sound she hadn't heard in days. The trees grew thicker, the shade more generous. How strange, she reflected, to have those sheer, unforgiving walls at her back and a cozy little forest in front of her. More unreality? Then, glancing down, she saw a patch of small white flowers. Lee picked three, leaving the rest for someone else. She hadn't come for them, she remembered as she tucked them in her hair, but she was glad, so very glad, to have found them.

"How's this?" He turned to see her secure the last flower in her hair. The need for her, the complete her, rose inside him so swiftly it took his breath away. Lenore. He had no trouble understanding why the man in Poe's verse had mourned the loss of her to the point of madness. "You grow lovelier. Impossible." Hunter touched a fingertip to her cheek. Would he, too, grow mad from mourning the loss of her?

Her face, lifted to the sun, needed nothing more than the luminescence of her skin to make it exquisite. But how long, he wondered, how long would she be content to shun the polish? How long would it be before she craved the life she'd begun to carve out for herself?

Lee didn't smile, because his eyes prevented her. He was looking into her again, for something… Something. She wasn't certain, even if she'd known what it was, that she could give him the answer he wanted. Instead, she did what he'd once done. Placing her hands on his shoulders, she touched her mouth to his. With her eyes squeezed shut, she dropped her head onto his chest.

How could she leave? How could she not? There seemed to be no direction she could go and not lose something essential. "I don't believe in magic," she murmured, "but if I did, I'd say this was a magic place. Now, in the day, it's quiet. Sleeping, perhaps. But at night, the air would be alive with spirits."

He held her closer as he rested his neck on top of her head. Did she realize how romantic she was? he wondered. Or just how hard she fought not to be? A week ago, she might have had such a thought, but she'd never have said it aloud. A week from now… Hunter bit back a sigh. A week from now, she'd give no more thought to magic.

"I want to make love with you here," he said quietly. "With the sunlight streaming through the leaves and onto your skin. In the evening, just before the dew falls. At dawn, when the light's caught somewhere between rose and gray."

Moved, ruled by love, she smiled up at him. "And at midnight, when the moon's high and anything's possible."

"Anything's always possible." He kissed one cheek, then the other. "You only have to believe it."

She laughed, a bit shakily. "You almost make me believe it. You make my knees weak."

His grin flashed as he swept her up in his arms. "Better?"

Would she ever feel this free again? Throwing her arms around his neck, Lee kissed him with all the feeling that welled inside her. "Yes. And if you don't put me down, I'll want you to carry me back to camp."

The half smile touched his lips. "Decided you aren't hungry after all?"

"Since I doubt you've got anything in that bag but dried fruit and sunflower seeds, I don't have any illusions about lunch."

"I've still got a couple pieces of fudge."

"Let's eat."

Hunter dropped her unceremoniously on the ground. "It shows the woman's basic lust centers around food."

"Just chocolate," Lee disagreed. "You can have my share of the sunflower seeds."

"They're good for you." Digging into the pack, he pulled out some small clear plastic bags.

"I can handle the raisins," Lee said unenthusiastically. "But I can do without the seeds."

Shrugging, Hunter popped two in his mouth. "You'll be hungry before dinner."

"I've been hungry before dinner for two weeks," she tossed back, and began to root through the pack herself for the fudge. "No matter how good seeds and nuts and little dried pieces of apricot are for you, they don't take the place of red meat—" she found a small square of fudge "—or chocolate."

Hunter watched her close her eyes in pure pleasure as she chewed the candy. "Hedonist."

"Absolutely." Her eyes were laughing when she opened them. "I like silk blouses, French champagne and lobster with warm butter sauce." She sighed as she sat back, wondering if Hunter had any emotional attachment to the last piece of fudge. "I especially enjoy them after I've worked all week to justify having them."

He understood that, perhaps too well. She wasn't a woman who wanted to be taken care of, nor was he a man who believed anyone should have a free ride. But what future was there in a relationship when two people couldn't acclimate to each other's lifestyle? He'd never imposed his on anyone else, nor would be permit anyone to sway him from his own. And yet, now that he felt the clock ticking the hours away, the days away, he wondered if it would be as simple to go back, alone, as he'd once expected it to be.

"You enjoy living in the city?" he asked casually.

"Of course." It wasn't possible to tell him that she hated the thought of going back, alone, to what she'd always thought was perfect for her. "My apartment's twenty minutes from the magazine."

"Convenient." And practical, he mused. It seemed she would always choose the practical, even if she had a whim for the fanciful. He opened the canteen and drank. When he passed it to Lee, she accepted. She'd learned to make a number of adjustments.

"I suppose you work at home."

"Yes."

She touched a hand absently to one of the flowers in her hair. "That takes discipline. I think most people need the structure of an office away from their living space to accomplish anything."

"You wouldn't."

She looked over then, wishing they could talk about more personal things without bringing on that quiet sense of panic. Better that they talked of work or the weather, or of nothing at all. "No?"

"You'd drive yourself harder than any supervisor or time clock." He bit into an apple slice. "If you put your mind to it, you'd have that manuscript finished within a month."

Restlessly, she moved her shoulders. "If I worked eight hours a day, without any other obligations."

"The story's your only obligation."

She held back a sigh. She didn't want to argue or even debate, not when they had so little time left together. Yet if they didn't discuss her work, she might not be able to prevent herself from talking about her feelings. That was a circle without any meeting point.

"Hunter, as a writer, you can feel that way about a book. I suppose you have to. I have a job, a career that demands blocks of time and a great deal of my attention. I can't simply put that into hiatus while I speculate on my chances of getting a manuscript published."

"You're afraid to risk it."

It was a direct hit to her most sensitive area. Both of them knew her anger was a defense. "What if I am? I've worked hard for my position at *Celebrity*. Everything I've done there, and every benefit I've received, I've earned on my own. I've already taken enough risks."

"By not marrying Jonathan Willoby?"

The fury leaped into her eyes quickly, interesting him. So, it was still a sore point, Hunter realized. A very sore point.

"Do you find that amusing?" Lee demanded. "Does the fact that I reneged on an unspoken agreement appeal to your sense of humor?"

"Not particularly. But it intrigues me that you'd consider it possible to renege on something unspoken."

From the meticulous way she recapped the canteen, he gauged just how angry she was. Her voice was cool and detached, as he hadn't heard it for days. "My family and the Willobys have been personally and professionally involved for years. The marriage was expected of me and I knew it from the time I was sixteen."

Hunter leaned back against the trunk of a tree until he was comfortable. "And at sixteen you didn't consider that sort of expectation antiquated?"

"How could you possibly understand?" Fuming, she rose. The nerves that had been dormant for days began to jump again. Hunter could almost see them spring to life. "You said your father was a dreamer who made his living as a salesman. My father was a realist who made his living socializing and delegating. He socialized with the Willobys. He delegated me to complete the social and professional merger with them by marrying Jonathan." Even now, the tidy, unemotional plans gave her a twinge of distaste. "Jonathan was attractive, intelligent, already successful. My father never considered that I'd object."

"But you did," Hunter pointed out. "Why do you continue to insist on paying for something that was your right?"

Lee whirled to him. It was no longer possible for her to answer coolly, to rebuff with aloofness. "Do you know what it cost me not to do what was expected of me? Everything I did, all my life, was ultimately for their approval."

"Then you did something for yourself." Without hurry, he rose to face her. "Is your career for yourself, Lenore, or are you still trying to win their approval?"

He had no right to ask, no right to make her search for the answer. Pale, she turned away from him. "I don't want to discuss this with you. It's none of your concern."

"Isn't it?" Abruptly as angry as she, Hunter spun her around again. "Isn't it?" he repeated.

Her hands curled around his arms—whether in protest or for support, she wasn't certain. Now, she thought, now perhaps she'd reached that edge where she had to make a stand, no matter how unsteady the ground under her feet. "My life and the way I live it are my business, Hunter."

"Not anymore."

"You're being ridiculous." She threw back her head, the better to meet his eyes. "This argument doesn't even have a point."

Something was building inside him so quickly he didn't have a chance to fight it or reason it through. "You're wrong."

She was beginning to tremble without knowing why. Along with the anger came the quick panic she recognized too well. "I don't know what you want."

"You." She was crushed against him before she understood her own reaction. "All of you."

His mouth closed over hers with none of the gentle patience he usually showed. Lee felt a lick of fear that was almost immediately swallowed by raging need.

He'd made her feel passion before, but not so swiftly. Desire had burst inside her before, but not so painfully. Everything was as it always was whenever he touched her, and yet everything was so different.

Was it anger she felt from him? Frustration? Passion? She only knew that the control he mastered so finely was gone. Something strained inside him, something more primitive than he'd let free before. This time, they both knew it could break loose. Her blood swam with the panicked excitement of anticipation.

Then they were on the ground, with the scent of sun-warmed leaves and cool water. She felt his beard scrape over her cheek before he buried his mouth in her throat. Whatever drove him left her no choice but to race with him to the end that waited for both of them.

He didn't question his own desperation. He couldn't. If she held off sharing certain pieces of herself with him, she still shared her body willingly. He wanted more, all, though he told himself it wasn't reasonable. Even now, as he felt her body heat and melt for him, he knew he wouldn't be satisfied. When would she give her feelings to him as freely? For the first time in his life, he wanted too much.

He struggled back to the edge of reason, resisting the wave after wave of need that raged through him. This wasn't the time, the place or the way. In his mind, he knew it, but emotion battled to betray him. Still holding her close, he buried his face in her hair and waited for the madness to pass.

Stunned, as much by his outburst of passion as by her unquestioning response, Lee lay still. Instinctively, she stroked a hand down his back to soothe. She knew him well enough to understand that his temper was rarely unguarded. Now she knew why.

Hunter lifted his head to look at her, seeing on a surge of self-disgust that her eyes were wary again. The flowers had fallen from her hair. Taking one, he pressed it into her hand. "You're much too fragile to be handled so clumsily."

His eyes were so intense, so dark, it was impossible for her to relax again. Against his back, her fingers curled and uncurled. There was a warning somewhere in her brain that he wanted more than she'd expected him to want, more than she knew how to give. Play it light, Lee ordered herself, and deliberately stilled the movement of her fingers. She smiled, though her eyes remained cautious.

"I should've waited until we were back in the tent before I made you angry."

Understanding what she was trying to do, Hunter lifted a brow. Under his voice, and hers, was a strain both of them pretended not to hear. "We can go back now. I can toss you around a bit more."

As the panic subsided, she sent him a mild glance. "I'm stronger than I look."

"Yeah?" He sent her a smile of his own. He had the long hours of night to think about what had happened and what he was going to do about it. "Show me."

More confident than she should've been, Lee pushed against him, intent on rolling him off her. He didn't budge. The look of calm amusement on his face had her doubling her efforts. Breathless, unsuccessful, she lay back and frowned at him. "You're heavier than you look," she complained. "It must be all those sunflower seeds."

"Your muscles are full of chocolate," he corrected.

"I only had one piece," she began.

"Today. By my count, you've polished off—"

"Never mind." Her brow arched elegantly. The nerves in her stomach hadn't completely subsided. "If you want to talk about unhealthy habits, you're the one who smokes too much."

He shrugged, accepting the truth. "Everyone's entitled to one vice."

Her grin became wicked, then sultry. "Is that your only one?"

If she'd planned to make her mouth irresistible, she'd succeeded. Hunter lowered his to nibble at the sweetness. "I've never been one to consider pleasures vices."

Sighing, she linked her arms around his neck. They didn't have enough time left to waste it arguing, or even thinking. "Why don't we go back to the tent so you can show me what you mean?"

He laughed softly and shifted to kiss the curve of her shoulder. Her laugh echoed his, then Lee's smile froze when she glanced down the length of his body to what stood at their feet.

Fear ripped through her. She couldn't have screamed. Her short, unpainted nails dug into Hunter's back.

"What—" He lifted his head. Her face was ice-white

and still. Though her body was rigid beneath his, there was lively fear in the hands that dug into his back. Muscles tense, he turned to look in the direction she was staring. "Damn." The word was hardly out of his mouth before a hundred pounds of fur and muscle leaped on him. This time, Lee's scream tore free.

Adrenaline born of panic gave her the strength to send the three of them rolling to the edge of the bank. As she struck out blindly, Lee heard Hunter issue a sharp command. A whimper followed it.

"Lenore." Her shoulders were gripped before she could spring to her feet. In her mind, the only thought was to find a weapon to defend them. "It's all right." Without giving her a choice, Hunter held her close. "It's all right, I promise. He won't hurt you."

"My God, Hunter, it's a wolf!" Every nightmare she'd ever read or heard about fangs and claws spun in her mind. With her arms wrapped around him to protect him, as much as for protection for herself, Lee turned her head. Silver eyes stared back at her from a silver coat.

"No." He felt the fresh fear jump through her and continued to soothe. "He's only half wolf."

"We've got to do something." Should they run? Should they sit perfectly still? "He attacked—"

"Greeted," Hunter corrected. "Trust me, Lenore. He's not vicious." Annoyed and resigned, Hunter held out a hand. "Here, Santanas."

A bit embarrassed at having lost control of himself, the dog crawled forward, head down. Speechless, Lee watched Hunter stroke the thick silver-gray fur.

"He's usually better behaved," Hunter said mildly. "But he hasn't seen me for nearly two weeks."

"Seen you?" She pressed herself closer to Hunter.

"But..." Logic began to seep through her panic as she saw the dog lick Hunter's extended hand. "You called him by name," she said shakily. "What did you call him?"

Before Hunter could answer, there was a rustling in the trees behind them. Lee had nearly mustered the breath to scream again when another voice, young and high, shouted out. "Santanas! You come back here. I'm going to get in trouble."

"Damn right," Hunter mumbled under his breath.

Lee drew back far enough to look into Hunter's face. "Just what the hell's going on?"

"A reunion," he said simply.

Puzzled, with her heart still pounding in her ears, Lee watched the girl break through the trees. The dog's tail began to thump the ground.

"Santanas!" She stopped, her dark braids whipping back and forth. Smiling, she uninhibitedly showed her braces. "Whoops." The quick exclamation trailed off as Lee was treated to a long intense stare that was hauntingly familiar. The girl stuck her hands in the pockets of cutoff jeans, scuffing the ground with battered sneakers. "Well, hi." Her gaze shifted to Hunter briefly before it focused on Lee again. "I guess you wonder what I'm doing here."

"We'll get into that later," Hunter said in a tone both females recognized as basic male annoyance.

"Hunter—" Lee drew farther away, traces of anger and anxiety working their way through the confusion. She couldn't bring herself to look away from the dark, dark eyes of the girl who stared at her. "What's going on here?"

"Apparently a lesson in manners should be," he returned easily. "Lenore, the creature currently sniffing at your hand is Santanas, my dog." At the gesture of his hand, the large, lean animal sat and lifted a friendly paw. Dazed, Lee found herself taking it while she turned to watch the dog's master. She saw Hunter's gaze travel beyond her with a smile that held both irony and pride. "The girl rudely staring at you is Sarah. My daughter."

Chapter 10

Daughter...Sarah...

Lee turned her head to meet the dark, direct eyes that were a duplicate of Hunter's. Yes, they were a duplicate. It struck her like a blast of air. He had a child? This lovely, slender girl with a tender mouth and braids secured by mismatched rubber bands was Hunter's daughter? So many opposing emotions moved through her that she said nothing. Nothing at all.

"Sarah." Hunter spoke into the drumming silence. "This is Ms. Radcliffe."

"Sure, I know, the reporter. Hi."

Still sitting on the ground, with the dog now sniffing around her shoulder, Lee felt like a complete fool. "Hello." She hoped the word wasn't as ridiculously formal as it sounded to her.

"Dad said I shouldn't call you pretty because pretty

was like a bowl of fruit." Sarah didn't tilt her head as one might to study from a new angle, but Lee had the impression she was being weighed and dissected like a still life. "I like your hair," Sarah declared. "Is it a real color?"

"A definite lesson in manners," Hunter put in, more amused than annoyed. "I'm afraid Sarah's a bit of a brat."

"He always says that." Sarah moved thin, expressive shoulders. "He doesn't mean it, though."

"Until today." He ruffled the dog's fur, wondering just how he would handle the situation. Lee was still silent, and Sarah's eyes were all curiosity. "Take Santanas back to the house. I assume Bonnie's there."

"Yeah. We came back yesterday because I remembered I had a soccer game and she had an inspiration and couldn't do anything with it in Phoenix with all the kids running around like monkeys."

"I see." And though he did, perfectly, Lee was left floundering in the dark. "Go ahead, then, we'll be right along."

"Okay. Come on, Santanas." Then she shot Lee a quick grin. "He looks pretty ferocious, but he doesn't bite." As the girl darted away, Lee wondered if she'd been speaking of the dog or her father. When she was once again alone with Hunter, Lee remained still and silent.

"I'll apologize for the rudeness of my family, if you'd like."

Family. The word struck her, a dose of reality that flung her out of the dream. Rising, Lee meticulously dusted off her jeans. "There's no need." Her voice was cool, almost chill. Her muscles were wire-taut. "Since the game's over, I'd like you to drive me into Sedona so I can arrange for transportation back to L.A."

"Game?" In one long, easy motion, he came to his feet, then took her hand, stopping its nervous movement. It was a gesture that had become so much of a habit, neither of them noticed. "There's no game, Lenore."

"Oh, you played it very well." The hurt she wouldn't permit in her voice showed clearly in her eyes. Her hand remained cold and rigid in his. "So well, in fact, I completely forgot we were playing."

Patience deserted him abruptly and without warning. Anger he could handle, with more anger or with amusement. But hurt left him with no defense, no attack. "Don't be an idiot. Whatever game there was ended a few nights ago in the tent."

"Ended." Tears sprang to her eyes, stunning her. Furiously she blinked them back, filled with self-disgust, but not before he'd seen them. "No, it never ended. You're an excellent strategist, Hunter. You seemed to be so open with me that I didn't think you were holding anything back." She jerked her hand from his, longing for the luxury of dissolving into those hot, cleansing tears. "How could you?" she demanded. "How could you touch me that way and lie?"

"I never lied to you." His voice was as calm as hers, his eyes were as full of passion.

"You have a child." Something snapped inside her, so that she had to grip her hands together to prevent herself from wringing them. "You have a half-grown daughter you never mentioned to me. You told me you'd never been married."

"I haven't been," he said simply, and waited for the inevitable questions.

They leaped into her mind, but Lee found she couldn't ask them. She didn't want to know. If she was to put him out of her life immediately and completely, she couldn't ask. "You said her name once, and when I asked, you avoided answering."

"Who asked?" he countered. "You or the reporter?"

She paled, and her step away from him said more than a dozen words.

"If that was an unfair question," he said, feeling his way carefully, "I'm sorry."

Lee stifled a bitter answer. He'd just said it all. "I want to go back to Sedona. Will you drive me, or do I have to arrange for a car?"

"Stop this." He gripped her shoulders before she could back farther away. "You've been a part of my life for a few days. Sarah's been my life for ten years. I take no risks with her." She saw the fury come and go in his eyes as he fought against it. "She's off the record, do you understand? She stays off the record. I won't have her childhood disturbed by photographers dogging her at soccer games or hanging from trees at school picnics. Sarah's not an item for the glossy pages of any magazine."

"Is that what you think of me?" she whispered. "We've come no further than that?" She swallowed a mixture of pain and betrayal. "Your daughter won't be mentioned in any article I write. You have my word. Now let me go."

She wasn't speaking only of the hands that held her there, and they both knew it. He felt a bubble of panic he'd never expected, a twist of guilt that left him baffled. Frustrated, he stared down at her. He'd never realized she could be a complication. "I can't." It was said with such simplicity her skin iced. "I want you to understand, and I need time for that."

"You've had nearly two weeks to make me understand, Hunter."

"Damn it, you came here as a reporter." He paused, as if waiting for her to confirm or deny, but she said nothing. "What happened between us wasn't planned or expected by either one of us. I want you to come back with me to my home."

Somehow she met his eyes levelly. "I'm still a reporter."

"We have two days left in our agreement." His voice softened, his hands gentled. "Lenore, spend those two days with me at home, with my daughter."

"You have no problem asking for everything, do you?"

"No." She was still holding herself away from him. No matter how badly he wanted to, Hunter knew better than to try to draw her closer. Not yet. "It's important to me that you understand. Give me two days."

She wanted to say no. She wanted to believe she could deny him even that and turn away, go away, without regrets. But there'd be regrets, Lee realized, if she went back to L.A. without taking whatever was left. "I can't promise to understand, but I'll stay two more days."

Though she was reluctant, he held her hand to his lips. "Thank you. It's important to me."

"Don't thank me," she murmured. The anger had slipped away so quietly, she couldn't recall it. "Things have changed."

"Things changed days ago." Still holding her hand, he drew her in the direction Sarah had gone. "I'll come back for the gear."

Now that the first shock had passed, the second occurred to her. "But you live here in the canyon."

"That's right."

"You mean to tell me you have a house, with hot and

cold running water and a normal bed, but you chose to spend two weeks in a tent?"

"It relaxes me."

"That's just dandy," she muttered. "You've had me showering with lukewarm water and waking up with aching muscles, when you knew I'd've given a week's pay for one tub bath."

"Builds character," he claimed, more comfortable with her annoyance.

"The hell it does. You did it deliberately." She stopped, turning to him as the sun dappled light through the trees. "You did it all deliberately to see just how much I could tolerate."

"You were very impressive." He smiled infuriatingly. "I admit I never expected you to last out a week, much less two."

"You sonofa—"

"Don't get cranky now," he said easily. "You can take as many baths as you like over the next couple of days." He swung a friendly arm over her shoulder before she could prevent it. And he'd have time, he thought, to explain to her about Sarah. Time, he hoped, to make her understand. "I'll even see to it that you have that red meat you've been craving."

Fury threatened. Control strained. "Don't you dare patronize me."

"I'm not. You're not a woman a man could patronize." Though she mistrusted his answer, his voice was bland with sincerity and he wasn't smiling. "I'm enjoying you and, I suppose, the foul-up of my own plans. Believe me, I hadn't intended for you to find out I lived a couple miles from the campsite in quite this way."

"Just how did you intend for me to find out?"

"By offering you a quiet candlelight dinner on our last night. I'd hoped you'd see the—ah—humor in the situation."

"You'd've been wrong," she said precisely, then caught sight of the house cocooned in the trees.

It was smaller than she'd expected, but with the large areas of glass in the wood, it seemed to extend into the land. It made her think of dolls' houses and fairy tales, though she didn't know why. Dolls' houses were tidy and formal and laced with gingerbread. Hunter's house was made up of odd angles and unexpected peaks. A porch ran across the front, where the roof arched to a high pitch. Plants spilled over the banister—bloodred geraniums in jade-green pots. The roof sloped down again, then ran flat over a parallelogram with floor-to-ceiling windows. On the patio that jutted out from it, a white wicker chair lay overturned next to a battered soccer ball.

The trees closed in around it. Closed it in, Lee thought. Protected, sheltered, hid. It was like a house out of a play, or… Stopping, she narrowed her eyes and studied it again. "This is Jonas Thorpe's house in *Silent Scream*."

Hunter smiled, rather pleased she'd seen it so quickly. "More or less. I wanted to put him in isolation, miles away from what would normally be considered civilized, but in reality, the only safe place left."

"Is that how you look at it?" she wondered aloud. "As the only safe place left?"

"Often." Then a shriek, which after a heart-stopping moment Lee identified as laughter, ripped through the silence. It was followed by an excited bout of barking and a woman's frazzled voice. "Then there're other times," Hunter murmured as he led Lee toward the front door.

Even as he opened it, Sarah came bounding out. Unsure of her own feelings, Lee watched the girl throw her arms around her father's waist. She saw Hunter stroke a hand over the dark hair at the crown of Sarah's head.

"Oh, Dad, it's so funny! Aunt Bonnie was making a bracelet out of glazed dough and Santanas ate it—or he chewed on it until he found out it tasted awful."

"I'm sure Bonnie thinks it's a riot."

Her eyes, so like her father's, lit with a wicked amusement that would've made a veteran fifth-grade teacher nervous. "She said she had to take that sort of thing from art critics, but not from half-breed wolves. She said she'd make some tea for Lenore, but there aren't any cookies because we ate them yesterday. And she said—"

"Never mind, we'll find out for ourselves." He stepped back so that Lee could walk into the house ahead of him. She hesitated for a moment, wondering just what she was walking into, and his eyes lit with the same wicked amusement as Sarah's. They were quite a pair, Lee decided, and stepped forward.

She hadn't expected anything so, well, normal in Hunter Brown's home. The living room was airy, sunny in the afternoon light. *Cheerful.* Yes, Lee realized, that was precisely the word that came to mind. No shadowy corners or locked doors. There were wildflowers in an enameled vase and plump pillows on the sofa.

"Were you expecting witches' brooms and a satin-lined coffin?" he murmured in her ear.

Annoyed, she stepped away from him. "Of course not. I suppose I didn't expect you to have something quite so…domesticated."

He arched a brow at the word. "I am domesticated."

Lee looked at him, at the face that was half rugged, half aristocratic. On one level, perhaps, she mused. But only on one.

"I guess Aunt Bonnie's got the mess in the kitchen pretty well cleaned up." Sarah kept one arm around her father as she gave Lee another thorough going-over. "She'd like to meet you because Dad doesn't see nearly enough women and never talks to reporters. So maybe you're special because he decided to talk to you."

While she spoke, she watched Lee steadily. She was only ten, but already she'd sensed there was something between her father and this woman with the dark blue eyes and nifty hair. What she didn't know was exactly how she felt about it yet. In the manner of her father, Sarah decided to wait and see.

Equally unsure of her own feelings, Lee went with them into the kitchen. She had an impression of sunny walls, white trim and confusion.

"Hunter, if you're going to keep a wolf in the house, you should at least teach him to appreciate art. Hi, I'm Bonnie."

Lee saw a tall, thin woman with dark brown shoulder-length hair streaked liberally with blond. She wore a purple T-shirt with faded pink printing over cutoffs as ragged as her niece's. Her bare feet were tipped at the toes with hot-pink polish. Studying her thin model's face, Lee couldn't be sure if she was years older than Hunter or years younger. Automatically she held out her hand in response to Bonnie's outstretched one.

"How do you do?"

"I'd be doing a lot better if Santanas hadn't tried to make a snack of my latest creation." She held up a golden-brown half circle with ragged ends. "Just lucky for him it was a dreadful idea. Anyway, sit." She gestured to a table piled with bowls and canisters and dusted with flour. "I'm making tea."

"You didn't turn the kettle on," Sarah pointed out, and did so herself.

"Hunter, the child's always picking on details. I worry about her."

With a shrug of acceptance, he picked up what looked like a small doughnut and might, with imagination, have been an earring. "You're finding gold and silver too traditional to work with these days?"

"I thought I might start a trend." When Bonnie smiled, she became abruptly and briefly stunning. "In any case, it was a small failure. Probably cost you less than three dollars in flour. Sit," she repeated as she began to transfer the mess from the table to the counter behind her. "So, how was the camping trip?"

"Enlightening. Wouldn't you say, Lenore?"

"Educational," she corrected, but thought the last half hour had been the most educational of all.

"So, you work for *Celebrity.*" Bonnie's long, twisted gold earrings swung when she walked, much like Sarah's braids. "I'm a faithful reader."

"That's because she's had a couple of embarrassingly flattering write-ups."

"Write-ups?" Lee watched Bonnie dust her flour-covered hands on her cutoffs.

Hunter smiled as he watched his sister reach for a tin of tea and send others clattering to the counter. "Professionally she's known as B. B. Smithers."

The name rang a bell. For years, B. B. Smithers had been considered the queen of avant-garde jewelry. The elite, the wealthy and the trendy flocked to her for personal designs. They paid, and paid well, for her talent, her creativity, and the tiny *B*s etched into the finished product. Lee stared at the thin, somewhat clumsy woman with something close to wonder. "I've admired your work."

"But you wouldn't wear it," Bonnie put in with a smile as she shoved tumbled boxes and tins out of her way. "No, it's the classics for you. What a fabulous face. Do you want lemon in your tea? Do we have any lemons, Hunter?"

"Probably not."

Taking this in stride, Bonnie set the teapot on the table to let the tea steep. "Tell me, Lenore, how did you talk the hermit into coming out of his cave?"

"By making him furious, I believe."

"That might work." She sat down across from Lee as Sarah walked to her father's side. Her eyes were softer than her brother's, less intense, but not, Lee thought, less perceptive. "Did the two weeks playing pioneer in the canyon give you the insight to write an article on him?"

"Yes." Lee smiled, because there was humor in Bonnie's eyes. "Plus I gained a growing affection for box springs and mattresses."

The quick, stunning smile flashed again. "My husband takes the children camping once a year. That's when I go to Elizabeth Arden's for the works. When we come home, both of us feel we've accomplished several small miracles."

"Camping's not so bad," Sarah commented in her father's defense.

"Is that so?" He patted her bottom as he drew her

closer. "Why is it that you always have this all-consuming desire to visit Bonnie in Phoenix whenever I start packing gear?"

She giggled, and her arm went easily around his shoulder. "Must be coincidence," she said in a dry tone that echoed his. "Did he make you go fishing?" Sarah wanted to know. "And sit around for just *hours?*"

Lee watched Hunter's brow lift before she answered. "Actually, he did, ah, suggest fishing several days running."

"Ugh" was Sarah's only comment.

"But I caught a bigger fish than he did."

Unimpressed, Sarah shook her head. "It's awfully boring." She sent her father an apologetic glance. "I guess somebody's got to do it." Leaning her head against her father's, she smiled at Lee. "Mostly he's never boring, he just likes some weird stuff. Like fishing and beer."

"Sarah doesn't consider Hunter's shrunken-head collection at all unusual." Bonnie picked up the teapot. "Are you having some?" she asked her brother.

"I'll pass. Sarah and I'll go and break camp."

"Take your wolf with you," Bonnie told him as she poured tea into Lee's cup. "He's still on my hit list. By the way, a couple of calls from New York came in for you yesterday."

"They'll keep." As he rose, he ran a careless hand down Lee's hair, a gesture not lost on either of the other females in the room. "I'll be back shortly."

She started to offer her help, but it was so comfortable in the sunny, cluttered kitchen, and the tea smelled like heaven. "All right." She saw the proprietary hand Sarah put on her father's arm and thought it just as well to stay where she was.

Together, father and daughter walked to the back door. Hunter whistled for the dog, then they were gone.

Bonnie stirred her tea. "Sarah adores her father."

"Yes." Lee thought of the way they'd looked, side by side.

"And so do you."

Lee had started to lift her cup; now it only rattled in the saucer. "I beg your pardon?"

"You're in love with Hunter," Bonnie said mildly. "I think it's marvelous."

She could've denied it—vehemently, icily, laughingly, but hearing it said aloud seemed to put her in some kind of trance. "I don't—that is, it doesn't..." Lee stopped, realizing she was running the spoon handle through her hands. "I'm not sure how I feel."

"A definite symptom. Does being in love worry you?"

"I didn't say I was." Again, Lee stopped. Could anyone make evasions with those soft doe eyes watching? "Yes, it worries me a lot."

"Only natural. I used to fall in and out of love like some people change clothes. Then I met Fred." Bonnie laughed into her tea before she sipped. "I went around with a queasy stomach for weeks."

Lee pressed a hand to her own before she rose. Tea wasn't going to help. She had to move. "I have no illusions about Hunter and myself," she said, more firmly than she'd expected to. "We have different priorities, different tastes." She looked through the kitchen window to the high red walls far beyond the clustering trees. "Different lives. I have to get back to L.A."

Bonnie calmly continued to drink tea. "Of course." If Lee heard the irony, she didn't respond to it. "There are people who have it fixed in their heads that in order to have a relationship, the two parties involved must be on the same wavelength. If one adores sixteenth-century French poetry and the other detests it, there's no hope." She noticed Lee's frown but continued, lightly. "Fred's an accountant who gets a primal thrill out of interest rates." She wiped absently at a smudge of flour on the table. "Statistically, I suppose we should've divorced years ago."

Lee turned back, unable to be angry, unable to smile. "You're a great deal like Hunter, aren't you?"

"I suppose. Is your mother Adreanne Radcliffe?"

Though she no longer wanted it, Lee came back to the table for her tea. "Yes."

"I met her at a party in Palm Springs two, no, must've been three years ago. Yes, three," Bonnie said decisively, "because I was still nursing Carter, my youngest, and he's currently terrorizing everyone at nursery school. Just last week he tried to cook a goldfish in a toy oven. You're not at all like your mother, are you?"

It took a moment for Lee to catch up. She set down her tea again, untasted. "Aren't I?"

"Do you think you are?" Bonnie tossed her tousled, streaked hair behind her shoulder. "I don't mean any offense, but she wouldn't know what to say to anyone not born to the blue, so to speak. I'd've considered her a very sheltered woman. She's very lovely—you certainly appear to've inherited her looks. But that seems to be all."

Lee stared down at her tea. How could she explain that, because of the strong physical resemblance between her and her mother, she'd always figured there were other resemblances. Hadn't she spent her childhood and adolescence trying to find them, and all of her adult life trying to repress them? A sheltered woman. She found it a terrifying phrase, and too close to what she herself could have become.

"My mother has standards," she answered, at length. "She never seems to have any trouble living up to them."

"Oh, well, everyone should do what they do best." Bonnie propped her elbows on the table, lacing her fingers so that the three rings on her right hand gleamed and winked. "According to Hunter, the thing you do best is write. He mentioned your novel to me."

The irritation came so quickly Lee hadn't the chance to mask it. "He's the kind of man who can't admit when he's made a mistake. I'm a reporter, not a novelist."

"I see." Still smiling blandly, Bonnie dropped her chin onto her laced fingers. "So, what are you going to report about Hunter?"

Was there a challenge under the smile? A trace of mockery? Whatever there was at the edges, Lee couldn't help but respond to it. Yes, she thought again, Bonnie Smithers was a great deal like her brother.

"That he's a man who considers writing both a sacred duty and a skilled profession. That he has a sense of humor that's often so subtle it takes you hours to catch up. That he believes in choices and luck with the same stubbornness that he believes in fate." Pausing, she lifted her cup. "He values the written word, whether it's in comic books or Chaucer, and he works desperately hard to do what he considers his job—to tell the story."

"I like you."

Cautiously, Lee smiled. "Thank you."

"I love my brother," Bonnie went on easily. "More

than that, I admire him, for personal and professional reasons. You understand him. Not everyone would."

"Understand him?" Lee shook her head. "It seems to me that the more I find out about him, the less I understand. He's shown me more beauty in a pile of rocks than I'd ever have found for myself, yet he writes about horror and fears."

"And you consider that a contradiction?" Bonnie shrugged as she leaned back in her chair. "It's just that Hunter sees both sides of life very clearly. He writes about the dark side because it's the most intriguing."

"Yet he lives…" Lee gestured as she glanced around the kitchen.

"In a cozy little house nestled in the woods."

The laugh came naturally. "I wouldn't precisely call it cozy, but it's certainly not what you'd expect from the country's leading author of horror and occult fiction."

"The country's leading author of horror and occult fiction has a child to raise."

"Yes." Lee's smile faded. "Yes, Sarah. She's lovely."

"Will she be in your article?"

"No." Again, she lifted her gaze to Bonnie's. "No, Hunter made it clear he objected to that."

"She's the focal point of his life. If he seems a bit overprotective in certain ways, believe me, it's a completely unselfish act." When Lee merely nodded, Bonnie felt a stirring of sympathy. "He hasn't told you about her?"

"No, nothing."

There were times Bonnie's love and admiration for Hunter became clouded with frustration. A great many times. This woman was in love with him, was one step away from being irrevocably committed to him. Any fool could see it, Bonnie mused. Any fool except

Hunter. "As I said, there are times he's overly protective. He has his reasons, Lenore."

"And will you tell me what they are?"

She was tempted. It was time Hunter opened that part of his life, and she was certain this was the woman he should open it to. "The story's Hunter's," Bonnie said at length. "You should hear it from him." She glanced around idly as she heard the Jeep pull up in the drive. "They're back."

"I guess I'm glad you brought her back," Sarah commented as they drove the last mile toward home.

"You guess?" Hunter turned his head, to see his daughter looking pensively through the windshield.

"She's beautiful, like a princess." For the first time in months, Sarah worried her braces with her tongue. "You like her a lot, I can tell."

"Yes, I like her a lot." He knew every nuance of his daughter's voice, every expression, every gesture. "That doesn't mean I like you any less."

Sarah gave him one long look. She needed no other words from him to reaffirm love. "I guess you have to like me," she decided, half teasing, "'cause we're stuck with each other. But I don't think she does."

"Why shouldn't Lenore like you?" Hunter countered, able to follow her winding statement without any trouble.

"She doesn't smile much."

Not enough, he silently agreed, but more each day. "When she relaxes, she does."

Sarah shrugged, unconvinced. "Well, she looked at me awful funny."

"Your grammar's deteriorating."

"She did."

Hunter frowned a bit as he turned into the dirt drive to their house. "It's only that she was surprised. I hadn't mentioned you to her."

Sarah stared at him a moment, then put her scuffed sneakers on the dash. "That wasn't very nice of you."

"Maybe not."

"You'd better apologize."

He sent his daughter a mild glance. "Really?"

She patted Santanas's head when he leaned over the back of her seat and dropped it on her shoulder. "Really. You always make me apologize when I'm rude."

"I didn't consider that you were any of her business." At first, Hunter amended silently. Things changed. Everything changed.

"You always make me apologize, even when I make up excuses," Sarah pointed out unmercifully. When they pulled up by the house, she grinned at him. "And even when I hate apologizing."

"Brat," he mumbled, setting the brake.

With a squeal of laughter, Sarah launched herself at him. "I'm glad you're home."

He held her close a moment, absorbing her scent—youthful sweat, grass and flowery shampoo. It seemed impossible that ten years had passed since he'd first held her. Then she'd smelled of powder and fragility and fresh linen. It seemed impossible that she was half-grown and the time had been so short.

"I love you, Sarah."

Content, she cuddled against him a moment, then, lifting her head, she grinned. "Enough to make pizza for dinner?"

He pinched her subtly pointed chin. "Maybe just enough for that."

Chapter 11

When Lee thought of family dinners, she thought of quiet meals at a glossy mahogany table laid with heavy Georgian silver, meals where conversation was subdued and polite. It had always been that way for her.

Not this dinner.

The already confused kitchen became chaotic while Sarah dashed around, half dancing, half bobbing, as she filled her father in on every detail of the past two weeks. Oblivious to the noise, Bonnie used the kitchen phone to call home and check in with her husband and children. Santanas, forgiven, lay sprawled on the floor, dozing. Hunter stood at the counter, preparing what Sarah claimed was the best pizza in the stratosphere. Somehow he managed to keep up with his daughter's disjointed conversation, answer the questions Bonnie tossed at him and cook at the same time.

Feeling like oil poured heedlessly on a rub of churning water, Lee began to clear the table. If she didn't do something, she decided, she'd end up standing in the middle of the room with her head swiveling back and forth, like a fan at a tennis match.

"I'm supposed to do that."

Awkwardly, Lee set down the teapot she'd just lifted and looked at Sarah. "Oh." Stupid, she berated herself. Haven't you any conversation for a child?

"You can help, I guess," Sarah said after a moment. "But if I don't do my chores, I don't get my allowance." Her gaze slid to her father, then back again. "There's this album I want to buy. You know, the Total Wrecks."

"I see." Lee searched her mind for even a wispy knowledge of the group but came up blank.

"They're actually not as bad as the name makes them sound," Bonnie commented on her way out to the kitchen. "Anyway, Hunter won't dock your pay if you take on an assistant, Sarah. It's considered good business sense."

Turning his head, Hunter caught his sister's quick grin before she waltzed out of the room. "I suppose Lee should earn her supper as well," he said easily. "Even if it isn't red meat."

The smile made it difficult for her to casually lift the teapot again.

"You'll like the pizza better," Sarah stated confidently. "He puts *everything* on it. Anytime I have friends over for dinner, they always want Dad's pizza." As she continued to clear the table, Lee tried to imagine Hunter competently preparing meals for several young, chattering girls. She simply couldn't. "I think he was a cook in another life."

Good Lord, Lee thought, did the child already have views on reincarnation?

"The same way you were a gladiator," Hunter said dryly.

Sarah laughed, childlike again. "Aunt Bonnie was a slave sold at an Arabian auction for thousands and thousands of drachmas."

"Bonnie has a very fluid ego."

With a clatter, Sarah set the cups in the sink. "I think Lenore must've been a princess."

With a damp cloth in her hands, Lee looked up, not certain if she should smile.

"A medieval princess," Sarah went on. "Like with King Arthur."

Hunter seemed to consider the idea a moment, while he studied his daughter and the woman under discussion. "It's a possibility. One of those delicate jeweled crowns and filmy veils would suit her."

"And dragons." Obviously enjoying the game, Sarah leaned back against the counter, the better to imagine Lee in a flowing pastel gown. "A knight would have to kill at least one full-grown male dragon before he could ask for her hand."

"True enough," Hunter murmured, thinking that dragons came in many forms.

"Dragons aren't easy to kill." Though she spoke lightly, Lee wondered why her stomach was quivering. It was entirely too easy to imagine herself in a great torchlit hall, with jewels winking from her hair and from the bodice of a rich silk gown.

"It's the best way to prove valor," Sarah told her, nibbling on a slice of green pepper she'd snitched from her father. "A princess can't marry just anyone, you know. The king would either give her to a worthy knight, or marry her off to a neighboring prince so he could have more land with peace and prosperity."

Incredibly, Lee pictured her father, staff in hand, decreeing that she would marry Jonathan of Willoby.

"I bet you never had to wear braces."

Cast from one century to another in the blink of an eye, Lee merely stared. Sarah was frowning at her with the absorbed, absorbing concentration she could have inherited only from Hunter. It was all so foolish, Lee thought. Knights, princesses, dragons. For the first time, she was able to smile naturally at the slim, dark girl who was a part of the man she loved.

"Two years."

"You did?" Interest sprang into Sarah's solemn face. She stepped forward, obviously to get a better look at Lee's teeth. "It worked good," she decided. "Did you hate them?"

"Every minute."

Sarah giggled, so that the silver flashed. "I don't mind too much, 'cept I can't chew gum." She sent a sulky look over her shoulder in Hunter's direction. "Not even one stick."

"Neither could I." Ever, she thought, but didn't add it. Gum chewing was not permitted in the Radcliffe household.

Sarah studied her another moment, then nodded. "I guess you can help me set the table, too."

Acceptance, Lee was to discover, was just that simple.

The sun was streaming into the kitchen while they ate. It was rich and golden, without those harsh, stunning flashes of white she remembered from the cliffs of the canyon. She found it peaceful, despite all the talk and laughter and arguments swimming around her.

Her fantasies had run to eating a thick, rare steak and a crisp chef's salad in a dimly lit, quiet restaurant where the hovering waiter saw that your glass of Bordeaux was never empty. She found herself in a bright, noisy kitchen, eating pizza stringy with cheese, chunky with slices of green pepper and mushroom, spiced with pepperoni and hot sausage. And while she did, she found herself agreeing with Sarah's accolade. The best in the stratosphere.

"If only Fred could learn how to make one of these." Bonnie cut into her second slice with the same dedication she'd cut into her first. "On a good day he makes a superior egg salad, but it's not the same."

"With a family the size of yours," Hunter commented, "you'd need to set up an assembly line. Five hungry children could keep a pizzeria hopping."

"And do," Bonnie agreed. "In a bit less than seven months, it'll be six."

She grinned as Hunter's knife paused. "Another?"

"Another." Bonnie winked across the table at her niece. "I always said I'd have half a dozen kids," she said casually to Lee. "People should do what they do best."

Hunter reached over to take her hand. Lee saw the fingers interlock. "Some might call it overachievement."

"Or sibling rivalry," she tossed back. "I'll have as many kids as you do bestsellers." With a laugh, she squeezed her brother's hand. "It takes us about the same length of time to produce."

"When you bring the baby to visit, she should sleep in my room." Sarah bit off another mouthful of pizza.

"She?" Hunter ruffled her hair before he started to eat again.

"It'll be a girl." With the confidence of youth, Sarah nodded. "Aunt Bonnie already has three boys, so another girl makes it even."

"I'll see what I can do," Bonnie told her. "Anyway, I'll be heading back in the morning. Cassandra, she's my oldest," she put in for Lee's benefit, "has decided she wants a tattoo." She closed her eyes as she leaned back. "Ah, it's nice to be needed."

"A tattoo?" Sarah wrinkled her nose. "That's gross. Cassie's nuts."

"Fred and I are forced to agree."

Interested, Hunter lifted his wine. "Where does she want it?"

"On the curve of her right shoulder. She insists it'll be very tasteful."

"Dumb." Sarah handed out the decree with a shrug. "Cassie's thirteen," she added, rolling her eyes. "Boy, is she a case."

Lee choked back a laugh at both the facial and verbal expressions. "How will you handle it?"

Bonnie only smiled. "Oh, I think I'll take her to the tattoo parlor."

"But you wouldn't—" Lee broke off, seeing Bonnie's liberally streaked hair and shoulder-length earrings. Perhaps she would.

With a laugh, Bonnie patted Lee's hand. "No, I wouldn't. But it'll be a lot more effective if Cassie makes the decision herself—which she will, the minute she gets a good look at all those nasty little needles."

"Sneaky," Sarah approved with a grin.

"Clever," Bonnie corrected.

"Same thing." With her mouth half-full, she turned to Lee. "There's always a crisis at Aunt Bonnie's house," she said confidentially. "Did you have brothers and sisters?"

"No." Was that wistfulness she saw in the child's eyes? She'd often had the same wish herself. "There was only me."

"I think it's better to have them, even though it gets crowded." She slanted her father a guileless smile. "Can I have another piece?"

The rest of the evening passed, not quietly but, for all the noise, peacefully. Sarah dragged her father outside for soccer practice, which Bonnie declined, grinning. Her condition, she claimed, was too delicate. Lee, over her protests, found herself drafted. She learned, though her aim was never very accurate, to kick a ball with the side of her foot and bounce it off her head. She enjoyed it, which surprised her, and didn't feel like a fool, which surprised her more.

Dusk came quickly, then a dark that flickered with fireflies. Though her eyes were heavy, Sarah groaned about going to bed until Hunter agreed to carry her up on his back. Lee didn't have to be told it was a nightly ritual; she only had to see them together.

He'd said Sarah was his life, and though she'd only seen them together for a matter of hours, Lee believed it.

She'd never have expected the man whose books she'd read to be a devoted father, content to spend his time with a ten-year-old girl. She'd never have imagined him here, in a house so far away from the excitement of the city. Even the man she'd grown to know over the past two weeks didn't quite fit the structure of being parent, disciplinarian and mentor to a ten-year-old. Yet he was.

If she superimposed the image of Sarah's father

over those of her lover and the author of *Silent Scream,* they all seemed to meld into one. The problem was dealing with it.

Righting the overturned chair on the patio, Lee sat. She could hear Sarah's sleepy laughter drift through the open window above her. Hunter's voice, low and indistinct, followed it. It was an odd way to spend her last hours with Hunter, here in his home, only a few miles from the campsite where they'd become lovers. And yes, she realized as she stared up at the stars, friends. She very much wanted to be his friend.

Now, when she wrote the article, she'd be able to do so with knowledge of both sides of him. It was what she'd come for. Lee closed her eyes because the stars were suddenly too bright. She was going back with much more and, because of it, much less.

"Tired?"

Opening her eyes, she looked up at Hunter. This was how she'd always remember him, cloaked in shadows, coming out of the darkness. "No. Is Sarah asleep?"

He nodded, coming around behind her to put his hands on her shoulders. This was where he wanted her. Here, when night was closing in. "Bonnie, too."

"You'd work now," she guessed. "When the house was quiet and the windows dark."

"Yes, most of the time. I finished my last book on a night like this." He hadn't been lonely then, but now… "Let's walk. The moon's full.

"Afraid? I'll give you a talisman." He slipped his ring off his pinky, sliding it onto her finger.

"I'm not superstitious," she said loftily, but curled her fingers into her palm to hold the ring in place.

"Of course you are." He drew her against his side as they walked. "I like the night sounds."

Lee listened to them—the faintest breeze through the trees, the murmur of water, the singsong of insects. "You've lived here a long time." As the day had passed, it had become less feasible to think of his living anywhere else.

"Yes. I moved here the year Sarah was born."

"It's a lovely spot."

He turned her into his arms. Moonlight spilled over her, silver, jewel-like in her hair, marbling her skin, darkening her eyes. "It suits you," he murmured. He ran a hand through her hair, then watched it fall back into place. "The princess and the dragon."

Her heart had already begun to flutter. Like a teenager's, Lee thought. He made her feel like a girl on her first date. "These days women have to kill their own dragons."

"These days—" his mouth brushed over hers "—there's less romance. If these were the Dark Ages, and I came upon you in a moonlit wood, I'd take you because it was my right. I'd woo you because I'd have no choice." His voice darkened like the shadows in the trees surrounding them. "Let me love you now, Lenore, as if it were the first time."

Or the last, she thought dimly as his lips urged her to soften, to yield, to demand. With his arms around her, she could let her consciousness go. Imagine and feel. Lovemaking consisted of nothing more. Even as her head tilted back in submission, her arms strengthened around him, challenging him to take whatever he wanted, to give whatever she asked.

Then his hands were on her face, gently, as gently as

they'd ever been, memorizing the slope and angle of her bones, the softness of her skin. His lips followed, tasting, drinking in each separate flavor. The pleasure that could come so quickly ran liquid through her. Bonelessly, she slid with him to the ground.

He'd wanted to love her like this, in the open, with the moon silvering the trees and casting purple shadows. He'd wanted to feel her muscles coil and go fluid under the touch of his hand. What she gave to him now was something out of his own dreams and much, much more real than anything he'd ever had. Slowly, he undressed her, while his lips and the tips of his fingers both pleasured and revered her. This would be the night when he gave her all of him and when he asked for all of her.

Moonlight and shadows washed over her, making his heart pound in his ears. He heard the creek bubble nearby to mix with her quiet sighs. The woods smelled of night. And so, as she buried his face against her neck, did she.

She felt the surging excitement in him, the growing, straining need that swept her up. Willingly, she went into the whirlpool he created. There the air was soft to the touch and streaked with color. There she would stay, endlessly possessed.

His skin was warm against hers. She tasted, her head swimming from pleasure, power and newly awakened dizzying speed. Ravenous for more, she raced over him, acutely aware of every masculine tremble beneath her, every drawn breath, every murmur of her name.

Silver and shadows. Lee felt them every bit as tangibly as she saw them flickering around her. The silver streak of power. The dark shadow of desire. With them, she could take him to that trembling precipice.

When he swore, breathlessly, she laughed. Their needs were tangled together, twining tighter. She felt it. She celebrated it.

The air seemed to still, the breeze pause. The sounds that had grown to one long din around them seemed to hush. The fingers tangled in her hair tightened desperately. In the silence, their eyes met and held, moment after moment.

Her lips curved as she opened for him.

She could have slept there, effortlessly, with the bare ground beneath her, the sky overhead and his body pressed to hers. She might have slept there, endlessly, like a princess under a spell, if he hadn't drawn her up into his arms.

"You fall asleep like a child," he murmured. "You should be in bed. My bed."

Lee sighed, content to stay where she was. "Too far."

With a low laugh, he kissed the hollow between her neck and shoulder. "Should I carry you?"

"Mmm." She nestled against him. "'Kay."

"Not that I object, but you might be a bit disconcerted if Bonnie happened to walk downstairs while I was carrying you in, naked."

She opened her eyes, so that her irises were dusky blue slits under her lashes. Reality was returning. "I guess we have to get dressed."

"It might be advisable." His gaze skimmed over her, then back to her face. "Should I help you?"

She smiled. "I think that we might have the same result with you dressing me as we do with you undressing me."

"An interesting theory." Hunter reached over her for the brief strip of ivory lace.

"But this isn't the time to test it out." Lee plucked her panties out of his hand and wiggled into them. "How long have we been out here?"

"Centuries."

She shot him a look just before her head disappeared into her shirt. She wasn't completely certain he was exaggerating. "The least I deserve after these past two weeks is a real mattress."

He took her hand, pressing her palm to his lips. "You're welcome to share mine."

Lee curled her fingers around his briefly, then released them. "I don't think that's wise."

"You're worried about Sarah."

It wasn't a question. Lee took her time, making certain all the clouds of romance were out of her head before she spoke. "I don't know a great deal about children, but I imagine she's unprepared for someone sharing her father's bed."

Silence lay for a moment, like the eye of a storm. "I've never brought a woman to our home before."

The statement caused her to look at him quickly, then, just as quickly, look away. "All the more reason."

"All the more reason for many things." He dressed without speaking while Lee stared out into the trees. So beautiful, she thought. And more and more distant.

"You wanted to ask me about Sarah, but you didn't."

She moistened her lips. "It's not my business."

Her chin was captured quickly, not so gently. "Isn't it?" he demanded.

"Hunter—"

"This time you'll have the answer without asking." He dropped his hand, but his gaze never faltered. She needed nothing else to tell her the calm was over. "I met a woman, almost a dozen years ago. I was writing as Laura Miles by then, so that I could afford a few luxuries. Dinner out occasionally, the theater now and then. I was still living in L.A., alone, enjoying my work and the benefits it brought me. She was a student in her last year. Brains and ambition she had in abundance, money she didn't have at all. She was on scholarship and determined to be the hottest young attorney on the West Coast."

"Hunter, what happened between you and another woman all those years ago isn't my business."

"Not just another woman. Sarah's mother."

Lee began to pull at the tuft of grass by her side. "All right, if it's important for you to tell me, I'll listen."

"I cared about her," he continued. "She was bright, lovely and full of dreams. Neither of us had ever considered becoming too serious. She still had law school to finish, the bar to pass. I had stories to tell. But then, no matter how much we plan, fate has a way of taking over."

He drew out a cigarette, thinking back, remembering each detail. His tiny, cramped apartment with the leaky plumbing, the battered typewriter with its hiccuping carriage, the laughter from the couple next door that would often seep through the thin walls.

"She came by one afternoon. I knew something was wrong because she had afternoon classes. She was much too dedicated to skip classes. It was hot, one of those sultry, breathless days. The windows were up, and I had a little portable fan that stirred the air around without doing much to cool it. She'd come to tell me she was pregnant."

He could remember the way she'd looked if he concentrated. But he never chose to. But whether he chose to or not, he'd always be able to remember the tone of her voice when she'd told him. Despair, laced with fury and accusation.

"I said I cared about her, and that was true. I didn't love her. Still, our parents' values do trickle down. I offered to marry her." He laughed then, not humorously, but not, Lee reflected, bitterly. It was the laugh of a man who'd accepted the joke life had played on him. "She refused, almost as angry with the solution I'd offered as she was with the pregnancy. She had no intention of taking on a husband and a child when she had a career to carve out. It might be difficult to understand, but she wasn't being cold, simply practical, when she asked me to pay for the abortion."

Lee felt all of her muscles contract. "But, Sarah—"

"That's not the end of the story." Hunter blew out a stream of smoke and watched it fade into darkness. "We had a memorable fight, threats, accusations, blame-casting. At the time, I couldn't see her end of it, only the fact that she had part of me inside her that she wanted to dispose of. We parted then, both of us furious, both of us desperate enough to know we each needed time to think."

She didn't know what to say, or how to say it. "You were young," she began.

"I was twenty-four," Hunter corrected. "I'd long since stopped being a boy. I was—we were—responsible for our own actions. I didn't sleep for two days. I thought of a dozen answers and rejected them all, over and over. Only one thing stuck with me in that whole sweaty, terrified time. I wanted the child. It's not something I can explain, because I did enjoy my life, the lack of responsibilities, the possibility of becoming really successful. I simply knew I had to have the child. I called her and asked her to come back.

"We were both calmer the second time, and both more frightened than either of us had ever been in our lives. Marriage couldn't be considered, so we set it aside. She didn't want the child, so we dealt with that. I did. That was something a bit more complex to deal with. She needed freedom from the responsibility we'd made together, and she needed money. In the end, we resolved it all."

Dry-mouthed, Lee turned to him. "You paid her."

He saw, as he'd expected to see, the horror in her eyes. When he continued, his voice was calm, but it took a great deal of effort to make it so. "I paid all the medical expenses, her living expenses up until she delivered, and I gave her ten thousand dollars for my daughter."

Stunned, heartsick, Lee stared at the ground. "How could she—"

"We each wanted something. In the only way open, we gave it to each other. I've never resented that young law student for what she did. It was her choice, and she could've taken another without consulting me."

"Yes." She tried to understand, but all Lee could see was that slim, dark little girl. "She chose, but she lost."

It meant everything just to hear her say it. "Sarah's been mine, only mine, from the first moment she breathed. The woman who carried her gave me a priceless gift. I only gave her money."

"Does Sarah know?"

"Only that her mother had choices to make."

"I see." She let out a long breath. "The reason you're so careful about keeping publicity away from her is to keep speculation away."

"One of them. The other is simply that I want her to have the uncomplicated life every child's entitled to."

"You didn't have to tell me." She reached a hand for his. "I'm glad you did. It can't have been easy for you, raising a baby by yourself."

There was nothing but understanding in her eyes now. Every taut muscle in his body relaxed as if she'd stroked them. He knew now, with utter certainty, that she was what he'd been waiting for. "No, not easy, but always a pleasure." His fingers tightened on hers. "Share it with me, Lenore."

Her thoughts froze. "I don't know what you mean."

"I want you here, with me, with Sarah. I want you here with the other children we'll have together." He looked down at the ring he'd put on her hand. When his eyes came back to hers, she felt them reach inside her. "Marry me."

Marry? She could only stare at him blankly while the panic quietly built and built. "You don't—you don't know what you're asking."

"I do," he corrected, holding her hand more firmly when she tried to draw it away. "I've asked only one other woman, and that out of obligation. I'm asking you because you're the first and only woman I've ever loved. I want to share your life. I want you to share mine."

Panic steadily turned into fear. He was asking her to change everything she'd aimed for. To risk everything. "Our lives are too far apart," she managed. "I have to go back. I have my job."

"A job you know you weren't made for." Urgency slipped into his voice as he took her shoulders. "You know you were made to write about the images you have in your head, not about other people's social lives and tomorrow's trends."

"It's what I know!" Trembling, she jerked away from him. "It's what I've been working for."

"To prove a point. Damn it, Lenore, do something for yourself. For yourself."

"It is for myself," she said desperately. You love him, a voice shouted inside her. Why are you pushing away what you need, what you want? Lee shook her head, as if to block the voice out. Love wasn't enough, needs weren't enough. She knew that. She had to remember it. "You're asking me to give it all up, every hard inch I've climbed in five years. I have a life in L.A., I know who I am, where I'm going. I can't live here and risk—"

"Finding out who you really are?" he finished. He wouldn't allow despair. He barely controlled anger. "If it was only myself, I'd go anywhere you liked, live anywhere that suited you, even if I knew it was a mistake. But there's Sarah. I can't take her away from the only home she's ever known."

"You're asking for everything again." Her voice was hardly a whisper, but he'd never heard anything more clearly. "You're asking me to risk everything, and I can't. I won't."

He rose, so that shadows shifted around him. "I'm asking you to risk everything," he agreed. "Do you love me?" And by asking, he'd already risked it all.

Torn by emotions, pushed by fear, she stared at him. "Yes. Damn you, Hunter, leave me alone."

She streaked back toward the house until the darkness closed in between them.

Chapter 12

"If you're not going to break for lunch, at least take this." Bryan held out one of her inexhaustible supply of candy bars.

"I'll eat when I've finished the article." Lee kept her eyes on the typewriter and continued to pound at the keys, lightly, rhythmically.

"Lee, you've been back for two days and I haven't seen you so much as nibble on a Danish." And her photographer's eye had seen beneath the subtle use of cosmetics to the pale bruises under Lee's eyes. That must've been some interview, she thought, as the brisk, even clickity-click of the typewriter keys went on.

"Not hungry." No, she wasn't hungry any more than she was tired. She'd been working steadily on Hunter's article for the better part of forty-eight hours. It was going to be perfect, she promised herself. It was going to be polished like a fine piece of glass. And oh, God, when she finished it, *finished it,* she'd have purged her system of him.

She'd gripped that thought so tightly, it often skidded away.

If she'd stayed… If she went back…

The oath came quickly, under her breath, as her fingers faltered. Meticulously, Lee reversed the carriage to make the correction. She couldn't go back. Hadn't she made that clear to Hunter? She couldn't just toss everything over her shoulder and go. But the longer she stayed away, the larger the hole in her life became. In the life, Lee was ruthlessly reminded, that she'd so carefully carved out for herself.

So she'd work in a nervous kind of fury until the article was finished. Until, she told herself, it was all finished. Then it would be time to take the next step. When she tried to think of that next step, her mind went stunningly, desperately blank. Lee dropped her hands into her lap and stared at the paper in front of her.

Without a word, Bryan bumped the door with her hip so that it closed and muffled the noise. Dropping down into the chair across from Lee, she folded her hands and waited a beat. "Okay, now why don't you tell me the story that's not for publication?"

Lee wanted to be able to shrug and say she didn't have time to talk. She was under a deadline, after all. The article was under a deadline. But then, so was her life. Drawing a breath, she turned in her chair. She didn't want to see the neat, clever little words she'd typed. Not now.

"Bryan, if you'd taken a picture, one that required a great deal of your time and all of your skill to set up, then once you'd developed it, it had come out in a completely different way than you'd planned, what would you do?"

"I'd take a good hard look at the way it had come out," she said immediately. "There'd be a good possibility I should've planned it that way in the first place."

"But wouldn't you be tempted to go back to your original plans? After all, you'd worked very, very hard to set it up in a certain way, wanting certain specific results."

"Maybe, maybe not. It'd depend on just what I'd seen when I looked at the picture." Bryan sat back, crossing long, jeans-clad legs. "What's in your picture, Lee?"

"Hunter." Her troubled gaze shifted, and locked on Bryan's. "You know me."

"As well as you let anyone know you."

With a short laugh, Lee began to push at a paper clip on her desk. "Am I as difficult as all that?"

"Yeah." Bryan smiled a bit to soften the quick answer. "And, I've always thought, as interesting. Apparently, Hunter Brown thinks the same thing."

"He asked me to marry him." The words came out in a jolt that left both women staring.

"Marry?" Bryan leaned forward. "As in 'till death do us part'?"

"Yes."

"Oh." The word came out like a breath of air as Bryan leaned back again. "Fast work." Then she saw Lee's unhappy expression. Just because Bryan didn't smell orange blossoms when the word *marriage* came up was no reason to be flippant. "Well, how do you feel? About Hunter, I mean."

The paper clip twisted in Lee's fingers. "I'm in love with him."

"Really?" Then she smiled, because it sounded nice when said so simply. "Did all this happen in the canyon?"

"Yes." Lee's fingers moved restlessly. "Maybe it started to happen before, when we were in Flagstaff. I don't know anymore."

"Why aren't you happy?" Bryan narrowed her eyes as she did when checking the light and angle. "When the man you love, really love, wants to build a life with you, you should be ecstatic."

"How do two people build a life together when they've both already built separate ones, completely different ones?" Lee demanded. "It isn't just a matter of making more room in the closet or shifting furniture around." The end of the paper clip broke off in her fingers as she rose. "Bryan, he lives in Arizona, in the canyon. I live in L.A."

Lifting booted feet, Bryan rested them on Lee's polished desk, crossing her ankles. "You're not going to tell me it's all a matter of geography."

"It just shows how impossible it all is!" Angry, Lee whirled around. "We couldn't be more different, almost opposites. I do things step-by-step, Hunter goes in leaps and bounds. Damn it, you should see his house. It's like something out of a sophisticated fairy tale. His sister's B. B. Smithers—" Before Bryan could fully register that, Lee was blurting out, "He has a daughter."

"A daughter?" Her attention fully caught, Bryan dropped her feet again. "Hunter Brown has a child?"

Lee pressed her fingers to her eyes and waited for calm. True, it wouldn't have come out if she hadn't been so agitated, and she'd never discuss such personal agitations with anyone but Bryan, but now she had to deal with it. "Yes, a ten-year-old girl. It's important that it not be publicized."

"All right."

Lee needed no promises from Bryan. Trying to calm herself, she took a quiet breath. "She's bright, lovely and quite obviously the center of his life. I saw something in him when they were together, something incredibly beautiful. It scared the hell out of me."

"Why?"

"Bryan, he's capable of so much talent, brilliance, emotion. He's put them together to make a complete success of himself, in all ways."

"That bothers you?"

"I don't know what I'm capable of. I only know I'm afraid I'd never be able to balance it all out, make it all work."

Bryan said something short, quick and rude. "You won't marry him because you don't think you can juggle? You should know yourself better."

"I thought I did." Shaking her head, she took her seat again. "It's ridiculous, in the first place," she said more briskly. "Our lives are miles apart."

Bryan glanced out the window at the tall, sleek building that was part of Lee's view of the city. "So, he can move to L.A. and close the distance."

"He won't." Swallowing, Lee looked at the pages on her desk. The article was finished, she knew it, just as she knew that if she didn't let it go, she'd polish it to death. "He belongs there. He wants to raise his daughter there. I understand that."

"So, you move to the canyon. Great scenery."

Why did it always sound so simple, so plausible, when spoken aloud? The little trickle of fear returned, and her voice firmed. "My job's here."

"I guess it comes down to priorities, doesn't it?" Bryan knew she wasn't being sympathetic, just as she knew it wasn't sympathy that Lee needed. Because she cared a great deal, she spoke without any compassion. "You can keep your job and your apartment in L.A. and be miserable. Or you can take a few chances."

Chances. Lee ran a finger down the slick surface of her desk. But you were supposed to test the ground before you stepped forward. Even Hunter had said that. But… She looked at the mangled paper clip in the center of her spotless blotter. How long did you test it before you took the jump?

It was barely two weeks later that Lee sat in her apartment in the middle of the day. She was so rarely there during the day, during the week, that she somehow expected everything to look different. Everything looked precisely the same. Even, she was forced to admit, herself. Yet nothing was.

Quit. She tried to digest the word as she dealt with the panic she'd held off the past few days. There was a leafy, blooming African violet on the table in front of her. It was well-tended, as every area of her life had been well-tended. She'd always water it when the soil was dry and feed it when it required nourishing. As she stared at the plant, Lee knew she would never be capable of pulling it ruthlessly out by the roots. But wasn't that what she'd done to herself?

Quit, she thought again, and the word reverberated in her brain. She'd actually handed in her resignation, served her two weeks' notice and summarily turned her back on her steadily thriving career—ripped out its roots.

For what? she demanded of herself as panic trickled through. To follow some crazy dream that had planted itself in her mind years ago. To write a book that would probably never be published. To take a ridiculous risk and plunge headlong into the unknown.

Because Hunter had said she was good. Because he'd fed that dream, just as she fed the violet. More than that, Lee thought, he'd made it impossible for her to stop thinking about the "what ifs" in her life. And he was one of them. The most important one of them.

Now that the step was taken and she was here, alone in her impossibly quiet midweek, midmorning apartment, Lee wanted to run. Out there were people, noise, distractions. Here, she'd have to face those "what-ifs." Hunter would be the first.

He hadn't tried to stop her when she left the morning after he'd asked her to marry him. He'd said nothing when she'd made her goodbyes to Sarah. Nothing at all. Perhaps they'd both known that he'd said all there was to say the night before. He'd looked at her once, and she'd nearly wavered. Then Lee had climbed into the car with Bonnie, who'd driven her to the airport that was one step closer to L.A.

He hadn't phoned her since she'd returned. Had she expected him to? Lee wondered. Maybe she had, but she'd hoped he wouldn't. She didn't know how long it would take before she'd be able to hear his voice without going to pieces.

Glancing down, she stared at the twisted gold-and-silver ring on her hand. Why had she kept it? It wasn't hers. It should've been left behind. It was easy to tell herself she'd simply forgotten to take it off in the confusion, but it wasn't the truth. She'd known the ring was still on her finger as she packed, as she walked out of Hunter's house, as she stepped into the car. She just hadn't been capable of taking it off.

She needed time, and it was time, Lee realized, that she now had. She had to prove something again, but not to her parents, not to Hunter. Now there was only herself. If she could finish the book. If she could give it her very best and really finish it…

Rising, Lee went to her desk, sat down at the typewriter and faced the fear of the blank page.

Lee had known pressure in her work on *Celebrity*. The minutes ticking away while deadlines drew closer and closer. There was the pressure of making not-so-fascinating seem fascinating, in a limited space, and of having to do it week after week. And yet, after nearly a month of being away from it, and having only herself and the story to account for, Lee had learned the full meaning of pressure. And of delight.

She hadn't believed—truly believed—that it would be possible for her to sit down, hour after hour, and finish a book she'd begun on a whim so long ago. And it was true that for the first few days she'd met with nothing but frustration and failure. There'd been a ring of terror in her head. Why had she left a job where she was respected and knowledgeable to stumble in the dark this way?

Time after time, she was tempted to push it all aside and go back, even if it would mean starting over at *Celebrity*. But each time, she could see Hunter's face—lightly mocking, challenging and somehow encouraging.

"It takes a certain amount of stamina and endurance. If you've reached your limit and want to quit..."

The answer was no, just as grimly, just as determinedly as it had been in that little tent. Perhaps she'd fail. She shut her eyes as she struggled to deal with the thought. Perhaps she'd fail miserably, but she wouldn't quit. Whatever happened, she'd made her own choice, and she'd live with it.

The longer she worked, the more of a symbol those typewritten pages became. If she could do this, and do it well, she could do anything. The rest of her life balanced on it.

By the end of the second week, Lee was so absorbed she rarely noticed the twelve- and fourteen-hour days she was putting in. She plugged in her phone machine and forgot to return the calls as often as she forgot to eat.

It was as Hunter had once said. The characters absorbed her, drove her, frustrated and delighted her. As time passed, Lee discovered she wanted to finish the story, not only for her sake but for theirs. She wanted, as she'd never wanted before, for these words to be read. The excitement of that, and the dread, kept her going.

She felt a queer little thrill when the last word was typed, a euphoria mixed with an odd depression. She'd finished. She'd poured her heart into her story. Lee wanted to celebrate. She wanted to weep. It was over. As she pressed her fingers against her tired eyes, she realized abruptly that she didn't even know what day it was.

He'd never had a book race so frantically, so quickly. Hunter could barely keep up with his own zooming thoughts. He knew why, and flowed with it because he had no choice. The main character of this story was Lenore, though her name would be changed to Jennifer. She was Lenore, physically, emotionally, from the elegantly groomed red-gold hair to the nervously bitten fingernails. It was the only way he had of keeping her.

It had cost him more than she'd ever know to let her go. When he'd watched her climb into the car, he'd told himself she wouldn't stay away. She couldn't. If he was wrong about her feelings for him, then he'd been wrong about everything in his life.

Two women had crashed into his life with importance. The first, Sarah's mother, he hadn't loved, yet she'd changed everything. After that, she'd gone away, unable to find it possible to mix her ambition with a life that included children and commitment.

Lee, he loved, and she'd changed everything again. She, too, had gone away. Would she stay away, for the same reasons? Was he fated to bind himself to women who wouldn't share the tie? He wouldn't believe it.

So he'd let her go, aches and fury under the calm. She'd be back.

But a month had passed, and she hadn't come. He wondered how long a man could live when he was starving.

Call her. Go after her. You were a fool to ever let her go. Drag her back if necessary. You need her. You need…

His thoughts ran this way like clockwork. Every day at dusk. Every day at dusk, Hunter fought the urge to follow through on them. He needed; God, he needed. But if she didn't come to him willingly, he'd never have what he needed, only the shell of it. He looked down at his naked finger. She hadn't left everything behind. It was more, much more, than a piece of metal that she'd taken with her.

He'd given her a talisman, and she'd kept it. As long as she had it, she didn't sever the bond. Hunter was a man who believed in fate, omens and magic.

"Dinner's ready." Sarah stood in the doorway, her hair pulled back in a ponytail, her narrow face streaked with a bit of flour.

He didn't want to eat. He wanted to go on writing. As long as the story moved through him, he had a part of Lenore with him. Just as, whenever he stopped, the need to have all of her tore him apart. But Sarah smiled at him.

"Nearly ready," she amended. She came into the room, barefoot. "I made this meat loaf, but it looks more like a pancake. And the biscuits." She grinned, shrugging. "They're pretty hard, but we can put some jam or something on them." Sensing his mood, she wrapped her arms around his neck, resting her cheek against his. "I like it better when you cook."

"Who turned her nose up at the broccoli last night?"

"It looks like little trees that got sick." She wrinkled her nose, but when she drew back from him, her face was serious. "You really miss her a lot, huh?"

He could've evaded with anyone else. But this was Sarah. She was ten. She knew him inside out. "Yeah, I miss her a lot."

Thinking, Sarah fiddled with the hair that fell over his forehead. "I guess maybe you wanted her to marry you."

"She turned me down."

Her brows lowered, not so much from annoyance that anyone could say no to her father, but in concentration. Donna's father hardly had any hair at all, she thought, touching Hunter's again, and Kelly's dad's stomach bounced over his belt. Shelley's mother never got jokes. She didn't know anybody who was as neat to look at or as neat to be with as her dad. Anybody would want to marry him. When she'd been little, she'd wanted to marry him herself. But of course, she knew now that was just silly stuff.

Her brows were still drawn together when she brought her gaze to his. "I guess she didn't like me."

He heard everything just as clearly as if she'd spoken her thoughts aloud. He was greatly touched, and not a little impressed. "Couldn't stand you."

Her eyes widened, then brightened with laughter. "Because I'm such a brat."

"Right. I can barely stand you myself."

"Well." Sarah huffed a moment. "She didn't look stupid, but I guess she is if she wouldn't marry you." She cuddled against him, and knowing it was to comfort, Hunter warmed with love. "I liked her," Sarah murmured. "She was nice, kinda quiet, but really nice when she smiled. I guess you love her."

"Yes, I do." He didn't offer her any words of reassurance—it's different from the way I love you, you'll always be my little girl. Hunter simply held her, and it was enough. "She loves me, too, but she has to make her own life."

Sarah didn't understand that, and personally thought it was foolish, but decided not to say so. "I guess I wouldn't mind if she decided to marry you after all. It might be nice to have somebody who'd be like a mother."

He lifted a brow. She never asked about her own mother, knowing with a child's intuition, he supposed, that there was nothing to ask about. "Aren't I?"

"You're pretty good," she told him graciously. "But you don't know a whole lot about lady stuff." Sarah sniffed the air, then grinned. "Meat loaf's done."

"Overdone, from the smell of it."

"Picky, picky." She jumped off his lap before he could retaliate. "I hear a car coming. You can ask them to dinner so we can get rid of all the biscuits."

He didn't want company, Hunter thought as he watched his daughter dash out of the room. An evening with Sarah was enough, then he'd go back to work. After switching off his machine, he rose to go to the door. It was probably one of her friends, who'd talked her parents into dropping by on their way home from town. He'd brush them off, as politely as he could manage, then see if anything could be done about Sarah's meat loaf.

When he opened the door, she was standing there, her hair caught in the light of a late summer's evening. He was, quite literally, knocked breathless.

"Hello, Hunter." How calm a voice could sound, Lee thought, even when a heart's hammering against ribs. "I'd've called, but your number's unlisted." When he said nothing, Lee felt her heart move from her ribs to her throat. Somehow, she managed to speak over it. "May I come in?"

Silently, he stepped back. Perhaps he was dreaming, like the character in "The Raven." All he needed was a bust of Pallas and a dying fire.

She'd used up nearly all of her courage just coming back. If he didn't speak soon, they'd end up simply staring at each other. Like a nervous speaker about to lecture on a subject she hadn't researched, Lee cleared her throat. "Hunter…"

"Hey, I think we'd better just give the biscuits to Santanas because—" Sarah stopped her headlong flight into the room. "Well, gee."

"Sarah, hello." Lee was able to smile now. The child looked so comically surprised, not cool and distant like her father.

"Hi." Sarah glanced uncertainly from one adult to the other. She supposed they were going to make a mess of things. Aunt Bonnie said that people who loved each other usually made a mess of things, for at least a little while. "Dinner's ready. I made meat loaf. It's probably not too bad."

Understanding the invitation, Lee grasped at it. At least it would give her more time before Hunter tossed her out again. "It smells wonderful."

"Okay, come on." Imperiously, Sarah held out her hand, waiting until Lee took it. "It doesn't look very good," she went on, as she led Lee into the kitchen. "But I did everything I was supposed to."

Lee looked at the flattened meat loaf and smiled. "Better than I could do."

"Really?" Sarah digested this with a nod. "Well, Dad and I take turns." And if they got married, Sarah figured, she'd only have to cook every third day. "You'd better set another place," she said lightly to her father. "The biscuits didn't work, but we've got potatoes."

The three of them sat down, very much as if it were the natural thing to do. Sarah served, carrying on a babbling conversation that alleviated the need for either adult to speak to the other. They each answered her, smiled, ate, while their thoughts were in a frenzy.

He doesn't want me anymore.

Why did she come?

He hasn't even spoken to me.

What does she want? She looks lovely. So lovely.

What can I do? He looks wonderful. So wonderful.

Sarah lifted the casserole containing the rest of the meat loaf. "I'll give this to Santanas." Like most children, she detested leftovers—unless it was spaghetti. "Dad has to do the dishes," she explained to Lee. "You can help him if you like." After she'd dumped Santanas's dinner in his bowl, she danced out of the room. "See you later."

Then they were alone, and Lee found she was gripping her hands together so tightly they were numb. Deliberately, she unlaced her fingers. He saw the ring, still on her finger, and felt something twist, loosen, then tighten again in his chest.

"You're angry," she said in that same calm, even voice. "I'm sorry, I shouldn't have come this way."

Hunter rose and began to stack dishes. "No, I'm not angry." Anger was possibly the only emotion he hadn't experienced in the last hour. "Why did you?"

"I..." Lee looked down helplessly at her hands. She should help him with the dishes, keep busy, stay natural. She didn't think her legs would hold her just yet. "I finished the book," she blurted out.

He stopped and turned. For the first time since she'd opened the door, she saw that hint of a smile around his mouth. "Congratulations."

"I wanted you to read it. I know I could've mailed it—I sent a copy on to your editor—but..." She lifted her eyes to his again. "I didn't want to mail it. I wanted to give it to you. Needed to."

Hunter put the dishes in the sink and came back to the table, but he didn't sit. He had to stand. If this was what she'd come for, all she'd come for, he wasn't certain he could face it. "You know I want to read it. I expect you to autograph the first copy for me."

She managed a smile. "I'm not as optimistic as that, but you were right. I had to finish it. I wanted to thank you for showing me." Her lips remained curved, but the smile left her eyes. "I quit my job."

He hadn't moved, but it seemed that he suddenly became very still. "Why?"

"I had to try to finish the book. For me." If only he'd touch her, just her hand, she wouldn't feel so cold. "I knew if I could do that, I could do anything. I needed to prove that to myself before I…" Lee trailed off, not able to say it all. "I've been reading your work, your earlier work as Laura Miles."

If he could just touch her… But once he did, he'd never let her go again. "Did you enjoy it?"

"Yes." There was enough lingering surprise in her voice to make him smile. "I'd never have believed there could be a similarity of styles between a romance novel and a horror story, but there was. Atmosphere, tension, emotion." Taking a deep breath, she stood so that she could face him. It was perhaps the most difficult step she'd taken so far. "You understand how a woman feels. It shows in your work."

"*Writer*'s a word without gender."

"Still, it's a rare gift, I think, for a man to be able to understand and appreciate the kinds of emotions and insecurities that go on inside a woman." Her eyes met his again, and this time held. "I'm hoping you can do the same with me."

He was looking into her again. She could feel it.

"It's more difficult when your own emotions are involved."

She gripped her fingers together, tightly. "Are they?"

He didn't touch her, not yet, but she thought she could almost feel his hand against her cheek. "Do you need me to tell you I love you?"

"Yes, I—"

"You've finished your book, quit your job. You've taken a lot of risks, Lenore." He waited. "But you've yet to put it all on the line."

Her breath trembled out. No, he'd never make things easy for her. There'd always be demands, expectations. He'd never pamper. "You terrified me when you asked me to marry you. I thought about it a great deal, like the small child thinks about a dark closet. I don't know what's in there—it might be dream or nightmare. You understand that."

"Yes." Though it hadn't been a question. "I understand that."

She breathed a bit easier. "I used what I had in L.A. as an excuse because it was logical, but it wasn't the real reason. I was just afraid to walk into that closet."

"And are you still?"

"A little." It took more effort than she'd imagined to relax her fingers. She wondered if he knew it was the final step. She held out her hand. "But I want to try. I want to go there with you."

His fingers laced with hers, and she felt the nerves melt away. Of course he knew. "It won't be dream or nightmare, Lenore. Every minute of it will be real."

She laughed then, because his hand was in hers.

"Now you're really trying to scare me." Stepping closer, she kissed him softly, until desire built to a quiet roar. It was so easy, like sliding into a warm, clear stream. "You won't scare me off," she whispered.

The arms around her were tight, but she barely noticed. "No, I won't scare you off." He breathed in the scent of her hair, wallowed in the texture of it. She'd come to him. Completely. "I won't let you go, either. I've waited too long for you to come back."

"You knew I would," she murmured.

"I had to, I'd've gone mad otherwise."

She closed her eyes, content, but with a thrill of excitement underneath. "Hunter, if Sarah doesn't, that is, if she isn't able to adjust..."

"Worried already." He drew her back. "Sarah gave me a pep talk just this evening. You do, I assume, know quite a bit about lady stuff?"

"Lady stuff?"

He drew her back just a bit farther, to look her up and down. "Every inch the lady. You'll do, Lenore, for me, and for Sarah."

"Okay." She let out a long breath, because as usual, she believed him. "I'd like to be with you when you tell her."

"Lenore." Framing her face, he kissed both cheeks, gently, with a hint of a laugh beneath. "She already knows."

A brow lifted. "Her father's daughter."

"Exactly." He grabbed her, swinging her around once in a moment of pure, irrepressible joy. "The lady's going to find it interesting living in a house with real and imaginary monsters."

"The lady can handle that," she tossed back. "And anything else you dream up."

"Is that so?" He shot her a wicked look—amusement, desire, knowledge—as he released her. "Then let's get these dishes done and I'll see what I can do."

* * * * *

LESSONS LEARNED

For Jill Gregory, aka The Baby,
one of my favorite roommates.

Chapter 1

So he was gorgeous. And rich...and talented. And sexy; you shouldn't forget that he was outrageously sexy.

It hardly mattered to Juliet. She was a professional, and to a professional, a job was a job. In this case, great looks and personality were bound to help, but that was business. Strictly business.

No, personally it didn't matter a bit. After all, she'd met a few gorgeous men in her life. She'd met a few rich ones, too, and so forth, though she had to admit she'd never met a man with all those elusive qualities rolled up in one. She'd certainly never had the opportunity to work with one. Now she did.

The fact was, Carlo Franconi's looks, charm, reputation and skill were going to make her job a pleasure. So she was told. Still, with her office door closed, Juliet scowled down at the eight-by-ten glossy black-and-white publicity photo. It looked to her as though he'd be more trouble than pleasure.

Carlo grinned cockily up at her, dark, almond-shaped eyes amused and appreciative. She wondered if the photographer had been a woman. His full thick hair was appealingly disheveled with a bit of curl along the nape of his neck and over his ears. Not too much—just enough to disarm. The strong facial bones, jauntily curved mouth, straight nose and expressive brows combined to create a face destined to sabotage any woman's common sense. Gift or cultivated talent, Juliet wasn't certain, but she'd have to use it to her advantage. Author tours could be murder.

A cookbook. Juliet tried, and failed, not to sigh. Carlo Franconi's *The Italian Way* was, whether she liked it or not, her biggest assignment to date. Business was business.

She loved her job as publicist and was content for the moment with Trinity Press, the publisher she currently worked for, after a half-dozen job changes and upward jumps since the start of her career. At twenty-eight, the ambition she'd started with as a receptionist nearly ten years before had eased very little. She'd worked, studied, hustled and sweated for her own office and position. She had them, but she wasn't ready to relax.

In two years, by her calculations, she'd be ready to make the next jump: her own public relations firm. Naturally, she'd have to start out small, but it was building the business that was exciting. The contacts and experience she gained in her twenties would help her solidify her ambitions in her thirties. Juliet was content with that.

One of the first things she'd learned in public relations was that an account was an account, whether it was a big blockbuster bestseller already slated to be a big blockbuster film or a slim volume of poetry that would barely earn out its advance. Part of the challenge, and the fun, was finding the right promotional hook.

Now, she had a cookbook and a slick Italian chef. Franconi, she thought wryly, had a track record—with women and in publishing. The first was a matter of hot interest to the society and gossip sections of the international press. It wasn't necessary to cook to be aware of Franconi's name. The second was the reason he was being pampered on the road with a publicist.

His first two cookbooks had been solid bestsellers. For good reason, Juliet admitted. It was true she couldn't fry an egg without creating a gooey inedible glob, but she recognized quality and style. Franconi could make linguini sound like a dish to be prepared while wearing black lace. He turned a simple spaghetti dish into an erotic event.

Sex. Juliet tipped back in her chair and wiggled her stockinged toes. That's what he had. That's just what they'd use. Before the twenty-one-day author tour was finished, she'll have made Carlo Franconi the world's sexiest cook. Any red-blooded American woman would fantasize about him preparing an intimate dinner for two. Candlelight, pasta and romance.

One last study of his publicity shot and the charmingly crooked grin assured her he could handle it.

In the meantime, there was a bit more groundwork to cover. Creating a schedule was a pleasure, adhering to one a challenge. She thrived on both.

Juliet lifted the phone, noticed with resignation that

she'd broken another nail, then buzzed her assistant. "Terry, get me Diane Maxwell. She's program coordinator on the *Simpson Show* in L.A."

"Going for the big guns?"

Juliet gave a quick, unprofessional grin. "Yeah." She replaced the phone and started making hurried notes. No reason not to start at the top, she told herself. That way, if you fell on your face, at least the trip would be worth it.

As she waited, she looked around her office. Not the top, but a good ways from the bottom. At least she had a window. Juliet could still shudder thinking of some of the walled-in cubicles she'd worked in. Now, twenty stories below, New York rushed, bumped, pushed and shoved its way through another day. Juliet Trent had learned how to do the same thing after moving from the relatively easygoing suburb of Harrisburg, Pennsylvania.

She might've grown up in a polite little neighborhood where only a stranger drove over twenty-five miles per hour and everyone kept the grass clipped close to their side of the chain-link fences, but Juliet had acclimated easily. The truth was she liked the pace, the energy and the "I dare you" tone of New York. She'd never go back to the bee-humming, hedge-clipping quiet of suburbia where everyone knew who you were, what you did and how you did it. She preferred the anonymity and the individuality of crowds.

Perhaps her mother had molded herself into the perfect suburban wife, but not Juliet. She was an eighties woman, independent, self-sufficient and moving up. There was an apartment in the west Seventies that she'd furnished, slowly, meticulously and, most important, personally. Juliet had enough patience to move step by step as long as the result was perfect. She had a career she could be proud of and an office she was gradually altering to suit her own tastes. Leaving her mark wasn't something she took lightly. It had taken her four months to choose the right plants for her work space, from the four-foot split-leaf philodendron to the delicate white-blossomed African violet.

She'd had to make do with the beige carpet, but the six-foot Dali print on the wall opposite her window added life and energy. The narrow-beveled mirror gave an illusion of space and a touch of elegance. She had her eye on a big, gaudy Oriental urn that would be perfect for a spray of equally gaudy peacock feathers. If she waited a bit longer, the price might come down from exorbitant to ridiculous. Then she'd buy it.

Juliet might put on a very practical front to everyone, including herself, but she couldn't resist a sale. As a result, her bank balance wasn't as hefty as her bedroom closet. She wasn't frivolous. No, she would have been appalled to hear the word applied to her. Her wardrobe was organized, well tended and suitable. Perhaps twenty pairs of shoes could be considered excessive, but Juliet rationalized that she was often on her feet ten hours a day and deserved the luxury. In any case, she'd earned them, from the sturdy sneakers, the practical black pumps to the strappy evening sandals. She'd earned them with innumerable long meetings, countless waits in airports and endless hours on the phone. She'd earned them on author tours, where the luck of the draw could have you dealing with the brilliant, the funny, the inept, the boring or the rude. Whatever she had to deal with, the results had to be the same. Media, media and more media.

She'd learned how to deal with the press, from the *New York Times* reporter to the stringer on the small-town weekly. She knew how to charm the staff of talk shows, from the accepted masters to the nervous imitators. Learning had been an adventure, and since she'd allowed herself very few in her personal life, professional success was all the sweeter.

When the intercom buzzed, she caught her tongue between her teeth. Now, she was going to apply everything she'd learned and land Franconi on the top-rated talk show in the States.

Once she did, she thought as she pressed the button, he'd better make the most of it. Or she'd slit his sexy throat with his own chef's knife.

"Ah, *mi amore. Squisito.*" Carlo's voice was a low purr designed to accelerate the blood pressure. The bedroom voice wasn't something he'd had to develop, but something he'd been born with. Carlo had always thought a man who didn't use God-given gifts was less than a fool. *"Bellisimo,"* he murmured and his eyes were dark and dreamy with anticipation.

It was hot, almost steamy, but he preferred the heat. Cold slowed down the blood. The sun coming through the window had taken on the subtle gold texture with tints of red that spoke of the end of the day and hinted at the pleasures of night. The room was rich with scent so he breathed it in. A man was missing a great deal of life if he didn't use and appreciate all of his senses. Carlo believed in missing nothing.

He watched his love of the moment with a connoisseur's eye. He'd caress, whisper to, flatter—it never mattered to him if it took moments or hours to get what he wanted. As long as he got what he wanted. To Carlo, the process, the anticipation, the moves themselves were equally as satisfying as the result. Like a dance, he'd always thought. Like a song. An aria from *The Marriage of Figaro* played in the background while he seduced.

Carlo believed in setting the scene because life was a play not simply to be enjoyed, but to be relished.

"Bellisimo," he whispered and bent nearer what he adored. The clam sauce simmered erotically as he stirred it. Slowly, savoring the moment, Carlo lifted the spoon to his lips and with his eyes half-closed, tasted. The sound of pleasure came from low in his throat. *"Squisito."*

He moved from the sauce to give the same loving attention to his *zabaglione.* He believed there wasn't a woman alive who could resist the taste of that rich, creamy custard with the zing of wine. As usual, it was a woman he was expecting.

The kitchen was as much a den of pleasure to him as the bedroom. It wasn't an accident that he was one of the most respected and admired chefs in the world, or that he was one of the most engaging lovers. Carlo considered it a matter of destiny. His kitchen was cleverly arranged, as meticulously laid out for the seduction of sauces and spices as his bedroom was for the seduction of women. Yes, Carlo Franconi believed life was to be relished. Every drop of it.

When the knock on the front door reverberated through the high-ceilinged rooms of his home, he murmured to his pasta before he removed his apron. As hc went to answer, he rolled down the silk sleeves of his shirt but didn't stop for adjustments in any of the antique mirrors that lined the walls. He wasn't so much vain, as confident.

He opened the door to a tall, stately woman with honey-toned skin and dark glossy eyes. Carlo's heart moved as it did whenever he saw her. *"Mi amore."* Taking her hand, he pressed his mouth to the palm, while his eyes smiled into hers. *"Bella. Molto bella."*

She stood in the evening light for a moment, dark, lovely, with a smile only for him. Only a fool wouldn't have known he'd welcomed dozens of women in just this way. She wasn't a fool. But she loved him.

"You're a scoundrel, Carlo." The woman reached out to touch his hair. It was dark and thick and difficult to resist. "Is this the way you greet your mother?"

"This is the way—" he kissed her hand again "—I greet a beautiful woman." Then he wrapped both arms around her and kissed her cheeks. "This is the way I greet my mother. It's a fortunate man who can do both."

Gina Franconi laughed as she returned her son's hug. "To you, all women are beautiful."

"But only one is my mother." With his arm around her waist, he led her inside.

Gina approved, as always, the fact that his home was spotless, if a bit too exotic for her taste. She often wondered how the poor maid managed to keep the ornately carved archways dusted and polished and the hundreds of windowpanes unstreaked. Because she was a woman who'd spent fifteen years of her life cleaning other people's homes and forty cleaning her own, she thought of such things.

She studied one of his new acquisitions, a three-foot ivory owl with a small rodent captured in one claw. A good wife, Gina mused, would guide her son's tastes toward less eccentric paths.

"An aperitif, Mama?" Carlo walked over to a tall smoked-glass cabinet and drew out a slim black bottle. "You should try this," he told her as he chose two small glasses and poured. "A friend sent it to me."

Gina set aside her red snakeskin bag and accepted the glass. The first sip was hot, potent, smooth as a lover's kiss and just as intoxicating. She lifted a brow as she took the second sip. "Excellent."

"Yes, it is. Anna has excellent taste."

Anna, she thought, with more amusement than exasperation. She'd learned years before that it didn't do any good to be exasperated with a man, especially if you loved him. "Are all your friends women, Carlo?"

"No." He held his glass up, twirling it. "But this one was. She sent me this as a wedding present."

"A—"

"Her wedding," Carlo said with a grin. "She wanted a husband, and though I couldn't accommodate her, we parted friends." He held up the bottle as proof.

"Did you have it analyzed before you drank any?" Gina asked dryly.

He touched the rim of his glass to hers. "A clever man turns all former lovers into friends, Mama."

"You've always been clever." With a small movement of her shoulders she sipped again and sat down. "I hear you're seeing the French actress."

"As always, your hearing's excellent."

As if it interested her, Gina studied the hue of the liqueur in her glass. "She is, of course, beautiful."

"Of course."

"I don't think she'll give me grandchildren."

Carlo laughed and sat beside her. "You have six grandchildren and another coming, Mama. Don't be greedy."

"But none from my son. My only son," she reminded him with a tap of her finger on his shoulder. "Still, I haven't given you up yet."

"Perhaps if I could find a woman like you."

She shot him back arrogant look for arrogant look. "Impossible, *caro*."

His feeling exactly, Carlo thought as he guided her into talk about his four sisters and their families. When he looked at this sleek, lovely woman, it was difficult to think of her as the mother who'd raised him, almost single-handedly. She'd worked, and though she'd been known to storm and rage, she'd never complained. Her clothes had been carefully mended, her floors meticulously scrubbed while his father had spent endless months at sea.

When he concentrated, and he rarely did, Carlo could recall an impression of a dark, wiry man with a black mustache and an easy grin. The impression didn't bring on resentment or even regret. His father had been a seaman before his parents had married, and a seaman he'd remained. Carlo's belief in meeting your destiny was unwavering. But while his feelings for his father were ambivalent, his feelings for his mother were set and strong.

She'd supported each of her children's ambitions, and when Carlo had earned a scholarship to the Sorbonne in Paris and the opportunity to pursue his interest in haute cuisine, she'd let him go. Ultimately, she'd supplemented the meager income he could earn between studies with part of the insurance money she'd received when her husband had been lost in the sea he'd loved.

Six years before, Carlo had been able to pay her back in his own way. The dress shop he'd bought for her birthday had been a lifelong dream for both of them. For him, it was a way of seeing his mother happy at last. For Gina it was a way to begin again.

He'd grown up in a big, boisterous, emotional family. It gave him pleasure to look back and remember. A man who grows up in a family of women learns to understand them, appreciate them, admire them. Carlo knew about women's dreams, their vanities, their insecurities. He never took a lover he didn't have affection for as well as desire. If there was only desire, he knew there'd be no friendship at the end, only resentment. Even now, the comfortable affair he was having with the French actress was ending. She'd be starting a film in a few weeks, and he'd be going on tour in America. That, Carlo thought with some regret, would be that.

"Carlo, you go to America soon?"

"Hmm. Yes." He wondered if she'd read his mind, knowing women were capable of doing so. "Two weeks."

"You'll do me a favor?"

"Of course."

"Then notice for me what the professional American woman is wearing. I'm thinking of adding some things to the shop. The Americans are so clever and practical."

"Not too practical, I hope." He swirled his drink. "My publicist is a Ms. Trent." Tipping back his glass, he accepted the heat and the punch. "I'll promise you to study every aspect of her wardrobe."

She gave his quick grin a steady look. "You're so good to me, Carlo."

"But of course, Mama. Now I'm going to feed you like a queen."

* * *

Carlo had no idea what Juliet Trent looked like, but put himself in the hands of fate. What he did know, from the letters he'd received from her, was that Juliet Trent was the type of American his mother had described. Practical and clever. Excellent qualities in a publicist.

Physically was another matter. But again, as his mother had said, Carlo could always find beauty in a woman. Perhaps he did prefer, in his personal life, a woman with a lovely shell, but he knew how to dig beneath to find inner beauty. It was something that made life interesting as well as aesthetically pleasing.

Still, as he stepped off the plane into the terminal in L.A., he had his hand on the elbow of a stunning redhead.

Juliet did know what he looked like, and she first saw him, shoulder to shoulder with a luxuriously built woman in pencil-thin heels. Though he carried a bulky leather case in one hand, and a flight bag over his shoulder, he escorted the redhead through the gate as though they were walking into a ballroom. Or a bedroom.

Juliet took a quick assessment of the well-tailored slacks, the unstructured jacket and open-collared shirt. The well-heeled traveler. There was a chunk of gold and diamond on his finger that should've looked ostentatious and vulgar. Somehow it looked as casual and breezy as the rest of him. She felt formal and sticky.

She'd been in L.A. since the evening before, giving herself time to see personally to all the tiny details. Carlo Franconi would have nothing to do but be charming, answer questions and sign his cookbook.

As she watched him kiss the redhead's knuckles,

Juliet thought he'd be signing plenty of them. After all, didn't women do the majority of cookbook buying? Carefully smoothing away a sarcastic smirk, Juliet rose. The redhead was sending one last wistful look over her shoulder as she walked away.

"Mr. Franconi?"

Carlo turned away from the woman who'd proven to be a pleasant traveling companion on the long flight from New York. His first look at Juliet brought a quick flutter of interest and a subtle tug of desire he often felt with a woman. It was a tug he could either control or let loose, as was appropriate. This time, he savored it.

She didn't have merely a lovely face, but an interesting one. Her skin was very pale, which should have made her seem fragile, but the wide, strong cheekbones undid the air of fragility and gave her face an intriguing diamond shape. Her eyes were large, heavily lashed and artfully accented with a smoky shadow that only made the cool green shade of the irises seem cooler. Her mouth was only lightly touched with a peach-colored gloss. It had a full, eye-drawing shape that needed no artifice. He gathered she was wise enough to know it.

Her hair was caught somewhere between brown and blond so that its shade was soft, natural and subtle. She wore it long enough in the back to be pinned up in a chignon when she wished, and short enough on the top and sides so that she could style it from fussy to practical as the occasion, and her whim, demanded. At the moment, it was loose and casual, but not windblown. She'd stopped in the ladies' room for a quick check just after the incoming flight had been announced.

"I'm Juliet Trent," she told him when she felt he'd stared long enough. "Welcome to California." As he took the hand she offered, she realized she should've expected him to kiss it rather than shake. Still, she stiffened, hardly more than an instant, but she saw by the lift of brow, he'd felt it.

"A beautiful woman makes a man welcome anywhere."

His voice was incredible—the cream that rose to the top and then flowed over something rich. She told herself it only pleased her because it would record well and took his statement literally. Thinking of the redhead, she gave him an easy, not entirely friendly smile. "Then you must have had a pleasant flight."

His native language might have been Italian, but Carlo understood nuances in any tongue. He grinned at her. "Very pleasant."

"And tiring," she said remembering her position. "Your luggage should be in by now." Again, she glanced at the large case he carried. "Can I take that for you?"

His brow lifted at the idea of a man dumping his burden on a woman. Equality, to Carlo, never crossed the border into manners. "No, this is something I always carry myself."

Indicating the way, she fell into step beside him. "It's a half-hour ride to the Beverly Wilshire, but after you've settled in, you can rest all afternoon. I'd like to go over tomorrow's schedule with you this evening."

He liked the way she walked. Though she wasn't tall, she moved in long, unhurried strides that made the red side-pleated skirt she wore shift over her hips. "Over dinner?"

She sent him a quick sidelong look. "If you like."

She'd be at his disposal, Juliet reminded herself, for the next three weeks. Without appearing to think about it, she skirted around a barrel-chested man hefting a bulging garment bag and a briefcase. Yes, he liked the way she walked, Carlo thought again. She was a woman who could take care of herself without a great deal of fuss.

"At seven? You have a talk show in the morning that starts at seven-thirty so we'd best make it an early evening."

Seven-thirty a.m. Carlo thought, only briefly, about jet lag and time changes. "So, you put me to work quickly."

"That's what I'm here for, Mr. Franconi." Juliet said it cheerfully as she stepped up to the slowly moving baggage belt. "You have your stubs?"

An organized woman, he thought as he reached into the inside pocket of his loose-fitting buff-colored jacket. In silence, he handed them to her, then hefted a Pullman and a garment bag from the belt himself.

Gucci, she observed. So he had taste as well as money. Juliet handed the stubs to a skycap and waited while Carlo's luggage was loaded onto the pushcart. "I think you'll be pleased with what we have for you, Mr. Franconi." She walked through the automatic doors and signaled for her limo. "I know you've always worked with Jim Collins in the past on your tours in the States. He sends his best."

"Does Jim like his executive position?"

"Apparently."

Though Carlo expected her to climb into the limo first, she stepped back. With a bow to women professionals, Carlo ducked inside and took his seat. "Do you like yours, Ms. Trent?"

She took the seat across from him then sent him a straight-shooting, level look. Juliet could have no idea how much he admired it. "Yes, I do."

Carlo stretched out his legs—legs his mother had once said that had refused to stop growing long after it was necessary. He'd have preferred driving himself, particularly after the long, long flight from Rome where someone else had been at the controls. But if he couldn't, the plush laziness of the limo was the next best thing. Reaching over, he switched on the stereo so that Mozart poured out, quiet but vibrant. If he'd been driving, it would've been rock, loud and rambunctious.

"You've read my book, Ms. Trent?"

"Yes, of course. I couldn't set up publicity and promotion for an unknown product." She sat back. It was easy to do her job when she could speak the simple truth. "I was impressed with the attention to detail and the clear directions. It seemed a very friendly book, rather than simply a kitchen tool."

"Hmm." He noticed her stockings were very pale pink and had a tiny line of dots up one side. It would interest his mother that the practical American businesswoman could enjoy the frivolous. It interested him that Juliet Trent could. "Have you tried any of the recipes?"

"No, I don't cook."

"You don't…" His lazy interest came to attention. "At all?"

She had to smile. He looked so sincerely shocked.

As he watched the perfect mouth curve, he had to put the next tug of desire in check.

"When you're a failure at something, Mr. Franconi, you leave it to someone else."

"I could teach you." The idea intrigued him. He never offered his expertise lightly.

"To cook?" She laughed, relaxing enough to let her

heel slip out of her shoe as she swung her foot. "I don't think so."

"I'm an excellent teacher," he said with a slow smile.

Again, she gave him the calm, gunslinger look. "I don't doubt it. I, on the other hand, am a poor student."

"Your age?" When her look narrowed, he smiled charmingly. "A rude question when a woman's reached a certain stage. You haven't."

"Twenty-eight," she said so coolly his smile became a grin.

"You look younger, but your eyes are older. I'd find it a pleasure to give you a few lessons, Ms. Trent."

She believed him. She, too, understood nuances. "A pity our schedule won't permit it."

He shrugged easily and glanced out the window. But the L.A. freeway didn't interest him. "You put Philadelphia in the schedule as I requested?"

"We'll have a full day there before we fly up to Boston. Then we'll finish up in New York."

"Good. I have a friend there. I haven't seen her in nearly a year."

Juliet was certain he had—friends—everywhere.

"You've been to Los Angeles before?" he asked her.

"Yes. Several times on business."

"I've yet to come here for pleasure myself. What do you think of it?"

As he had, she glanced out the window without interest. "I prefer New York."

"Why?"

"More grit, less gloss."

He liked her answer, and her phrasing. Because of it, he studied her more closely. "Have you ever been to Rome?"

"No." He thought he heard just a trace of wistfulness in her voice. "I haven't been to Europe at all."

"When you do, come to Rome. It was built on grit."

Her mind drifted a bit as she thought of it, and her smile remained. "I think of fountains and marble and cathedrals."

"You'll find them—and more." She had a face exquisite enough to be carved in marble, he thought. A voice quiet and smooth enough for cathedrals. "Rome rose and fell and clawed its way back up again. An intelligent woman understands such things. A romantic woman understands the fountains."

She glanced out again as the limo pulled up in front of the hotel. "I'm afraid I'm not very romantic."

"A woman named Juliet hasn't a choice."

"My mother's selection," she pointed out. "Not mine."

"You don't look for Romeo?"

Juliet gathered her briefcase. "No, Mr. Franconi. I don't."

He stepped out ahead of her and offered his hand. When Juliet stood on the curb, he didn't move back to give her room. Instead, he experimented with the sensation of bodies brushing, lightly, even politely on a public street. Her gaze came up to his, not wary but direct.

He felt it, the pull. Not the tug that was impersonal and for any woman, but the pull that went straight to the gut and was for one woman. So he'd have to taste her mouth. After all, he was a man compelled to judge a great deal by taste. But he could also bide his time. Some creations took a long time and had complicated preparations to perfect. Like Juliet, he insisted on perfection.

"Some women," he murmured, "never need to look, only to evade and avoid and select."

"Some women," she said just as quietly, "choose not to select at all." Deliberately, she turned her back on him to pay off the driver. "I've already checked you in, Mr. Franconi," she said over her shoulder as she handed his key to the waiting bellboy. "I'm just across the hall from your suite."

Without looking at him, Juliet followed the bellboy into the hotel and to the elevators. "If it suits you, I'll make reservations here in the hotel for dinner at seven. You can just tap on my door when you're ready." With a quick check of her watch she calculated the time difference and figured she could make three calls to New York and one to Dallas before office hours were over farther east. "If you need anything, you've only to order it and charge it to the room."

She stepped from the elevator, unzipping her purse and pulling out her own room key as she walked. "I'm sure you'll find your suite suitable."

He watched her brisk, economic movements. "I'm sure I will."

"Seven o'clock then." She was already pushing her key into the lock as the bellboy opened the first door to the suite across the hall. As she did, her mind was already on the calls she'd make the moment she'd shed her jacket and shoes.

"Juliet."

She paused, her hair swinging back as she looked over her shoulder at Carlo. He held her there, a moment longer, in silence. "Don't change your scent," he murmured. "Sex without flowers, femininity without vulnerability. It suits you."

While she continued to stare over her shoulder, he disappeared inside the suite. The bellboy began his polite introductions to the accommodations of the suite. Something Carlo said caused him to break off and laugh.

Juliet turned her key with more strength than necessary, pushed open her door, then closed it again with the length of her body. For a minute, she just leaned there, waiting for her system to level.

Professional training had prevented her from stammering and fumbling and making a fool of herself. Professional training had helped her to keep her nerves just at the border where they could be controlled and concealed. Still, under the training, there was a woman. Control had cost her. Juliet was dead certain there wasn't a woman alive who would be totally unaffected by Carlo Franconi. It wasn't balm for her ego to admit she was simply part of a large, varied group.

He'd never know it, she told herself, but her pulse had been behaving badly since he'd first taken her hand. It was still behaving badly. Stupid, she told herself and threw her bag down on a chair. Then she thought it best if she followed it. Her legs weren't steady yet. Juliet let out a long, deep breath. She'd just have to wait until they were.

So he was gorgeous. And rich…and talented. And outrageously sexy. She'd already known that, hadn't she? The trouble was, she wasn't sure how to handle him. Not nearly as sure as she had to be.

Chapter 2

She was a woman who thrived on tight scheduling, minute details and small crises. These were the things that kept you alert, sharp and interested. If her job had been simple, there wouldn't have been much fun to it.

She was also a woman who liked long, lazy baths in mountains of bubbles and big, big beds. These were the things that kept you sane. Juliet felt she'd earned the second after she'd dealt with the first.

While Carlo amused himself in his own way, Juliet spent an hour and a half on the phone, then another hour revising and fine-tuning the next day's itinerary. A print interview had come through and had to be shuffled in. She shuffled. Another paper was sending a reporter and photographer to the book signing. Their names had to be noted and remembered. Juliet noted, circled and committed to memory. The way things were shaping up, they'd be lucky to manage a two-hour breather the next day. Nothing could've pleased her more.

By the time she'd closed her thick, leather-bound notebook, she was more than ready for the tub. The bed, unfortunately, would have to wait. Ten o'clock, she promised herself. By ten, she'd be in bed, snuggled in, curled up and unconscious.

She soaked, designating precisely forty-five minutes for her personal time. In the bath, she didn't plot or plan or estimate. She clicked off the busy, business end of her brain and enjoyed.

Relaxing—it took the first ten minutes to accomplish that completely. Dreaming—she could pretend the white, standard-size tub was luxurious, large and lush. Black marble perhaps and big enough for two. It was a secret ambition of Juliet's to own one like it eventually. The symbol, she felt, of ultimate success. She'd have bristled if anyone had called her goal romantic. Practical, she'd insist. When you worked hard, you needed a place to unwind. This was hers.

Her robe hung on the back of the door—jade green, teasingly brief and silk. Not a luxury as far as she was concerned, but a necessity. When you often had only short snatches to relax, you needed all the help you could get. She considered the robe as much an aid in keeping pace as the bottles of vitamins that lined the counter by the sink. When she traveled, she always took them.

After she'd relaxed and dreamed a bit, she could appreciate soft, hot water against her skin, silky bubbles hissing, steam rising rich with scent.

He'd told her not to change her scent.

Juliet scowled as she felt the muscles in her shoulders tense. Oh no. Deliberately she picked up the tiny cake of hotel soap and rubbed it up and down her arms. Oh no, she wouldn't let Carlo Franconi intrude on her personal time. That was rule number one.

He'd purposely tried to unravel her. He'd succeeded. Yes, he had succeeded, Juliet admitted with a stubborn nod. But that was over now. She wouldn't let it happen again. Her job was to promote his book, not his ego. To promote, she'd go above and beyond the call of duty with her time, her energy and her skill, but not with her emotions.

Franconi wasn't flying back to Rome in three weeks with a smug smile on his face unless it was professionally generated. That instant knife-sharp attraction would be dealt with. Priorities, Juliet mused, were the order of the day. He could add all the American conquests to his list he chose—as long as she wasn't among them.

In any case, he didn't seriously interest her. It was simply that basic, primal urge. Certainly there wasn't any intellect involved. She preferred a different kind of man—steady rather than flashy, sincere rather than charming. That was the kind of man a woman of common sense looked for when the time was right. Juliet judged the time would be right in about three years. By then, she'd have established the structure for her own firm. She'd be financially independent and creatively content. Yes, in three years she'd be ready to think about a serious relationship. That would fit her schedule nicely.

Settled, she decided, and closed her eyes. It was a nice, comfortable word. But the hot water, bubbles and steam didn't relax her any longer. A bit resentful, she released the plug and stood up to let the water drain off her. The wide mirror above the counter and sink was fogged, but only lightly. Through the mist she could see Juliet Trent.

Odd, she thought, how pale and soft and vulnerable a naked woman could look. In her mind, she was strong, practical, even tough. But she could see, in the damp, misty mirror, the fragility, even the wistfulness.

Erotic? Juliet frowned a bit as she told herself she shouldn't be disappointed that her body had been built on slim, practical lines rather than round and lush ones. She should be grateful that her long legs got her where she was going and her narrow hips helped keep her silhouette in a business suit trim and efficient. Erotic would never be a career plus.

Without makeup, her face looked too young, too trusting. Without careful grooming, her hair looked too wild, too passionate.

Fragile, young, passionate. Juliet shook her head. Not qualities for a professional woman. It was fortunate that clothes and cosmetics could play down or play up certain aspects. Grabbing a towel, she wrapped it around herself, then taking another she wiped the steam from the mirror. No more mists, she thought. To succeed you had to see clearly.

With a glance at the tubes and bottles on the counter she began to create the professional Ms. Trent.

Because she hated quiet hotel rooms, Juliet switched on the television as she started to dress. The old Bogart–Bacall movie pleased her and was more relaxing than a dozen bubble baths. She listened to the well-known dialogue while she drew on her smoke-colored stockings. She watched the shimmering restrained passion as she adjusted the straps of a sheer black teddy. While the plot twisted and turned, she zipped on the narrow black dress and knotted the long strand of pearls under her breasts.

Caught up, she sat on the edge of the bed, running a brush through her hair as she watched. She was smiling, absorbed, distracted, but it would've shocked her if anyone had said she was romantic.

When the knock sounded at her door, she glanced at her watch. 7:05. She'd lost fifteen minutes dawdling. To make up for it, Juliet had her shoes on, her earrings clipped and her bag and notebook at hand in twelve seconds flat. She went to the door ready with a greeting and an apology.

A rose. Just one, the color of a young girl's blush. When Carlo handed it to her, she didn't have anything to say at all. Carlo, however, had no problem.

"*Bella.*" He had her hand to his lips before she'd thought to counter the move. "Some women look severe or cold in black. Others…" His survey was long and male, but his smile made it gallant rather than calculating. "On others it simply enhances their femininity. I'm disturbing you?"

"No, no, of course not. I was just—"

"Ah, I know this movie."

Without waiting for an invitation, he breezed past her into the room. The standard, single hotel room didn't seem so impersonal any longer. How could it? He brought life, energy, passion into the air as if it were his mission.

"Yes, I've seen it many times." The two strong faces dominated the screen. Bogart's, creased, heavy-eyed, weary—Bacall's, smooth, steamy and challenging. "*Passione,*" he murmured and made the word seem like honey to be tasted. Incredibly, Juliet found herself swallowing. "A man and a woman can bring many things to each other, but without passion, everything else is tame. *Sì?*"

Juliet recovered herself. Franconi wasn't a man to discuss passion with. The subject wouldn't remain academic for long. "Perhaps." She adjusted her evening bag and her notebook. But she didn't put the rose down. "We've a lot to discuss over dinner, Mr. Franconi. We'd best get started."

With his thumbs still hooked in the pockets of his taupe slacks, he turned his head. Juliet figured hundreds of women had trusted that smile. She wouldn't. With a careless flick, he turned off the television. "Yes, it's time we started."

What did he think of her? Carlo asked himself the question and let the answer come in snatches, twined through the evening.

Lovely. He didn't consider his affection for beautiful women a weakness. He was grateful that Juliet didn't find the need to play down or turn her natural beauty into severity, nor did she exploit it until it was artificial. She'd found a pleasing balance. He could admire that.

She was ambitious, but he admired that as well. Beautiful women without ambition lost his interest quickly.

She didn't trust him. That amused him. As he drank his second glass of Beaujolais, he decided her wariness was a compliment. In his estimation, a woman like Juliet would only be wary of a man if she were attracted in some way.

If he were honest, and he was, he'd admit that most women were attracted to him. It seemed only fair, as he was attracted to them. Short, tall, plump, thin, old or young, he found women a fascination, a delight, an amusement. He respected them, perhaps only as a man who had grown up surrounded by women could do. But respect didn't mean he couldn't enjoy.

He was going to enjoy Juliet.

"*Hello, L.A.* is on first tomorrow." Juliet ran down her notes while Carlo nibbled on pâté. "It's the top-rated morning talk show on the coast, not just in L.A. Liz Marks hosts. She's very personable—not too bubbly. Los Angeles doesn't want bubbly at 8:00 a.m."

"Thank God."

"In any case, she has a copy of the book. It's important that you get the title in a couple of times if she doesn't. You have the full twenty minutes, so it shouldn't be a problem. You'll be autographing at Books, Incorporated on Wilshire Boulevard between one and three." Hastily, she made herself a note to contact the store in the morning for a last check. "You'll want to plug that, but I'll remind you just before airtime. Of course, you'll want to mention that you're beginning a twenty-one-day tour of the country here in California."

"Mmm-hmm. The pâté is quite passable. Would you like some?"

"No, thanks. Just go ahead." She checked off her list and reached for her wine without looking at him. The restaurant was quiet and elegant, but it didn't matter. If they'd been in a loud crowded bar on the Strip, she'd still have gone on with her notes. "Right after the morning show, we go to a radio spot. Then we'll have brunch with a reporter from the *Times*. You've already had an article in the *Trib.* I've got a clipping for you. You'd want to mention your other two books, but concentrate on the new one. It wouldn't hurt to bring up some of the major cities we'll hit. Denver, Dallas, Chicago, New York. Then there's the autographing, a spot on the evening news and dinner with two book reps. The next day—"

"One day at a time," he said easily. "I'll be less likely to snarl at you."

"All right." She closed her notebook and sipped at her wine again. "After all, it's my job to see to the details, yours to sign books and be charming."

He touched his glass to hers. "Then neither of us should have a problem. Being charming is my life."

Was he laughing at himself, she wondered, or at her? "From what I've seen, you excel at it."

"A gift, *cara*." Those dark, deep-set eyes were amused and exciting. "Unlike a skill that's developed and trained."

So, he was laughing at both of them, she realized. It would be both difficult and wise not to like him for it.

When her steak was served, Juliet glanced at it. Carlo, however, studied his veal as though it were a fine old painting. No, Juliet realized after a moment, he studied it as though it were a young, beautiful woman.

"Appearances," he told her, "in food, as in people, are essential." He was smiling at her when he cut into the veal. "And, as in people, they can be deceiving."

Juliet watched him sample the first bite, slowly, his eyes half-closed. She felt an odd chill at the base of her spine. He'd sample a woman the same way, she was certain. Slowly.

"Pleasant," he said after a moment. "No more, no less."

She couldn't prevent the quick smirk as she cut into her steak. "Yours is better of course."

He moved his shoulders. A statement of arrogance. "Of course. Like comparing a pretty young girl with a beautiful woman." When she glanced up he was holding out his fork. Over it, his eyes studied her. "Taste," he invited and the simple word made her blood shiver. "Nothing should ever go untasted, Juliet."

She shrugged, letting him feed her the tiny bite of veal. It was spicy, just bordering on rich and hot on her tongue. "It's good."

"Good, *sì*. Nothing Franconi prepares is ever merely good. Good, I'd pour into the garbage, feed to the dogs in the alley." She laughed, delighting him. "If something isn't special, then it's ordinary."

"True enough." Without realizing it, she slipped out of her shoes. "But then, I suppose I've always looked at food as a basic necessity."

"Necessity?" Carlo shook his head. Though he'd heard such sentiment before, he still considered it a sacrilege. "Oh, *madonna,* you have much to learn. When one knows how to eat, how to appreciate, it's second only to making love. Scents, textures, tastes. To eat only to fill your stomach? Barbaric."

"Sorry." Juliet took another bite of steak. It was tender and cooked well. But it was only a piece of meat. She'd never have considered it sensual or romantic, but simply filling. "Is that why you became a cook? Because you think food's sexy?"

He winced. "Chef, *cara mia.*"

She grinned, showing him for the first time a streak of humor and mischief. "What's the difference?"

"What's the difference between a plow horse and a thoroughbred? Plaster and porcelain?"

Enjoying herself, she touched her tongue to the rim of her glass. "Some might say dollar signs."

"No, no, no, my love. Money is only a result, not a cause. A cook makes hamburgers in a greasy kitchen that smells of onions behind a counter where people squeeze plastic bottles of ketchup. A chef creates…" He gestured, a circle of a hand. "An experience."

She lifted her glass and swept her lashes down, but she didn't hide the smile. "I see."

Though he could be offended by a look when he chose, and be ruthless with the offender, Carlo liked her style. "You're amused. But you haven't tasted Franconi." He waited until her eyes, both wry and wary, lifted to him. "Yet."

He had a talent for turning the simplest statement into something erotic, she observed. It would be a challenge to skirt around him without giving way. "But you haven't told me why you became a chef."

"I can't paint or sculpt. I haven't the patience or the talent to compose sonnets. There are other ways to create, to embrace art."

She saw, with surprise mixed with respect, that he was quite serious. "But paintings, sculpture and poetry remain centuries after they've been created. If you make a soufflé, it's here, then it's gone."

"Then the challenge is to make it again, and again. Art needn't be put behind glass or bronzed, Juliet, merely appreciated. I have a friend…" He thought of Summer Lyndon—no, Summer Cocharan now. "She makes pastries like an angel. When you eat one, you're a king."

"Then is cooking magic or art?"

"Both. Like love. And I think you, Juliet Trent, eat much too little."

She met his look as he'd hoped she would. "I don't believe in overindulgence, Mr. Franconi. It leads to carelessness."

"To indulgence then." He lifted his glass. The smile was back, charming and dangerous. "Carefully."

Anything and everything could go wrong. You had to expect it, anticipate it and avoid it. Juliet knew just how much could be botched in a twenty-minute, live interview at 7:30 a.m. on a Monday. You hoped for the best and made do with the not too bad. Even she didn't expect perfection on the first day of a tour.

It wasn't easy to explain why she was annoyed when she got it.

The morning spot went beautifully. There was no other way to describe it, Juliet decided as she watched Liz Marks talk and laugh with Carlo after the camera stopped taping. If a shrewd operator could be called a natural, Carlo was indeed a natural. During the interview, he'd subtly and completely dominated the show while charmingly blinding his host to it. Twice he'd made the ten-year veteran of morning talk shows giggle like a girl. Once, once, Juliet remembered with astonishment, she'd seen the woman blush.

Yeah. She shifted the strap of her heavy briefcase on her arm. Franconi was a natural. It was bound to make her job easier. She yawned and cursed him.

Juliet always slept well in hotel rooms. *Always.* Except for last night. She might've been able to convince someone else that too much coffee and first-day jitters had kept her awake. But she knew better. She could drink a pot of coffee at ten and fall asleep on command at eleven. Her system was very disciplined. Except for last night.

She'd nearly dreamed of him. If she hadn't shaken herself awake at 2:00 a.m., she would have dreamed of him. That was no way to begin a very important, very long author tour. She told herself now if she had to choose between some silly fantasies and honest fatigue, she'd take the fatigue.

Stifling another yawn, Juliet checked her watch. Liz had her arm tucked through Carlo's and looked as though she'd keep it there unless someone pried her loose. With a sigh, Juliet decided she'd have to be the crowbar.

"Ms. Marks, it was a wonderful show." As she crossed over, Juliet deliberately held out her hand. With obvious reluctance, Liz disengaged herself from Carlo and accepted it.

"Thank you, Miss…"

"Trent," Juliet supplied without a waver.

"Juliet is my publicist," Carlo told Liz, though the two women had been introduced less than an hour earlier. "She guards my schedule."

"Yes, and I'm afraid I'll have to rush Mr. Franconi along. He has a radio spot in a half hour."

"If you must." Juliet was easily dismissed as Liz turned back to Carlo. "You have a delightful way of starting the morning. A pity you won't be in town longer."

"A pity," Carlo agreed and kissed Liz's fingers. Like an old movie, Juliet thought impatiently. All they needed were violins.

"Thank you again, Ms. Marks." Juliet used her most diplomatic smile as she took Carlo's arm and began to lead him out of the studio. After all, she'd very likely need Liz Marks again. "We're in a bit of a hurry," she muttered as they worked their way back to the reception area. The taping was over and she had other fish to fry. "This radio show's one of the top-rated in the city. Since it leans heavily on top forties and classic rock, its audience, at this time of day, falls mainly in the eighteen to thirty-five range. Excellent buying power. That gives us a nice mix with the audience from this morning's show, which is generally in the twenty-five to fifty, primarily female category."

Listening with all apparent respect, Carlo reached the waiting limo first and opened the door himself. "You consider this important?"

"Of course." Because she was distracted by what she thought was a foolish question, Juliet climbed into the limo ahead of him. "We've a solid schedule in L.A." And she didn't see the point in mentioning there were some cities on the tour where they wouldn't be quite so busy. "A morning talk show with a good reputation, a popular radio show, two print interviews, two quick spots on the evening news and the *Simpson Show.*" She said the last with a hint of relish. The *Simpson Show* offset what she was doing to the budget with limos.

"So you're pleased."

"Yes, of course." Digging into her briefcase, she took out her folder to recheck the name of her contact at the radio station.

"Then why do you look so annoyed?"

"I don't know what you're talking about."

"You get a line right...here," he said as he ran a fingertip between her eyebrows. At the touch, Juliet jerked back before she could stop herself. Carlo only cocked his head, watching her. "You may smile and speak in a quiet, polite voice, but that line gives you away."

"I was very pleased with the taping," she said again.

"But?"

All right, she thought, he was asking for it. "Perhaps it annoys me to see a woman making a fool of herself." Juliet stuffed the folder back into her briefcase. "Liz Marks is married, you know."

"Wedding rings are things I try to be immediately aware of," he said with a shrug. "Your instructions were to be charming, weren't they?"

"Perhaps *charm* has a different meaning in Italy."

"As I said, you must come to Rome."

"I suppose you enjoy having women drooling all over you."

He smiled at her, easy, attractive, innocent. "But of course."

A gurgle of laughter bubbled in her throat but she swallowed it. She wouldn't be charmed. "You'll have to deal with some men on this tour as well."

"I promise not to kiss Simpson's fingers."

This time the laughter escaped. For a moment, she relaxed with it, let it come. Carlo saw, too briefly, the youth and energy beneath the discipline. He'd like to have kept her like that longer—laughing, at ease with him, and with herself. It would be a challenge, he mused, to find the right sequence of buttons to push to bring laughter to her eyes more often. He liked challenges—particularly when there was a woman connected to them.

"Juliet." Her name flowed off his tongue in a way only the European male had mastered. "You mustn't worry. Your tidily married Liz only enjoyed a mild flirtation with a man she'll more than than likely never see again. Harmless. Perhaps because of it, she'll find more romance with her husband tonight."

Juliet eyed him a moment in her straight-on, no-

nonsense manner. "You think quite of lot of yourself, don't you?"

He grinned, not sure if he was relieved or if he regretted the fact that he'd never met anyone like her before. "No more than is warranted, *cara.* Anyone who has character leaves a mark on another. Would you like to leave the world without making a ripple?"

No. No, that was one thing she was determined not to do. She sat back determined to hold her own. "I suppose some of us insist on leaving more ripples than others."

He nodded. "I don't like to do anything in a small way."

"Be careful, Mr. Franconi, or you'll begin to believe your own image."

The limo had stopped, but before Juliet could scoot toward the door, Carlo had her hand. When she looked at him this time, she didn't see the affable, amorous Italian chef, but a man of power. A man, she realized, who was well aware of how far it could take him.

She didn't move, but wondered how many other women had seen the steel beneath the silk.

"I don't need imagery, Juliet." His voice was soft, charming, beautiful. She heard the razor-blade cut beneath it. "Franconi is Franconi. Take me for what you see, or go to the devil."

Smoothly, he climbed from the limo ahead of her, turned and took her hand, drawing her out with him. It was a move that was polite, respectful, even ordinary. It was a move, Juliet realized, that expressed their positions. Man to woman. The moment she stood on the curb, she removed her hand.

With two shows and a business brunch under their belts, Juliet left Carlo in the bookstore, already swamped with women crowded in line for a glimpse at and a few words with Carlo Franconi. They'd handled the reporter and photographer already, and a man like Franconi wouldn't need her help with a crowd of women. Armed with change and her credit card, she went to find a pay phone.

For the first forty-five minutes, she spoke with her assistant in New York, filling her pad with times, dates and names while L.A. traffic whisked by outside the phone booth. As a bead of sweat trickled down her back, she wondered if she'd chosen the hottest corner in the city.

Denver still didn't look as promising as she'd hoped, but Dallas… Juliet caught her bottom lip between her teeth as she wrote. Dallas was going to be fabulous. She might need to double her daily dose of vitamins to get through that twenty-four-hour stretch, but it would be fabulous.

After breaking her connection with New York, Juliet dialed her first contact in San Francisco. Ten minutes later, she was clenching her teeth. No, her contact at the department store couldn't help coming down with a virus. She was sorry, genuinely sorry he was ill. But did he have to get sick without leaving someone behind with a couple of working brain cells?

The young girl with the squeaky voice knew about the cooking demonstration. Yes, she knew all about it and wasn't it going to be fun? Extension cords? Oh my, she really didn't know a thing about that. Maybe she could ask someone in maintenance. A table—chairs? Well golly, she supposed she could get something, if it was really necessary.

Juliet was reaching in her bag for her purse-size container of aspirin before it was over. The way it looked now, she'd have to get to the department store at least two hours before the demonstration to make sure everything was taken care of. That meant juggling the schedule.

After completing her calls, Juliet left the corner phone booth, aspirin in hand, and headed back to the bookstore, hoping they could give her a glass of water and a quiet corner.

No one noticed her. If she'd just crawled in from the desert on her belly, no one would have noticed her. The small, rather elegant bookstore was choked with laughter. No bookseller stood behind the counter. There was a magnet in the left-hand corner of the room. Its name was Franconi.

It wasn't just women this time, Juliet noticed with interest. There were men sprinkled in the crowd. Some of them might have been dragged along by their wives, but they were having a time of it now. It looked like a cocktail party, minus the cigarette smoke and empty glasses.

She couldn't even see him, Juliet realized as she worked her way toward the back of the store. He was surrounded, enveloped. Jingling the aspirin in her hand, she was glad she could find a little corner by herself. Perhaps he got all the glory, she mused. But she wouldn't trade places with him.

Glancing at her watch, she noted he had another hour and wondered whether he could dwindle the crowd down in the amount of time. She wished vaguely for a stool, dropped the aspirin in the pocket of her skirt and began to browse.

"Fabulous, isn't he?" Juliet heard someone murmur on the other side of a book rack.

"God, yes. I'm so glad you talked me into coming."

"What're friends for?"

"I thought I'd be bored to death. I feel like a kid at a rock concert. He's got such…"

"Style," the other voice supplied. "If a man like that ever walked into my life, he wouldn't walk out again."

Curious, Juliet walked around the stacks. She wasn't sure what she expected—young housewives, college students. What she saw were two attractive women in their thirties, both dressed in sleek professional suits.

"I've got to get back to the office." One woman checked a trim little Rolex watch. "I've got a meeting at three."

"I've got to get back to the courthouse."

Both women tucked their autographed books into leather briefcases.

"How come none of the men I date can kiss my hand without making it seem like a staged move in a one-act play?"

"Style. It all has to do with style."

With this observation, or complaint, the two women disappeared into the crowd.

At three-fifteen, he was still signing, but the crowd had thinned enough that Juliet could see him. Style, she was forced to agree, he had. No one who came up to his table, book in hand, was given a quick signature, practiced smile and brush-off. He talked to them. Enjoyed them, Juliet corrected, whether it was a grandmother who smelled of lavender or a young woman with a toddler on her hip. How did he know the right thing to say to each one of them, she wondered, that made them leave the table with a laugh or a smile or a sigh?

First day of the tour, she reminded herself. She wondered if he could manage to keep himself up to this level for three weeks. Time would tell, she decided and calculated she could give him another fifteen minutes before she began to ease him out the door.

Even with the half-hour extension, it wasn't easy. Juliet began to see the pattern she was certain would set the pace of the tour. Carlo would charm and delight, and she would play the less attractive role of drill sergeant. That's what she was paid for, Juliet reminded herself as she began to smile, chat and urge people toward the door. By four there were only a handful of stragglers. With apologies and an iron grip, Juliet disengaged Carlo.

"That went very well," she began, nudging him onto the street. "One of the booksellers told me they'd nearly sold out. Makes you wonder how much pasta's going to be cooked in L.A. tonight. Consider this just one more triumph today."

"Grazie."

"*Prego.* However, we won't always have the leeway to run an hour over," she told him as the door of the limo shut behind her. "It would help if you try to keep an eye on the time and pick up the pace say half an hour before finishing time. You've got an hour and fifteen minutes before airtime—"

"Fine." Pushing a button, Carlo instructed the driver to cruise.

"But—"

"Even I need to unwind," he told her, then opened up a small built-in cabinet to reveal the bar. "Cognac," he decided and poured two glasses without asking. "You've had two hours to window-shop and browse." Leaning back, he stretched out his legs.

Juliet thought of the hour and a half she'd spent on

the phone, then the time involved in easing customers along. She'd been on her feet for two and a half hours straight, but she said nothing. The cognac went down smooth and warm.

"The spot on the news should run four, four and a half minutes. It doesn't seem like much time, but you'd be surprised how much you can cram in. Be sure to mention the book title, and the autographing and demonstration at the college tomorrow afternoon. The sensual aspect of food, cooking and eating's a great angle. If you'll—"

"Would you care to do the interview for me?" he asked so politely she glanced up.

So, he could be cranky, she mused. "You handle interviews beautifully, Mr. Franconi, but—"

"Carlo." Before she could open her notebook, he had his hand on her wrist. "It's Carlo, and put the damn notes away for ten minutes. Tell me, my very organized Juliet Trent, why are we here together?"

She started to move her hand but his grip was firmer than she'd thought. For the second time, she got the full impression of power, strength and determination. "To publicize your book."

"Today went well, *sì?*"

"Yes, so far—"

"Today went well," he said again and began to annoy her with the frequency of his interruptions.

"I'll go on this local news show, talk for a few minutes, then have this necessary business dinner when I would much rather have a bottle of wine and a steak in my room. With you. Alone. Then I could see you without your proper little business suit and your proper little business manner."

She wouldn't permit herself to shudder. She wouldn't permit herself to react in any way. "Business is what we're here for. It's all I'm interested in."

"That may be." His agreement was much too easy. In direct contrast, he moved his hand to the back of her neck, gently, but not so gently she could move aside. "But we have an hour before business begins again. Don't lecture me on timetables."

The limo smelled of leather, she realized all at once. Of leather and wealth and Carlo. As casually as possible, she sipped from her glass. "Timetables, as you pointed out yourself this morning, are part of my job."

"You have an hour off," he told her, lifting a brow before she could speak. "So relax. Your feet hurt, so take your shoes off and drink your cognac." He set down his own drink, then moved her briefcase to the floor so there was nothing between them. "Relax," he said again but wasn't displeased that she'd stiffened. "I don't intend to make love with you in the back of a car. This time." He smiled as temper flared in her eyes because he'd seen doubt and excitement as well. "One day, one day soon, I'll find the proper moment for that, the proper place, the proper mood."

He leaned closer, so that he could just feel her breath flutter on his lips. She'd swipe at him now, he knew, if he took the next step. He might enjoy the battle. The color that ran along her cheekbones hadn't come from a tube or pot, but from passion. The look in her eyes was very close to a dare. She expected him to move an inch closer, to press her back against the seat with his mouth firm on hers. She was waiting for him, poised, ready.

He smiled while his lips did no more than hover

until he knew the tension in her had built to match the tension in him. He let his gaze shift down to her mouth so that he could imagine the taste, the texture, the sweetness. Her chin stayed lifted even as he brushed a thumb over it.

He didn't care to do the expected. In a long, easy move, he leaned back, crossed his feet at the ankles and closed his eyes.

"Take off your shoes," he said again. "My schedule and yours should merge very well."

Then, to her astonishment, he was asleep. Not feigning it, she realized, but sound asleep, as if he'd just flicked a switch.

With a click, she set her half-full glass down and folded her arms. Angry, she thought. Damn right she was angry because he hadn't kissed her. Not because she wanted him to, she told herself as she stared out the tinted window. But because he'd denied her the opportunity to show her claws.

She was beginning to think she'd love drawing some Italian blood.

Chapter 3

Their bags were packed and in the limo. As a precaution, Juliet had given Carlo's room a quick, last-minute going-over to make sure he hadn't left anything behind. She still remembered being on the road with a mystery writer who'd forgotten his toothbrush eight times on an eight-city tour. A quick look was simpler than a late-night search for a drugstore.

Checkout at the hotel had gone quickly and without any last-minute hitches. To her relief, the charges on Carlo's room bill had been light and reasonable. Her road budget might just hold. With a minimum of confusion, they'd left the Wilshire. Juliet could only hope check-in at the airport, then at the hotel in San Francisco would go as well.

She didn't want to think about the *Simpson Show.*

A list of demographics wasn't necessary here. She knew Carlo had spent enough time in the States off and on to know how important his brief demonstration on the proper way to prepare *biscuit tortoni* and his ten minutes on the air would be. It was the top-rated nighttime show in the country and had been for fifteen years. Bob Simpson was an American institution. A few minutes on his show could boost the sale of books even in the most remote areas. Or it could kill it.

And boy, oh boy, she thought, with a fresh gurgle of excitement, did it look impressive to have the *Simpson Show* listed on her itinerary. She offered a last-minute prayer that Carlo wouldn't blow it.

She checked the little freezer backstage to be certain the dessert Carlo had prepared that afternoon was in place and ready. The concoction had to freeze for four hours, so they'd play the before-and-after game for the viewers. He'd make it up on the air, then *voilà,* they'd produce the completed frozen dessert within minutes.

Though Carlo had already gone over the procedure, the tools and ingredients with the production manager and the director, Juliet went over them all again. The whipped cream was chilling and so far none of the crew had pilfered any macaroons. The brand of dry sherry Carlo had insisted on was stored and ready. No one had broken the seal for a quick sample.

Juliet nearly believed she could whip up the fancy frozen dessert herself if necessary and only thanked God she wouldn't have to give a live culinary demonstration in front of millions of television viewers.

He didn't seem to be feeling any pressure, she thought as they settled in the green room. No, he'd already given the little half-dressed blonde on the sofa a big smile and offered her a cup of coffee from the available machine.

Coffee? Even for Hollywood, it took a wild imagination to consider the contents of the pot coffee. Juliet had taken one sip of what tasted like lukewarm mud and set the cup aside.

The little blonde was apparently a new love interest on one of the popular nighttime soaps, and she was jittery with nerves. Carlo sat down on the sofa beside her and began chatting away as though they were old friends. By the time the green room door opened again, she was giggling.

The green room itself was beige—pale, unattractive beige and cramped. The air-conditioning worked, but miserably. Still Juliet knew how many of the famous and near-famous had sat in that dull little room chewing their nails. Or taking quick sips from a flask.

Carlo had exchanged the dubious coffee for plain water and was sprawled on the sofa with one arm tossed over the back. He looked as easy as a man entertaining in his own home. Juliet wondered why she hadn't tossed any antacids in her bag.

She made a pretense of rechecking the schedule while Carlo charmed the rising star and the *Simpson Show* murmured away on the twenty-five-inch color console across the room.

Then the monkey walked in. Juliet glanced up and saw the long-armed, tuxedoed chimpanzee waddle in with his hand caught in that of a tall thin man with harassed eyes and a nervous grin. Feeling a bit nervous herself, Juliet looked over at Carlo. He nodded to both newcomers, then went back to the blonde without missing a beat. Even as Juliet told herself to relax, the chimp grinned, threw back his head and let out a long, loud announcement.

The blonde giggled, but looked as though she'd cut and run if the chimp came one step closer—tux or no tux.

"Behave, Butch." The thin man cleared his throat as he swept his gaze around the room. "Butch just finished a picture last week," he explained to the room in general. "He's feeling a little restless."

With a jiggle of the sequins that covered her, the blonde walked to the door when her name was announced. With some satisfaction, Carlo noted that she wasn't nearly as edgy as she'd been when he'd sat down. She turned and gave him a toothy smile. "Wish me luck, darling."

"The best."

To Juliet's disgust, the blonde blew him a kiss as she sailed out.

The thin man seemed to relax visibly. "That's a relief. Blondes make Butch overexcited."

"I see." Juliet thought of her own hair that could be considered blond or brown depending on the whim. Hopefully Butch would consider it brown and unstimulating.

"But where's the lemonade?" The man's nerves came back in full force. "They know Butch wants lemonade before he goes on the air. Calms him down."

Juliet bit the tip of her tongue to hold back a snicker. Carlo and Butch were eyeing each other with a kind of tolerant understanding. "He seems calm enough," Carlo ventured.

"Bundle of nerves," the man disagreed. "I'll never be able to get him on camera."

"I'm sure it's just an oversight." Because she was used to soothing panic, Juliet smiled. "Maybe you should ask one of the pages."

"I'll do that." The man patted Butch on the head and went back through the door.

"But—" Juliet half rose, then sat again. The chimp stood in the middle of the room, resting his knuckles on the floor. "I'm not sure he should've left Cheetah."

"Butch," Carlo corrected. "I think he's harmless enough." He sent the chimp a quick grin. "He certainly has an excellent tailor."

Juliet looked over to see the chimp grinning and winking. "Is he twitching," she asked Carlo, "or is he flirting with me?"

"Flirting, if he's a male of any taste," he mused. "And, as I said, his tailoring is quite good. What do you say, Butch? You find my Juliet attractive?"

Butch threw back his head and let out a series of sounds Juliet felt could be taken either way.

"See? He appreciates a beautiful woman."

Appreciating the ridiculous, Juliet laughed. Whether he was attracted to the sound or simply felt it was time he made his move, Butch bowlegged his way over to her. Still grinning, he put his hand on Juliet's bare knee. This time, she was certain he winked.

"I never make so obvious a move on first acquaintance," Carlo observed.

"Some women prefer the direct approach." Deciding he was harmless, Juliet smiled down at Butch. "He reminds me of someone." She sent Carlo a mild look. "It must be that ingratiating grin." Before she'd finished speaking, Butch climbed into her lap and wrapped one of his long arms around her. "He's kind of sweet." With another laugh, she looked down into the chimp's face. "I think he has your eyes, Carlo."

"Ah, Juliet, I think you should—"

"Though his might be more intelligent."

"Oh, I think he's smart, all right." Carlo coughed into

his hand as he watched the chimp's busy fingers. "Juliet, if you'd—"

"Of course he's smart, he's in movies." Enjoying herself, Juliet watched the chimp grin up at her. "Have I seen any of your films, Butch?"

"I wouldn't be surprised if they're blue."

She tickled Butch under the chin. "Really, Carlo, how crude."

"Just a guess." He let his gaze run over her. "Tell me Juliet, do you feel a draft?"

"No. I'd say it's entirely too warm in here. This poor thing is all wrapped up in a tux." She clucked at Butch and he clacked his teeth at her.

"Juliet, do you believe people can reveal their personalities by the clothes they wear? Send signals, if you understand what I mean."

"Hmm?" Distracted, she shrugged and helped Butch straighten his tie. "I suppose so."

"I find it interesting that you wear pink silk under such a prim blouse."

"I beg your pardon?"

"An observation, *mi amore.*" He let his gaze wander down again. "Just an observation."

Sitting very still, Juliet moved only her head. In a moment, her mouth was as open as her blouse. The monkey with the cute face and excellent tailor had nimbly undone every one of the buttons.

Carlo gave Butch a look of admiration. "I must ask him how he perfected that technique."

"Why you son of a—"

"Not me." Carlo put a hand to his heart. "I'm an innocent bystander."

Juliet rose abruptly, dumping the chimp onto the floor.

As she ducked into the adjoining restroom, she heard the laughter of two males—one a chimp, the other a rat.

Juliet took the ride to the airport where they would leave for San Diego in excruciatingly polite silence.

"Come now, *cara,* the show went well. Not only was the title mentioned three times, but there was that nice close-up of the book. My *tortoni* was a triumph, and they liked my anecdote on cooking the long, sensual Italian meal."

"You're a real prince with anecdotes," she murmured.

"*Amore,* it was the monkey who tried to undress you, not I." He gave a long, self-satisfied sigh. He couldn't remember when he'd enjoyed a...demonstration quite so much. "If I had, we'd have missed the show altogether."

"You just had to tell that story on the air, didn't you?" She sent him a cool, killing look. "Do you know how many millions of people watch that show?"

"It was a good story." In the dim light of the limo, she saw the gleam in his eyes. "Most millions of people like good stories."

"Everyone I work with will have seen that show." She found her jaw was clenched and deliberately relaxed it. "Not only did you just—just *sit* there and let that happy-fingered little creature half strip me, but then you broadcast it on national television."

"*Madonna,* you'll remember I did try to warn you."

"I remember nothing of the kind."

"But you were so enchanted with Butch," he continued. "I confess, it was difficult not to be enchanted myself." He let his gaze roam down to her tidily buttoned blouse. "You've lovely skin, Juliet. Perhaps I was momentarily distracted. I throw myself, a simple, weak man, on your mercy."

"Oh, shut up." She folded her arms and stared straight ahead, not speaking again until the driver pulled to the curb at their airline.

Juliet pulled her carry-on bag out of the trunk. She knew the chance was always there that the bags could be lost—sent to San Jose while she went to San Diego—so she always carried her absolute essentials with her. She handed over both her ticket and Carlo's so the check-in could get under way while she paid off the driver. It made her think of her budget. She'd managed to justify limo service in L.A., but it would be cabs and rented cars from here on. Goodbye glamour, she thought as she pocketed her receipt. Hello reality.

"No, this I'll carry."

She turned to see Carlo indicate his leather-bound box of about two feet in length, eight inches in width. "You're better off checking something that bulky."

"I never check my tools." He slung a flight bag over his shoulder and picked up the box by its handle.

"Suit yourself," she said with a shrug and moved through the automatic doors with him. Fatigue was creeping in, she realized, and she hadn't had to prepare any intricate desserts. If he were human, he'd be every bit as weary as she. He might annoy her in a dozen ways, but he didn't gripe. Juliet bit back a sigh. "We've a half hour before they'll begin boarding. Would you like a drink?"

He gave her an easy smile. "A truce?"

She returned it despite herself. "No, a drink."

"Okay."

They found a dark, crowded lounge and worked their

way through to a table. She watched Carlo maneuver his box, with some difficulty, around people, over chairs and ultimately under their table. "What's in there?"

"Tools," he said again. "Knives, properly weighted, stainless-steel spatulas of the correct size and balance. My own cooking oil and vinegar. Other essentials."

"You're going to lug oil and vinegar through airport terminals from coast to coast?" With a shake of her head, she glanced up at a waitress. "Vodka and grapefruit juice."

"Brandy. Yes," he said, giving his attention back to Juliet after he'd dazzled the waitress with a quick smile. "Because there's no brand on the American market to compare with my own." He picked up a peanut from the bowl on the table. "There's no brand on any market to compare with my own."

"You could still check it," she pointed out. "After all, you check your shirts and ties."

"I don't trust my tools to the hands of baggage carriers." He popped the peanut into his mouth. "A tie is a simple thing to replace, even a thing to become bored with. But an excellent whisk is entirely different. Once I teach you to cook, you'll understand."

"You've got as much chance teaching me to cook as you do flying to San Diego without the plane. Now, you know you'll be giving a demonstration of preparing linguini and clam sauce on *A.M. San Diego.* The show airs at eight, so we'll have to be at the studio at six to get things started."

As far as he could see, the only civilized cooking to be done at that hour would be a champagne breakfast for two. "Why do Americans insist on rising at dawn to watch television?"

"I'll take a poll and find out," she said absently. "In

the meantime, you'll make up one dish that we'll set aside, exactly as we did tonight. On the air you'll be going through each stage of preparation, but of course we don't have enough time to finish—that's why we need the first dish. Now, for the good news." She sent a quick smile to the waitress as their drinks were served. "There's been a bit of a mix-up at the studio, so we'll have to bring the ingredients along ourselves. I need you to give me a list of what you'll need. Once I see you settled into the hotel, I'll run out and pick them up. There's bound to be an all-night market."

In his head, he went over the ingredients for his *linguini con vongole biance.* True, the American market would have some of the necessities, but he considered himself fortunate that he had a few of his own in the case at his feet. The clam sauce was his specialty, not to be taken lightly.

"Is shopping for groceries at midnight part of a publicist's job?"

She smiled at him. Carlo thought it was not only lovely, but perhaps the first time she'd smiled at him and meant it. "On the road, anything that needs to be done is the publicist's job. So, if you'll run through the ingredients, I'll write them down."

"Not necessary." He swirled and sipped his brandy. "I'll go with you."

"You need your sleep." She was already rummaging for a pencil. "Even with a quick nap on the plane you're only going to get about five hours."

"So are you," he pointed out. When she started to speak again, he lifted his brow in that strange silent way he had of interrupting. "Perhaps I don't trust an amateur to pick out my clams."

Juliet watched him as she drank. Or perhaps he was a gentleman, she mused. Despite his reputation with women, and a healthy dose of vanity, he was one of that rare breed of men who knew how to be considerate of women without patronizing them. She decided to forgive him for Butch after all.

"Drink up, Franconi." And she toasted him, perhaps in friendship. "We've a plane to catch."

"*Salute.*" He lifted his glass to her.

They didn't argue again until they were on the plane.

Grumbling only a little, Juliet helped him stow his fancy box of tools under the seat. "It's a short flight." She checked her watch and calculated the shopping would indeed go beyond midnight. She'd have to take some of the vile-tasting brewer's yeast in the morning. "I'll see you when we land."

He took her wrist when she would have gone past him. "Where are you going?"

"To my seat."

"You don't sit here?" He pointed to the seat beside him.

"No, I'm in coach." Impatient, she had to shift to let another oncoming passenger by.

"Why?"

"Carlo, I'm blocking the aisle."

"Why are you in coach?"

She let out a sigh of a parent instructing a stubborn child. "Because the publisher is more than happy to spring for a first-class ticket for a bestselling author and celebrity. There's a different style for publicists. It's called coach." Someone bumped a briefcase against her hip. Damn if she wouldn't have a bruise. "Now if you'd let me go, I could stop being battered and go sit down."

"First class is almost empty," he pointed out. "It's a simple matter to upgrade your ticket."

She managed to pull her arm away. "Don't buck the system, Franconi."

"I always buck the system," he told her as she walked down the aisle to her seat. Yes, he did like the way she moved.

"Mr. Franconi." A flight attendant beamed at him. "May I get you a drink after takeoff?"

"What's your white wine?"

When she told him he settled into his seat. A bit pedestrian, he thought, but not entirely revolting. "You noticed the young woman I was speaking with. The honey-colored hair and the stubborn chin."

Her smile remained bright and helpful though she thought it was a shame that he had his mind on another woman. "Of course, Mr. Franconi."

"She'll have a glass of wine, with my compliments."

Juliet would have considered herself fortunate to have an aisle seat if the man beside her hadn't already been sprawled out and snoring. Travel was so glamorous, she thought wryly as she slipped her toes out of her shoes. Wasn't she lucky to have another flight to look forward to the very next night?

Don't complain, Juliet, she warned herself. When you have your own agency, you can send someone else on the down-and-dirty tours.

The man beside her snored through takeoff. On the other side of the aisle a woman held a cigarette in one hand and a lighter in the other in anticipation of the No Smoking sign blinking off. Juliet took out her pad and began to work.

"Miss?"

Stifling a yawn, Juliet glanced up at the flight attendant. "I'm sorry, I didn't order a drink."

"With Mr. Franconi's compliments."

Juliet accepted the wine as she looked up toward first class. He was sneaky, she told herself. Trying to get under her defenses by being nice. She let her notebook close as she sighed and sat back.

It was working.

She barely finished the wine before touchdown, but it had relaxed her. Relaxed her enough, she realized, that all she wanted to do was find a soft bed and a dark room. In an hour—or two, she promised herself and gathered up her flight bag and briefcase.

She found Carlo was waiting for her in first class with a very young, very attractive flight attendant. Neither of them seemed the least bit travel weary.

"Ah, Juliet, Deborah knows of a marvelous twenty-four-hour market where we can find everything we need."

Juliet looked at the willowy brunette and managed a smile. "How convenient."

He took the flight attendant's hand and, inevitably Juliet thought, kissed it. *"Arrivederci."*

"Don't waste time, do you?" Juliet commented the moment they deplaned.

"Every moment lived is a moment to be enjoyed."

"What a quaint little sentiment." She shifted her bag and aimed for baggage claim. "You should have it tattooed."

"Where?"

She didn't bother to look at his grin. "Where it would be most attractive, naturally."

They had to wait longer than she liked for their luggage, and by then the relaxing effects of the wine had worn off. There was business to be seen to. Because he enjoyed watching her in action, Carlo let her see to it.

She secured a cab, tipped the skycap and gave the driver the name of the hotel. Scooting in beside Carlo, she caught his grin. "Something funny?"

"You're so efficient, Juliet."

"Is that a compliment or an insult?"

"I never insult women." He said it so simply, she was absolutely certain it was true. Unlike Juliet, he was completely relaxed and not particularly sleepy. "If this was Rome, we'd go to a dark little café, drink heavy red wine and listen to American music."

She closed her window because the air was damp and chilly. "The tour interfering with your night life?"

"So far I find myself enjoying the stimulating company."

"Tomorrow you're going to find yourself worked to a frazzle."

Carlo thought of his background and smiled. At nine, he'd spent the hours between school and supper washing dishes and mopping up kitchens. At fifteen he'd waited tables and spent his free time learning of spices and sauces. In Paris he'd combined long, hard study with work as an assistant chef. Even now, his restaurant and clients had him keeping twelve-hour days. Not all of his background was in the neatly typed bio Juliet had in her briefcase.

"I don't mind work, as long as it interests me. I think you're the same."

"I have to work," she corrected. "But it's easier when you enjoy it."

"You're more successful when you enjoy it. It shows with you. Ambition, Juliet, without a certain joy, is cold, and when achieved leaves a flat taste."

"But I am ambitious."

"Oh, yes." He turned to look at her, starting off flutters she'd thought herself too wise to experience. "But you're not cold."

For a moment, she thought she'd be better off if he were wrong. "Here's the hotel." She turned from him, relieved to deal with details. "We need you to wait," she instructed the driver. "We'll be going out again as soon as we check in. The hotel has a lovely view of the bay, I'm told." She walked into the lobby with Carlo as the bellboy dealt with their luggage. "It's a shame we won't have time to enjoy it. Franconi and Trent," she told the desk clerk.

The lobby was quiet and empty. Oh, the lucky people who were sleeping in their beds, she thought and pushed at a strand of hair that had come loose.

"We'll be checking out first thing tomorrow, and we won't be able to come back, so be sure you don't leave anything behind in your room."

"But of course you'll check anyway."

She sent him a sidelong look as she signed the form. "Just part of the service." She pocketed her key. "The luggage can be taken straight up." Discreetly, she handed the bellboy a folded bill. "Mr. Franconi and I have an errand."

"Yes, ma'am."

"I like that about you." To Juliet's surprise, Carlo linked arms with her as they walked back outside.

"What?"

"Your generosity. Many people would've slipped out without tipping the bellboy."

She shrugged. "Maybe it's easier to be generous when it's not your money."

"Juliet." He opened the door to the waiting cab and gestured her in. "You're intelligent enough. Couldn't you—how is it—stiff the bellboy then write the tip down on your expense account?"

"Five dollars isn't worth being dishonest."

"Nothing's worth being dishonest." He gave the driver the name of the market and settled back. "Instinct tells me if you tried to tell a lie—a true lie—your tongue would fall out."

"Mr. Franconi." She planted the tongue in question in her cheek. "You forget, I'm in public relations. If I didn't lie, I'd be out of a job."

"A true lie," he corrected.

"Isn't that a contradiction in terms?"

"Perhaps you're too young to know the variety of truths and lies. Ah, you see? This is why I'm so fond of your country." Carlo leaned out the window as they approached the big, lighted all-night market. "In America, you want cookies at midnight, you can buy cookies at midnight. Such practicality."

"Glad to oblige. Wait here," she instructed the driver, then climbed out opposite Carlo. "I hope you know what you need. I'd hate to get into the studio at dawn and find I had to run out and buy whole peppercorns or something."

"Franconi knows linguini." He swung an arm around her shoulder and drew her close as they walked inside. "Your first lesson, my love."

He led her first to the seafood section where he clucked and muttered and rejected and chose until he had the proper number of clams for two dishes. She'd seen women give as much time and attention to choosing an engagement ring.

Juliet obliged him by pushing the cart as he walked along beside her, looking at everything. And touching. Cans, boxes, bottles—she waited as he picked up, examined and ran his long artist's fingers over the labels as he read every ingredient. Somewhat amused, she watched his diamond wink in the fluorescent light.

"Amazing what they put in this prepackaged garbage," he commented as he dropped a box back on the shelf.

"Careful, Franconi, you're talking about my staple diet."

"You should be sick."

"Prepackaged food's freed the American woman from the kitchen."

"And destroyed a generation of taste buds." He chose his spices carefully and without haste. He opened three brands of oregano and sniffed before he settled on one. "I tell you, Juliet, I admire your American convenience, its practicality, but I would rather shop in Rome where I can walk along the stalls and choose vegetables just out of the ground, fish fresh from the sea. Everything isn't in a can, like the music."

He didn't miss an aisle, but Juliet forgot her fatigue in fascination. She'd never seen anyone shop like Carlo Franconi. It was like strolling through a museum with an art student. He breezed by the flour, scowling at each sack. She was afraid for a moment he'd rip one open and test the contents. "This is a good brand?"

Juliet figured she bought a two-pound bag of flour about once a year. "Well, my mother always used this, but—"

"Good. Always trust a mother."

"She's a dreadful cook."

Carlo set the flour firmly in the basket. "She's a mother."

"An odd sentiment from a man no mother can trust."

"For mothers, I have the greatest respect. I have one myself. Now, we need garlic, mushrooms, peppers. Fresh."

Carlo walked along the stalls of vegetables, touching, squeezing and sniffing. Cautious, Juliet looked around for clerks, grateful they'd come at midnight rather than midday. "Carlo, you really aren't supposed to handle everything quite so much."

"If I don't handle, how do I know what's good and what's just pretty?" He sent her a quick grin over his shoulder. "I told you, food is much like a woman. They put mushrooms in this box with wrap over it." Disgusted, he tore the wrapping off before Juliet could stop him.

"Carlo! You can't open it."

"I want only what I want. You can see, some are too small, too skimpy." Patiently, he began to pick out the mushrooms that didn't suit him.

"Then we'll throw out what you don't want when we get back to the hotel." Keeping an eye out for the night manager, she began to put the discarded mushrooms back in the box. "Buy two boxes if you need them."

"It's a waste. You'd waste your money?"

"The publisher's money," she said quickly, as she put the broken box into the basket. "He's glad to waste it. Thrilled."

He paused for a moment, then shook his head. "No, no, I can't do it." But when he started to reach into the basket, Juliet moved and blocked his way.

"Carlo, if you break open another package, we're going to be arrested."

"Better to go to jail than to buy mushrooms that will do me no good in the morning."

She grinned at him and stood firm. "No, it's not."

He ran a fingertip over her lips before she could react. "For you, then, but against my better judgment."

"*Grazie.* Do you have everything now?"

His gaze followed the path his finger had traced just as slowly. "No."

"Well, what next?"

He stepped closer and because she hadn't expected it, she found herself trapped between him and the grocery cart. "Tonight is for first lessons," he murmured then ran his hands along either side of her face.

She should laugh. Juliet told herself it was ludicrous that he'd make a pass at her under the bright lights of the vegetable section of an all-night market. Carlo Franconi, a man who'd made seduction as much an art as his cooking, wouldn't choose such a foolish setting.

But she saw what was in his eyes, and she didn't laugh.

Some women, he thought as he felt her skin soft and warm under his hands, were made to be taught slowly. Very slowly. Some women were born knowing; others were born wondering.

With Juliet, he would take time and care because he understood. Or thought he did.

She didn't resist, but her lips had parted in surprise. He touched his to hers gently, not in question, but with patience. Her eyes had already given him the answer.

He didn't hurry. It didn't matter to him where they were, that the lights were bright and the music manufactured. It only mattered that he explore the tastes that waited for him. So he tasted again, without pressure. And again.

She found she was bracing herself against the cart

with her fingers wrapped around the metal. Why didn't she walk away? Why didn't she just brush him aside and stalk out of the store? He wasn't holding her there. On her face his hands were light, clever but not insistent. She could move. She could go. She should.

She didn't.

His thumbs trailed under her chin, tracing there. He felt the pulse, rapid and jerky, and kept his hold easy. He meant to keep it so, but even he hadn't guessed her taste would be so unique.

Neither of them knew who took the next step. Perhaps they took it together. His mouth wasn't so light on hers any longer, nor was hers so passive. They met, triumphantly, and clung.

Her fingers weren't wrapped around the cart now, but gripping his shoulders, holding him closer. Their bodies fit. Perfectly. It should have warned her. Giving without thought was something she never did, until now. In giving, she took, but she never thought to balance the ledger.

His mouth was warm, full. His hands never left her face, but they were firm now. She couldn't have walked away so easily. She wouldn't have walked away at all.

He'd thought he had known everything there was to expect from a woman—fire, ice, temptation. But a lesson was being taught to both. Had he ever felt this warmth before? This kind of sweetness? No, because if he had, he'd remember. No tastes, no sensations ever experienced were forgotten.

He knew what it was to desire a woman—many women—but he hadn't known what it was to crave. For a moment, he filled himself with the sensation. He wouldn't forget.

But he knew that a cautious man takes a step back and a second breath before he steps off a cliff. With a murmur in his own language, he did.

Shaken, Juliet gripped the cart again for balance. Cursing herself for an idiot, she waited for her breath to even out.

"Very nice," Carlo said quietly and ran a finger along her cheek. "Very nice, Juliet."

An eighties woman, she reminded herself as her heart thudded. Strong, independent, sophisticated. "I'm so glad you approve."

He took her hand before she could slam the cart down the aisle. Her skin was still warm, he noted, her pulse still unsteady. If they'd been alone… Perhaps it was best this way. For now. "It isn't a matter of approval, *cara mia,* but of appreciation."

"From now on, just appreciate me for my work, okay?" A jerk, and she freed herself of him and shoved the cart away. Without regard for the care he'd taken in selecting them, Juliet began to drop the contents of the cart on the conveyor belt at checkout.

"You didn't object," he reminded her. He'd needed to find his balance as well, he realized. Now he leaned against the cart and gave her a cocky grin.

"I didn't want a scene."

He took the peppers from the basket himself before she could wound them. "Ah, you're learning about lies."

When her head came up, he was surprised her eyes didn't bore right through him. "You wouldn't know truth if you fell into it."

"Darling, mind the mushrooms," he warned her as she swung the package onto the belt. "We don't want them bruised. I've a special affection for them now."

She swore at him, loudly enough that the checker's eyes widened. Carlo continued to grin and thought about lesson two.

He thought they should have it soon. Very soon.

Chapter 4

There were times when you knew everything could go wrong, should go wrong, and probably would go wrong, but somehow it didn't. Then there were the other times.

Perhaps Juliet was grouchy because she'd spent another restless night when she couldn't afford to lose any sleep. That little annoyance she could lay smack at Carlo's door, even though it didn't bring any satisfaction. But even if she'd been rested and cheerful, the ordeal at Gallegher's Department Store would have had her steaming. With a good eight hours' sleep, she might have kept things from boiling over.

First, Carlo insisted on coming with her two hours before he was needed. Or wanted. Juliet didn't care to spend the first two hours of what was bound to be a long, hectic day with a smug, self-assured, egocentric chef who looked as though he'd just come back from two sun-washed weeks on the Riviera.

Obviously, *he* didn't need any sleep, she mused as they took the quick, damp cab ride from hotel to mall.

Whatever the tourist bureau had to say about sunny California, it was raining—big, steady drops of it that immediately made the few minutes she'd taken to fuss with her hair worthless.

Prepared to enjoy the ride, Carlo looked out the window. He liked the way the rain plopped in puddles. It didn't matter to him that he'd heard it start that morning, just past four. "It's a nice sound," he decided. "It makes things more quiet, more…subtle, don't you think?"

Breaking away from her own gloomy view of the rain, Juliet turned to him. "What?"

"The rain." Carlo noted she looked a bit hollow-eyed. Good. She hadn't been unaffected. "Rain changes the look of things."

Normally, she would have agreed. Juliet never minded dashing for the subway in a storm or strolling along Fifth Avenue in a drizzle. Today, she considered it her right to look on the dark side. "This one might lower the attendance in your little demonstration by ten percent."

"So?" He gave an easy shrug as the driver swung into the parking lot of the mall.

What she didn't need at that moment was careless acceptance. "Carlo, the purpose of all this is exposure."

He patted her hand. "You're only thinking of numbers. You should think instead of my *pasta con pesto*. In a few hours, everyone else will."

"I don't think about food the way you do," she muttered. It still amazed her that he'd lovingly prepared the first linguini at 6:00 a.m., then the second two hours later for the camera. Both dishes had been an exquisite example of Italian cooking at its finest. He'd looked more like a film star on holiday than a working chef, which was precisely the image Juliet had wanted to project. His spot on the morning show had been perfect. That only made Juliet more pessimistic about the rest of the day. "It's hard to think about food at all on this kind of a schedule."

"That's because you didn't eat anything this morning."

"Linguini for breakfast doesn't suit me."

"My linguini is always suitable."

Juliet gave a mild snort as she stepped from the cab into the rain. Though she made a dash for the doors, Carlo was there ahead of her, opening one. "Thanks." Inside, she ran a hand through her hair and wondered how soon she could come by another cup of coffee. "You don't need to do anything for another two hours." And he'd definitely be in the way while things were being set up on the third floor.

"So, I'll wander." With his hands in his pockets, he looked around. As luck would have it, they'd entered straight into the lingerie department. "I find your American malls fascinating."

"I'm sure." Her voice was dry as he fingered the border of lace on a slinky camisole. "You can come upstairs with me first, if you like."

"No, no." A saleswoman with a face that demanded a second look adjusted two negligees and beamed at him. "I think I'll just roam around and see what your shops have to offer." He beamed back. "So far, I'm charmed."

She watched the exchange and tried not to clench her teeth. "All right, then, if you'll just be sure to—"

"Be in Special Events on the third floor at eleven-forty-five," he finished. In his friendly, casual way, he kissed her forehead. She wondered why he could touch her like a cousin and make her think of a lover. "Believe me, Juliet, nothing you say to me is forgotten." He took her hand, running his thumb over her knuckles. That was definitely not the touch of a cousin. "I'll buy you a present."

"It isn't necessary."

"A pleasure. Things that are necessary are rarely a pleasure."

Juliet disengaged her hand while trying not to dwell on the pleasure he could offer. "Please, don't be later than eleven-forty-five, Carlo."

"Timing, *mi amore,* is something I excel in."

I'll bet, she thought as she started toward the escalator. She'd have bet a week's pay he was already flirting with the lingerie clerk.

It only took ten minutes in Special Events for Juliet to forget Carlo's penchant for romancing anything feminine.

The little assistant with the squeaky voice was still in charge as her boss continued his battle with the flu. She was young, cheerleader pretty and just as pert. She was also in completely over her head.

"Elise," Juliet began because it was still early on enough for her to have some optimism. "Mr. Franconi's going to need a working area in the kitchen department. Is everything set?"

"Oh, yes." Elise gave Juliet a toothy, amiable grin. "I'm getting a nice folding table from Sporting Goods."

Diplomacy, Juliet reminded herself, was one of the primary rules of PR. "I'm afraid we'll need something a bit sturdier. Perhaps one of the islands where Mr.

Franconi could prepare the dish and still face the audience. Your supervisor and I had discussed it."

"Oh, is that what he meant?" Elise looked blank for a moment, then brightened. Juliet began to think dark thoughts about mellow California. "Well, why not?"

"Why not," Juliet agreed. "We've kept the dish Mr. Franconi is to prepare as simple as possible. You do have all the ingredients listed?"

"Oh, yes. It sounds just delicious. I'm a vegetarian, you know."

Of course she was, Juliet thought. Yogurt was probably the high point of her day. "Elise, I'm sorry if it seems I'm rushing you along, but I really need to work out the setup as soon as possible."

"Oh, sure." All cooperation, Elise flashed her straight-toothed smile. "What do you want to know?"

Juliet offered up a prayer. "How sick is Mr. Francis?" she asked, thinking of the levelheaded, businesslike man she had dealt with before.

"Just miserable." Elise swung back her straight California-blond hair. "He'll be out the rest of the week."

No help there. Accepting the inevitable, Juliet gave Elise her straight, no-nonsense look. "All right, what have you got so far?"

"Well, we've taken a new blender and some really lovely bowls from Housewares."

Juliet nearly relaxed. "That's fine. And the range?"

Elise smiled. "Range?"

"The range Mr. Franconi needs to cook the spaghetti for this dish. It's on the list."

"Oh. We'd need elecricity for that, wouldn't we?"

"Yes." Juliet folded her hands to keep them from clenching. "We would. For the blender, too."

"I guess I'd better check with maintenance."

"I guess you'd better." Diplomacy, tact, Juliet reminded herself as her fingers itched for Elise's neck. "Maybe I'll just go over to the kitchen layouts and see which one would suit Mr. Franconi best."

"Terrific. He might want to do his interview right there."

Juliet had taken two steps before she stopped and turned back. "Interview?"

"With the food editor of the *Sun.* She'll be here at eleven-thirty."

Calm, controlled, Juliet pulled out her itinerary of the San Diego stop. She skimmed it, though she knew every word by heart. "I don't seem to have anything listed here."

"It came up at the last minute. I called your hotel at nine, but you'd already checked out."

"I see." Should she have expected Elise to phone the television studio and leave a message? Juliet looked into the personality-plus smile. No, she supposed not. Resigned, she checked her watch. The setup could be dealt with in time if she started immediately. Carlo would just have to be paged. "How do I call mall management?"

"Oh, you can call from my office. Can I do anything?"

Juliet thought of and rejected several things, none of which were kind. "I'd like some coffee, two sugars."

She rolled up her sleeves and went to work.

By eleven, Juliet had the range, the island and the ingredients Carlo had specified neatly arranged. It had taken only one call, and some finesse, to acquire two vivid flower arrangements from a shop in the mall.

She was on her third coffee and considering a fourth when Carlo wandered over. "Thank God." She drained the last from the foam cup. "I thought I was going to have to send out a search party."

"Search party?" Idly he began looking around the kitchen set. "I came when I heard the page."

"You've been paged five times in the last hour."

"Yes?" He smiled as he looked back at her. Her hair was beginning to stray out of her neat bun. He might have stepped off the cover of *Gentlemen's Quarterly.* "I only just heard. But then, I spent some time in the most fantastic record store. Such speakers. Quadraphonic."

"That's nice." Juliet dragged a hand through her already frazzled hair.

"There's a problem?"

"Her name's Elise. I've come very close to murdering her half a dozen times. If she smiles at me again, I just might." Juliet gestured with her hand to brush it off. This was no time for fantasies, no matter how satisfying. "It seems things were a bit disorganized here."

"But you've seen to that." He bent over to examine the range as a driver might a car before Le Mans. "Excellent."

"You can be glad you've got electricity rather than your imagination," she muttered. "You have an interview at eleven-thirty with a food editor, Marjorie Ballister, from the *Sun.*"

He only moved his shoulders and examined the blender. "All right."

"If I'd known it was coming up, I'd have bought a paper so we could have seen her column and gauged her style. As it is—"

"*Non importante.* You worry too much, Juliet."

She could have kissed him. Strictly in gratitude, but she could have kissed him. Considering that unwise, she smiled instead. "I appreciate your attitude, Carlo. After the last hour of dealing with the inept, the insane and the unbearable, it's a relief to have someone take things in stride."

"Franconi always takes things in stride." Juliet started to sink into a chair for a five-minute break.

"*Dio!* What joke is this?" She was standing again and looking down at the little can he held in his hand. "Who would sabotage my pasta?"

"Sabotage?" Had he found a bomb in the can? "What are you talking about?"

"This!" He shook the can at her. "What do you call this?"

"It's basil," she began, a bit unsteady when she lifted her gaze and caught the dark, furious look in his eyes. "It's on your list."

"Basil!" He went off in a stream of Italian. "You dare call this basil?"

Soothe, Juliet reminded herself. It was part of the job. "Carlo, it says basil right on the can."

"On the can." He said something short and rude as he dropped it into her hand. "Where in your clever notes does it say Franconi uses basil from a can?"

"It just says basil," she said between clenched teeth. "B-a-s-i-l."

"Fresh. On your famous list you'll see fresh. *Accidenti!* Only a philistine uses basil from a can for *pasta con pesto*. Do I look like a philistine?"

She wouldn't tell him what he looked like. Later, she might privately admit that temper was spectacular on him. Dark and unreasonable, but spectacular. "Carlo, I realize things aren't quite as perfect here as both of us would like, but—"

"I don't need perfect," he tossed at her. "I can cook in a sewer if I have to, but not without the proper ingredients."

She swallowed—though it went down hard—pride, temper and opinion. She only had fifteen minutes left until the interview. "I'm sorry, Carlo. If we could just compromise on this—"

"Compromise?" When the word came out like an obscenity, she knew she'd lost the battle. "Would you ask Picasso to compromise on a painting?"

Juliet stuck the can into her pocket. "How much fresh basil do you need?"

"Three ounces."

"You'll have it. Anything else?"

"A mortar and pestle, marble."

Juliet checked her watch. She had forty-five minutes to handle it. "Okay. If you'll do the interview right here, I'll take care of this and we'll be ready for the demonstration at noon." She sent up a quick prayer that there was a gourmet shop within ten miles. "Remember to get in the book title and the next stop on the tour. We'll be hitting another Gallegher's in Portland, so it's a good tie-in. Here." Digging into her bag she brought out an eight-by-ten glossy. "Take the extra publicity shot for her in case I don't get back. Elise didn't mention a photographer."

"You'd like to chop and dice that bouncy little woman," Carlo observed, noting that Juliet was swearing very unprofessionally under her breath.

"You bet I would." She dug in again. "Take a copy of the book. The reporter can keep it if necessary."

"I can handle the reporter," he told her calmly enough. "You handle the basil."

It seemed luck was with her when Juliet only had to make three calls before she found a shop that carried what she needed. The frenzied trip in the rain didn't improve her disposition, nor did the price of a marble pestle. Another glance at her watch reminded her she didn't have time for temperament. Carrying what she considered Carlo's eccentricities, she ran back to the waiting cab.

At exactly ten minutes to twelve, dripping wet, Juliet rode up to the third floor of Gallegher's. The first thing she saw was Carlo, leaning back in a cozy wicker dinette chair laughing with a plump, pretty middle-aged woman with a pad and pencil. He looked dashing, amiable and most of all, dry. She wondered how it would feel to grind the pestle into his ear.

"Ah, Juliet." All good humor, Carlo rose as she walked up to the table. "You must meet Marjorie. She tells me she's eaten my pasta in my restaurant in Rome."

"Loved every sinful bite. How do you do? You must be the Juliet Trent Carlo bragged about."

Bragged about? No, she wouldn't be pleased. But Juliet set her bag on the table and offered her hand. "It's nice to meet you. I hope you can stay for the demonstration."

"Wouldn't miss it." She twinkled at Carlo. "Or a sample of Franconi's pasta."

Juliet felt a little wave of relief. Something would be salvaged out of the disaster. Unless she was way off the mark, Carlo was about to be given a glowing write-up.

Carlo was already taking the little sack of basil out of the bag. "Perfect," he said after one sniff. "Yes, yes, this is excellent." He tested the pestle weight and size. "You'll see over at our little stage a crowd is gathering," he said easily to Juliet. "So we moved here to talk, knowing you'd see us as soon as you stepped off the escalator."

"Very good." They'd both handled things well, she decided. It was best to take satisfaction from that. A quick glance showed her that Elise was busy chatting away with a small group of people. Not a worry in the world, Juliet thought nastily. Well, she'd already resigned herself to that. Five minutes in the restroom for some quick repairs, she calculated, and she could keep everything on schedule.

"You have everything you need now, Carlo?"

He caught the edge of annoyance, and her hand, smiling brilliantly. "*Grazie, cara mia.* You're wonderful."

Perhaps she'd rather have snarled, but she returned the smile. "Just doing my job. You have a few more minutes before we should begin. If you'll excuse me, I'll just take care of some things and be right back."

Juliet kept up a brisk, dignified walk until she was out of sight, then made a mad dash for the restroom, pulling out her brush as she went in.

"What did I tell you?" Carlo held the bag of basil in his palm to judge the weight. "She's fantastic."

"And quite lovely," Marjorie agreed. "Even when she's damp and annoyed."

With a laugh, Carlo leaned forward to grasp both of Marjorie's hands. He was a man who touched, always. "A woman of perception. I knew I liked you."

She gave a quick dry chuckle, and for a moment felt twenty years younger. And twenty pounds lighter. It was a talent of his that he was generous with. "One last question, Carlo, before your fantastic Ms. Trent rushes you off. Are you still likely to fly off to Cairo or Cannes to prepare one of your dishes for an appreciative client and a stunning fee?"

"There was a time this was routine." He was silent a moment, thinking of the early years of his success. There'd been mad, glamorous trips to this country and to that, preparing fettuccine for a prince or cannelloni for a tycoon. It had been a heady, spectacular time.

Then he'd opened his restaurant and had learned that the solid continuity of his own place was so much more fulfilling than the flash of the single dish.

"From time to time I would still make such trips. Two months ago there was Count Lequine's birthday. He's an old client, an old friend, and he's fond of my spaghetti. But my restaurant is more rewarding to me." He gave her a quizzical look as a thought occurred to him. "Perhaps I'm settling down?"

"A pity you didn't decide to settle in the States." She closed her pad. "I guarantee if you opened a Franconi's right here in San Diego, you'd have clientele flying in from all over the country."

He took the idea, weighed it in much the same way he had the basil, and put it in a corner of his mind. "An interesting thought."

"And a fascinating interview. Thank you." It pleased her that he rose as she did and took her hand. She was a tough outspoken feminist who appreciated genuine manners and genuine charm. "I'm looking forward to a taste of your pasta. I'll just ease over and try to get a good seat. Here comes your Ms. Trent."

Marjorie had never considered herself particularly romantic, but she'd always believed where there was smoke, there was fire. She watched the way Carlo turned his head, saw the change in his eyes and the slight tilt of his mouth. There was fire all right, she mused. You only had to be within five feet to feel the heat.

Between the hand dryer and her brush, Juliet had managed to do something with her hair. A touch here, a dab there, and her makeup was back in shape. Carrying her raincoat over her arm, she looked competent and collected. She was ready to admit she'd had one too many cups of coffee.

"Your interview went well?"

"Yes." He noticed, and approved, that she'd taken the time to dab on her scent. "Perfectly."

"Good. You can fill me in later. We'd better get started."

"In a moment." He reached in his pocket. "I told you I'd buy you a present."

There was a flutter of surprised pleasure she tried to ignore. Just wired from the coffee, she told herself. "Carlo, I told you not to. We don't have time—"

"There's always time." He opened the little box himself and drew out a small gold heart with an arrow of diamonds running through it. She'd been expecting something along the line of a box of chocolates.

"Oh, I—" Words were her business, but she'd lost them. "Carlo, really, you can't—"

"Never say can't to Franconi," he murmured and began to fasten the pin to her lapel. He did so smoothly, with no fumbling. After all, he was a man accustomed to such feminine habits. "It's very delicate, I thought, very elegant. So it suits you." Narrowing his eyes, he stood back, then nodded. "Yes, I was sure it would."

It wasn't possible to remember her crazed search for fresh basil when he was smiling at her in just that way. It was barely possible to remember how furious she was over the lackadaisical setup for the demonstration. Instinctively, she put up her hand and ran a finger over the pin. "It's lovely." Her lips curved, easily, sweetly, as he thought they didn't do often enough. "Thank you."

He couldn't count or even remember the number of presents he'd given, or the different styles of gratitude he'd received. Somehow, he was already sure this would be one he wouldn't forget.

"Prego."

"Ah, Ms. Trent?"

Juliet glanced over to see Elise watching her. Present or no present, it tightened her jaw. "Yes, Elise. You haven't met Mr. Franconi yet."

"Elise directed me from the office to you when I answered the page," Carlo said easily, more than appreciating Juliet's aggravation.

"Yes." She flashed her touchdown smile. "I thought your cookbook looked just super, Mr. Franconi. Everyone's dying to watch you cook something." She opened a little pad of paper with daisies on the cover. "I thought you could spell what it is so I could tell them when I announce you."

"Elise, I have everything." Juliet managed charm and diplomacy to cover a firm nudge out the door. "Why don't I just announce Mr. Franconi?"

"Great." She beamed. Juliet could think of no other word for it. "That'll be a lot easier."

"We'll get started now. Carlo, if you'd just step over there behind those counters, I'll go give the announcements." Without waiting for an assent, she gathered up the basil, mortar and pestle and walked over to the area that she'd prepared. In the most natural of moves, she set everything down and turned to the audience. Three hundred, she judged. Maybe even over. Not bad for a rainy day in a department store.

"Good afternoon." Her voice was pleasant and well pitched. There'd be no need for a microphone in the relatively small space. Thank God, because Elise had botched that minor detail as well. "I want to thank you all for coming here today, and to thank Gallegher's for providing such a lovely setting for the demonstration."

From a few feet away, Carlo leaned on a counter and watched her. She was, as he'd told the reporter, fantastic. No one would guess she'd been up and on her feet since dawn.

"We all like to eat." This drew the murmured laughter she'd expected. "But I've been told by an expert that eating is more than a basic necessity, it's an experience. Not all of us like to cook, but the same expert told me that cooking is both art and magic. This afternoon, the expert, Carlo Franconi, will share with you the art, the magic and the experience with his own *pasta con pesto.*"

Juliet started the applause herself, but it was picked up instantly. As Carlo stepped out, she melted back. Center stage was his the moment he stepped on it.

"It's a fortunate man," he began, "who has the opportunity to cook for so many beautiful women. Some of you have husbands?" At the question there was a smatter of chuckles and the lifting of hands. "Ah, well." He gave a very European shrug. "Then I must be content to cook."

She knew Carlo had chosen that particular dish because it took little time in preparation. After the first five minutes, Juliet was certain not one member of the audience would have budged if he'd chosen something that took hours. She wasn't yet convinced cooking was magic, but she was certain he was.

His hands were as skilled and certain as a surgeon's, his tongue as glib as a politician's. She watched him measure, grate, chop and blend and found herself just as entertained as she might have been with a well-produced one-act play.

One woman was bold enough to ask a question. It opened the door and dozens of others followed. Juliet needn't have worried that the noise and conversations would disturb him. Obviously he thrived on the interaction. He wasn't, she decided, simply doing his job or fulfilling an obligation. He was enjoying himself.

Calling one woman up with him, Carlo joked about all truly great chefs requiring both inspiration and assistance. He told her to stir the spaghetti, made a fuss out of showing her the proper way to stir by putting his hand over hers and undoubtedly sold another ten books then and there.

Juliet had to grin. He'd done it for fun, not for sales. He was fun, Juliet realized, even if he did take his basil too seriously. He was sweet. Unconsciously, she began to toy with the gold and diamonds on her lapel. Uncommonly considerate and uncommonly demanding. Simply uncommon.

As she watched him laugh with his audience, something began to melt inside her. She sighed with it, dreaming. There were certain men that prompted a woman, even a practical woman, to dream.

One of the women seated closer to her leaned toward a companion. "Good God, he's the sexiest man I've ever seen. He could keep a dozen lovers patiently waiting."

Juliet caught herself and dropped her hand. Yes, he could keep a dozen lovers patiently waiting. She was sure he did. Deliberately she tucked her hands in the pockets of her skirt. She'd be better off remembering she was encouraging this public image, even exploiting it. She'd be better off remembering that Carlo himself had told her he needed no imagery.

If she started believing half the things he said to her, she might just find herself patiently waiting. The thought of that was enough to stop the melting. Waiting didn't fit into her schedule.

When every last bite of pasta had been consumed, and every last fan had been spoken with, Carlo allowed himself to think of the pleasures of sitting down with a cool glass of wine.

Juliet already had his jacket.

"Well done, Carlo." As she spoke, she began to help him into it. "You can leave California with the satisfaction of knowing you were a smashing success."

He took her raincoat from her when she would've shrugged into it herself. "The airport."

She smiled at his tone, understanding. "We'll pick up our bags in the holding room at the hotel on the way. Look at it this way. You can sit back and sleep all the way to Portland if you like."

Because the thought had a certain appeal, he cooperated. They rode down to the first floor and went out the west entrance where Juliet had told the cab to wait. She let out a quick sigh of relief when it was actually there.

"We get into Portland early?"

"Seven." Rain splattered against the cab's windshield. Juliet told herself to relax. Planes took off safely in the rain every day. "You have a spot on *People of Interest,* but not until nine-thirty. That means we can have breakfast at a civilized hour and go over the scheduling."

Quickly, efficiently, she checked off her San Diego list and noted everything had been accomplished. She had time for a quick, preliminary glance at her Portland schedule before the cab pulled up to the hotel.

"Just wait here," she ordered both the driver and Carlo. She was up and out of the cab and, because they were running it close, managed to have the bags installed in the trunk within seven minutes. Carlo knew because it amused him to time her.

"You, too, can sleep all the way to Portland."

She settled in beside him again. "No, I've got some work to do. The nice thing about planes is that I can pretend I'm in my office and forget I'm thousands of feet off the ground."

"I didn't realize flying bothered you."

"Only when I'm in the air." Juliet sat back and closed her eyes, thinking to relax for a moment. The next thing she knew, she was being kissed awake.

Disoriented, she sighed and wrapped her arms around Carlo's neck. It was soothing, so sweet. And then the heat began to rise.

"*Cara.*" She'd surprised him, but that had brought its own kind of pleasure. "Such a pity to wake you."

"Hmm?" When she opened her eyes, his face was close, her mouth still warm, her heart still thudding. She jerked back and fumbled with the door handle. "That was uncalled for."

"True enough." Leisurely, Carlo stepped out into the rain. "But it was illuminating. I've already paid the driver, Juliet," he continued when she started to dig into her purse. "The baggage is checked. We board from gate five." Taking her arm, and his big leather case, he led her into the terminal.

"You didn't have to take care of all that." She'd have pulled her arm away if she'd had the energy. Or so she told herself. "The reason I'm here is to—"

"Promote my book," he finished easily. "If it makes you feel better, I've been known to do the same when I traveled with your predecessor."

The very fact that it did made her feel foolish as well. "I appreciate it, Carlo. It's not that I mind you lending a hand, it's that I'm not used to it. You'd be surprised how many authors are either helpless or careless on the road."

"You'd be surprised how many chefs are temperamental and rude."

She thought of the basil and grinned. "No!"

"Oh, yes." And though he'd read her thoughts perfectly, his tone remained grave. "Always flying off the handle, swearing, throwing things. It leads to a bad reputation for all of us. Here, they're boarding. If only they have a decent Bordeaux."

Juliet stifled a yawn as she followed him through. "I'll need my boarding pass, Carlo."

"I have it." He flashed them both for the flight attendant and nudged Juliet ahead. "Do you want the window or the aisle?"

"I need my pass to see which I've got."

"We have 2A and B. Take your pick."

Someone pushed past her and bumped her solidly. It brought a sinking sensation of déjà vu. "Carlo, I'm in coach, so—"

"No, your tickets are changed. Take the window."

Before she could object, he'd maneuvered her over

and slipped in beside her. "What do you mean my ticket's been changed? Carlo, I have to get in the back before I cause a scene."

"Your seat's here." After handing Juliet her boarding pass he stretched out his legs. "*Dio,* what a relief."

Frowning, Juliet studied her stub—2A. "I don't know how they could've made a mistake like this. I'd better see to it right away."

"There's no mistake. You should fasten your belt," he advised, then did so himself. "I changed your tickets for the remaining flights on the tour."

Juliet reached to undo the clasp he'd just secured. "You— But you can't."

"I told you, don't say *can't* to Franconi." Satisfied with her belt, he dealt with his own. "You work as hard as I do—why should you travel in tourist?"

"Because I'm paid to work. Carlo, let me out so I can fix this before we take off."

"No." For the first time, his voice was blunt and final. "I prefer your company to that of a stranger or an empty seat." When he turned his head, his eyes were like his voice. "I want you here. Leave it."

Juliet opened her mouth and closed it again. Professionally, she was on shaky ground either direction she went. She was supposed to see to his needs and wants within reason. Personally, she'd counted on the distance, at least during flight time, to keep her balanced. With Carlo, even a little distance could help.

He was being kind, she knew. Considerate. But he was also being stubborn. There was always a diplomatic way to handle such things.

She gave him a patient smile. "Carlo—"

He stopped her by simply closing his mouth over

hers, quietly, completely and irresistibly. He held her there a moment, one hand on her cheek, the other over the fingers which had frozen in her lap. Juliet felt the floor tilt and her head go light.

We're taking off, she thought dimly, but knew the plane hadn't left the ground.

His tongue touched hers briefly, teasingly; then it was only his lips again. After brushing a hand through her hair, he leaned back. "Now, go back to sleep awhile," he advised. "This isn't the place I'd choose to seduce you."

Sometimes, Juliet decided, silence was the best diplomacy. Without another word, she closed her eyes and slept.

Chapter 5

Colorado. The Rockies, Pike's Peak, Indian ruins, aspens and fast-running streams. It sounded beautiful, exciting. But a hotel room was a hotel room after all.

They'd been busy in Washington State. For most of their three-day stay, Juliet had had to work and think on her feet. But the media had been outstanding. Their schedule had been so full her boss back in New York had probably done handstands. Her report on their run on the coast would be a publicist's dream. Then there was Denver.

What coverage she'd managed to hustle there would barely justify the plane fare. One talk show at the ungodly hour of 7:00 a.m. and one miserly article in the food section of a local paper. No network or local news coverage of the autographing, no print reporter who'd confirm an appearance. Lousy.

It was 6:00 a.m. when Juliet dragged herself out of the shower and began to search through her unpacked garment bag for a suit and a fresh blouse. The cleaners was definitely a priority the minute they moved on to Dallas.

At least Carlo wasn't cooking this morning. She didn't think she could bear to look at food in any form for at least two hours.

With any luck she could come back to the hotel after the show, catch another hour's sleep and then have breakfast in her room while she made her morning calls. The autographing wasn't until noon, and their flight out wasn't until early the next morning.

That was something to hold on to, Juliet told herself as she looked for the right shade of stockings. For the first time in a week, they had an evening free with no one to entertain, no one to be entertained by. A nice, quiet meal somewhere close by and a full night's sleep. With that at the end of the tunnel, she could get through the morning.

With a grimace, she gulped down her daily dose of brewer's yeast.

It wasn't until she was fully dressed that she woke up enough to remember she hadn't dealt with her makeup. With a shrug Juliet slipped out of her little green jacket and headed for the bathroom. She stared at the front door with a combination of suspicion and bad temper when she heard the knock. Peeking through the peephole, she focused on Carlo. He grinned at her, then crossed his eyes. She only swore a little as she pulled open the door.

"You're early," she began, then caught the stirring aroma of coffee. Looking down, she saw that he carried a tray with a small pot, cups and spoons. "Coffee," she murmured, almost like a prayer.

"Yes." He nodded as he stepped into the room. "I thought you'd be ready, though room service isn't." He walked over to a table, saw that her room could fit into one section of his suite and set down the tray. "So, we deliver."

"Bless you." It was so sincere he grinned again as she crossed the room. "How did you manage it? Room service doesn't open for half an hour."

"There's a small kitchen in my suite. A bit primitive, but adequate to brew coffee."

She took the first sip, black and hot, and she closed her eyes. "It's wonderful. Really wonderful."

"Of course. I fixed it."

She opened her eyes again. No, she decided, she wouldn't spoil gratitude with sarcasm. After all, they'd very nearly gotten along for three days running. With the help of her shower, the yeast and the coffee, she was feeling almost human again.

"Relax," she suggested. "I'll finish getting ready." Expecting him to sit, Juliet took her cup and went into the bathroom to deal with her face and hair. She was dotting on foundation when Carlo leaned on the doorjamb.

"*Mi amore,* doesn't this arrangement strike you as impractical?"

She tried not to feel self-conscious as she smoothed on the thin, translucent base. "Which arrangement is that?"

"You have this—broom closet," he decided as he gestured toward her room. Yes, it was small enough that the subtle, feminine scent from her shower reached all the corners. "While I have a big suite with two baths, a bed big enough for three friends and one of those sofas that unfold."

"You're the star," she murmured as she brushed color over the slant of her cheeks.

"It would save the publisher money if we shared the suite."

She shifted her eyes in the mirror until they met his. She'd have sworn, absolutely sworn, he meant no more than that. That is, if she hadn't known him. "He can afford it," she said lightly. "It just thrills the accounting department at tax time."

Carlo moved his shoulders then sipped from his cup again. He'd known what her answer would be. Of course, he'd enjoy sharing his rooms with her for the obvious reason, but neither did it sit well with him that her accommodations were so far inferior to his.

"You need a touch more blusher on your left cheek," he said idly, not noticing her surprised look. What he'd noticed was the green silk robe that reflected in the mirror from the back of the door. Just how would she look in that? Carlo wondered. How would she look out of it?

After a narrowed-eyed study, Juliet discovered he'd been right. She picked up her brush again and evened the color. "You're a very observant man."

"Hmm?" He was looking at her again, but mentally, he'd changed her neat, high-collared blouse and slim skirt for the provocative little robe.

"Most men wouldn't notice unbalanced blusher." She picked up a grease pencil to shadow her eyes.

"I notice everything when it comes to a woman." There was still a light fog near the top of the mirror from the steam of her shower. Seeing it gave Carlo other, rather pleasant mental images. "What you're doing now gives you a much different look."

Relaxed again, she laughed. "That's the idea."

"But, no." He stepped in closer so he could watch over her shoulder. The small, casual intimacy was as natural for him as it was uncomfortable for her. "Without the pots of paint, your face is younger, more vulnerable, but no less attractive than it is with them. Different..." Easily, he picked up her brush and ran it through her hair. "It's not more, not less, simply different. I like both of your looks."

It wasn't easy to keep her hand steady. Juliet set down the eye shadow and tried the coffee instead. Better to be cynical than be moved, she reminded herself and gave him a cool smile. "You seem right at home in the bathroom with a woman fixing her face."

He liked the way her hair flowed as he brushed it. "I've done it so often."

Her smile became cooler. "I'm sure."

He caught the tone, but continued to brush as he met her eyes in the glass. "Take it as you like, *cara,* but remember, I grew up in a house with five women. Your powders and bottles hold no secrets from me."

She'd forgotten that, perhaps because she'd chosen to forget anything about him that didn't connect directly with the book. Yet now it made her wonder. Just what sort of insight did a man get into women when he'd been surrounded by them since childhood? Frowning a bit, she picked up her mascara.

"Were you a close family?"

"We are a close family," he corrected. "My mother's a widow who runs a successful dress shop in Rome." It was typical of him not to mention that he'd bought it for her. "My four sisters all live within thirty kilometers. Perhaps I no longer share the bathroom with them, but little else changes."

She thought about it. It sounded cozy and easy and

rather sweet. Juliet didn't believe she could relate at all. "Your mother must be proud of you."

"She'd be prouder if I added to her growing horde of grandchildren."

She smiled at that. It sounded more familiar. "I know what you mean."

"You should leave your hair just like this," he told her as he set down the brush. "You have a family?"

"My parents live in Pennsylvania."

He struggled with geography a moment. "Ah, then you'll visit them when we go to Philadelphia."

"No." The word was flat as she recapped the tube of mascara. "There won't be time for that."

"I see." And he thought he was beginning to. "You have brothers, sisters?"

"A sister." Because he was right about her hair, Juliet let it be and slipped out for her jacket. "She married a doctor and produced two children, one of each gender, before she was twenty-five."

Oh yes, he was beginning to see well enough. Though the words had been easy, the muscles in her shoulders had been tight. "She makes an excellent doctor's wife?"

"Carrie makes a perfect doctor's wife."

"Not all of us are meant for the same things."

"I wasn't." She picked up her briefcase and her purse. "We'd better get going. They said it would take about fifteen minutes to drive to the studio."

Strange, he thought, how people always believed their tender spots could go undetected. For now, he'd leave her with the illusion that hers had.

Because the directions were good and the traffic was light, Juliet drove the late model Chevy she'd rented with confidence. Carlo obliged by navigating because he enjoyed the poised, skilled way she handled the wheel.

"You haven't lectured me on today's schedule," he pointed out. "Turn right here at this light."

Juliet glanced in the mirror, switched lanes, then made the turn. She wasn't yet sure what his reaction would be to the fact that there barely was one. "I've decided to give you a break," she said brightly, knowing how some authors snarled and ranted when they had a dip in exposure. "You have this morning spot, then the autographing at World of Books downtown."

He waited, expecting the list to go on. When he turned to her, his brow was lifted. "And?"

"That's all." She heard the apology in her voice as she stopped at a red light. "It happens sometimes, Carlo. Things just don't come through. I knew it was going to be light here, but as it happens they've just started shooting a major film using Denver locations. Every reporter, every news team, every camera crew is covering it this afternoon. The bottom line is we got bumped."

"Bumped? Do you mean there is no radio show, no lunch with a reporter, no dinner engagement?"

"No, I'm sorry. It's just—"

"Fantastico!" Grabbing her face with both hands he kissed her hard. "I'll find out the name of this movie and go to its premiere."

The little knot of tension and guilt vanished. "Don't take it so hard, Carlo."

He felt as though he'd just been paroled. "Juliet, did you think I'd be upset? *Dio,* for a week it's been nothing but go here, rush there."

She spotted the TV tower and turned left. "You've been

wonderful," she told him. The best time to admit it, she decided, was when they only had two minutes to spare. "Not everyone I've toured with has been as considerate."

She surprised him. He preferred it when a woman could do so. He twined a lock of the hair he'd brushed around his finger. "So, you've forgiven me for the basil?"

She smiled and had to stop herself from reaching up to touch the heart on her lapel. "I'd forgotten all about it."

He kissed her cheek in a move so casual and friendly she didn't object. "I believe you have. You've a kind heart, Juliet. Such things are beauty in themselves."

He could soften her so effortlessly. She felt it, fought it and, for the moment, surrendered to it. In an impulsive, uncharacteristic move, she brushed the hair on his forehead. "Let's go in. You've got to wake up Denver."

Professionally, Juliet should've been cranky at the lack of obligations and exposure in Denver. It was going to leave a few very obvious blanks on her overall report. Personally, she was thrilled.

According to schedule, she was back in her room by eight. By 8:03, she'd stripped out of her suit and had crawled, naked and happy, into her still-rumpled bed. For exactly an hour she slept deeply, and without any dreams she could remember. By ten-thirty, she'd gone through her list of phone calls and an enormous breakfast. After freshening her makeup, she dressed in her suit then went downstairs to meet Carlo in the lobby.

It shouldn't have surprised her that he was huddled in one of the cozy lounging areas with three women. It shouldn't have irked her. Pretending it did neither, Juliet strolled over. It was then she noticed that all three women were built stupendously. That shouldn't have surprised her, either.

"Ah, Juliet." He smiled, all grace, all charm. She didn't stop to wonder why she'd like to deck him. "Always prompt. Ladies." He turned to bow to all three of them. "It's been a pleasure."

"Bye-bye, Carlo." One of them sent him a look that could have melted lead. "Remember, if you're ever in Tucson…"

"How could I forget?" Hooking his arm with Juliet's, he strolled outside. "Juliet," he murmured, "where is Tucson?"

"Don't you ever quit?" she demanded.

"Quit what?"

"Collecting women."

He lifted a brow as he pulled open the door on the driver's side. "Juliet, one collects matchbooks, not women."

"It would seem there are some who consider them on the same level."

He blocked her way before she could slip inside. "Any who do are too stupid to matter." He walked around the side of the car and opened his own door before she spoke again.

"Who were they anyhow?"

Soberly, Carlo adjusted the brim of the buff-colored fedora he wore. "Female bodybuilders. It seems they're having a convention."

A muffled laugh escaped before she could prevent it. "Figures."

"Indeed yes, but such muscular ones." His expression was still grave as he lowered himself into the car.

Juliet remained quiet a moment, then gave up and

laughed out loud. Damn, she'd never had as much fun on tour with anyone. She might as well accept it. "Tucson's in Arizona," she told him with another laugh. "And it's not on the itinerary."

They would have been on time for the autographing if they hadn't run into the detour. Traffic was clogged, rerouted and bad tempered as roads were blocked off for the film being shot. Juliet spent twenty minutes weaving, negotiating and cursing until she found she'd done no more than make a nice big circle.

"We've been here before," Carlo said idly and received a glowering look.

"Oh, really?" Her sweet tone had an undertone of arsenic.

He merely shifted his legs into a less cramped position. "It's an interesting city," he commented. "I think perhaps if you turn right at the next corner, then left two corners beyond, we'll find ourselves on the right track."

Juliet meticulously smoothed her carefully written directions when she'd have preferred to crumple them into a ball. "The book clerk specifically said—"

"I'm sure she's a lovely woman, but things seem a bit confused today." It didn't particularly bother him. The blast of a horn made her jolt. Amused, Carlo merely looked over. "As someone from New York City, you should be used to such things."

Juliet set her teeth. "I never drive in the city."

"I do. Trust me, *innamorata.*"

Not on your life, Juliet thought, but turned right. It took nearly ten minutes in the crawling traffic to manage the next two blocks, but when she turned left she found herself, as Carlo had said, on the right track. She waited, resigned, for him to gloat.

"Rome moves faster" was all he said.

How could she anticipate him? she wondered. He didn't rage when you expected, didn't gloat when it was natural. With a sigh, she gave up. "Anything moves faster." She found herself in the right block, but parking space was at a premium. Weighing the ins and outs, Juliet swung over beside a car at the curb. "Look, Carlo, I'm going to have to drop you off. We're already running behind. I'll find a place to park and be back as soon as I can."

"You're the boss," he said, still cheerful after forty-five minutes of teeth-grinding traffic.

"If I'm not there in an hour, send up a flare."

"My money's on you."

Still cautious, she waited until she saw him swing into the bookstore before she fought her way into traffic again.

Twenty frustrating minutes later, Juliet walked into the dignified little bookstore herself. It was, she noted with a sinking stomach, too quiet and too empty. A clerk with a thin-striped tie and shined shoes greeted her.

"Good morning. May I help you?"

"I'm Juliet Trent, Mr. Franconi's publicist."

"Ah yes, right this way." He glided across the carpet to a set of wide steps. "Mr. Franconi's on the second level. It's unfortunate that the traffic and confusion have discouraged people from coming out. Of course, we rarely do these things." He gave her a smile and brushed a piece of lint from the sleeve of his dark blue jacket. "The last time was…let me see, in the fall. J. Jonathan Cooper was on tour. I'm sure you've heard of him. He wrote *Metaphysical Force and You.*"

Juliet bit back a sigh. When you hit dry ground, you just had to wait for the tide.

She spotted Carlo in a lovely little alcove on a curvy love seat. Beside him was a woman of about forty with a neat suit and pretty legs. Such things didn't warrant even a raised brow. But to Juliet's surprise, Carlo wasn't busy charming her. Instead, he was listening intently to a young boy who sat across from him.

"I've worked in the kitchens there for the last three summers. I'm not allowed to actually prepare anything, but I can watch. At home, I cook whenever I can, but with school and the job, it's mostly on weekends."

"Why?"

The boy stopped in midstream and looked blank. "Why?"

"Why do you cook?" Carlo asked. He acknowledged Juliet with a nod, then gave his attention back to the boy.

"Because…" The boy looked at his mother, then back at Carlo. "Well, it's important. I like to take things and put them together. You have to concentrate, you know, and be careful. But you can make something really terrific. It looks good and it smells good. It's…I don't know." His voice lowered in embarrassment. "Satisfying, I guess."

"Yes." Pleased, Carlo smiled at him. "That's a good answer."

"I have both your other books," the boy blurted out. "I've tried all your recipes. I even made your *pasta al tre formaggi* for this dinner party at my aunt's."

"And?"

"They liked it." The boy grinned. "I mean they really liked it."

"You want to study."

"Oh yeah." But the boy dropped his gaze to where his hands rubbed nervously over his knees. "Thing is we can't really afford college right now, so I'm hoping to get some restaurant work."

"In Denver?"

"Any place where I could start cooking instead of wiping up."

"We've taken up enough of Mr. Franconi's time." The boy's mother rose, noting there was now a handful of people milling around on the second level with Carlo's books in hand. "I want to thank you." She offered her hand to Carlo as he rose with her. "It meant a great deal to Steven to talk with you."

"My pleasure." Though he was gracious as always, he turned back to the boy. "Perhaps you'd give me your address. I know of some restaurant owners here in the States. Perhaps one of them needs an apprentice chef."

Stunned, Steven could do nothing but stare. "You're very kind." His mother took out a small pad and wrote on it. Her hand was steady, but when she handed the paper to Carlo and looked at him, he saw the emotion. He thought of his own mother. He took the paper, then her hand.

"You have a fortunate son, Mrs. Hardesty."

Thoughtful, Juliet watched them walk away, noting that Steven looked over his shoulder with the same blank, baffled expression.

So he has a heart, Juliet decided, touched. A heart that wasn't altogether reserved for *amore.* But she saw Carlo slip the paper into his pocket and wondered if that would be the end of it.

The autographing wasn't a smashing success. Six books by Juliet's count. That had been bad enough, but then there'd been The Incident.

Looking at the all but empty store, Juliet had considered hitting the streets with a sign on her back, then the homey little woman had come along bearing all three of Carlo's books. Good for the ego, Juliet thought. That was before the woman had said something that caused Carlo's eyes to chill and his voice to freeze. All Juliet heard was the name LaBare.

"I beg your pardon, Madame?" Carlo said in a tone Juliet had never heard from him. It could've sliced through steel.

"I said I keep all your books on a shelf in my kitchen, right next to André LaBare's. I love to cook."

"LaBare?" Carlo put his hand over his stack of books as a protective parent might over a threatened child. "You would dare put my work next to that—that peasant's?"

Thinking fast, Juliet stepped up and broke into the conversation. If ever she'd seen a man ready to murder, it was Carlo. "Oh, I see you have all of Mr. Franconi's books. You must love to cook."

"Well, yes I—"

"Wait until you try some of his new recipes. I had the *pasta con pesto* myself. It's wonderful." Juliet started to take the woman's books from under Carlo's hand and met with resistance and a stubborn look. She gave him one of her own and jerked the books away. "Your family's going to be just thrilled when you serve it," Juliet went on, keeping her voice pleasant as she led the woman out of the line of fire. "And the fettuccine…"

"LaBare is a swine." Carlo's voice was very clear and reached the stairs. The woman glanced back nervously.

"Men." Juliet made her voice a conspiratorial whisper. "Such egos."

"Yes." Gathering up her books, the woman hurried

down the stairs and out of the store. Juliet waited until she was out of earshot before she pounced on Carlo.

"How could you?"

"How could I?" He rose, and though he skimmed just under six feet, he looked enormous. "She would *dare* speak that name to me? She would *dare* associate the work of an artist with the work of a jackass? LaBare—"

"At the moment, I don't give a damn who or what this LaBare is." Juliet put a hand on his shoulder and shoved him back onto the love seat. "What I do care about is you scaring off the few customers we have. Now behave yourself."

He sat where he was only because he admired the way she'd ordered him to. Fascinating woman, Carlo decided, finding it wiser to think of her than LaBare. It was wiser to think of flood and famine than of LaBare.

The afternoon had dragged on and on, except for the young boy, Carlo thought and touched the paper in his pocket. He'd call Summer in Philadelphia about young Steven Hardesty.

But other than Steven and the woman who upped his blood pressure by speaking of LaBare, Carlo had found himself perilously close to boredom. Something he considered worse than illness.

He needed some activity, a challenge—even a small one. He glanced over at Juliet as she spoke with a clerk. That was no small challenge. The one thing he'd yet to be in Juliet's company was bored. She kept him interested. Sexually? Yes, that went without saying. Intellectually. That was a plus, a big one.

He understood women. It wasn't a matter of pride, but to Carlo's thinking, a matter of circumstance. He enjoyed women. As lovers, of course, but he also enjoyed them as companions, as friends, as associates. It was a rare thing when a man could find a woman to be all of those things. That's what he wanted from Juliet. He hadn't resolved it yet, only felt it. Convincing her to be his friend would be as challenging, and as rewarding, as it would be to convince her to be his lover.

No, he realized as he studied her profile. With this woman, a lover would come easier than a friend. He had two weeks left to accomplish both. With a smile, he decided to start the campaign in earnest.

Half an hour later, they were walking the three blocks to the parking garage Juliet had found.

"This time I drive," he told Juliet as they stepped inside the echoing gray building. When she started to object, he held out his hand for the keys. "Come, my love, I've just survived two hours of boredom. Why should you have all the fun?"

"Since you put it that way." She dropped the keys in his hand, relieved that whatever had set him off before was forgotten.

"So now we have a free evening."

"That's right." With a sigh she leaned back in her seat and waited for him to start the engine.

"We'll have dinner at seven. Tonight, I make the arrangements."

A hamburger in her room, an old movie and bed. Juliet let the wish come and go. Her job was to pamper and entertain as much as possible. "Whatever you like."

Carlo pulled out of the parking space with a squeal of tires that had Juliet bolting up. "I'll hold you to that, *cara.*"

He zoomed out of the garage and turned right with hardly a pause. "Carlo—"

"We should have champagne to celebrate the end of our first week. You like champagne?"

"Yes, I— Carlo, the light's changing."

He breezed through the amber light, skimmed by the bumper of a battered compact and kept going. "Italian food. You have no objection?"

"No." She gripped the door handle until her knuckles turned white. "That truck!"

"Yes, I see it." He swerved around it, zipped through another light and cut a sharp right. "You have plans for the afternoon?"

Juliet pressed a hand to her throat, thinking she might be able to push out her voice. "I was thinking of making use of the hotel spa. If I live."

"Good. Me, I think I'll go shopping."

Juliet's teeth snapped together as he changed lanes in bumper-to-bumper traffic. "How do I notify next of kin?"

With a laugh, Carlo swung in front of their hotel. "Don't worry, Juliet. Have your whirlpool and your sauna. Knock on my door at seven."

She looked back toward the street. Pamper and entertain, she remembered. Did that include risking your life? Her supervisor would think so. "Maybe I should go with you."

"No, I insist." He leaned over, cupping her neck before she'd recovered enough to evade. "Enjoy," he murmured lightly against her lips. "And think of me as your skin grows warm and your muscles grow lax."

In self-defense, Juliet hurried out of the car. Before she could tell him to drive carefully, he was barreling back out into the street. She offered a prayer for Italian maniacs, then went inside.

By seven, she felt reborn. She'd sweated out fatigue

in the sauna, shocked herself awake in the pool and splurged on a massage. Life, she thought as she splashed on her scent, had its good points after all. Tomorrow's flight to Dallas would be soon enough to draft her Denver report. Such as it was. Tonight, all she had to worry about was eating. After pressing a hand to her stomach, Juliet admitted she was more than ready for that.

With a quick check, she approved the simple ivory dress with the high collar and tiny pearly buttons. Unless Carlo had picked a hot dog stand it would suit. Grabbing her evening bag, she slipped across the hall to knock on Carlo's door. She only hoped he'd chosen someplace close by. The last thing she wanted to do was fight Denver's downtown traffic again.

The first thing she noticed when Carlo opened his door were the rolled-up sleeves of his shirt. It was cotton, oversized and chic, but her eyes were drawn to the surprising cord of muscles in his forearms. The man did more than lift spoons and spatulas. The next thing she noticed was the erotic scents of spices and sauce.

"Lovely." Carlo took both hands and drew her inside. She pleased him, the smooth, creamy skin, the light, subtle scent, but more, the confused hesitation in her eyes as she glanced over to where the aroma of food was strongest.

"An interesting cologne," she managed after a moment. "But don't you think you've gotten a bit carried away?"

"*Innamorata,* you don't wear Franconi's spaghetti sauce, you absorb it." He kissed the back of her hand. "Anticipate it." Then the other. "Savor it." This time her palm.

A smart woman wasn't aroused by a man who used such flamboyant tactics. Juliet told herself that as the chills raced up her arms and down again. "Spaghetti sauce?" Slipping her hands from his, she linked them behind her back.

"I found a wonderful shop. The spices pleased me very much. The burgundy was excellent. Italian, of course."

"Of course." Cautious, she stepped farther into the suite. "You spent the day cooking?"

"Yes. Though you should remind me to speak to the hotel owner about the quality of this stove. All in all, it went quite well."

She told herself it wasn't wise to encourage him when she had no intention of eating alone with him in his suite. Perhaps if she'd been made out of rock she could have resisted wandering toward the little kitchenette. Her mouth watered. "Oh, God."

Delighted, Carlo slipped an arm around her waist and led her to the stove. The little kitchen itself was in shambles. She'd never seen so many pots and bowls and spoons jammed into a sink before. Counters were splattered and streaked. But the smells. It was heaven, pure and simple.

"The senses, Juliet. There's not one of us who isn't ruled by them. First, you smell, and you begin to imagine." His fingers moved lightly over her waist. "Imagine. You can almost taste it on your tongue from that alone."

"Hmm." Knowing she was making a mistake, she watched him take the lid off the pot on the stove. The tang made her close her eyes and just breathe. "Oh, Carlo."

"Then we look, and the imagination goes one step further." His fingers squeezed lightly at her waist until she opened her eyes and looked into the pot. Thick, red, simmering, the sauce was chunky with meat, peppers and spice. Her stomach growled.

"Beautiful, yes?"

"Yes." She wasn't aware that her tongue slid out over her lips in anticipation. He was.

"And we hear." Beside the sauce a pot of water began to boil. In an expert move, he measured pasta by sight and slid it in. "Some things are destined to be mated." With a slotted spoon, he stirred gently. "Without each other, they are incomplete. But when merged—" he adjusted the flame "—a treasure. Pasta and the sauce. A man and a woman. Come, you'll have some burgundy. The champagne's for later."

It was time to take a stand, even though she took it by the stove. "Carlo, I had no idea this was what you intended. I think—"

"I like surprises." He handed her a glass half-filled with dark, red wine. "And I wanted to cook for you."

She wished he hadn't put it quite that way. She wished his voice wasn't so warm, so deep, like his eyes. Like the feelings he could urge out of her. "I appreciate that, Carlo, it's just that—"

"You had your sauna?"

"Yes, I did. Now—"

"It relaxed you. It shows."

She sighed, sipping at the wine without thinking. "Yes."

"This relaxes me. We eat together tonight." He tapped his glass to hers. "Men and women have done so for centuries. It has become civilized."

Her chin tilted. "You're making fun of me."

"Yes." Ducking into the refrigerator, he pulled out a small tray. "First you'll try my antipasto. Your palate should be prepared."

Juliet chose a little chunk of zucchini. "I'd think you'd prefer being served in a restaurant."

"Now and then. There are times I prefer privacy." He set down the tray. As he did, she took a small step back. Interested, he lifted a brow. "Juliet, do I make you nervous?"

She swallowed zucchini. "Don't be absurd."

"Am I?" On impulse, he set his wine down as well and took another step toward her. Juliet found her back pressed into the refrigerator.

"Carlo—"

"No, shh. We experiment." Gently, watching her, he brushed his lips over one cheek, then the other. He heard her breath catch then shudder out. Nerves—these he accepted. When a man and woman were attracted and close, there had to be nerves. Without them, passion was bland, like a sauce without spice.

But fear? Wasn't that what he saw in her eyes? Just a trace of it, only briefly. Nerves he'd use, play on, exploit. Fear was something different. It disturbed him, blocked him and, at the same time, moved him.

"I won't hurt you, Juliet."

Her eyes were direct again, level, though her hand was balled into a fist. "Won't you?"

He took her hand, slowly working it open. "No." In that moment, he promised both of them. "I won't. Now we'll eat."

Juliet held off the shudder until he'd turned around to stir and drain his pasta. Perhaps he wouldn't hurt her, she thought and recklessly tossed back her wine. But she might hurt herself.

He didn't fuss. He merely perfected. It occurred to Juliet, as she watched him put the last touches on the meal, that he was no different here in the little hotel kitchen than he'd been before the camera. Juliet added her help in the only way she'd have dared. She set the table.

Yes, it was a mistake, she told herself as she arranged plates. But no one but a fool would walk away from anything that smelled like that sauce. She wasn't a fool. She could handle herself. The moment of weak fear she'd felt in the kitchen was past. She'd enjoy a take-your-shoes-off meal, drink two glasses of really excellent burgundy, then go across the hall and catch eight hours' sleep. The merry-go-round would continue the next day.

She selected a marinated mushroom as Carlo brought in the platter of spaghetti. "Better," he said when she smiled at him. "You're ready to enjoy yourself."

With a shrug, Juliet sat. "If one of the top chefs in the world wants to cook me dinner, why should I complain?"

"*The* top," he corrected and gestured for her to serve herself. She did, barely conquering greed.

"Does it really relax you to stand in a kitchen?"

"It depends. Sometimes it relaxes, sometimes it excites. Always it pleases. No, don't cut." With a shake of his head, he reached over. "Americans. You roll it onto the fork."

"It falls off when I do."

"Like this." With his hands on her wrists, he guided her. Her pulse was steady, he noted, but not slow. "Now." Still holding her hand, he lifted the fork toward her mouth. "Taste."

As she did, he had the satisfaction of watching her face. Spices exploded on her tongue. Heat seeped through, mellowing to warmth. She savored it, even as she thought of the next bite. "Oh, this is no little sin."

Nothing could have delighted him more. With a laugh, he sat back and started on his own plate. "Small sins are only small pleasures. When Franconi cooks for you, food is not a basic necessity."

She was already rolling the next forkful. "You win that one. Why aren't you fat?"

"Prego?"

"If I could cook like this..." She tasted again and sighed. "I'd look like one of your meatballs."

With a chuckle, he watched her dig in. It pleased him to see someone he cared for enjoying what he'd created. After years of cooking, he'd never tired of it. "So, your mother didn't teach you to cook?"

"She tried." Juliet accepted a piece of the crusty bread he offered but set it aside as she rolled more spaghetti. First things first. "I never seemed to be very good at the things she wanted me to be good at. My sister plays the piano beautifully. I can barely remember the scales."

"So, what did you want to do instead of taking piano lessons?"

"Play third base." It came out so easily, it stunned her. Juliet had thought she'd buried that along with a dozen other childhood frustrations. "It just wasn't done," she said with a shrug. "My mother was determined to raise two well-rounded ladies who would become two well-rounded, successful wives. Win some, lose some."

"You think she's not proud of you?"

The question hit a target she hadn't known was exposed. Juliet reached for her wine. "It's not a matter of pride, but of disappointment, I suppose. I disappointed her. I confused my father. They still wonder what they did wrong."

"What they did wrong was not to accept what you are."

"Maybe," she murmured. "Or maybe I was determined to be something they couldn't accept. I've never worked it out."

"Are you unhappy with your life?"

Surprised, she glanced up. Unhappy? Sometimes frustrated, harassed and pressured. But unhappy? "No. No, I'm not."

"Then perhaps that's your answer."

Juliet took a moment to study him. He was more than gorgeous, more than sexy, more than all those qualities she'd once cynically attributed to him. "Carlo." For the first time she reached out to touch him, just his hand, but he thought it a giant step. "You're a very nice man."

"But of course I am." His fingers curled over hers because he couldn't resist. "I could give you references."

With a laugh, Juliet backed off. "I'm sure you could." With concentration, dedication and just plain greed, she cleared off her plate.

"Time for dessert."

"Carlo!" Moaning, Juliet pressed a hand to her stomach. "Please, don't be cruel."

"You'll like it." He was up and in the kitchen before she found the strength to refuse again. "It's an old, old, Italian tradition. Back to the empire. American cheesecake is sometimes excellent, but this…" He brought out a small, lovely cake with cherries dripping lavishly over it.

"Carlo, I'll die."

"Just a taste with the champagne." He popped the cork with an expert twist and poured two fresh glasses. "Go, sit on the sofa, be comfortable."

As she did, Juliet realized why the Romans traditionally slept after a meal. She could've curled up in a happy little ball and been unconscious in moments. But the champagne was lively, insistent.

"Here." He brought over one plate with a small slice. "We'll share."

"One bite," she told him, prepared to stand firm. Then she tasted. Creamy, smooth, not quite sweet, more nutty. Exquisite. With a sigh of surrender, Juliet took another. "Carlo, you're a magician."

"Artist," he corrected.

"Whatever you want." Using all the willpower she had left, Juliet exchanged the cake for champagne. "I really can't eat another bite."

"Yes, I remember. You don't believe in overindulgence." But he filled her glass again.

"Maybe not." She sipped, enjoying that rich, luxurious aura only champagne could give. "But now I've gotten a different perspective on indulgence." Slipping out of her shoes, she laughed over the rim of her glass. "I'm converted."

"You're lovely." The lights were low, the music soft, the scents lingering and rich. He thought of resisting. The fear that had been in her eyes demanded he think of it. But just now, she was relaxed, smiling. The desire he'd felt tug the moment he'd seen her had never completely gone away.

Senses were aroused, heightened, by a meal. That was something he understood perfectly. He also understood that a man and a woman should never ignore whatever pleasure they could give to each other.

So he didn't resist, but took her face in his hands. There he could watch her eyes, feel her skin, nearly taste her. This time he saw desire, not fear but wariness. Perhaps she was ready for lesson two.

She could have refused. The need to do so went through her mind. But his hands were so strong, so gentle on her skin. She'd never been touched like that before. She knew how he'd kiss her and the sense of anticipation mixed with nerves. She knew, and wanted.

Wasn't she a woman who knew her own mind? She took her hands to his wrists, but didn't push away. Her fingers curled around and held as she touched her mouth to his. For a moment they stayed just so, allowing themselves to savor that first taste, that first sensation. Then slowly, mutually, they asked for more.

She seemed so small when he held her that a man could forget how strong and competent she was. He found himself wanting to treasure. Desire might burn, but when she was so pliant, so vulnerable, he found himself compelled to show only gentleness.

Had any man ever shown her such care? Juliet's head began to swim as his hands moved into her hair. Was there another man so patient? His heart was pounding against hers. She could feel it, like something wild and desperate. But his mouth was so soft, his hands so gentle. As though they'd been lovers for years, she thought dimly. And had all the time left in the world to continue to love.

No hurry, no rush, no frenzy. Just pleasure. Her heart opened reluctantly, but it opened. He began to pour through. When the phone shrilled, he swore and she sighed. They'd both been prepared to take all the chances.

"Only a moment," he murmured.

Still dreaming, she touched his cheek. "All right."

As he went to answer, she leaned back, determined not to think.

"Cara!" The enthusiasm in his voice, and the endearment, had her opening her eyes again. With a warm laugh, Carlo went into a stream of Italian. Juliet had no choice but to think.

Affection. Yes, it was in his voice. She didn't have to understand the words. She looked around to see him smiling as he spoke to the woman on the other end. Resigned, Juliet picked up her champagne. It wasn't easy for her to admit she'd been a fool. Or for her to admit she'd been hurt.

She knew who he was. What he was. She knew how many women he'd seduced. Perhaps she was a woman who knew her own mind, and perhaps she wanted him. But she would never be eased into a long line of *others.* Setting down the champagne, she rose.

"*Sì, sì.* I love you."

Juliet turned away at the phrase *I love you.* How well it slid off his tongue, in any language. How little it meant, in any language.

"Interruptions. I'm sorry."

Juliet turned back and gave him her uncompromising look. "Don't be. The dinner was marvelous, Carlo, thank you. You should be ready to check out by eight."

"A moment," he murmured. Crossing over, he took her by the arms. "What's this? You're angry."

"Of course not." She tried to back away and failed. It was easy to forget just how strong he was. "Why should I be?"

"Reasons aren't always necessary for a woman."

Though he'd said it in a simple tone that offered no insult, her eyes narrowed. "The expert. Well, let me tell you something about *this* woman, Franconi. She doesn't think much of a man who makes love to her one minute then pushes another lover in her face the next."

He held up his hand as he struggled to follow her drift. "I'm not following you. Maybe my English is failing."

"Your English is perfect," she spat at him. "From what I just heard, so's your Italian."

"My…" His grin broke out. "The phone."

"Yes. The phone. Now, if you'll excuse me."

He let her get as far as the door. "Juliet, I admit I'm hopelessly enamored of the woman I was speaking to. She's beautiful, intelligent, interesting and I've never met anyone quite like her."

Furious, Juliet whirled around. "How marvelous."

"I think so. It was my mother."

She walked back to snatch up the purse she'd nearly forgotten. "I'd think a man of your experience and imagination could do better."

"So I could." He held her again, not so gently, not so patiently. "If it was necessary. I don't make a habit to explain myself, and when I do, I don't lie."

She took a deep breath because she was abruptly certain she was hearing the truth. Either way, she'd been a fool. "I'm sorry. It's none of my business in any case."

"No, it's not." He took her chin in his hand and held it. "I saw fear in your eyes before. It concerned me. Now I think it wasn't me you were afraid of, but yourself."

"That's none of your business."

"No, it's not," he said again. "You appeal to me, Juliet, in many ways, and I intend to take you to bed. But we'll wait until you aren't afraid."

She wanted to rage at him. She wanted to weep. He saw both things clearly. "We have an early flight in the morning, Carlo."

He let her go, but stood where he was for a long time after he'd heard her door shut across the hall.

Chapter 6

Dallas was different. Dallas was Dallas without apology. Texas rich, Texas big and Texas arrogant. If it was the city that epitomized the state, then it did so with flair. Futuristic architecture and mind-twisting freeways abounded in a strange kind of harmony with the more sedate buildings downtown. The air was hot and carried the scents of oil, expensive perfumes and prairie dust. Dallas was Dallas, but it had never forgotten its roots.

Dallas held the excitement of a boomtown that was determined not to stop booming. It was full of down-home American energy that wasn't about to lag. As far as Juliet was concerned they could have been in downtown Timbuktu.

He acted as though nothing had happened—no intimate dinner, no arousal, no surrender, no cross words. Juliet wondered if he did it to drive her crazy.

Carlo was amiable, cooperative and charming. She knew better now. Under the amiability was a shaft of steel that wouldn't bend an inch. She'd seen it. One could say she'd felt it. It would have been a lie to say she didn't admire it.

Cooperative, sure. In his favor, Juliet had to admit that she'd never been on tour with anyone as willing to work without complaint. And touring was hard work, no matter how glamorous it looked on paper. Once you were into your second full week, it became difficult to smile unless you were cued. Carlo never broke his rhythm.

But he expected perfection—spelled his way—and wouldn't budge an inch until he got it.

Charming. No one could enchant a group of people with more style than Franconi. That alone made her job easier. No one would deny his charm unless they'd seen how cold his eyes could become. She had.

He had flaws like any other man, Juliet thought. Remembering that might help her keep an emotional distance. It always helped her to list the pros and cons of a situation, even if the situation was a man. The trouble was, though flawed, he was damn near irresistible.

And he knew it. That was something else she had to remind herself of.

His ego was no small matter. That was something she'd be wise to balance against his unrestricted generosity. Vanity about himself and his work went over the border into arrogance. It didn't hurt her sense of perspective to weigh that against his innate consideration for others.

But then, there was the way he smiled, the way he said her name. Even the practical, professional Juliet

Trent had a difficult time finding a flaw to balance those little details.

The two days in Dallas were busy enough to keep her driving along on six hours' sleep, plenty of vitamins and oceans of coffee. They were making up for Denver, all right. She had the leg cramps to prove it.

Four minutes on the national news, an interview with one of the top magazines in the country, three write-ups in the Dallas press and two autograph sessions that sold clean out. There was more, but those headed up her report. When she went back to New York, she'd go back in triumph.

She didn't want to think of the dinners with department store executives that started at 10:00 p.m. and lasted until she was falling asleep in her bananas flambé. She couldn't bear to count the lunches of poached salmon or shrimp salad. She'd had to refill her pocket aspirin bottles and stock up on antacids. But it was worth it. She should have been thrilled.

She was miserable.

She was driving him mad. Polite, Carlo thought as they prepared to sit through another luncheon interview. Yes, she was polite. Her mother had taught her perfect manners even if she hadn't taught her to cook.

Competent? As far as he was concerned, he'd never known anyone, male or female, who was as scrupulously competent as Juliet Trent. He'd always admired that particular quality in a companion, insisted on it in an associate. Of course, Juliet was both. Precise, prompt, cool in a crisis and unflaggingly energetic. Admirable qualities all.

For the first time in his life he gave serious thought to strangling a woman.

Indifferent. That's what he couldn't abide. She acted as though there was nothing more between them than the next interview, the next television spot, the next plane. She acted as though there'd been no flare of need, of passion, of understanding between them. One would think she didn't want him with the same intensity that he wanted her.

He knew better. Didn't he?

He could remember her ripe, unhesitating response to him. Mouth to mouth, body to body. There'd been no indifference in the way her arms had held him. No, there'd been strength, pliancy, need, demand, but no indifference. Yet now…

They'd spent nearly two days exclusively in each other's company, but he'd seen nothing in her eyes, heard nothing in her voice that indicated more than a polite business association. They ate together, drove together, worked together. They did everything but sleep together.

He'd had his fill of polite. But he hadn't had his fill of Juliet.

He thought of her. It didn't bruise Carlo's pride to admit he thought of her a great deal. He often thought of women, and why not? When a man didn't think of a woman, he was better off dead.

He wanted her. It didn't worry him to admit that he wanted her more every time he thought of her. He'd wanted many women. He'd never believed in self-denial. When a man didn't want a woman, he *was* dead.

But… Carlo found it odd that "buts" so often followed any thoughts he had on Juliet. But he found himself dwelling on her more often than he'd have once considered healthy. Though he didn't mind wanting a woman until he ached, he found Juliet could make him ache more than he'd have once considered comfortable.

He might have been able to rationalize the threat to his health and comfort. But…she was so damn indifferent.

If he did nothing else in the short time they had left in Dallas, he was going to change that.

Lunch was white linen, heavy silver flatware and thin crystal. The room was done in tones of dusty rose and pastel greens. The murmur of conversation was just as quiet.

Carlo thought it a pity they couldn't have met the reporter at one of the little Tex-Mex restaurants over Mexican beer with chili and nachos. Briefly, he promised himself he'd rectify that in Houston.

He barely noticed the reporter was young and running on nerves as they took their seats. He'd decided, no matter what it took, he'd break through Juliet's inflexible shield of politeness before they stood up again. Even if he had to play dirty.

"I'm so happy you included Dallas on your tour, Mr. Franconi," the reporter began, already reaching for her water glass to clear her throat. "Mr. Van Ness sends his apologies. He was looking forward to meeting you."

Carlo smiled at her, but his mind was on Juliet. "Yes?"

"Mr. Van Ness is the food editor for the *Tribune.*" Juliet spread her napkin over her lap as she gave Carlo information she'd related less than fifteen minutes before. She sent him the friendliest of smiles and hoped he felt the barbs in it. "Ms. Tribly is filling in for him."

"Of course." Carlo smoothed over the gap of attention. "Charmingly, I'm sure."

As a woman she wasn't immune to that top-cream voice. As a reporter, she was well aware of the importance of her assignment. "It's all pretty confused." Ms. Tribly wiped damp hands on her napkin. "Mr. Van Ness is having a baby. That is, what I mean is, his wife went into labor just a couple of hours ago."

"So, we should drink to them." Carlo signaled a waiter. "Margaritas?" He phrased the question as a statement, earned a cool nod from Juliet and a grateful smile from the reporter.

Determined to pull off her first really big assignment, Ms. Tribly balanced a pad discreetly on her lap. "Have you been enjoying your tour through America, Mr. Franconi?"

"I always enjoy America." Lightly he ran a finger over the back of Juliet's hand before she could move it out of reach. "Especially in the company of a beautiful woman." She started to slide her hand away then felt it pinned under his. For a man who could whip up the most delicate of soufflés, his hands were as strong as a boxer's.

Wills sparked, clashed and fumed. Carlo's voice remained mild, soft and romantic. "I must tell you, Ms. Tribly, Juliet is an extraordinary woman. I couldn't manage without her."

"Mr. Franconi's very kind." Though Juliet's voice was as mild and quiet as his, the nudge she gave him under the table wasn't. "I handle the details. Mr. Franconi's the artist."

"We make an admirable team, wouldn't you say, Ms. Tribly?"

"Yes." Not quite sure how to handle that particular line, she veered off to safer ground. "Mr. Franconi, besides writing cookbooks, you own and run a successful restaurant in Rome and occasionally travel to prepare a special dish. A few months ago, you flew to a yacht in the Aegean to cook minestrone for Dimitri Azares, the shipping magnate."

"His birthday," Carlo recalled. "His daughter arranged a surprise." Again, his gaze skimmed over the woman whose hand he held. "Juliet will tell you, I'm fond of surprises."

"Yes, well." Ms. Tribly reached for her water glass again. "Your schedule's so full and exciting. I wonder if you still enjoy the basics as far as cooking."

"Most people think of cooking as anything from a chore to a hobby. But as I've told Juliet—" His fingers twined possessively with hers "—food is a basic need. Like making love, it should appeal to all the senses. It should excite, arouse, satisfy." He slipped his thumb around to skim over her palm. "You remember, Juliet?"

She'd tried to forget, had told herself she could. Now with that light, insistent brush of thumb, he was bringing it all back. "Mr. Franconi is a strong believer in the sensuality of food. His unusual flair for bringing this out has made him one of the top chefs in the world."

"Grazie, mi amore," he murmured and brought her stiff hand to his lips.

She pressed her shoe down on the soft leather of his loafers and hoped she ground bones. "I think you, and your readers, will find that Mr. Franconi's book, *The Italian Way,* is a really stunning example of his technique, his style and his opinions, written in such a way that the average person following one of his recipes step-by-step can create something very special."

When their drinks were served, Juliet gave another tug on her hand thinking she might catch him off guard. She should have known better.

"To the new baby." He smiled over at Juliet. "It's always a pleasure to drink to life in all its stages."

Ms. Tribly sipped lightly at her margarita in a glass the size of a small birdbath. "Mr. Franconi, have you actually cooked and tasted every recipe that's in your book?"

"Of course." Carlo enjoyed the quick tang of his drink. There was a time for the sweet, and a time for the tart. His laugh came low and smooth as he looked at Juliet. "When something's mine, there's nothing I don't learn about it. A meal, Ms. Tribly, is like a love affair."

She broke the tip of her pencil and hurriedly dug out another. "A love affair?"

"Yes. It begins slowly, almost experimentally. Just a taste, to whet the appetite, to stir the anticipation. Then the flavor changes, perhaps something light, something cool to keep the senses stirred, but not overwhelmed. Then there's the spice, the meat, the variety. The senses are aroused—the mind is focused on the pleasure. It should be lingered over. But finally, there's dessert, the time of indulgence." When he smiled at Juliet, there was no mistaking his meaning. "It should be enjoyed slowly, savored, until the palate is satisfied and the body sated."

Ms. Tribly swallowed. "I'm going to buy a copy of your book for myself."

With a laugh, Carlo picked up his menu. "Suddenly, I have a huge appetite."

Juliet ordered a small fruit salad and picked at it for thirty minutes.

"I've really got to get back." After polishing off her meal and an apricot tart, Ms. Tribly gathered up her pad. "I can't tell you how much I've enjoyed this, Mr.

Franconi. I'm never going to sit down to pot roast with the same attitude again."

Amused, Carlo rose. "It was a pleasure."

"I'll be glad to send a clipping of the article to your office, Ms. Trent."

"I'd appreciate that." Juliet offered her hand, surprised when the reporter held it an extra moment.

"You're a lucky woman. Enjoy the rest of your tour, Mr. Franconi."

"Arrivederci." He was still smiling when he sat down to finish his coffee.

"You put on a hell of a show, Franconi."

He'd been expecting the storm. Anticipating it. "Yes, I think I did my—what was it you called it? Ah yes, my spiel very well."

"It was more like a three-act play." With calm, deliberate movements, she signed the check. "But the next time, don't cast me unless you ask first."

"Cast you?"

His innocence was calculated to infuriate. He never missed his mark. "You gave that woman the very clear impression that we were lovers."

"Juliet, I merely gave her the very correct impression that I respect and admire you. What she takes from that isn't my responsibility."

Juliet rose, placed her napkin very carefully on the table and picked up her briefcase. "Swine."

Carlo watched her walk out of the restaurant. No endearment could have pleased him more. When a woman called a man a swine, she wasn't indifferent. He was whistling when he walked out to join her. It pleased him even more to see her fumbling with the keys of the rented car parked at the curb. When a woman was indifferent, she didn't swear at inanimate objects.

"Would you like me to drive to the airport?"

"No." Swearing again, she jabbed the key into the lock. She'd control her temper. She would control it. Like hell. Slamming both hands down on the roof of the car, she stared at him. "Just what was the point of that little charade?"

Squisito, he thought briefly. Her eyes were a dangerous blade-sharp green. He'd discovered he preferred a woman with temper. "Charade?"

"All that hand-holding, those intimate looks you were giving me?"

"It's not a charade that I enjoy holding your hand, and that I find it impossible not to look at you."

She refused to argue with the car between them. In a few quick steps she was around the hood and toe-to-toe with him. "It was completely unprofessional."

"Yes. It was completely personal."

It was going to be difficult to argue at all if he turned everything she said to his own advantage.

"Don't ever do it again."

"Madonna." His voice was very mild, his move very calculated. Juliet found herself boxed in between him and the car. "Orders I'll take from you when they have to do with schedules and plane flights. When it comes to more personal things, I do as I choose."

It wasn't something she'd expected; that's why she lost her advantage. Juliet would tell herself that again and again—later. He had her by both shoulders and his eyes never left hers as he gave her a quick jerk. It wasn't the smooth, calculated seduction she'd have anticipated from him. It was rough, impulsive and enervating.

His mouth was on hers, all demand. His hands held her still, all power. She had no time to stiffen, to struggle or to think. He took her with him quickly, through a journey of heat and light. She didn't resist. Later, when she would tell herself she had, it would be a lie.

There were people on the sidewalk, cars in the street. Juliet and Carlo were unaware of everything. The heat of a Dallas afternoon soaked into the concrete beneath them. It blasted the air until it hummed. They were concerned with a fire of their own.

Her hands were at his waist, holding on, letting go. A car streaked by, country rock blasting through open windows. She never heard it. Though she'd refused wine at lunch, she tasted it on his tongue and was intoxicated.

Later, much later, he'd take time to think about what was happening. It wasn't the same. Part of him already knew and feared because it wasn't the same. Touching her was different than touching other women. Tasting her—lightly, deeply, teasingly—just tasting her was different than tasting other women. The feelings were new, though he'd have sworn he'd experienced all the feelings that any man was capable of.

He knew about sensations. He incorporated them in his work and in his life. But they'd never had this depth before. A man who found more and didn't reach for it was a fool.

He knew about intimacy. He expected, demanded it in everything he did. But it had never had this strength before.

New experiences were not to be refused, but explored and exploited. If he felt a small, nagging fear, he could ignore it. For now.

Later. They clung to each other and told themselves they'd think later. Time was unimportant after all. Now held all the meaning necessary.

He took his mouth from hers, but his hands held her still. It shocked him to realize they weren't quite steady. Women had made him ache. Women had made him burn. But no woman had ever made him tremble. "We need a place," he murmured. "Quiet, private. It's time to stop pretending this isn't real."

She wanted to nod, to simply put herself completely in his hands. Wasn't that the first step in losing control over your own life? "No, Carlo." Her voice wasn't as strong as she would have liked but she didn't back away. "We've got to stop mixing personal feelings with business. We've got just under two weeks to go on the road."

"I don't give a damn if it's two days or two years. I want to spend it making love with you."

She brought herself back enough to remember they were standing on a public street in the middle of afternoon traffic. "Carlo, this isn't the time to discuss it."

"Now is always the time. Juliet—" He cupped her face in his hand. "It's not me you're fighting."

He didn't have to finish the thought. She was all too aware that the war was within herself. What she wanted, what was wise. What she needed, what was safe. The tug-of-war threatened to split her apart, and the two halves, put back together, would never equal the whole she understood.

"Carlo, we have a plane to catch."

He said something soft and pungent in Italian. "You'll talk to me."

"No." She lifted her hands to grip his forearms. "Not about this."

"Then we'll stay right here until you change your mind."

They could both be stubborn, and with stubbornness, they could both get nowhere. "We have a schedule."

"We have a great deal more than that."

"No, we don't." His brow lifted. "All right then, we can't. We have a plane to catch."

"We'll catch your plane, Juliet. But we'll talk in Houston."

"Carlo, don't push me into a corner."

"Who pushes?" he murmured. "Me or you?"

She didn't have an easy answer. "What I'll do is arrange for someone else to come out and finish the tour with you."

He only shook his head. "No, you won't. You're too ambitious. Leaving a tour in the middle wouldn't look good for you."

She set her teeth. He knew her too well already. "I'll get sick."

This time he smiled. "You're too proud. Running away isn't possible for you."

"It's not a matter of running." But of survival, she thought and quickly changed the phrase. "It's a matter of priorities."

He kissed her again, lightly. "Whose?"

"Carlo, we have business."

"Yes, of different sorts. One has nothing to do with the other."

"To me they do. Unlike you, I don't go to bed with everyone I'm attracted to."

Unoffended, he grinned. "You flatter me, *cara*."

She could have sighed. How like him to make her want to laugh while she was still furious. "Purely unintentional."

"I like you when you bare your teeth."

"Then you're going to enjoy the next couple of weeks." She pushed his hands away. "It's a long ride to the airport, Carlo. Let's get going."

Amiable as ever, he pulled his door open. "You're the boss."

A foolish woman might've thought she'd won a victory.

Chapter 7

Juliet was an expert on budgeting time. It was her business every bit as much as promotion. So, if she could budget time, she could just as easily overbudget it when the circumstances warranted. If she did her job well enough, hustled fast enough, she could create a schedule so tight that there could be no time for talk that didn't directly deal with business. She counted on Houston to cooperate.

Juliet had worked with Big Bill Bowers before. He was a brash, warmhearted braggart who handled special events for Books, Etc., one of the biggest chains in the country. Big Bill had Texas sewed up and wasn't ashamed to say so. He was partial to long, exaggerated stories, ornate boots and cold beer.

Juliet liked him because he was sharp and tough and invariably made her job easier. On this trip, she blessed him because he was also long-winded and gregarious. He wouldn't give her or Carlo many private moments.

From the minute they arrived at Houston International, the six-foot-five, two-hundred-and-sixty-pound Texan made it his business to entertain. There was a crowd of people waiting at the end of the breezeway, some already packed together and chatting, but there was no overlooking Big Bill. You only had to look for a Brahma bull in a Stetson.

"Well now, there's little Juliet. Pretty as ever."

Juliet found herself caught in a good-natured, rib-cracking bear hug. "Bill." She tested her lungs gingerly as she drew away. "It's always good to be back in Houston. You look great."

"Just clean living, honey." He let out a boom of a laugh that turned heads. Juliet found her mood lifting automatically.

"Carlo Franconi, Bill Bowers. Be nice to him," she added with a grin. "He's not only big, he's the man who'll promote your books for the largest chain in the state."

"Then I'll be very nice." Carlo offered his hand and met an enormous, meaty paw.

"Glad you could make it." The same meaty hand gave Carlo a friendly pat on the back that could have felled a good-sized sapling. Juliet gave Carlo points for not taking a nosedive.

"It's good to be here" was all he said.

"Never been to Italy myself, but I'm partial to Eye-talian cooking. The wife makes a hell of a pot of spaghetti. Let me take that for you." Before Carlo could object, Bill had hefted his big leather case. Juliet couldn't prevent the smirk when Carlo glanced down at the case as though it were a small child boarding a school bus for the first time.

"Car's outside. We'll just pick up your bags and get going. Airports and hospitals, can't stand 'em." Bill started toward the terminal in his big, yard-long strides. "Hotel's all ready for you. I checked this morning."

Juliet managed to keep up though she still wore three-inch heels. "I knew I could depend on you, Bill. How's Betty?"

"Mean as ever," he said proudly of his wife. "With the kids up and gone, she's only got me to order around."

"But you're still crazy about her."

"A man gets used to mean after a while." He grinned, showing one prominent gold tooth. "No need to go by the hotel straight off. We'll show Carlo here what Houston's all about." As he walked he swung Carlo's case at his side.

"I'd like that." Diplomatically, Carlo moved closer to his side. "I could take that case..."

"No need for that. What you got in here, boy? Weighs like a steer."

"Tools," Juliet put in with an innocent smile. "Carlo's very temperamental."

"Man can't be too temperamental about his tools," Bill said with a nod. He tipped his hat at a young woman with a short skirt and lots of leg. "I've still got the same hammer my old man gave me when I was eight."

"I'm just as sentimental about my spatulas," Carlo murmured. But he hadn't, Juliet noted, missed the legs, either.

"You got a right." A look passed between the two men that was essential male and pleased. Juliet decided it had more to do with long smooth thighs than tools. "Now, I figured you two must've had your fill of fancy restaurants and creamed chicken by now. Having a little barbecue over at my place. You can take off your shoes, let down your hair and eat real food."

Juliet had been to one of Bill's *little* barbecues before. It meant grilling a whole steer along with several chickens and the better part of a pig, then washing it all down with a couple hundred gallons of beer. It also meant she wouldn't see her hotel room for a good five hours. "Sounds great. Carlo, you haven't lived until you've tasted one of Bill's steaks grilled over mesquite."

Carlo slipped a hand over her elbow. "Then we should live first." The tone made her turn her head and meet the look. "Before we attend to business."

"That's the ticket." Bill stopped in front of the conveyor belt. "Just point 'em out and we'll haul 'em in."

They lived, mingling at Bill's little barbecue with another hundred guests. Music came from a seven-piece band that never seemed to tire. Laughter and splashing rose up from a pool separated from the patio by a spread of red flowering bushes that smelled of spice and heat. Above all was the scent of grilled meat, sauce and smoke. Juliet ate twice as much as she would normally have considered because her host filled her plate then kept an eagle eye on her.

It should have pleased her that Carlo was surrounded by a dozen or so Texas ladies in bathing suits and sundresses who had suddenly developed an avid interest in cooking. But, she thought nastily, most of them wouldn't know a stove from a can opener.

It should have pleased her that she had several men

dancing attendance on her. She was barely able to keep the names and faces separate as she watched Carlo laugh with a six-foot brunette in two minuscule ribbons of cloth.

The music was loud, the air heavy and warm. Giving in to necessity, Juliet had dug a pair of pleated shorts and a crop top out of her bag and changed. It occurred to her that it was the first time since the start of the tour that she'd been able to sit out in the sun, soak up rays and not have a pad and pencil in her hand.

Though the blond beside her with the gleaming biceps was in danger of becoming both a bore and a nuisance, she willed herself to enjoy the moment.

It was the first time Carlo had seen her in anything other than her very proper suits. He'd already concluded, by the way she walked, that her legs were longer than one might think from her height. He hadn't been wrong. They seemed to start at her waist and continued down, smooth, slim and New York pale. The statuesque brunette beside him might not have existed for all the attention he paid her.

It wasn't like him to focus on a woman yards away when there was one right beside him. Carlo knew it, but not what to do about it. The woman beside him smelled of heat and musk—heavy and seductive. It made him think that Juliet's scent was lighter, but held just as much punch.

She had no trouble relaxing with other men. Carlo tipped back a beer as he watched her fold those long legs under her and laugh with the two men sitting on either side of her. She didn't stiffen when the young, muscle-bound hunk on her left put his hand on her shoulder and leaned closer.

It wasn't like him to be jealous. As emotional as he

was, Carlo had never experienced that particular sensation. He'd also felt that a woman had just as much right to flirt and experiment as he did. He found that particular rule didn't apply to Juliet. If she let that slick-skinned, weight-lifting *buffone* put his hand on her again…

He didn't have time to finish the thought. Juliet laughed again, set aside her plate and rose. Carlo couldn't hear whatever she'd said to the man beside her, but she strolled into the sprawling ranch house. Moments later, the burnished, bare-chested man rose and followed her.

"Maledetto!"

"What?" The brunette stopped in the middle of what she'd thought was an intimate conversation.

Carlo barely spared her a glance. *"Scusi."* Muttering, he strode off in the direction Juliet had taken. There was murder in his eye.

Fed up with fending off the attentions of Big Bill's hotshot young neighbor, Juliet slipped into the house through the kitchen. Her mood might have been foul, but she congratulated herself on keeping her head. She hadn't taken a chunk out of the free-handed, self-appointed Adonis. She hadn't snarled out loud even once in Carlo's direction.

Attending to business always helped steady her temper. With a check of her watch, Juliet decided she could get one collect call through to her assistant at home. She'd no more than picked up the receiver from the kitchen wall phone than she was lifted off her feet.

"Ain't much to you. But it sure is a pleasure to look at what there is."

She barely suppressed the urge to come back with

her elbow. "Tim." She managed to keep her voice pleasant while she thought how unfortunate it was that most of his muscle was from the neck up. "You're going to have to put me down so I can make my call."

"It's a party, sweetheart." Shifting her around with a flex of muscle, he set her on the counter. "No need to go calling anybody when you've got me around."

"You know what I think?" Juliet gauged that she could give him a quick kick below the belt, but tapped his shoulder instead. After all, he was Bill's neighbor. "I think you should get back out to the party before all the ladies miss you."

"Got a better idea." He leaned forward, boxing her in with a hand on each side. His teeth gleamed in the style of the best toothpaste ads. "Why don't you and I go have a little party of our own? I imagine you New York ladies know how to have fun."

If she hadn't considered him such a jerk, she'd have been insulted for women in general and New York in particular. Patiently, Juliet considered the source. "We New York ladies," she said calmly, "know how to say no. Now back off, Tim."

"Come on, Juliet." He hooked a finger in the neck of her top. "I've got a nice big water bed down the street."

She put a hand on his wrist. Neighbor or not, she was going to belt him. "Why don't you go take a dive."

He only grinned as his hand slid up her leg. "Just what I had in mind."

"Excuse me." Carlo's voice was soft as a snake from the doorway. "If you don't find something else to do with your hands quickly, you might lose the use of them."

"Carlo." Her voice was sharp, but not with relief. She wasn't in the mood for a knight-in-armor rescue.

"The lady and I're having a private conversation." Tim flexed his pectorals. "Take off."

With his thumbs hooked in his pockets, Carlo strolled over. Juliet noted he looked as furious as he had over the canned basil. In that mood, there was no telling what he'd do. She swore, let out a breath and tried to avoid a scene. "Why don't we all go outside."

"Excellent." Carlo held out a hand to help her down. Before she could reach for it, Tim blocked her way.

"You go outside, buddy. Juliet and I haven't finished talking."

Carlo inclined his head then shifted his gaze to Juliet. "Have you finished talking?"

"Yes." She'd have slid off the counter, but that would have put her on top of Tim's shoulders. Frustrated, she sat where she was.

"Apparently Juliet is finished." Carlo's smile was all amiability, but his eyes were flat and cold. "You seem to be blocking her way."

"I told you to take off." Big and annoyed, he grabbed Carlo by the lapels.

"Cut it out, both of you." With a vivid picture of Carlo bleeding from the nose and mouth, Juliet grabbed a cookie jar shaped like a ten-gallon hat. Before she could use it, Tim grunted and bent over from the waist. As he gasped, clutching his stomach, Juliet only stared.

"You can put that down now," Carlo said mildly. "It's time we left." When she didn't move, he took the jar himself, set it aside, then lifted her from the counter. "You'll excuse us," he said pleasantly to the groaning Tim, then led Juliet outside.

"What did you do?"

"What was necessary."

Juliet looked back toward the kitchen door. If she hadn't seen it for herself… "You hit him."

"Not very hard." Carlo nodded to a group of sunbathers. "All his muscle is in his chest and his brain."

"But—" She looked down at Carlo's hands. They were lean-fingered and elegant with the flash of a diamond on the pinky. Not hands one associated with self-defense. "He was awfully big."

Carlo lifted a brow as he took his sunglasses back out of his pocket. "Big isn't always an advantage. The neighborhood where I grew up was an education. Are you ready to leave?"

No, his voice wasn't pleasant, she realized. It was cold. Ice cold. Instinctively hers mirrored it. "I suppose I should thank you."

"Unless of course you enjoyed being pawed. Perhaps Tim was just acting on the signals you were sending out."

Juliet stopped in her tracks. "What signals?"

"The ones women send out when they want to be pursued."

Thinking she could bring her temper to order, she gave herself a moment. It didn't work. "He might have been bigger than you," she said between her teeth. "But I think you're just as much of an ass. You're very much alike."

The lenses of his glasses were smoky, but she saw his eyes narrow. "You compare what's between us with what happened in there?"

"I'm saying some men don't take no for an answer graciously. You might have a smoother style, Carlo, but you're after the same thing, whether it's a roll in the hay or a cruise on a water bed."

He dropped his hand from her arm, then very deliberately tucked both in his pockets. "If I've mistaken your feelings, Juliet, I apologize. I'm not a man who finds it necessary or pleasurable to pressure a woman. Do you wish to leave or stay?"

She felt a great deal of pressure—in her throat, behind her eyes. She couldn't afford the luxury of giving in to it. "I'd like to get to the hotel. I still have some work to do tonight."

"Fine." He left her there to find their host.

Three hours later, Juliet admitted working was impossible. She'd tried all the tricks she knew to relax. A half hour in a hot tub, quiet music on the radio while she watched the sun set from her hotel window. When relaxing failed, she went over the Houston schedule twice. They'd be running from 7:00 a.m. to 5:00 p.m., almost nonstop. Their flight to Chicago took off at 6:00.

There'd be no time to discuss, think or worry about anything that had happened within the last twenty-four hours. That's what she wanted. Yet when she tried to work on the two-day Chicago stand, she couldn't. All she could do was think about the man a few steps across the hall.

She hadn't realized he could be so cold. He was always so full of warmth, of life. True, he was often infuriating, but he infuriated with verve. Now, he'd left her in a vacuum.

No. Tossing her notebook aside, Juliet dropped her chin in her hand. No, she'd put herself there. Maybe she could have stood it if she'd been right. She'd been dead wrong. She hadn't sent any signals to the idiot Tim, and Carlo's opinion on that still made her steam, but… But she hadn't even thanked him for helping her when, whether she liked to admit it or not, she'd needed help. It didn't sit well with her to be in debt.

With a shrug, she rose from the table and began to pace the room. It might be better all around if they finished off the tour with him cold and distant. There'd certainly be fewer personal problems that way because there'd be nothing personal between them. There'd be no edge to their relationship because they wouldn't have a relationship. Logically, this little incident was probably the best thing that could have happened. It hardly mattered if she'd been right or wrong as long as the result was workable.

She took a glimpse around the small, tidy, impersonal room where she'd spend little more than eight hours, most of it asleep.

No, she couldn't stand it.

Giving in, Juliet stuck her room key in the pocket of her robe.

Women had made him furious before. Carlo counted on it to keep life from becoming too tame. Women had frustrated him before. Without frustrations, how could you fully appreciate success?

But hurt. That was something no woman had ever done to him before. He'd never considered the possibility. Frustration, fury, passion, laughter, shouting. No man who'd known so many women—mother, sisters, lovers—expected a relationship without them. Pain was a different matter.

Pain was an intimate emotion. More personal than passion, more elemental than anger. When it went deep, it found places inside you that should have been left alone.

It had never mattered to him to be considered a rogue, a rake, a playboy—whatever term was being used for a man who appreciated women. Affairs came and went, as affairs were supposed to. They lasted no longer than the passion that conceived them. He was a careful man, a caring man. A lover became a friend as desire waned. There might be spats and hard words during the storm of an affair, but he'd never ended one that way.

It occurred to him that he'd had more spats, more hard words with Juliet than with any other woman. Yet they'd never been lovers. Nor would they be. After pouring a glass of wine, he sat back in a deep chair and closed his eyes. He wanted no woman who compared him with a muscle-bound idiot, who confused passion for lust. He wanted no woman who compared the beauty of lovemaking to—what was it?—a cruise on a water bed. *Dio!*

He wanted no woman who could make him ache so—in the middle of the night, in the middle of the day. He wanted no woman who could bring him pain with a few harsh words.

God, he wanted Juliet.

He heard the knock on the door and frowned. By the time he'd set his glass aside and stood, it came again.

If Juliet hadn't been so nervous, she might have thought of something witty to say about the short black robe Carlo wore with two pink flamingos twining up one side. As it was, she stood in her own robe and bare feet with her fingers linked together.

"I'm sorry," she said when he opened the door.

He stepped back. "Come in, Juliet."

"I had to apologize." She let out a deep breath as she walked into the room. "I was awful to you this afternoon, and you'd helped me out of a very tricky situation with a minimum of fuss. I was angry when you insinuated that I'd led that—that idiot on in some way. I had a right to be." She folded her arms under her chest and paced the room. "It was an uncalled-for remark, and insulting. Even if by the remotest possibility it had been true, you had no right to talk. After all, you were basking in your own harem."

"Harem?" Carlo poured another glass of wine and offered it.

"With that amazon of a brunette leading the pack." She sipped, gestured with the glass and sipped again. "Everywhere we go, you've got half a dozen women nipping at your ankles, but do I say a word?"

"Well, you—"

"And once, just once, I have a problem with some creep with an overactive libido, and you assume I asked for it. I thought that kind of double standard was outdated even in Italy."

Had he ever known a woman who could change his moods so quickly? Thinking it over, and finding it to his taste, Carlo studied his wine. "Juliet, did you come here to apologize, or demand that I do so?"

She scowled at him. "I don't know why I came, but obviously it was a mistake."

"Wait." He held up a hand before she could storm out again. "Perhaps it would be wise if I simply accepted the apology you came in with."

Juliet sent him a killing look. "You can take the apology I came in with and—"

"And offer you one of my own," he finished. "Then we'll be even."

"I didn't encourage him," she murmured. And pouted. He'd never seen that sulky, utterly feminine look on her face before. It did several interesting things to his system.

"And I'm not looking for the same thing he was." He came to her then, close enough to touch. "But very much more."

"Maybe I know that," she whispered, but took a step away. "Maybe I'd like to believe it. I don't understand affairs, Carlo." With a little laugh, she dragged her hand through her hair and turned away. "I should—my father had plenty of them. Discreet," she added with a lingering taste of bitterness. "My mother could always turn a blind eye as long as they were discreet."

He understood such things, had seen them among both friends and relatives, so he understood the scars and disillusionments that could be left. "Juliet, you're not your mother."

"No." She turned back, head up. "No, I've worked long and hard to be certain I'm not. She's a lovely, intelligent woman who gave up her career, her self-esteem, her independence to be no more than a glorified housekeeper because my father wanted it. He didn't want a wife of his to work. A wife of his," she repeated. "What a phrase. Her job was to take care of him. That meant having dinner on the table at six o'clock every night, and his shirts folded in his drawer. He—damn, he's a good father, attentive, considerate. He simply doesn't believe a man should shout at a woman or a girl. As a husband, he'd never forget a birthday, an anniversary. He's always seen to it that she was provided for in the best material fashion, but he dictated my mother's lifestyle. While he was about it, he enjoyed a very discreet string of women."

"Why does your mother stay his wife?"

"I asked her that a few years ago, before I moved away to New York. She loves him." Juliet stared into her wine. "That's reason enough for her."

"Would you rather she'd have left him?"

"I'd rather she'd have been what she could be. What she might've been."

"The choice was hers, Juliet. Just as your life is yours."

"I don't want to ever be bound to anyone, *anyone* who could humiliate me that way." She lifted her head again. "I won't put myself in my mother's position. Not for anyone."

"Do you see all relationships as being so imbalanced?"

With a shrug, she drank again. "I suppose I haven't seen so many of them."

For a moment he was silent. Carlo understood fidelity, the need for it, and the lack of it. "Perhaps we have something in common. I don't remember my father well, I saw him little. He, too, was unfaithful to my mother."

She looked over at him, but he didn't see any surprise in her face. It was as though she expected such things. "But he committed his adultery with the sea. For months he'd be gone, while she raised us, worked, waited. When he'd come home, she'd welcome him. Then he'd go again, unable to resist. When he died, she mourned. She loved him, and made her choice."

"It's not fair, is it?"

"No. Did you think love was?"

"It's not something I want."

He remembered once another woman, a friend, telling him the same thing when she was in turmoil. "We all want love, Juliet."

"No." She shook her head with the confidence born of desperation. "No, affection, respect, admiration, but not love. It steals something from you."

He looked at her as she stood in the path of the

lamplight. "Perhaps it does," he murmured. "But until we love, we can't be sure we needed what was lost."

"Maybe it's easier for you to say that, to think that. You've had many lovers."

It should have amused him. Instead, it seemed to accent a void he hadn't been aware of. "Yes. But I've never been in love. I have a friend—" again he thought of Summer "—once she told me love was a merry-go-round. Maybe she knew best."

Juliet pressed her lips together. "And an affair?"

Something in her voice had him looking over. For the second time he went to her, but slowly. "Perhaps it's just one ride on the carousel."

Because her fingers weren't steady, Juliet set down the glass. "We understand each other."

"In some ways."

"Carlo—" She hesitated, then admitted the decision had already been made before she crossed the hall. "Carlo, I've never taken much time for carousels, but I do want you."

How should he handle her? Odd, he'd never had to think things through so carefully before. With some women, he'd have been flamboyant, sweeping her up, carrying her off. With another he might have been impulsive, tumbling with her to the carpet. But nothing he'd ever done seemed as important as the first time with Juliet.

Words for a woman had always come easily to him. The right phrase, the right tone had always come as naturally as breathing. He could think of nothing. Even a murmur might spoil the simplicity of what she'd said to him and how she'd said it. So he didn't speak.

He kissed her where they stood, not with the raging

passion he knew she could draw from him, not with the hesitation she sometimes made him feel. He kissed her with the truth and the knowledge that longtime lovers often experience. They came to each other with separate needs, separate attitudes, but with this, they locked out the past. Tonight was for the new, and for renewing.

She'd expected the words, the flash and style that seemed so much a part of him. Perhaps she'd even expected something of triumph. Again, he gave her the different and the fresh with no more than the touch of mouth to mouth.

The thought came to her, then was discounted, that he was no more certain of his ground than she. Then he held out his hand. Juliet put hers in it. Together they walked to the bedroom.

If he'd set the scene for a night of romance, Carlo would've added flowers with a touch of spice, music with the throb of passion. He'd have given her the warmth of candlelight and the fun of champagne. Tonight, with Juliet, there was only silence and moonlight. The maid had turned down the bed and left the drapes wide. White light filtered through shadows and onto white sheets.

Standing by the bed, he kissed her palms, one by one. They were cool and carried a hint of her scent. At her wrist her pulse throbbed. Slowly, watching her, he loosened the tie of her robe. With his eyes still on hers, he brought his hands to her shoulders and slipped the material aside. It fell silently to pool at her feet.

He didn't touch her, nor did he yet look at anything but her face. Through nerves, through needs, something like comfort began to move through her. Her lips curved, just slightly, as she reached for the tie of his robe and drew the knot. With her hands light and sure on his shoulders, she pushed the silk aside.

They were both vulnerable, to their needs, to each other. The light was thin and white and washed with shadows. No other illumination was needed this first time that they looked at each other.

He was lean but not thin. She was slender but soft. Her skin seemed only more pale when he touched her. Her hand seemed only more delicate when she touched him.

They came together slowly. There was no need to rush.

The mattress gave, the sheets rustled. Quietly. Side by side they lay, giving themselves time—all the time needed to discover what pleasures could come from the taste of mouth to mouth, the touch of flesh to flesh.

Should she have known it would be like this? So easy. Inevitable. Her skin was warm, so warm wherever he brushed it. His lips demanded, they took, but with such patience. He loved her gently, slowly, as though it were her first time. As she drifted deeper, Juliet thought dimly that perhaps it was.

Innocence. He felt it from her, not physical, but emotional. Somehow, incredibly, he discovered it was the same for himself. No matter how many had come before, for either of them, they came to each other now in innocence.

Her hands didn't hesitate as they moved over him, but stroked as though she were blind and could only gain her own picture through other senses. He smelled of a shower, water and soap, but he tasted richer, of wine. Then he spoke for the first time, only her name. It was to her more moving, more poetic than any endearment.

Her body moved with his, in rhythm, keeping pace.

She seemed to know, somehow, where he would touch her just before she felt his fingers trace, his palms press. Then his lips began a long, luxurious journey she hoped would never end.

She was so small. Why had he never noticed before how small she was? It was easy to forget her strength, her control, her stamina. He could give her tenderness and wait for the passion.

The line of her neck was slender and so white in the moonlight. Her scent was trapped there, at her throat. Intensified. Arousing. He could linger there while blood heated. His and hers.

He slid his tongue over the subtle curve of her breast to find the peak. When he drew it into his mouth, she moaned his name, giving them both a long, slow nudge to the edge.

But there was more to taste, more to touch. Passion, when heated, makes a mockery of control. Sounds slipped into the room—a catch of breath, a sigh, a moan—all pleasure. Their scents began to mix together—a lover's fragrance. In the moonlight, they were one form. The sheets were hot, twisted. When with tongue and fingertips he drove her over the first peak, Juliet gripped the tousled sheets as her body arched and shuddered with a torrent of sensations.

While she was still weak, still gasping, he slipped into her.

His head was spinning—a deliciously foreign sensation to him. He wanted to bury himself in her, but he wanted to see her. Her eyes were shut; her lips just parted as the breath hurried in and out. She moved with him, slowly, then faster, still faster until her fingers dug into his shoulders.

On a cry of pleasure, her eyes flew open. Looking into them, he saw the dark, astonished excitement he'd wanted to give her.

At last, giving in to the rushing need of his own body, he closed his mouth over hers and let himself go.

Chapter 8

Were there others who understood true passion? Wrapped in Carlo, absorbing and absorbed by Carlo, Juliet knew she hadn't until moments ago. Should it make you weak? She felt weak, but not empty.

Should she feel regret? Yes, logically she should. She'd given more of herself than she'd intended, shared more than she'd imagined, risked more than she should have dared. But she had no regrets. Perhaps later she'd make her list of the whys and why nots. For now, she wanted only to enjoy the soft afterglow of loving.

"You're quiet." His breath whispered across her temple, followed by his lips.

She smiled a little, content to let her eyes close. "So are you."

Nuzzling his cheek against her hair, he looked over to the slant of moonlight through the window. He wasn't sure which words to use. He'd never felt quite like this before with any woman. He'd never expected to. How could he tell her that and expect to be believed? He was having a hard time believing it himself. And yet...perhaps truth was the hardest thing to put into words.

"You feel very small when I hold you like this," he murmured. "It makes me want to hold you like this for a long, long time."

"I like having you hold me." The admission was much easier to make than she'd thought. With a little laugh, she turned her head so that she could see his face. "I like it very much."

"Then you won't object if I go on holding you for the next few hours."

She kissed his chin. "The next few minutes," she corrected. "I have to get back to my room."

"You don't like my bed?"

She stretched and cuddled and thought how wonderful it would be never to move from that one spot. "I think I'm crazy about it, but I've got a little work to do before I call it a night, then I have to be up by six-thirty, and—"

"You work too much." He cut her off, then leaned over her to pick up the phone. "You can get up in the morning just as easily from my bed as yours."

Finding she liked the way his body pressed into hers, she prepared to be convinced. "Maybe. What're you doing?"

"Shh. Yes, this is Franconi in 922. I'd like a wake-up call for six." He replaced the phone and rolled, pulling her on top of him. "There now, everything is taken care of. The phone will ring at dawn and wake us up."

"It certainly will." Juliet folded her hands over his

chest and rested her chin on them. "But you told them to call at six. We don't have to get up until six-thirty."

"Yes." He slid his hands down low over her back. "So we have a half hour to—ah—wake up."

With a laugh, she pressed her lips to his shoulder. This once, she told herself, just this once, she'd let someone else do the planning. "Very practical. Do you think we might take a half hour or so to—ah—go to sleep?"

"My thoughts exactly."

When the phone did ring, Juliet merely groaned and slid down under the sheets. For the second time, she found herself buried under Carlo as he rolled over to answer it. Without complaint, she lay still, hoping the ringing of the phone had been part of a dream.

"Come now, Juliet." Shifting most of his weight from her, Carlo began to nibble on her shoulder. "You're playing mole."

She murmured in drowsy excitement as he slid his hand down to her hip. "Mole? I don't have a mole."

"Playing mole." She was so warm and soft and pliant. He'd known she would be. Mornings were made for lazy delights and waking her was a pleasure just begun.

Juliet stretched under the stroke and caress of his hands. Mornings were for a quick shower and a hasty cup of coffee. She'd never known they could be luxurious. "Playing mole?"

"An American expression." The skin over her rib cage was soft as butter. He thought there was no better time to taste it. "You pretend to be dead."

Because her mind was clouded with sleep, her

system already churning with passion, it took a moment. "Possum."

"Prego?"

"Playing possum," she repeated and, guided by his hands, shifted. "A mole's different."

"So, they're both little animals."

She opened one eye. His hair was rumpled around his face, his chin darkened with a night's growth of beard. But when he smiled he looked as though he'd been awake for hours. He looked, she admitted, absolutely wonderful.

"You want an animal?" With a sudden burst of energy, she rolled on top of him. Her hands were quick, her mouth avid. In seconds, she'd taken his breath away.

She'd never been aggressive, but found the low, surprised moan and the fast pump of his heart to her liking. Her body reacted like lightning. She didn't mind that his hands weren't as gentle, as patient as they'd been the night before. This new desperation thrilled her.

He was Franconi, known for his wide range of expertise in the kitchen and the bedroom. But she was making him wild and helpless at the same time. With a laugh, she pressed her mouth to his, letting her tongue find all the dark, lavish tastes. When he tried to shift her, to take her because the need had grown too quickly to control, she evaded. His breathless curse whispered into her mouth.

He never lost finesse with a woman. Passion, his passion, had always been melded with style. Now, as she took her frenzied journey over him, he had no style, only needs. He'd never been a man to rush. When he cooked, he went slowly, step-by-step. Enjoy, experience, experiment. He made love the same way. Such things were meant to be savored, to be appreciated by each of the five senses.

It wasn't possible to savor when you were driven beyond the civilized. When your senses were whirling and tangled, it wasn't possible to separate them. Being driven was something new for him, something intoxicating. No, he wouldn't fight it, but pull her with him.

Rough and urgent, he grabbed her hips. Within moments, they were both beyond thought, beyond reason….

His breath was still unsteady, but he held her close and tight. Whatever she'd done, or was doing to him, he didn't want to lose it. The thought flickered briefly that he didn't want to lose her. Carlo pushed it aside. It was a dangerous thought. They had now. It was much wiser to concentrate on that.

"I have to go." Though she wanted nothing more than to curl up against him, Juliet made herself shift away. "We have to be downstairs at checkout in forty minutes."

"To meet Big Bill."

"That's right." Juliet reached onto the floor for her robe, slipping it onto her arms before she stood up. Carlo's lips trembled at the way she turned her back to him to tie it. It was rather endearing to see the unconscious modesty from a woman who'd just exploited every inch of his body. "You don't know how grateful I am that Bill volunteered to play chauffeur. The last thing I want to do is fight the freeway system in this town. I've had to do it before, and it's not a pretty sight."

"I could drive," he murmured, enjoying the way the rich green silk reached the top of her thighs.

"Staying alive is another reason I'm grateful for Bill.

I'll call and have a bellman come up for the bags in—thirty-five minutes. Be sure—"

"You check everything because we won't be coming back," he finished. "Juliet, haven't I proven my competency yet?"

"Just a friendly reminder." She checked her watch before she remembered she wasn't wearing it. "The TV spot should be a breeze. Jacky Torrence hosts. It's a jovial sort of show that goes after the fast, funny story rather than nuts and bolts."

"Hmm." He rose, stretching. The publicist was back, he noted with a half smile, but as he reached down for his own robe, he noticed that she'd broken off. Lifting his head, he looked up at her.

Good God, he was beautiful. It was all she could think. Schedules, planning, points of information all went out of her head. In the early-morning sun, his skin was more gold than brown, smooth and tight over his rib cage, nipped in at the waist to a narrow line of hip. Letting out a shaky breath, she took a step back.

"I'd better go," she managed. "We can run through today's schedule on the way to the studio."

It pleased him enormously to understand what had broken her concentration. He held the robe loosely in one hand as he took a step closer. "Perhaps we'll get bumped."

"Bite your tongue." Aiming for a light tone, she succeeded with a whisper. "That's an interesting robe."

The tone of her voice was a springboard to an arousal already begun. "You like the flamingos? My mother has a sense of humor." But he didn't put it on as he stepped closer.

"Carlo, stay right where you are. I mean it." She held up a hand as she walked backward to the doorway.

He grinned, and kept on grinning after he heard the click of the hallway door.

Between Juliet cracking the whip and Bill piloting, their Houston business went like clockwork. TV, radio and print, the media was responsive and energetic. The midafternoon autograph party turned out to be a party in the true sense of the word and was a smashing success. Juliet found herself a spot in a storeroom and ripped open the oversized envelope from her office that had been delivered to the hotel. Settling back, she began to go through the clippings her assistant had air expressed.

L.A. was excellent, as she'd expected. Upbeat and enthusiastic. San Diego might've tried for a little more depth, but they'd given him page one of the *Food* section in one spread and a below-the-fold in the *Style* section in another. No complaints. Portland and Seattle listed a recipe apiece and raved shamelessly. Juliet could've rubbed her hands together with glee if she hadn't been drinking coffee. Then she hit Denver.

Coffee sloshed out of the cup and onto her hand.

"Damn!" Fumbling in her briefcase, she found three crumpled tissues and began to mop up. A gossip column. Who'd have thought it? She gave herself a moment to think then relaxed. Publicity was publicity, after all. And the truth of the matter was, Franconi was gossip. Looking at it logically, the more times his name was in print, the more successful the tour. Resolved, Juliet began to read.

She nodded absently as she skimmed the first paragraph. Chatty, shallow, but certainly not offensive. A lot of people who might not glance at the food or cooking sections would give the gossip columns a working over. All in all, it was probably an excellent break. Then she read the second paragraph.

Juliet was up out of her folding chair. This time the coffee that dripped onto the floor went unnoticed. Her expression changed from surprised astonishment to fury in a matter of seconds. In the same amount of time, she stuffed the clippings back into their envelope. It wasn't easy, but she gave herself five minutes for control before she walked back into the main store.

The schedule called for another fifteen minutes, but Carlo had more than twenty people in line, and that many again just milling around. Fifteen minutes would have to be stretched to thirty. Grinding her teeth, Juliet stalked over to Bill.

"There you are." Friendly as always, he threw his arm over her shoulder and squeezed. "Going great guns out here. Old Carlo knows how to twinkle to the ladies without setting the men off. Damn clever sonofabitch."

"I couldn't have said it better myself." Her knuckles were white on the strap of her briefcase. "Bill, is there a phone I can use? I have to call the office."

"No problem at all. Y'all just come on back with me." He led her through Psychology, into Westerns and around Romances to a door marked Private. "You just help yourself," he invited and showed her into a room with a cluttered metal desk, a goosenecked lamp and stacks upon stacks of books. Juliet headed straight for the phone.

"Thanks, Bill." She didn't even wait until the door closed before she started dialing. "Deborah Mortimor, please," she said to the answering switchboard. Tapping her foot, Juliet waited.

"Ms. Mortimor."

"Deb, it's Juliet."

"Hi. I've been waiting for you to call in. Looks like

we've got a strong nibble with the *Times* when you come back to New York. I just—"

"Later." Juliet reached into her briefcase for a roll of antacids. "I got the clippings today."

"Great, aren't they?"

"Oh sure. They're just dandy."

"Uh-huh." Deb waited only a beat. "It's the little number in Denver, isn't it?"

She gave the rolling chair a quick kick. "Of course it is."

"Sit down, Juliet." Deb didn't have to see to know her boss was pacing.

"Sit down? I'm tempted to fly back to Denver and ring Chatty Cathy's neck."

"Killing columnists isn't good for PR, Juliet."

"It was garbage."

"No, no, it wasn't that bad. Trash maybe, but not garbage."

She struggled for control and managed to get a very slippery rein on her temper. Popping the first antacid into her mouth, she crunched down. "Don't be cute, Deb. I didn't like the insinuations about Carlo and me. *Carlo Franconi's lovely American traveling companion,*" she quoted between her teeth. "Traveling companion. It makes me sound as though I'm just along for the ride. And then—"

"I read it," Deb interrupted. "So did Hal," she added, referring to the head of publicity.

Juliet closed her eyes a moment. "And?"

"Well, he went through about six different reactions. In the end, he decided a few comments like that were bound to come up and only added to Franconi's—well, *mystique* might be the best term."

"I see." Her jaw clenched, her fingers tight around the little roll of stomach pills. "That's fine then, isn't it? I'm just thrilled to add to a client's mystique."

"Now, Juliet—"

"Look, just tell dear old Hal that Houston went perfectly." She was definitely going to need two pills. Juliet popped another out of the roll with her thumb. "I don't even want you to mention to him that I called about this—this tripe in Denver."

"Whatever you say."

Taking a pen, she sat down and made space on the desk. "Now, give me what you have with the *Times*."

A half hour later, Juliet was just finishing up her last call when Carlo poked his head in the office. Seeing she was on the phone, he rolled his eyes, closed the door and leaned against it. His brow lifted when he spotted the half-eaten roll of antacids.

"Yes, thank you, Ed, Mr. Franconi will bring all the necessary ingredients and be in the studio at 8:00. Yes." She laughed, though her foot was tapping out a rhythm on the floor. "It's absolutely delicious. Guaranteed. See you in two days."

When she hung up the receiver, Carlo stepped forward. "You didn't come to save me."

She gave him a long, slow look. "You seemed to be handling the situation without me."

He knew the tone, and the expression. Now all he had to do was find the reason for them. Strolling over, he picked up the roll of pills. "You're much too young to need these."

"I've never heard that ulcers had an age barrier."

His brows drew together as he sat on the edge of the desk. "Juliet, if I believed you had an ulcer, I'd pack you off to my home in Rome and keep you in bed on bland foods for the next month. Now…" He slipped the roll into his pocket. "What problem is there?"

"Several," she said briskly as she began to gather up her notes. "But they're fairly well smoothed out now. We'll need to go shopping again in Chicago for that chicken dish you'd planned to cook. So, if you've finished up here, we can just—"

"No." He put a hand on her shoulder and held her in the chair. "We're not finished. Shopping for chicken in Chicago isn't what had you reaching for pills. What?"

The best defense was always ice. Her voice chilled. "Carlo, I've been very busy."

"You think after two weeks I don't know you?" Impatient, he gave her a little shake. "You dig in that briefcase for your aspirin or your little mints only when you feel too much pressure. I don't like to see it."

"It comes with the territory." She tried to shrug off his hand and failed. "Carlo, we've got to get to the airport."

"We have more than enough time. Tell me what's wrong."

"All right then." In two sharp moves, she pulled the clipping out of her case and pushed it into his hands.

"What's this?" He skimmed it first without really reading it. "One of those little columns about who is seen with whom and what they wear while they're seen?"

"More or less."

"Ah." As he began to read from the top, he nodded. "And you were seen with me."

Closing her notebook, she slipped it neatly into her briefcase. Twice she reminded herself that losing her temper would accomplish nothing. "As your publicist, that could hardly be avoided."

Because he'd come to expect logic from her, he only nodded again. "But you feel this intimates something else."

"It *says* something else," she tossed back. "Something that isn't true."

"It calls you my traveling companion." He glanced up, knowing that wouldn't sit well with her. "It's perhaps not the full story, but not untrue. Does it upset you to be known as my companion?"

She didn't want him to be reasonable. She had no intention of emulating him. "When *companion* takes on this shade of meaning, it isn't professional or innocent. I'm not here to have my name linked with you this way, Carlo."

"In what way, Juliet?"

"It gives my name and goes on to say that I'm never out of arm's length, that I guard you as though you were my own personal property. And that you—"

"That I kiss your hand in public restaurants as though I couldn't wait for privacy," Carlo read at a glance. "So? What difference does it make what it says here?"

She dragged both hands through her hair. "Carlo, I'm here, with you, to do a job. This clipping came through my office, through my supervisor. Don't you know something like this could ruin my credibility?"

"No," he said simply enough, "This is no more than gossip. Your supervisor, he's upset by this?"

She laughed, but it had little to do with humor. "No, actually, it seems he's decided it's just fine. Good for your image."

"Well, then?"

"I don't want to be good for your image," she threw back with such passion, it shocked both of them. "I won't be one of the dozens of names and faces linked with you."

"So," he murmured. "Now, we push away to the truth. You're angry with me for this." He set the clipping down. "You're angry because there's more truth in it now than there was when it was written."

"I don't want to be on anyone's list, Carlo." Her voice had lowered, calmed. She dug balled fists into the pockets of her skirt. "Not yours, not anyone's. I haven't come this far in my life to let that happen now."

He stood, wondering if she understood how insulting her words were. No, she'd see them as facts, not as darts. "I haven't put you on a list. If you have one in your own mind, it has nothing to do with me."

"A few weeks ago it was the French actress, a month before that a widowed countess."

He didn't shout, but it was only force of will that kept his voice even. "I never pretended you were the first woman in my bed. I never expected I was the first man in yours."

"That's entirely different."

"Ah, now you find the double standard convenient." He picked up the clipping, balled it in his fist then dropped it into the wastebasket. "I've no patience for this, Juliet."

He was to the door again before she spoke. "Carlo, wait." With a polite veneer stretched thinly over fury he turned. "Damn." Hands still in her pockets, she paced from one stack of books to the other. "I never intended to take this out on you. It's totally out of line and I'm sorry, really. You might guess I'm not thinking very clearly right now."

"So it would seem."

Juliet let out a sigh, knowing she observed the cutting edge of his voice. "I don't know how to explain, except to say that my career's very important to me."

"I understand that."

"But it's no more important to me than my privacy. I don't want my personal life discussed around the office water cooler."

"People talk, Juliet. It's natural and it's meaningless."

"I can't brush it off the way you do." She picked up her briefcase by the strap then set it down again. "I'm used to staying in the background. I set things up, handle the details, do the legwork, and someone else's picture gets in the paper. That's the way I want it."

"You don't always get what you want." With his thumbs hooked in his pockets, he leaned back against the door and watched her. "Your anger goes deeper than a few lines in a paper people will have forgotten tomorrow."

She closed her eyes a moment, then turned back to him. "All right, yes, but it's not a matter of being angry. Carlo, I've put myself in a delicate position with you."

Carefully, he weighed the phrase, tested it, judged it. "Delicate position?"

"Please, don't misunderstand. I'm here, with you, because of my job. It's very important to me that that's handled in the best, the most professional manner I can manage. What's happened between us…"

"What has happened between us?" he prompted when she trailed off.

"Don't make it difficult."

"All right, we'll make it easy. We're lovers."

She let out a long, unsteady breath, wondering if he really believed that was easy. For him it might be just another stroll through the moonlight. For her, it was a race through a hurricane. "I want to keep that aspect of our relationship completely separate from the professional area."

It surprised him he could find such a statement endearing. Perhaps the fact that she was half romanticist and half businesswoman was part of her appeal to him. "Juliet, my love, you sound as though you're negotiating a contract."

"Maybe I do." Nerves were beginning to run through her too quickly again. "Maybe I am, in a way."

His own anger had disappeared. Her eyes weren't nearly as certain as her voice. Her hands, he noted, were twisting together. Slowly, he walked toward her, pleased that though she didn't back away, the wariness was back. "Juliet…" He lifted a hand to brush through her hair. "You can negotiate terms and times, but not emotion."

"You can—regulate it."

He took both her hands, kissing them. "No."

"Carlo, please—"

"You like me to touch you," he murmured. "Whether we stand here alone, or we stand in a group of strangers. If I touch your hand, like this, you know what's in my mind. It's not always passion. There are times, I see you, I touch you, and I think only of being with you—talking, or sitting silently. Will you negotiate now how I am to touch your hand, how many times a day it's permitted?"

"Don't make me sound like a fool."

His fingers tightened on hers. "Don't make what I feel for you sound foolish."

"I—" No, she couldn't touch that. She didn't dare. "Carlo, I just want to keep things simple."

"Impossible."

"No, it's not."

"Then tell me, is this simple?" With just his fingertips on her shoulder, he leaned down to kiss her. So softly, so lightly, it was hardly a kiss at all. She felt her legs dissolve from the knees down.

"Carlo, we're not staying on the point."

He slipped his arms around her. "I like this point much better. When we get to Chicago…" His fingers slipped up and down her spine as he began to brush his lips over her face. "I want to spend the evening alone with you."

"We—have an appointment for drinks at ten with—"

"Cancel it."

"Carlo, you know I can't."

"Very well." He caught the lobe of her ear between his teeth. "I'll plead fatigue and make certain we have a very quick, very early evening. Then, I'll spend the rest of the night doing little things, like this."

His tongue darted inside her ear, then retreated to the vulnerable spot just below. The shudder that went through her was enough to arouse both of them. "Carlo, you don't understand."

"I understand that I want you." In a swift mood swing, he had her by the shoulders. "If I told you now that I want you more than I've wanted any other woman, you wouldn't believe me."

She backed away from that, but was caught close again. "No, I wouldn't. It isn't necessary to say so."

"You're afraid to hear it, afraid to believe it. You won't get simple with me, Juliet. But you'll get a lover you'll never forget."

She steadied a bit, meeting his look levelly. "I've already resigned myself to that, Carlo. I don't apologize to myself, and I don't pretend to have any regrets about coming to you last night."

"Then resign yourself to this." The temper was back

in his eyes, hot and volatile. "I don't care what's written in the paper, what's whispered about in offices in New York. You, this moment, are all I care about."

Something shattered quietly inside her. A defense built instinctively through years. She knew she shouldn't take him literally. He was Franconi, after all. If he cared about her, it was only in his way, and in his time. But something had shattered, and she couldn't rebuild it so quickly. Instead, she chose to be blunt.

"Carlo, I don't know how to handle you. I haven't the experience."

"Then don't handle me." Again, he took her by the shoulders. "Trust me."

She put her hands on his, held them a moment, then drew them away. "It's too soon, and too much."

There were times, in his work, where he had to be very, very patient. As a man, it happened much more rarely. Yet he knew if he pushed now, as for some inexplicable reason he wanted to, he'd only create more distance between them. "Then, for now, we just enjoy each other."

That's what she wanted. Juliet told herself that was exactly what she wanted—no more, no less. But she felt like weeping.

"We'll enjoy each other," she agreed. Letting out a sigh, she framed his face with her hands as he so often did with her. "Very much."

He wondered, when he lowered his brow to hers, why it didn't quite satisfy.

Chapter 9

Burned out from traveling, ready for a drink and elevated feet, Juliet walked up to the front desk of their Chicago hotel. Taking a quick glimpse around the lobby, she was pleased with the marble floors, sculpture and elegant potted palms. Such places usually lent themselves to big, stylish bathrooms. She intended to spend her first hour in Chicago with everything from the neck down submerged.

"May I help you?"

"You have a reservation for Franconi and Trent."

With a few punches on the keyboard, the clerk brought up their reservations on the screen. "You'll both be staying for two nights, Miss Trent?"

"Yes, that's right."

"It's direct bill. Everything's set. If you and Mr.

Franconi will just fill out these forms, I'll ring for a bellman."

As he scrawled the information on the form, Carlo glanced over. From the profile, she looked lovely, though perhaps a bit tired. Her hair was pinned up in the back, fluffed out on the sides and barely mussed from traveling. She looked as though she could head a three-hour business meeting without a whimper. But then she arched her back, closing her eyes briefly as she stretched her shoulders. He wanted to take care of her.

"Juliet, there's no need for two rooms."

She shifted her shoulder bag and signed her name. "Carlo, don't start. Arrangements have already been made."

"But it's absurd. You'll be staying in my suite, so the extra room is simply extra."

The desk clerk stood at a discreet distance and listened to every word.

Juliet pulled her credit card out of her wallet and set it down on the counter with a snap. Carlo noted, with some amusement, that she no longer looked the least bit tired. He wanted to make love with her for hours.

"You'll need the imprint on this for my incidentals," she told the clerk calmly enough. "All Mr. Franconi's charges will be picked up."

Carlo pushed his form toward the clerk then leaned on the counter. "Juliet, won't you feel foolish running back and forth across the hall? It's ridiculous, even for a publisher, to pay for a bed that won't be slept in."

With her jaw clenched, she picked up her credit card again. "I'll tell you what's ridiculous," she said under her breath. "It's ridiculous for you to be standing here deliberately embarrassing me."

"You have rooms 1102 and 1108." The clerk pushed the keys toward them. "I'm afraid they're just down the hall from each other rather than across."

"That's fine." Juliet turned to find the bellman had their luggage packed on the cart and his ears open. Without a word, she strode toward the bank of elevators.

Strolling along beside her, Carlo noted that the cashier had a stunning smile. "Juliet, I find it odd that you'd be embarrassed over something so simple."

"I don't think it's simple." She jabbed the up button on the elevator.

"Forgive me." Carlo put his tongue in his cheek. "It's only that I recall you specifically saying you wanted our relationship to be simple."

"Don't tell me what I said. What I said has nothing to do with what I meant."

"Of course not," he murmured and waited for her to step inside the car.

Seeing the look on Juliet's face, the bellman began to worry about his tip. He put on a hospitality-plus smile. "So, you in Chicago long?"

"Two days," Carlo said genially enough.

"You can see a lot in a couple of days. You'll want to get down to the lake—"

"We're here on business," Juliet interrupted. "Only business."

"Yes, ma'am." With a smile, the bellman pushed his cart into the hall. "1108's the first stop."

"That's mine." Juliet dug out her wallet again and pulled out bills as the bellman unlocked her door.

"Those two bags," she pointed out then turned to Carlo. "We'll meet Dave Lockwell in the bar for drinks at 10:00. You can do as you like until then."

"I have some ideas on that," he began but Juliet moved past him. After stuffing the bills in the bellman's hand, she shut the door with a quick click.

Thirty minutes, to Carlo's thinking, was long enough for anyone to cool down. Juliet's stiff-backed attitude toward their room situation had caused him more exasperation than annoyance. But then, he expected to be exasperated by women. On one hand, he found her reaction rather sweet and naive. Did she really think the fact that they were lovers would make the desk clerk or a bellman blink twice?

The fact that she did, and probably always would, was just another aspect of her nature that appealed to him. In whatever she did, Juliet Trent would always remain proper. Simmering passion beneath a tidy, clean-lined business suit. Carlo found her irresistible.

He'd known so many kinds of women—the bright young ingenue greedy to her fingertips, the wealthy aristocrat bored both by wealth and tradition, the successful career woman who both looked for and was wary of marriage. He'd known so many—the happy, the secure, the desperate and seeking, the fulfilled and the grasping. Juliet Trent with the cool green eyes and quiet voice left him uncertain as to what pigeonhole she'd fit into. It seemed she had all and none of the feminine qualities he understood. The only thing he was certain of was that he wanted her to fit, somehow, into his life.

The best way, the only way, he knew to accomplish

that was to distract her with charm until she was already caught. After that, they'd negotiate the next step.

Carlo lifted the rose he'd had sent up from the hotel florist out of its bud vase, sniffed its petals once, then walked down the hall to Juliet's room.

She was just drying off from a hot, steamy bath. If she'd heard the knock five minutes before, she'd have growled. As it was, she pulled on her robe and went to answer.

She'd been expecting him. Juliet wasn't foolish enough to believe a man like Carlo would take a door in the face as final. It had given her satisfaction to close it, just as it gave her satisfaction to open it again. When she was ready.

She hadn't been expecting the rose. Though she knew it wasn't wise to be moved by a single long-stemmed flower with a bud the color of sunshine, she was moved nonetheless. Her plans to have a calm, serious discussion with him faltered.

"You look rested." Rather than giving her the rose, he took her hand. Before she could decide whether or not to let him in, he was there.

A stand, Juliet reminded herself even as she closed the door behind him. If she didn't take a stand now, she'd never find her footing. "Since you're here, we'll talk. We have an hour."

"Of course." As was his habit, he took a survey of her room. Her suitcase sat on a stand, still packed, but with its top thrown open. It wasn't practical to unpack and repack when you were bouncing around from city to city. Though they were starting their third week on the road, the contents of the case were still neat and organized. He'd have expected no less from her. Her notebook and two pens were already beside the phone. The only things remotely out of place in the tidy, impersonal room were the Italian heels that sat in the middle of the rug where she'd stepped out of them. The inconsistency suited her perfectly.

"I can discuss things better," she began, "if you weren't wandering around."

"Yes?" All cooperation, Carlo sat and waved the rose under his nose. "You want to talk about our schedule here in Chicago?"

"No—yes." She had at least a dozen things to go over with him. For once she let business take a backseat. "Later." Deciding to take any advantage, Juliet remained standing. "First, I want to talk about that business down at the desk."

"Ah." The sound was distinctly European and as friendly as a smile. She could have murdered him.

"It was totally uncalled for."

"Was it?" He'd learned that strategy was best plotted with friendly questions or simple agreement. That way, you could swing the final result to your own ends without too much blood being shed.

"Of course it was." Forgetting her own strategy, Juliet dropped down on the edge of the bed. "Carlo, you had no right discussing our personal business in public."

"You're quite right."

"I—" His calm agreement threw her off. The firm, moderately angry speech she'd prepared in the tub went out the window.

"I must apologize," he continued before she could balance herself. "It was thoughtless of me."

"Well, no." As he'd planned, she came to his defense. "It wasn't thoughtless, just inappropriate."

With the rose, he waved her defense away. "You're too kind, Juliet. You see, I was thinking only of how practical you are. It's one of the things I most admire about you." In getting his way, Carlo had always felt it best to use as much truth as possible. "You see, besides my own family, I've known very few truly practical women. This trait in you appeals to me, as much as the color of your eyes, the texture of your skin."

Because she sensed she was losing ground, Juliet sat up straighter. "You don't have to flatter me, Carlo. It's simply a matter of establishing ground rules."

"You see." As if she'd made his point, he sat forward to touch her fingertips. "You're too practical to expect flattery or to be swayed by it. Is it any wonder I'm enchanted by you?"

"Carlo—"

"I haven't made my point." He retreated just enough to keep his attack in full gear. "You see, knowing you, I thought you would agree that it was foolish and impractical to book separate rooms when we want to be together. You do want to be with me, don't you, Juliet?"

Frustrated, she stared at him. He was turning the entire situation around. Certain of it, Juliet groped for a handhold. "Carlo, it has nothing to do with my wanting to be with you."

His brow lifted. "No?"

"No. It has to do with the line that separates our business and our personal lives."

"A line that's difficult to draw. Perhaps impossible for me." The truth came out again, though this time unplanned. "I want to be with you, Juliet, every moment we have. I find myself resenting even the hour that you're here and I'm there. A few hours at night isn't enough for me. I want more, much more for us."

Saying it left him stunned. It hadn't been one of his clever moves, one of his easy catch-phrases. That little jewel had come from somewhere inside where it had quietly hidden until it could take him by surprise.

He rose, and to give himself a moment, stood by the window to watch a stream of Chicago traffic. It rushed, then came to fitful stops, wound and swung then sped on again. Life was like this, he realized. You could speed right along but you never knew when something was going to stop you dead in your tracks.

Juliet was silent behind him, torn between what he'd said, what he'd meant and what she felt about it. From the very beginning, she'd kept Carlo's definition of an affair in the front of her mind. Just one ride on the carousel. When the music stopped, you got off and knew you'd gotten your money's worth. Now, with a few words he was changing the scope. She wondered if either of them was ready.

"Carlo, since you say I am, I'll be practical." Drawing together her resources, she rose. "We have a week left on tour. During that time, we've got Chicago and four other cities to deal with. To be honest, I'd rather if our only business right now was with each other."

He turned, and though she thought the smile was a bit odd, at least he smiled. "That's the nicest thing you've said to me in all these days and all these cities, Juliet."

She took a step toward him. It seemed foolish to think about risks when they had such little time. "Being with you isn't something I'll ever forget, no matter how much I might want to in years to come."

"Juliet—"

"No, wait. I want to be with you, and part of me

hates the time we lose with other people, in separate rooms, in all the demands that brought us to each other in the first place. But another part of me knows that all of those things are completely necessary. Those things will still be around after we're each back in our separate places."

No, don't think about that now, she warned herself. If she did, her voice wouldn't be steady.

"No matter how much time I spend with you in your suite, I need a room of my own if for no other reason than to know it's there. Maybe that's the practical side of me, Carlo."

Or the vulnerable one, he mused. But hadn't he just discovered he had a vulnerability of his own? Her name was Juliet. "So, it will be as you want in this." And for the best perhaps. He might just need a bit of time to himself to think things through.

"No arguing?"

"Do we argue ever, *cara?*"

Her lips curved. "Never." Giving in to herself as much as him, she stepped forward and linked her arms around his neck. "Did I ever tell you that when I first started setting up this tour I looked at your publicity shot and thought you were gorgeous?"

"No." He brushed his lips over hers. "Why don't you tell me now?"

"And sexy," she murmured as she drew him closer to the bed. "Very, very sexy."

"Is that so?" He allowed himself to be persuaded onto the bed. "So you decided in your office in New York that we'd be lovers?"

"I decided in my office in New York that we'd never be lovers." Slowly, she began to unbutton his shirt. "I decided that the last thing I wanted was to be romanced and seduced by some gorgeous, sexy Italian chef who had a string of women longer than a trail of his own pasta, but—"

"Yes." He nuzzled at her neck. "I think I'll prefer the 'but.'"

"But it seems to me that you can't make definitive decisions without all the facts being in."

"Have I ever told you that your practicality arouses me to the point of madness?"

She sighed as he slipped undone the knot in her robe. "Have I ever told you that I'm a sucker for a man who brings me flowers?"

"Flowers." He lifted his head then picked up the rosebud he'd dropped on the pillow beside them. "Darling, did you want one, too?"

With a laugh, she pulled him back to her.

Juliet decided she'd seen more of Chicago in the flight into O'Hare than during the day and a half she'd been there. Cab drives from hotel to television station, from television station to department store, from department store to bookstore and back to the hotel again weren't exactly leisurely sightseeing tours. Then and there she decided that when she took her vacation at the end of the month, she'd go somewhere steamy with sun and do nothing more energetic than laze by a pool from dawn to dusk.

The only hour remotely resembling fun was another shopping expedition where she watched Carlo select a plump three-pound chicken for his cacciatore.

He was to prepare his *pollastro alla cacciatora* from simmer to serve during a live broadcast of one of the country's top-rated morning shows. Next to the *Simpson Show* in L.A., Juliet considered this her biggest coup for the tour. *Let's Discuss It* was the hottest hour on daytime TV, and remained both popular and controversial after five consecutive seasons.

Despite the fact that she knew Carlo's showmanship abilities, Juliet was nervous as a cat. The show would air live in New York. She had no doubt that everyone in her department would be watching. If Carlo was a smash, it would be his triumph. If he bombed, the bomb was all hers. Such was the rationale in public relations.

It never occurred to Carlo to be nervous. He could make cacciatore in the dark, from memory with the use of only one hand. After watching Juliet pace the little green room for the fifth time, he shook his head. "Relax, my love, it's only chicken."

"Don't forget to bring up the dates we'll be in the rest of the cities. This show reaches all of them."

"You've already told me."

"And the title of the book."

"I won't forget."

"You should remember to mention you prepared this dish for the President when he visited Rome last year."

"I'll try to keep it in mind. Juliet, wouldn't you like some coffee?"

She shook her head and kept pacing. What else?

"I could use some," he decided on the spot.

She glanced toward the pot on a hot plate. "Help yourself."

He knew if she had something to do, she'd stop worrying, even for a few moments. And she'd stop pacing up and down in front of him. "Juliet, no one with a heart would ask a man to drink that poison that's been simmering since dawn."

"Oh." Without hesitation, she assumed the role of pamperer. "I'll see about it."

"Grazie."

At the door, she hesitated. "The reporter for the *Sun* might drop back before the show."

"Yes, you told mc. I'll bc charming."

Muttering to herself, she went to find a page.

Carlo leaned back and stretched his legs. He'd have to drink the coffee when she brought it back, though he didn't want any. He didn't want to board the plane for Detroit that afternoon, but such things were inevitable. In any case, he and Juliet would have the evening free in Detroit—what American state was that in?

They wouldn't be there long enough to worry about it.

In any case, he would soon be in Philadelphia and there, see Summer. He needcd to. Though he'd always had friends and was close to many of them, he'd never needed one as he felt he needed one now. He could talk to Summer and know what he said would be listened to carefully and not be repeated. Gossip had never bothered him in the past, but when it came to Juliet… When it came to Juliet, nothing was as it had been in the past.

None of his previous relationships with women had ever become a habit. Waking up in the morning beside a woman had always been pleasant, but never necessary. Every day, Juliet was changing that. He couldn't imagine his bedroom back in Rome without her, yet she'd never been there. He'd long since stopped imagining other women in his bed.

Rising, he began to pace as Juliet had.

When the door opened, he turned, expecting her. The tall, willowy blonde who entered wasn't Juliet, but she was familiar.

"Carlo! How wonderful to see you again."

"Lydia." He smiled, cursing himself for not putting the name of the *Sun*'s reporter with the face of the woman he'd spent two interesting days in Chicago with only eighteen months before. "You look lovely."

Of course she did. Lydia Dickerson refused to look anything less. She was sharp, sexy and uninhibited. She was also, in his memory, an excellent cook and critic of gourmet foods.

"Carlo, I was just thrilled when I heard you were coming into town. We'll do the interview after the show, but I just had to drop back and see you." She swirled toward him with the scent of spring lilacs and the swish of a wide-flared skirt. "You don't mind?"

"Of course not." Smiling, he took her outstretched hand. "It's always good to see an old friend."

With a laugh, she put her hands on his shoulders. "I should be angry with you, *caro*. You do have my number, and my phone didn't ring last night."

"Ah." He put his hands to her wrists, wondering just how to untangle himself. "You'll have to forgive us, Lydia. The schedule is brutal. And there's a…complication." He winced, thinking how Juliet would take being labeled a complication.

"Carlo." She edged closer. "You can't tell me you haven't got a few free hours for…an old friend. I've a tremendous recipe for *vitèllo tonnato*." She murmured the words and made the dish sound like something to be eaten in the moonlight. "Who else should I cook it for but the best chef in Italy?"

"I'm honored." He put his hands on her hips hoping to draw her away with the least amount of insult. It wouldn't occur to him until later that he'd felt none, absolutely none, of the casual desire he should have. "I haven't forgotten what a superb cook you are, Lydia."

Her laugh was low and full of memories. "I hope you haven't forgotten more than that."

"No." He let out a breath and opted to be blunt. "But you see I'm—"

Before he could finish being honest, the door opened again. With a cup of coffee in her hand, Juliet walked in, then came to a dead stop. She looked at the blonde wound around Carlo like an exotic vine. Her brow lifted as she took her gaze to Carlo's face. If only she had a camera.

Her voice was as cool and dry as her eyes. "I see you've met."

"Juliet, I—"

"I'll give you a few moments for the…pre-interview," she said blandly. "Try to wrap it up by 8:50, Carlo. You'll want to check the kitchen set." Without another word, she shut the door behind her.

Though her arms were still around Carlo's neck, Lydia looked toward the closed door. "Oops," she said lightly.

Carlo let out a long breath as they separated. "You couldn't have put it better."

At nine o'clock, Juliet had a comfortable seat midway back in the audience. When Lydia slipped into the seat beside her, she gave the reporter an easy nod, then looked back to the set. As far as she could tell, and she'd gone over every inch of it, it was perfect.

When Carlo was introduced to cheerful applause she

began to relax, just a little. But when he began preparations on the chicken, moving like a surgeon and talking to his host, his studio and television audience like a seasoned performer, her relaxation was complete. He was going to be fantastic.

"He's really something, isn't he?" Lydia murmured during the first break.

"Something," Juliet agreed.

"Carlo and I met the last time he was in Chicago."

"Yes, I gathered. I'm glad you could make it by this morning. You did get the press kit I sent in?"

She's a cool one, Lydia thought and shifted in her seat. "Yes. The feature should be out by the end of the week. I'll send you a clipping."

"I'd appreciate it."

"Miss Trent—"

"Juliet, please." For the first time, Juliet turned and smiled at her fully. "No need for formality."

"All right, Juliet, I feel like a fool."

"I'm sorry. You shouldn't."

"I'm very fond of Carlo, but I don't poach."

"Lydia, I'm sure there isn't a woman alive who wouldn't be fond of Carlo." She crossed her legs as the countdown for taping began again. "If I thought you'd even consider poaching, you wouldn't be able to pick up your pencil."

Lydia sat still for a moment, then leaned back with a laugh. Carlo had picked himself quite a handful. Served him right. "Is it all right to wish you luck?"

Juliet shot her another smile. "I'd appreciate it."

The two women might've come to amicable terms, but it wasn't easy for Carlo to concentrate on his job while they sat cozily together in the audience. His experience with Lydia had been a quick and energetic two days. He knew little more of her than her preference for peanut oil for cooking and blue bed linen. He understood how easy it was for a man to be executed without trial. He thought he could almost feel the prickle of the noose around his throat.

But he was innocent. Carlo poured the mixture of tomatoes, sauce and spices over the browned chicken and set the cover. If he had to bind and gag her, Juliet would listen to him.

He cooked his dish with the finesse of an artist completing a royal portrait. He performed for the audience like a veteran thespian. He thought the dark thoughts of a man already at the dock.

When the show was over, he spent a few obligatory moments with his host, then left the crew to devour one of his best cacciatores.

But when he went back to the green room, Juliet was nowhere in sight. Lydia was waiting. He had no choice but to deal with her, and the interview, first.

She didn't make it easy for him. But then, to his knowledge, women seldom did. Lydia chatted away as though nothing had happened. She asked her questions, noted down his answers, all the while with mischief gleaming in her eyes. At length, he'd had enough.

"All right, Lydia, what did you say to her?"

"To whom?" All innocence, Lydia blinked at him. "Oh, your publicist. A lovely woman. But then I'd hardly be one to fault your taste, darling."

He rose, swore and wondered what a desperate man should do with his hands. "Lydia, we had a few enjoyable hours together. No more."

"I know." Something in her tone made him pause and

glance back. "I don't imagine either of us could count the number of few enjoyable hours we've had." With a shrug, she rose. Perhaps she understood him, even envied what she thought she'd read in his eyes, but it wasn't any reason to let him off the hook. "Your Juliet and I just chatted, darling." She dropped her pad and pencil in her bag. "Girl talk, you know. Just girl talk. Thanks for the interview, Carlo." At the door, she paused and turned back. "If you're ever back in town without a…complication, give me a ring. *Ciao.*"

When she left he considered breaking something. Before he could decide what would be the most satisfying and destructive, Juliet bustled in. "Let's get moving, Carlo. The cab's waiting. It looks like we'll have enough time to get back to the hotel, check out and catch the earlier plane."

"I want to speak with you."

"Yes, fine. We'll talk in the cab." Because she was already heading down the winding corridor he had no choice but to follow.

"When you told me the name of the reporter, I simply didn't put it together."

"Put what together?" Juliet pulled open the heavy metal door and stepped out on the back lot. If it had been much hotter, she noted, Carlo could've browned his chicken on the asphalt. "Oh, that you'd known her. Well, it's so hard to remember everyone we've met, isn't it?" She slipped into the cab and gave the driver the name of the hotel.

"We've come halfway across the country." Annoyed, he climbed in beside her. "Things begin to blur."

"They certainly do." Sympathetic, she patted his hand. "Detroit and Boston'll be down and dirty. You'll be lucky to remember your own name." She pulled out her compact to give her makeup a quick check. "But then I can help out in Philadelphia. You've already told me you have a…friend there."

"Summer's different." He took the compact from her. "I've known her for years. We were students together. We never— Friends, we're only friends," he ended on a mutter. "I don't enjoy explaining myself."

"I can see that." She pulled out bills and calculated the tip as the cab drew up to the hotel. As she started to slide out, she gave Carlo a long look. "No one asked you to."

"Ridiculous." He had her by the arm before she'd reached the revolving doors. "You ask. It isn't necessary to ask with words to ask."

"Guilt makes you imagine all sorts of things." She swung through the doors and into the lobby.

"Guilt?" Incensed, he caught up with her at the elevators. "I've nothing to be guilty for. A man has to commit some crime, some sin, for guilt."

She listened calmly as she stepped into the elevator car and pushed the button for their floor. "That's true, Carlo. You seem to me to be a man bent on making a confession."

He went off on a fiery stream of Italian that had the other two occupants of the car edging into the corners. Juliet folded her hands serenely and decided she'd never enjoyed herself more. The other passengers gave Carlo a wide berth as the elevator stopped on their floor.

"Did you want to grab something quick to eat at the airport or wait until we land?"

"I'm not interested in food."

"An odd statement from a chef." She breezed into the hall. "Take ten minutes to pack and I'll call for a bellman." The key was in her hand and into the lock before his fingers circled her wrist. When she looked up at him, she thought she'd never seen him truly frustrated before. Good. It was about time.

"I pack nothing until this is settled."

"Until what's settled?" she countered.

"When I commit a crime or a sin, I do so with complete honesty." It was the closest he'd come to an explosion. Juliet lifted a brow and listened attentively. "It was Lydia who had her arms around me."

Juliet smiled. "Yes, I saw quite clearly how you were struggling. A woman should be locked up for taking advantage of a man that way."

His eyes, already dark, went nearly black. "You're sarcastic. But you don't understand the circumstances."

"On the contrary." She leaned against the door. "Carlo, I believe I understood the circumstances perfectly. I don't believe I've asked you to explain anything. Now, you'd better pack if we're going to catch that early plane." For the second time, she shut the door in his face.

He stood where he was for a moment, torn. A man expected a certain amount of jealousy from a woman he was involved with. He even, well, enjoyed it to a point. What he didn't expect was a smile, a pat on the head and breezy understanding when he'd been caught in another woman's arms. However innocently.

No, he didn't expect it, Carlo decided. He wouldn't tolerate it.

When the sharp knock came on the door, Juliet was still standing with a hand on the knob. Wisely, she counted to ten before she opened it.

"Did you need something?"

Carefully, he studied her face for a trap. "You're not angry."

She lifted her brows. "No, why?"

"Lydia's very beautiful."

"She certainly is."

He stepped inside. "You're not jealous?"

"Don't be absurd." She brushed a speck of lint from her sleeve. "If you found me with another man, under similar circumstances, you'd understand, I'm sure."

"No." He closed the door behind him. "I'd break his face."

"Oh?" Rather pleased, she turned away to gather a few things from her dresser. "That's the Italian temperament, I suppose. Most of my ancestors were rather staid. Hand me that brush, will you?"

Carlo picked it up and dropped it into her hand. "Staid—this means?"

"Calm and sturdy, I suppose. Though there was one—my great-great-grandmother, I think. She found her husband tickling the scullery maid. In her staid sort of way, she knocked him flat with a cast-iron skillet. I don't think he ever tickled any of the other servants." Securing the brush in a plastic case, she arranged it in the bag. "I'm said to take after her."

Taking her by the shoulders, he turned her to face him. "There were no skillets available."

"True enough, but I'm inventive. Carlo..." Still smiling, she slipped her arms around his neck. "If I hadn't understood exactly what was going on, the coffee I'd fetched for you would've been dumped over your head. *Capice?*"

"*Sì.*" He grinned as he rubbed his nose against hers. But he didn't really understand her. Perhaps that was why he was enchanted by her. Lowering his mouth to hers, he let the enchantment grow. "Juliet," he murmured. "There's a later plane for Detroit, yes?"

She had wondered if he would ever think of it. "Yes, this afternoon."

"Did you know it's unhealthy for the system to rush." As he spoke, he slipped the jacket from her arms so that it slid to the floor.

"I've heard something about that."

"Very true. It's much better, medically speaking, to take one's time. To keep a steady pace, but not a fast one. And, of course, to give the system time to relax at regular intervals. It could be very unhealthy for us to pack now and race to the airport." He unhooked her skirt so that it followed her jacket.

"You're probably right."

"Of course I'm right," he murmured in her ear. "It would never do for either of us to be ill on the tour."

"Disastrous," she agreed. "In fact, it might be best if we both just lay down for a little while."

"The very best. One must guard one's health."

"I couldn't agree more," she told him as his shirt joined her skirt and jacket.

She was laughing as they tumbled onto the bed.

He liked her this way. Free, easy, enthusiastic. Just as he liked her cooler, more enigmatic moods. He could enjoy her in a hundred different ways because she wasn't always the same woman. Yet she was always the same.

Soft, as she was now. Warm wherever he touched, luxurious wherever he tasted. She might be submissive one moment, aggressive the next, and he never tired of the swings.

They made love in laughter now, something he knew more than most was precious and rare. Even when the passion began to dominate, there was an underlying sense of enjoyment that didn't cloud the fire. She gave him more in a moment than he'd thought he'd ever find with a woman in a lifetime.

She'd never known she could be this way—laughing, churning, happy, desperate. There were so many things she hadn't known. Every time he touched her it was something new, though it was somehow as if his touch was all she'd ever known. He made her feel fresh and desirable, wild and weepy all at once. In the space of minutes, he could bring her a sense of contentment and a frantic range of excitements.

The more he brought, the more he gave, and the easier it became for her to give. She wasn't aware yet, nor was he, that every time they made love, the intimacy grew and spread. It was gaining a strength and weight that wouldn't break with simply walking away. Perhaps if they'd known, they would have fought it.

Instead, they loved each other through the morning with the verve of youth and the depth of familiarity.

Chapter 10

Juliet hung up the phone, dragged a hand through her hair and swore. Rising, she swore again then moved toward the wide spread of window in Carlo's suite. For a few moments she muttered at nothing and no one in particular. Across the room, Carlo lay sprawled on the sofa. Wisely, he waited until she'd lapsed into silence.

"Problems?"

"We're fogged in." Swearing again, she stared out the window. She could see the mist, thick and still hanging outside the glass. Detroit was obliterated. "All flights are cancelled. The only way we're going to get to Boston is to stick out our thumbs."

"Thumbs?"

"Never mind." She turned and paced around the suite.

Detroit had been a solid round of media and events, and the Renaissance Center a beautiful place to stay, but now it was time to move on. Boston was just a hop away by air, so that the evening could be devoted to drafting out reports and a good night's sleep. Except for the fact that fog had driven in from the lake and put the whole city under wraps.

Stuck, Juliet thought as she glared out the window again. Stuck when they had an 8:00 a.m. live demonstration on a well-established morning show in Boston.

He shifted a bit, but didn't sit up. If it hadn't been too much trouble, he could've counted off the number of times he'd been grounded for one reason or another. One, he recalled, had been a flamenco dancer in Madrid who'd distracted him into missing the last flight out. Better not to mention it. Still, when such things happened, Carlo reflected, it was best to relax and enjoy the moment. He knew Juliet better.

"You're worried about the TV in the morning."

"Of course I am." As she paced, she went over every possibility. Rent a car and drive—no, even in clear weather it was simply too far. They could charter a plane and hope the fog cleared by dawn. She took another glance outside. They were sixty-five floors up, but they might as well have been sixty-five feet under. No, she decided, no television spot was worth the risk. They'd have to cancel. That was that.

She dropped down on a chair and stuck her stockinged feet up by Carlo's. "I'm sorry, Carlo, there's no way around it. We'll have to scrub Boston."

"Scrub Boston?" Lazily he folded his arms behind his head. "Juliet, Franconi scrubs nothing. Cook, yes, scrub, no."

It took her a moment to realize he was serious. "I mean cancel."

"You didn't say cancel."

She heaved out a long breath. "I'm saying it now." She wiggled her toes, finding them a bit stiff after a ten-hour day. "There's no way we can make the television spot, and that's the biggest thing we have going in Boston. There're a couple of print interviews and an autographing. We didn't expect much to move there, and we were depending on the TV spot for that. Without it..." She shrugged and resigned herself. "It's a wash."

Letting his eyes half close, Carlo decided the sofa was an excellent place to spend an hour or so. "I don't wash."

She shot him a level look. "You're not going to have to do anything but lie on your—back," she decided after a moment, "for the next twenty-four hours."

"Nothing?"

"Nothing."

He grinned. Moving faster than he looked capable of, he sat up, grabbed her by the arms and pulled her down with him. "Good, you lie with me. Two backs, *madonna,* are better than one."

"Carlo." She couldn't avoid the first kiss. Or perhaps she didn't put her best effort into it, but she knew it was essential to avoid the second. "Wait a minute."

"Only twenty-four hours," he reminded her as he moved to her ear. "No time to waste."

"I've got to— Stop that," she ordered when her thoughts started to cloud. "There're arrangements to be made."

"What arrangements?"

She made a quick mental sketch. True, she'd already checked out of her room. They'd only kept the suite for convenience, and until six. She could book another separate room for the night, but—she might as well admit in this case it was foolish. Moving her shoulders, she gave in to innate practicality. "Like keeping the suite overnight."

"That's important." He lifted his head a moment. Her face was already flushed, her eyes already soft. Almost as if she'd spoken aloud, he followed the train of thought. He couldn't help but admire the way her mind worked from one point to the next in such straight lines.

"I have to call New York and let them know our status. I have to call Boston and cancel, then the airport and change our flight. Then I—"

"I think you have a love affair with the phone. It's difficult for a man to be jealous of an inanimate object."

"Phones are my life." She tried to slip out from under him, but got nowhere. "Carlo."

"I like it when you say my name with just a touch of exasperation."

"It's going to be more than a touch in a minute."

He'd thought he'd enjoy that as well. "But you haven't told me yet how fantastic I was today."

"You were fantastic." It was so easy to relax when he held her like this. The phone calls could wait, just a bit. After all, they weren't going anywhere. "You mesmerized them with your linguini."

"My linguini is hypnotic," he agreed. "I charmed the reporter from the *Free Press.*"

"You left him stupefied. Detroit'll never be the same."

"That's true." He kissed her nose. "Boston won't know what it's missing."

"Don't remind me," she began, then broke off. Carlo could almost hear the wheels turning.

"An idea." Resigned, he rolled her on top of him and watched her think.

"It might work," she murmured. "If everyone cooperates, it might work very well. In fact, it might just be terrific."

"What?"

"You claim to be a magician as well as an artist."

"Modesty prevents me from—"

"Save it." She scrambled up until she stradled him. "You told me once you could cook in a sewer."

Frowning, he toyed with the little gold hoop she wore in her ear. "Yes, perhaps I did. But this is only an expression—"

"How about cooking by remote control?"

His brows drew together, but he ran his hand idly to the hem of her skirt that had ridden high on her thigh. "You have extraordinary legs," he said in passing, then gave her his attention. "What do you mean by remote control?"

"Just that." Wound up with the idea, Juliet rose and grabbed her pad and pencil. "You give me all the ingredients—it's linguini again tomorrow, right?"

"Yes, my specialty."

"Good, I have all that in the file anyway. We can set up a phone session between Detroit and the studio in Boston. You can be on the air there while we're here."

"Juliet, you ask for a lot of magic."

"No, it's just basic electronics. The host of the show—Paul O'Hara—can put the dish together on the air while you talk him through it. It's like talking a plane in, you know. Forty degrees to the left—a cup of flour."

"No."

"Carlo."

Taking his time, he pried off his shoes. "You want him, this O'Hara who smiles for the camera, to cook my linguini?"

"Don't get temperamental on me," she warned, while her mind leaped ahead to possibilities. "Look, you write cookbooks so the average person can cook one of your dishes."

"Cook them, yes." He examined his nails. "Not like Franconi."

She opened her mouth, then closed it again. Tread softly on the ego, Juliet reminded herself. At least until you get your way. "Of course not, Carlo. No one expects that. But we could turn this inconvenience into a real event. Using your cookbook on the air, and some personal coaching from you via phone, O'Hara can prepare the linguini. He's not a chef or a gourmet, but an average person. Therefore, he'll be giving the audience thc average person's reactions. He'll make the average person's mistakes that you can correct. If we pull it off, the sales of your cookbook are going to soar. You know you can do it." She smiled winningly. "Why, you even said you could teach me to cook, and I'm helpless in the kitchen. Certainly you can talk O'Hara through one dish."

"Of course I can." Folding his arms again, he stared up at the ceiling. Her logic was infallible, her idea creative. To be truthful, he liked it—almost as much as he liked the idea of not having to fly to Boston. Still, it hardly seemed fair to give without getting. "I'll do it—on one condition."

"Which is?"

"Tomorrow morning, I talk this O'Hara through linguini. Tonight…" And he smiled at her. "We have a dress rehearsal. I talk you through it."

Juliet stopped tapping the end of her pencil on the pad. "You want me to cook linguini?"

"With my guidance, *cara mia,* you could cook anything."

Juliet thought it over and decided it didn't matter. The suite didn't have a kitchen this time, so he'd be counting on using the hotel's. That may or may not work. If it did, once she'd botched it, they could order room service. The bottom line was saving what she could of Boston. "I'd love to. Now, I've got to make those calls."

Carlo closed his eyes and opted for a nap. If he was going to teach two amateurs the secrets of linguini within twelve hours, he'd need his strength. "Wake me when you've finished," he told her. "We have to inspect the kitchen of the hotel."

It took her the best part of two hours, and when she hung up for the last time, Juliet's neck was stiff and her fingers numb. But she had what she wanted. Hal told her she was a genius and O'Hara said it sounded like fun. Arrangements were already in the works.

This time Juliet grinned at the stubborn fog swirling outside the window. Neither rain nor storm nor dark of night, she thought, pleased with herself. Nothing was going to stop Juliet Trent.

Then she looked over at Carlo. Something tilted inside her that had both her confidence and self-satisfaction wavering. Emotion, she reflected. It was something she hadn't written into the itinerary.

Well, maybe there was one catastrophe that wasn't in the books. Maybe it was one she couldn't work her way through with a creative idea and hustle. She simply had to take her feelings for Carlo one step at a time.

Four more days, she mused, and the ride would be

over. The music would stop and it would be time to get off the carousel.

It wasn't any use trying to see beyond that yet; it was all blank pages. She had to hold on to the belief that life was built one day at a time. Carlo would go, then she would pick up the pieces and begin her life again from that point.

She wasn't fool enough to tell herself she wouldn't cry. Tears would be shed over him, but they'd be shed quietly and privately. Schedule in a day for mourning, she thought then tossed her pad away.

It wasn't healthy to think of it now. There were only four days left. For a moment, she looked down at her empty hands and wondered if she'd have taken the steps she'd taken if she'd known where they would lead her. Then she looked over at him and simply watched him sleep.

Even with his eyes closed and that irrepressible inner life he had on hold, he could draw her. It wasn't simply a matter of his looks, she realized. She wasn't a woman who'd turn her life sideways for simple physical attraction. It was a matter of style. Smiling, she rose and walked closer to him as he slept. No matter how practical she was, how much common sense she possessed, she couldn't have resisted his style.

There'd be no regrets, she reaffirmed. Not now, nor in five days' time when an ocean and priorities separated them. As years passed, and their lives flowed and altered, she'd remember a handful of days when she'd had something special.

No time to waste, he'd said. Catching her tongue in her teeth Juliet decided she couldn't agree more. Reaching up, she began to unbutton her blouse. As a matter of habit, she draped it carefully over the back of a chair before she unhooked her skirt. When that fell, she lifted it, smoothed it out and folded it. The pins were drawn out of her hair, one by one, then set aside.

Dressed in a very impractical lace camisole and string bikini she moved closer.

Carlo awoke with his blood pumping and his head whirling. He could smell her scent lightly in her hair, more heady on her skin as her mouth took command of his. Her body was already heated as she lay full length on him. Before he could draw his first thoughts together, his own body followed suit.

She was all lace and flesh and passion. There wasn't time to steady his control or polish his style. Urgent and desperate, he reached for her and found silk and delicacy, strength and demand wherever he touched.

She unbuttoned his shirt and drew it aside so that their skin could meet and arouse. Beneath hers, she felt his heartbeat race and pound until power made her dizzy. Capturing his lips once again, she thought only of driving him to madness. She could feel it spread through him, growing, building, so that it would dominate both of them.

When he rolled so that she was trapped between the back of the sofa and his body, she was ready to relinquish control. With a moan, dark and liquid, she let herself enjoy what she'd begun.

No woman had ever done this to him. He understood that as his only thoughts were to devour everything she had. His fingers, so clever, so skilled, so gentle, pulled at the lace until the thin strap tore with hardly a sound.

He found her—small soft breasts that fit so perfectly in his hands, the strong narrow rib cage and slender waist. His. The word nearly drove him mad. She was his now, as she'd been in the dream she'd woken him from. Perhaps he was still dreaming.

She smelled of secrets, small, feminine secrets no man ever fully understood. She tasted of passion, ripe, shivering passion every man craved. With his tongue he tasted that sweet subtle valley between her breasts and felt her tremble. She was strong; he'd never doubted it. In her strength, she was surrendering completely to him, for the pleasure of each.

The lace smelled of her. He could have wallowed in it, but her skin was irresistible. He drew the camisole down to her waist and feasted on her.

With her hands tangled in his hair, her body on fire, she thought only of him. No tomorrows, no yesterdays. However much she might deny it in an hour, they'd become a single unit. One depended on the other for pleasure, for comfort, for excitement. For so much more she didn't dare think of it. She yearned for him; nothing would ever stop it. But now, he was taking her, fast and furious, through doors they'd opened together. Neither of them had gone there before with another, nor would again.

Juliet gave herself over to the dark, the heat, and to Carlo.

He drew the thin strings riding on her hips, craving the essence of her. When he'd driven her over the first peak, he knew and reveled in it. With endless waves of desire, he whipped her up again, and yet again, until they were both trembling. She called out his name as he ran his lips down her leg. All of her was the thought paramount in his mind. He'd have all of her until she was willing, ready to have all of him.

"Juliet, I want you." His face was above hers again, his breath straining. "Look at me."

She was staggering on that razor's edge between reason and madness. When she opened her eyes, his face filled her vision. It was all she wanted.

"I want you," he repeated while the blood raged in his head. "Only you."

She was wrapped around him, her head arched back. For an instant, their eyes met and held. What coursed through them wasn't something they could try to explain. It was both danger and security.

"Only," she murmured and took him into her.

They were both stunned, both shaken, both content. Naked, damp and warm, they lay tangled together in silence. Words had been spoken, Juliet thought. Words that were part of the madness of the moment. She would have to take care not to repeat them when passion was spent. They didn't need words; they had four days. Yet she ached to hear them again, to say them again.

She could set the tone between them, she thought. She had only to begin now and continue. No pressure. She kept her eyes closed a moment longer. No regrets. The extra moment she took to draw back her strength went unnoticed.

"I could stay just like this for a week," she murmured. Though she meant it, the words were said lazily. Turning her head, she looked at him, smiled. "Are you ready for another nap?"

There was so much he wanted to say. So much, he thought, she didn't want to hear. They'd set the rules; he had only to follow them. Nothing was as easy as it should've been.

"No." He kissed her forehead. "Though I've never found waking from a nap more delightful. Now, I think it's time for your next lesson."

"Really?" She caught her bottom lip between her teeth. "I thought I'd graduated."

"Cooking," he told her, giving her a quick pinch where Italian males were prone to.

Juliet tossed back her hair and pinched him back. "I thought you'd forget about that."

"Franconi never forgets. A quick shower, a change of clothes and down to the kitchen."

Agreeable, Juliet shrugged. She didn't think for one minute the management would allow him to give a cooking lesson in their kitchen.

Thirty minutes later, she was proven wrong.

Carlo merely bypassed management. He saw no reason to go through a chain of command. With very little fuss, he steered her through the hotel's elegant dining room and into the big, lofty kitchen. It smelled exotic and sounded like a subway station.

They'd stop him here, Juliet decided, still certain they'd be dining outside or through room service within the hour. Though she'd changed into comfortable jeans, she had no plans to cook. After one look at the big room with its oversized appliances and acres of counter, she was positive she wouldn't.

It shouldn't have surprised her to be proven wrong again.

"Franconi!" The name boomed out and echoed off the walls. Juliet jumped back three inches.

"Carlo, I think we should—" But as she spoke, she looked up at his face. He was grinning from ear to ear.

"Pierre!"

As she looked on, Carlo was enveloped by a wide, white-aproned man with a drooping mustache and a face as big and round as a frying pan. His skin glistened with sweat, but he smelt inoffensively of tomatoes.

"You Italian lecher, what do you do in my kitchen?"

"Honor it," Carlo said as they drew apart. "I thought you were in Montreal, poisoning the tourists."

"They beg me to take the kitchen here." The big man with the heavy French accent shrugged tanklike shoulders. "I feel sorry for them. Americans have so little finesse in the kitchen."

"They offered to pay you by the pound," Carlo said dryly. "Your pounds."

Pierre held both hands to his abundant middle and laughed. "We understand each other, old friend. Still, I find America to my liking. You, why aren't you in Rome pinching ladies?"

"I'm finishing up a tour for my book."

"But yes, you and your cookbooks." A noise behind him had him glancing around and bellowing in French. Juliet was certain the walls trembled. With a smile, he adjusted his hat and turned back to them. "That goes well?"

"Well enough." Carlo drew Juliet up. "This is Juliet Trent, my publicist."

"So it goes very well," Pierre murmured as he took Juliet's hand and brushed his lips over it. "Perhaps I will write a cookbook. Welcome to my kitchen, *mademoiselle.* I'm at your service."

Charmed, Juliet smiled. "Thank you, Pierre."

"Don't let this one fool you," Carlo warned. "He has a daughter your age."

"Bah!" Pierre gave him a lowered-brow look. "She's

but sixteen. If she were a day older I'd call my wife and tell her to lock the doors while Franconi is in town."

Carlo grinned. "Such flattery, Pierre." With his hands hooked in his back pockets, he looked around the room. "Very nice," he mused. Lifting his head, he scented the air. "Duck. Is that duck I smell?"

Pierre preened. "The specialty. *Canard au Pierre.*"

"*Fantastico.*" Carlo swung an arm around Juliet as he led her closer to the scent. "No one, absolutely no one, does to duck what Pierre can do."

The black eyes in the frying-pan face gleamed. "No, you flatter me, *mon ami.*"

"There's no flattery in truth." Carlo looked on while an assistant carved Pierre's duck. With the ease of experience, he took a small sliver and popped it into Juliet's mouth. It dissolved there, leaving behind an elusive flavor that begged for more. Carlo merely laid his tongue on his thumb to test. "Exquisite, as always. Do you remember, Pierre, when we prepared the Shah's engagement feast? Five, six years ago."

"Seven," Pierre corrected and sighed.

"Your duck and my cannelloni."

"Magnificent. Not so much paprika on that fish," he boomed out. "We are not in Budapest. Those were the days," he continued easily. "But..." The shrug was essentially Gallic. "When a man has his third child, he has to settle down, *oui?*"

Carlo gave another look at the kitchen, and with an expert's eye approved. "You've picked an excellent spot. Perhaps you'd let me have a corner of it for a short time."

"A corner?"

"A favor," Carlo said with a smile that would have

charmed the pearls from oysters. "I've promised my Juliet to teach her how to prepare linguini."

"Linguini con vongole biance?" Pierre's eyes glittered.

"Naturally. It is my specialty."

"You can have a corner of my kitchen, *mon ami,* in exchange for a plate."

Carlo laughed and patted Pierre's stomach. "For you, *amico,* two plates."

Pierre clasped him by the shoulders and kissed both cheeks. "I feel my youth coming back to me. Tell me what you need."

In no time at all, Juliet found herself covered in a white apron with her hair tucked into a chef's hat. She might have felt ridiculous if she'd been given the chance.

"First you mince the clams."

Juliet looked at Carlo, then down at the mess of clams on the cutting board. "Mince them?"

"Like so." Carlo took the knife and with a few quick moves had half of the clams in small, perfect pieces. "Try."

Feeling a bit like an executioner, Juliet brought the knife down. "They're not…well, alive, are they?"

"*Madonna,* any clam considers himself honored to be part of Franconi's linguini. A bit smaller there. Yes." Satisfied, he passed her an onion. "Chopped, not too fine." Again, he demonstrated, but this time Juliet felt more at home. Accepting the knife, she hacked again until the onion was in pieces and her eyes were streaming.

"I hate to cook," she muttered but Carlo only pushed a clove of garlic at her.

"This is chopped very fine. Its essence is what we need, not so much texture." He stood over her shoulder, watching until he approved. "You've good hands, Juliet. Now here, melt the butter."

Following instructions, she cooked the onion and garlic in the simmering butter, stirring until Carlo pronounced it ready.

"Now, it's tender, you see. We add just a bit of flour." He held her hand to direct it as she stirred it in. "So it thickens. We add the clams. Gently," he warned before she could dump them in. "We don't want them bruised. Ah…" He nodded with approval. "Spice," he told her. "It's the secret and the strength."

Bending over her, he showed her how to take a pinch of this, a touch of that and create. As the scent became more pleasing, her confidence grew. She'd never remember the amounts or the ingredients, but found it didn't matter.

"How about that?" she asked, pointing to a few sprigs of parsley.

"No, that comes just at the end. We don't want to drown it. Turn the heat down, just a little more. There." Satisfied, he nodded. "The cover goes on snug, then you let it simmer while the spices wake up."

Juliet wiped the back of her hand over her damp brow. "Carlo, you talk about the sauce as though it lived and breathed."

"My sauces do," he said simply. "While this simmers, you grate the cheese." He picked up a hunk and with his eyes closed, sniffed. *"Squisito."*

He had her grate and stir while the rest of the kitchen staff worked around them. Juliet thought of her mother's kitchen with its tidy counters and homey smells. She'd never seen anything like this. It certainly wasn't quiet. Pans were dropped, people and dishes were cursed, and fast was the order of the day. Busboys hustled in and out, weighed down with trays, waiters and waitresses breezed through demanding their orders. While she watched wide-eyed, Carlo ignored. It was time to create his pasta.

Unless it was already cooked and in a meal, Juliet thought of pasta as something you got off the shelf in a cardboard box. She learned differently, after her hands were white to the wrists with flour. He had her measure and knead and roll and spread until her elbows creaked. It was nothing like the five-minute throw-it-together kind she was used to.

As she worked, she began to realize why he had such stamina. He had to. In cooking for a living the way Franconi cooked for a living, he used as much energy as any athlete did. By the time the pasta had passed his inspection, her shoulder muscles ached the way they did after a brisk set of tennis.

Blowing the hair out of her eyes and mopping away sweat, Juliet turned to him. "What now?"

"Now you cook the pasta."

She tried not to grumble as she poured water into a Dutch oven and set it on to boil.

"One tablespoon salt," Carlo instructed.

"One tablespoon salt," she muttered and poured it in. When she turned around, he handed her a glass of wine.

"Until it boils, you relax."

"Can I turn down the heat?"

He laughed and kissed her, then decided it was only right to kiss her again. She smelled like heaven. "I like you in white." He dusted flour from her nose. "You're a messy cook, my love, but a stunning one."

It was easy to forget the noisy, bustling kitchen. "Cook?" A bit primly, she adjusted her hat. "Isn't it chef?"

He kissed her again. "Don't get cocky. One linguini doesn't make a chef."

She barely finished her wine when he put her back to work. "Put one end of the linguini in the water. Yes, just so. Now, as it softens coil them in. Careful. Yes, yes, you have a nice touch. A bit more patience and I might take you on in my restaurant."

"No, thanks," Juliet said definitely as the steam rose in her face. She was almost certain she felt each separate pore opening.

"Stir easily. Seven minutes only, not a moment more." He refilled her glass and kissed her cheek.

She stirred, and drained, measured parsley, poured and sprinkled cheese. By the time she was finished, Juliet didn't think she could eat a thing. Nerves, she discovered with astonishment. She was as nervous as a new bride on her first day in the kitchen.

With her hands clasped together, she watched Carlo take a fork and dip in. Eyes closed, he breathed in the aroma. She swallowed. His eyes remained closed as he took the first sample. Juliet bit her lip. Until then, she hadn't noticed that the kitchen had become as quiet as a cathedral. A quick glimpse around showed her all activity had stopped and all eyes were on Carlo. She felt as though she were waiting to be sentenced or acquitted.

"Well?" she demanded when she couldn't stand it any longer.

"Patience," Carlo reminded her without opening his eyes. A busboy rushed in and was immediately shushed. Carlo opened his eyes and carefully set down the fork. "*Fantastico!*" He took Juliet by the shoulders and gave her the ceremonial kiss on each cheek as applause broke out.

Laughing, she pulled off her hat with a flourish. "I feel like I won a gold medal in the decathlon."

"You've created." As Pierre boomed orders for plates, Carlo took both her hands. "We make a good team, Juliet Trent."

She felt something creeping too close to the heart. It just didn't seem possible to stop it. "Yes, we make a good team, Franconi."

Chapter 11

By twelve the next day, there was absolutely nothing left to be done. Carlo's remote control demonstration on the proper way to prepare linguini had gone far beyond Juliet's hopes for success. She'd stayed glued to the television, listening to Carlo's voice beside her and through the speakers. When her supervisor called personally to congratulate her, Juliet knew she had a winner. Relaxed and satisfied, she lay back on the bed.

"Wonderful." She folded her arms, crossed her ankles and grinned. "Absolutely wonderful."

"Did you ever doubt it?"

Still grinning, she shot a look at Carlo as he finished off the last of both shares of the late breakfast they'd ordered. "Let's just say I'm glad it's over."

"You worry too much, *mi amore.*" But he hadn't seen her dig for her little roll of pills in three days. It pleased him enormously to know that he relaxed her so that she didn't need them. "When it comes to Franconi's linguini, you have always a success."

"After this I'll never doubt it. Now we have five hours before flight time. Five full, completely unscheduled hours."

Rising, he sat on the end of the bed and ran his fingers along the arch of her foot. She looked so lovely when she smiled, so lovely when she let her mind rest. "Such a bonus," he murmured.

"It's like a vacation." With a sigh, she let herself enjoy the little tingles of pleasure.

"What would you like to do with our vacation of five full, unscheduled hours?"

She lifted a brow at him. "You really want to know?"

Slowly, he kissed each one of her toes. "Of course. The day is yours." He brushed his lips over her ankle. "I'm at your service."

Springing up, she threw her arms around his neck and kissed him, hard. "Let's go shopping."

Fifteen minutes later, Juliet strolled with Carlo through the first tower of the enormous circular shopping center attached to the hotel. People huddled around the maps of the complex, but she breezed around the curve and bypassed one. No maps, no schedules, no routes. Today, it didn't matter where they went.

"Do you know," she began, "with all the department stores, malls and cities we've been through, I haven't had a chance to shop?"

"You don't give yourself time."

"Same thing. Oh, look." She stopped at a window display and studied a long evening dress covered with tiny silver bangles.

"Very dashing," Carlo decided.

"Dashing," Juliet agreed. "If I were six inches taller it might not make me look like a scaled-down pillar. Shoes." She pulled him along to the next shop.

In short order, Carlo discovered Juliet's biggest weakness. The way to her heart wasn't through food, nor was it paved with furs and diamonds. Jewelry displays barely earned her glance. Evening clothes brought a brief survey while day wear and sports clothes won mild interest. But shoes were something different. Within an hour, she'd studied, fondled and critiqued at least fifty pairs. She found a pair of sneakers at thirty percent off and bought them to add to an already substantial collection. Then with a careful maneuver to pick and choose, she weeded her selection down to three pair of heels, all Italian.

"You show excellent taste." With the patience of a man accustomed to shopping expeditions, Carlo lounged in a chair and watched her vacillate between one pair then the other. Idly, he picked up one shoe and glanced at the signature inside. "He makes an elegant shoe and prefers my lasagna."

Wide-eyed, Juliet pivoted on the thin heels. "You know him?"

"Of course. Once a week he eats in Franconi's."

"He's my hero." When Carlo gave her his lifted-brow look, she laughed. "I know I can put on a pair of his shoes and go eight hours without needing emergency surgery. I'll take all three," she said on impulse, then sat down to exchange the heels for her newly bought sneakers.

"You make me surprised," he commented. "So many shoes when you have only two feet. This is not my practical Juliet."

"I'm entitled to a vice." Juliet pushed the Velcro closed. "Besides, I've always known Italians make the best shoes." She leaned closer to kiss his cheek. "Now I know they make the best…pasta." Without a blink at the total, she charged the shoes and pocketed the receipt.

Swinging the bag between them, they wandered from tower to tower. A group of women strolled by, earning Carlo's appreciation. Shopping during lunch hour, he gauged as he tossed an extra look over his shoulder. One had to admire the American workforce.

"You'll strain your neck that way," Juliet commented easily. She couldn't help but be amused by his blatant pleasure in anything female. He merely grinned.

"It's simply a matter of knowing just how far to go."

Comfortable, Juliet enjoyed the feel of his fingers laced with hers. "I'd never argue with the expert."

Carlo stopped once, intrigued by a choker in amethysts and diamonds. "This is lovely," he decided. "My sister, Teresa, always preferred purple."

Juliet leaned closer to the glass. The small, delicate jewels glimmered, hot and cold. "Who wouldn't? It's fabulous."

"She has a baby in a few weeks," he murmured, then nodded to the discreetly anxious clerk. "I'll see this."

"Of course, a lovely piece, isn't it?" After taking it out of the locked case, he placed it reverently in Carlo's hand. "The diamonds are all superior grade, naturally, and consist of one point three carat. The amethyst—"

"I'll have it."

Thrown off in the middle of his pitch, the clerk blinked. "Yes, sir, an excellent choice." Trying not to show surprise, he took the credit card Carlo handed him along with the choker and moved farther down the counter.

"Carlo." Juliet edged closer and lowered her voice. "You didn't even ask the price."

He merely patted her hand as he skimmed the other contents in the case. "My sister's about to make me an uncle again," he said simply. "The choker suits her. Now emeralds," he began, "would be your stone."

She glanced down at a pair of earrings with stones the color of dark, wet summer grass. The momentary longing was purely feminine and easily controlled. Shoes she could justify; emeralds, no. She shook her head and laughed at him. "I'll just stick with pampering my feet."

When Carlo had his present nicely boxed and his receipt in hand they wandered back out. "I love to shop," Juliet confessed. "Sometimes I'll spend an entire Saturday just roaming. It's one of the things I like best about New York."

"Then you'd love Rome." He'd like to see her there, he discovered. By the fountains, laughing, strolling through the markets and cathedrals, dancing in the clubs that smelled of wine and humanity. He wanted to have her there, with him. Going back alone was going back to nothing. He brought her hand to his lips as he thought of it, holding it there until she paused, uncertain.

"Carlo?" People brushed by them, and as his look became more intense, she swallowed and repeated his name. This wasn't the mild masculine appreciation she'd seen him send passing women, but something deep and dangerous. When a man looked at a woman this way, the woman was wise to run. But Juliet didn't know if it were toward him or away.

He shook off the mood, warning himself to tread carefully with her, and himself. "If you came," he said lightly, "I could introduce you to your hero. Enough of my lasagna and you'd have your shoes at cost."

Relieved, she tucked her arm through his again. "You tempt me to start saving for the airfare immediately. Oh, Carlo, look at this!" Delighted, she stopped in front of a window and pointed. In the midst of the ornate display was a three-foot Indian elephant done in high-gloss ceramic. Its blanket was a kaleidoscope of gilt and glitter and color. Opulent and regal, its head was lifted, its trunk curled high. Juliet fell in love. "It's wonderful, so unnecessarily ornate and totally useless."

He could see it easily in his living room along with the other ornate and useless pieces he'd collected over the years. But he'd never have imagined Juliet's taste running along the same path. "You surprise me again."

A bit embarrassed, she moved her shoulders. "Oh, I know it's awful, really, but I love things that don't belong anywhere at all."

"Then you must come to Rome and see my house." At her puzzled look, he laughed. "The last piece I acquired is an owl, this high." He demonstrated by holding out a palm. "It's caught a small, unfortunate rodent in its talons."

"Dreadful." With something close to a giggle, she kissed him. "I'm sure I'd love it."

"Perhaps you would at that," he murmured. "In any case, I believe the elephant should have a good home."

"You're going to buy it?" Thrilled, she clasped his hand as they went inside. The shop smelled of sandalwood and carried the tinkle of glass from wind chimes set swaying by a fan. She left him to make arrangements for shipping while she poked around, toying with long strings of brass bells, alabaster lions and ornamental tea services.

All in all, Juliet mused, it had been the easiest, most relaxing day she'd had in weeks, maybe longer. She'd remember it, that she promised herself, when she was alone again and life wound down to schedules and the next demand.

Turning, she looked at Carlo as he said something to make the clerk laugh. She hadn't thought there were men like him—secure, utterly masculine and yet sensitive to female moods and needs. Arrogant, he was certainly that, but generous as well. Passionate but gentle, vain but intelligent.

If she could have conjured up a man to fall in love with…oh no, Juliet warned herself with something like desperation. It wouldn't be Carlo Franconi. Couldn't be. He wasn't a man for one woman, and she wasn't a woman for any man. They both needed their freedom. To forget that would be to forget the plans she'd made and had been working toward for ten years. It was best to remember that Carlo was a ride on a carousel, and that the music only played so long.

She took a deep breath and waited for her own advice to sink in. It took longer than it should have. Determined, she smiled and walked to him. "Finished?"

"Our friend will be home soon, very soon after we are."

"Then we'll wish him bon voyage. We'd better start thinking airport ourselves."

With his arm around her shoulders, they walked out. "You'll give me our Philadelphia schedule on the plane."

"You're going to be a smash," she told him. "Though you might want to try my brewer's yeast before it's done."

* * *

"I can't believe it." At eight o'clock, Juliet dropped down into a chair outside customer service. Behind her, the conveyor belt of baggage was stopped. "The luggage went to Atlanta."

"Not so hard to believe," Carlo returned. He'd lost his luggage more times than he cared to remember. He gave his leather case a pat. His spatulas were safe. "So, when do we expect our underwear?"

"Maybe by ten tomorrow morning." Disgusted, Juliet looked down at the jeans and T-shirt she'd worn on the flight. She carried her toiletries and a few odds and ends in her shoulder bag, but nothing remotely resembling a business suit. No matter, she decided. She'd be in the background. Then she took a look at Carlo.

He wore a short-sleeved sweatshirt with the word *Sorbonne* dashed across it, jeans white at the stress points and a pair of sneakers that weren't nearly as new as hers. How the hell, she wondered, was he supposed to go on the air at 8:00 a.m. dressed like that?

"Carlo, we've got to get you some clothes."

"I have clothes," he reminded her, "in my bags."

"You're on *Hello, Philadelphia* in the morning at eight. From there we go directly to breakfast with reporters from the *Herald* and the *Inquirer*. At ten, when our bags may or may not be back, you're on *Midmorning Report*. After that—"

"You've already given me the schedule, my love. What's wrong with this?"

When he gestured toward what he wore, Juliet stood up. "Don't be cute, Carlo. We're heading for the closest department store."

"Department store?" Carlo allowed himself to be pulled outside. "Franconi doesn't wear department store."

"This time you do. No time to be choosey. What's in Philadelphia?" she muttered as she hailed a cab. "Wannamaker's." Holding the door open for him, she checked her watch. "We might just make it."

They arrived a half hour before closing. Though he grumbled, Carlo let her drag him through the old, respected Philadelphia institution. Knowing time was against them, Juliet pushed through a rack of slacks. "What size?"

"Thirty-one, thirty-three," he told her with his brow lifted. "Do I choose my own clothes?"

"Try this." Juliet held out a pair of dun-colored pleated slacks.

"I prefer the buff," he began.

"This is better for the camera. Now shirts." Leaving him holding the hanger, she pounced on the next rack. "Size?"

"What do I know from American sizes?" he grumbled.

"This should be right." She chose an elegant shade of salmon in a thin silk that Carlo was forced to admit he'd have looked twice at himself. "Go put these on while I look at the jackets."

"It's like shopping with your mother," he said under his breath as he headed for the dressing rooms.

She found a belt, thin and supple with a fancy little buckle she knew he wouldn't object to. After rejecting a half-dozen jackets she came across one in linen with a casual, unstructured fit in a shade between cream and brown.

When Carlo stepped out, she thrust them at him, then stood back to take in the entire view. "It's good," she decided as he shrugged the jacket on. "Yes, it's really good. The color of the shirt keeps the rest from being drab and the jacket keeps it just casual enough without being careless."

"The day Franconi wears clothes off the rack—"

"Only Franconi could wear clothes off the rack and make them look custom-tailored."

He stopped, meeting the laughter in her eyes. "You flatter me."

"Whatever it takes." Turning him around, she gave him a quick push toward the dressing room. "Strip it off, Franconi. I'll get you some shorts."

The look he sent her was cool, with very little patience. "There's a limit, Juliet."

"Don't worry about a thing," she said breezily. "The publisher'll pick up the tab. Make it fast. We've got just enough time to buy your shoes."

She signed the last receipt five minutes after the PA system announced closing. "You're set." Before he could do so himself, she bundled up his packages. "Now, if we can just get a cab to the hotel, we're in business."

"I wear your American shoes in protest."

"I don't blame you," she said sincerely. "Emergency measures, *caro*."

Foolishly, he was moved by the endearment. She'd never lowered her guard enough to use one before. Because of it, Carlo decided to be generous and forgive her for cracking the whip. "My mother would admire you."

"Oh?" Distracted, Juliet stood at the curb and held out her hand for a cab. "Why?"

"She's the only one who's ever poked and prodded

me through a store and picked out my clothes. She hasn't done so in twenty years."

"All publicists are mothers," she told him and switched to her other arm. "We have to be."

He leaned closer and caught her earlobe between his teeth. "I prefer you as a lover."

A cab screeched to a halt at the curb. Juliet wondered if it was that which had stolen her breath. Steadying, she bundled Carlo and the packages inside. "For the next few days, I'll be both."

It was nearly ten before they checked into the Cocharan House. Carlo managed to say nothing about the separate rooms, but he made up his mind on the spot that she'd spend no time in her own. They had three days and most of that time would be eaten up with business. Not a moment that was left would be wasted.

He said nothing as they got into the elevator ahead of the bellman. As they rode up, he hummed to himself as Juliet chatted idly. At the door of his suite, he took her arm.

"Put all the bags in here, please," he instructed the bellman. "Ms. Trent and I have some business to see to immediately. We'll sort them out." Before she could say a word, he took out several bills and tipped the bellman himself. She remained silent only until they were alone again.

"Carlo, just what do you think you're doing? I told you before—"

"That you wanted a room of your own. You still have it," he pointed out. "Two doors down. But you're staying here, with me. Now, we'll order a bottle of wine and relax." He took the packages she still carried out of her hands and tossed them on a long, low sofa. "Would you prefer something light?"

"I'd prefer not to be hustled around."

"So would I." With a grin, he glanced over at his new clothes. "Emergency measures."

Hopeless, she thought. He was hopeless. "Carlo, if you'd just try to understand—"

The knock on the door stopped her. She only muttered a little as he went to answer.

"Summer!" She heard the delight in his voice and turned to see him wrapped close with a stunning brunette.

"Carlo, I thought you'd be here an hour ago."

The voice was exotic, hints of France, a slight touch of British discipline. As she stepped away from Carlo, Juliet saw elegance, flash and style all at once. She saw Carlo take the exquisite face in his hands, as he had so often with hers, and kiss the woman long and hard.

"Ah, my little puff pastry, you're as beautiful as ever."

"And you, Franconi, are as full of..." Summer broke off as she spotted the woman standing in the center of the room. She smiled, and though it was friendly enough, she didn't attempt to hide the survey. "Hello. You must be Carlo's publicist."

"Juliet Trent." Odd, Carlo felt as nervous as a boy introducing his first heartthrob to his mother. "This is Summer Cocharan, the finest pastry chef on either side of the Atlantic."

Summer held out a hand as she crossed into the room. "He's flattering me because he hopes I'll fix him an éclair."

"A dozen of them," Carlo corrected. "Beautiful, isn't she, Summer?"

While Juliet struggled for the proper thing to say,

Summer smiled again. She'd heard something in Carlo's voice she'd never expected to. "Yes, she is. Horrid to work with, isn't he, Juliet?"

Juliet felt the laugh come easily. "Yes, he is."

"But never dull." Angling her head, she gave Carlo a quick, intimate look. Yes, there was something here other than business. About time, too. "By the way, Carlo, I should thank you for sending young Steven to me."

Interested, Carlo set down his leather case. "He's working out, then?"

"Wonderfully."

"The young boy who wanted to be a chef," Juliet murmured and found herself incredibly moved. He hadn't forgotten.

"Yes, did you meet him? He's very dedicated," Summer went on when Juliet nodded. "I think your idea of sending him to Paris for training will pay off. He's going to be excellent."

"Good." Satisfied, Carlo patted her hand. "I'll speak with his mother and make the arrangements."

Brows knit, Juliet stared at him. "You're going to send him to Paris?"

"It's the only place to study cordon bleu properly." Carlo gave a shrug as though the matter were everyday. "Then, when he's fully trained, I'll simply steal him away from Summer for my own restaurant."

"Perhaps you will." Summer smiled. "Then again, perhaps you won't."

He was going to pay for the education and training of a boy he'd met only once, Juliet thought, baffled. What sort of a man was it who could fuss for twenty minutes over the knot of his tie and give with such total generosity to a stranger? How foolish she'd been to think, even for a minute, that she really knew him.

"It's very kind of you, Carlo," she murmured after a moment.

He gave her an odd look, then shrugged it off. "Dues are meant to be paid, Juliet. I was young once and had only a mother to provide for me. Speaking of mothers," he went on smoothly, changing the topic. "How is Monique?"

"Gloriously happy still," Summer told him, and smiled thinking of her mother. "Keil was obviously the man she'd been looking for." With a laugh, she turned back to Juliet. "I'm sorry, Carlo and I go back a long way."

"Don't be. Carlo tells me you and he were students together."

"A hundred years ago, in Paris."

"Now Summer's married her big American. Where's Blake, *cara?* Does he trust you with me?"

"Not for long." Blake came through the open doorway, still elegant after a twelve-hour day. He was taller than Carlo, broader, but Juliet thought she recognized a similarity. Power, both sexual and intellectual.

"This is Juliet Trent," Summer began. "She's keeping Carlo in line on his American tour."

"Not an easy job." A waiter rolled in a bucket of champagne and glasses. Blake dismissed him with a nod. "Summer tells me your schedule in Philadelphia's very tight."

"She holds the whip," Carlo told him with a gesture toward Juliet. But when his hand came down, it brushed her shoulder in a gesture of casual and unmistakable intimacy.

"I thought I might run over to the studio in the

morning and watch your demonstration." Summer accepted the glass of champagne from her husband. "It's been a long time since I've seen you cook."

"Good." Carlo relaxed with the first sip of frosty wine. "Perhaps I'll have time to give your kitchen an inspection. Summer came here to remodel and expand Blake's kitchen, then stayed on because she'd grown attached to it."

"Quite right." Summer sent her husband an amused look. "In fact, I've grown so attached I've decided to expand again."

"Yes?" Interested, Carlo lifted his brow. "Another Cocharan House?"

"Another Cocharan," Summer corrected.

It took him a moment, but Juliet saw the moment the words had sunk in. Emotion she'd always expected from him, and it was there now, in his eyes as he set down his glass. "You're having a child."

"In the winter." Summer smiled and stretched out her hand. "I haven't figured out how I'm going to reach the stove for Christmas dinner."

He took her hand and kissed it, then kissed her cheeks, one by one. "We've come a long way, *cara mia.*"

"A very long way."

"Do you remember the merry-go-round?"

She remembered well her desperate flight to Rome to flee from Blake and her feelings. "You told me I was afraid to grab the brass ring, and so you made me try. I won't forget it."

He murmured something in Italian that made Summer's eyes fill. "And I've always loved you. Now make a toast or something before I disgrace myself."

"A toast." Carlo picked up his glass and slipped his free arm around Juliet. "To the carousel that doesn't end."

Juliet lifted her glass and, sipping, let the champagne wash away the ache.

Cooking before the camera was something Summer understood well. She spent several hours a year doing just that while handling the management of the kitchen in the Philadelphia Cocharan House, satisfying her own select clients with a few trips a year if the price and the occasion were important enough, and, most important of all, learning to enjoy her marriage.

Though she'd often cooked with Carlo, in the kitchen of a palace, in the less expensive area of the flat she still kept in Paris and dozens of other places, she never tired of watching him in action. While she was said to create with the intensity of a brain surgeon, Carlo had the flair of an artist. She'd always admired his expansiveness, his ease of manner, and especially his theatrics.

When he'd put the finishing touches on the pasta dish he'd named, not immodestly, after himself, she applauded with the rest of the audience. But she'd hitched a ride to the studio with him and Juliet for more reason than to feed an old friend's ego. If Summer knew anyone in the world as well as she did herself, it was Carlo. She'd often thought, in many ways, they'd risen from the same dough.

"*Bravo,* Franconi." As the crew began to serve his dish to the audience, Summer went up to give him a formal kiss on the cheek.

"Yes." He kissed her back. "I was magnificent."

"Where's Juliet?"

"On the phone." Carlo rolled his eyes to the ceiling. "*Dio,* that woman spends more time on the phone than a new bride spends in bed."

Summer checked her watch. She'd noted Carlo's schedule herself. "I don't imagine she'll be long. I know you're having a late breakfast at the hotel with reporters."

"You promised to make crêpes," he reminded her, thinking unapologetically of his own pleasure.

"So I did. In return, do you think you could find a small, quiet room for the two of us?"

He grinned and wiggled his brows. "My love, when Franconi can't oblige a lady with a quiet room, the world stops."

"My thoughts exactly." She hooked her arm through his and let him lead her down a corridor and into what turned out to be a storage room with an overhead light. "You've never lacked class, *caro.*"

"So." He made himself comfortable on a stack of boxes. "Since I know you don't want my body, superb as it is, what's on your mind?"

"You, of course, *cher.*"

"Of course."

"I love you, Carlo."

Her abrupt seriousness made him smile and take her hands. "And I you, always."

"You remember, not so long ago when you came through Philadelphia on tour for another book?"

"You were wondering how to take the job redoing the American's kitchen when you were attracted to him and determined not to be."

"In love with him and determined not to be," she corrected. "You gave me some good advice here, and when I visited you in Rome. I want to return the favor."

"Advice?"

"Grab the brass ring, Carlo, and hold on to it."

"Summer—"

"Who knows you better?" she interrupted.

He moved his shoulders. "No one."

"I saw you were in love with her the moment I stepped into the room, the moment you said her name. We understand each other too well to pretend."

He sat a moment, saying nothing. He'd been skirting around the word, and its consequences, very carefully for days. "Juliet is special," he said slowly. "I've thought perhaps what I feel for her is different."

"Thought?"

He let out a small sound and gave up. "Known. But the kind of love we're speaking of leads to commitment, marriage, children."

Instinctively Summer touched a hand to her stomach. Carlo would understand that she still had small fears. She didn't have to speak of them. "Yes. You told me once, when I asked you why you'd never married, that no woman had made your heart tremble. Do you remember what you told me you'd do if you met her?"

"Run for a license and a priest." Rising, he slipped his hands into the pockets of the slacks Juliet had selected for him. "Easy words *before* the heart trembles. I don't want to lose her." Once said, he sighed. "It's never mattered before, but now it matters too much to make the wrong move. She's elusive, Summer. There are times I hold her and feel part of her pull away. I understand her independence, her ambition, and even admire them."

"I have Blake, but I still have my independence and my ambition."

"Yes." He smiled at her. "Do you know, she's so like you. Stubborn." When Summer lifted a brow, he grinned. "Hard in the head and so determined to be the best. Qualities I've always found strangely appealing in a beautiful woman."

"Merci, mon cher ami," Summer said dryly. "Then where's your problem?"

"You'd trust me."

She looked surprised, then moved her shoulders as though he'd said something foolish. "Of course."

"She can't—won't," Carlo corrected. "Juliet would find it easier to give me her body, even part of her heart than her trust. I need it, Summer, as much as I need what she's already given me."

Thoughtful, Summer leaned against a crate. "Does she love you?"

"I don't know." A difficult admission for a man who'd always thought he understood women so well. He smiled a little as he realized a man never fully understood the woman most important to him. With any other woman he'd have been confident he could guide and mold the emotions to his own preference. With Juliet, he was confident of nothing.

"There are times she seems very close and times she seems very detached. Until yesterday I hadn't fully begun to know my own mind."

"Which is?"

"I want her with me," he said simply. "When I'm an old man sitting by the fountains watching the young girls, I'll still want her with me."

Summer moved over to put her hands on his shoulders. "Frightening, isn't it?"

"Terrifying." Yet somehow, he thought, easier now

that he'd admitted it. "I'd always thought it would be easy. There'd be love, romance, marriage and children. How could I know the woman would be a stubborn American?"

Summer laughed and dropped her forehead to his. "No more than I could know the man would be a stubborn American. But he was right for me. Your Juliet is right for you."

"So." He kissed Summer's temple. "How do I convince her?"

Summer frowned a moment, thinking. With a quick smile, she walked over to a corner. Picking up a broom, she held it out to him. "Sweep her off her feet."

Juliet was close to panic when she spotted Carlo strolling down the corridor with Summer on his arm. They might've been taking in the afternoon sun on the Left Bank. The first wave of relief evaporated into annoyance. "Carlo, I've turned this place upside down looking for you."

He merely smiled and touched a finger to her cheek. "You were on the phone."

Telling herself not to swear, she dragged a hand through her hair. "Next time you wander off, leave a trail of bread crumbs. In the meantime, I've got a very cranky cab driver waiting outside." As she pulled him along, she struggled to remember her manners. "Did you enjoy the show?" she asked Summer.

"I always enjoy watching Carlo cook. I only wish the two of you had more time in town. As it is, your timing's very wise."

"Yes?" Carlo pushed open the door and held it for both women.

"The French swine comes through next week."

The door shut with the punch of a bullet. "LaBare?"

Juliet turned back. She'd heard him snarl that name before. "Carlo—"

He held up a hand, silencing any interruption. "What does the Gallic slug do here?"

"Precisely what you've done," Summer returned. Tossing back her hair, she scowled at nothing. "He's written another book."

"Peasant. He's fit to cook only for hyenas."

"For rabid hyenas," Summer corrected.

Seeing that both of her charges were firing up, Juliet took an arm of each. "I think we can talk in the cab."

"He will not speak to you," Carlo announced, ignoring Juliet. "I will dice him into very small pieces."

Though she relished the image, Summer shook her head. "Don't worry. I can handle him. Besides, Blake finds it amusing.'

Carlo made a sound like a snake. Juliet felt her nerves fraying. "Americans. Perhaps I'll come back to Philadelphia and murder him."

Trying her best, Juliet nudged him toward the cab. "Come now, Carlo, you know you don't want to murder Blake."

"LaBare," he corrected with something close to an explosion.

"Who is LaBare?" Juliet demanded in exasperation.

"Swine," Carlo answered.

"Pig," Summer confirmed. "But I have plans of my own for him. He's going to stay at the Cocharan House." Summer spread her hands and examined her nails. "I'm going to prepare his meals personally."

With a laugh, Carlo lifted her from the ground and

kissed her. "Revenge, my love, is sweeter than even your meringue." Satisfied, he set her down again. "We were students with this slug," Carlo explained to Juliet. "His crimes are too numerous to mention." With a snap, Carlo adjusted his jacket. "I refuse to be on the same continent as he."

Running out of patience, Juliet glanced at the scowling cab driver. "You won't be," she reminded him. "You'll be back in Italy when he's here."

Carlo brightened and nodded. "You're right. Summer, you'll call me and tell me how he fell on his face?"

"Naturally."

"Then it's settled." His mood altered completely, he smiled and picked up the conversation as it ended before the mention of the Frenchman's name. "Next time we come to Philadelphia," Carlo promised. "You and I will make a meal for Blake and Juliet. My veal, your bombe. You haven't sinned, Juliet, until you've tasted Summer's bombe."

There wouldn't be a next time, Juliet knew, but she managed to smile. "I'll look forward to it."

Carlo paused as Juliet opened the door of the cab. "But tonight, we leave for New York."

Summer smiled as she stepped inside. "Don't forget to pack your broom."

Juliet started to climb into the front seat. "Broom?"

Carlo took Summer's hand in his and smiled. "An old French expression."

Chapter 12

New York hadn't changed. Perhaps it was hotter than when Juliet had left it, but the traffic still pushed, the people still rushed and the noise still rang. As she stood at her window at the Harley, she absorbed it.

No, New York hadn't changed, but she had.

Three weeks before, she'd looked out her office window at not so different a view. Her primary thought then had been the tour, to make a success of it. For herself, she admitted. She'd wanted the splash.

She realized she'd gotten it. At that moment, Carlo was in his suite, giving an interview to a reporter for the *Times*. She'd made a half-dozen excuses why she didn't have time to sit in on it. He'd accepted her usual list of phone calls and details, but the truth had been, she'd needed to be alone.

Later, there'd be another reporter and a photographer from one of the top magazines on the stands. They had network coverage of his demonstration at Bloomingdale's. *The Italian Way* had just climbed to number five on the bestsellers list. Her boss was ready to canonize her.

Juliet tried to remember when she'd ever been more miserable.

Time was running out. The next evening, Carlo would board a plane and she'd take the short cab ride back to her apartment. While she unpacked, he'd be thousands of miles above the Atlantic. She'd be thinking of him while he flirted with a flight attendant or a pretty seat companion. That was his way; she'd always known it.

It wasn't possible to bask in success, to begin plans on her next assignment when she couldn't see beyond the next twenty-four hours.

Wasn't this exactly what she'd always promised herself wouldn't happen? Hadn't she always picked her way carefully through life so that she could keep everything in perfect focus? She'd made a career for herself from the ground up, and everything she had, she'd earned. She'd never considered it ungenerous not to share it, but simply practical. After all, Juliet had what she considered the perfect example before her of what happened when you let go the reins long enough to let someone else pick them up.

Her mother had blindly handed over control and had never guided her own life again. Her promising career in nursing had dwindled down to doctoring the scraped knees of her children. She'd sacrificed hunks of herself for a man who'd cared for her but could never be faithful. How close had she come to doing precisely the same thing?

If she was still certain of anything, Juliet was certain she couldn't live that way. Exist, she thought, but not live.

So whether she wanted to or not, whether she thought she could or not, she had to think beyond the next twenty-four hours. Picking up her pad, she went to the phone. There were always calls to be made.

Before she could push the first button, Carlo strolled in. "I took your key," he said before she could ask. "So I wouldn't disturb you if you were napping. But I should've known." He nodded toward the phone, then dropped into a chair. He looked so pleased with himself she had to smile.

"How'd the interview go?"

"Perfectly." With a sigh, Carlo stretched out his legs. "The reporter had prepared my ravioli only last night. He thinks, correctly, that I'm a genius."

She checked her watch. "Very good. You've another reporter on the way. If you can convince him you're a genius—"

"He has only to be perceptive."

She grinned, then on impulse rose and went to kneel in front of him. "Don't change, Carlo."

Leaning down, he caught her face in his hands. "What I am now, I'll be tomorrow."

Tomorrow he'd be gone. But she wouldn't think of it. Juliet kissed him quickly then made herself draw away. "Is that what you're wearing?"

Carlo glanced down at his casual linen shirt and trim black jeans. "Of course it's what I'm wearing. If I wasn't wearing this, I'd be wearing something else."

"Hmm." She studied him, trying to judge him with a camera's eye. "Actually, I think it might be just right for this article. Something informal and relaxed for a magazine that's generally starched collars and ties. It should be a unique angle."

"*Grazie,*" he said dryly as he rose. "Now when do we talk about something other than reporters?"

"After you've earned it."

"You're a hard woman, Juliet."

"Solid steel." But she couldn't resist putting her arms around him and proving otherwise. "After you've finished being a hit across the hall, we'll head down to Bloomingdale's."

He nudged her closer, until their bodies fit. "And then?"

"Then you have drinks with your editor."

He ran the tip of his tongue down her neck. "Then?"

"Then you have the evening free."

"A late supper in my suite." Their lips met, clung, then parted.

"It could be arranged."

"Champagne?"

"You're the star. Whatever you want."

"You?"

She pressed her cheek against his. Tonight, this last night, there'd be no restriction. "Me."

It was ten before they walked down the hall to his suite again. Juliet had long since lost the urge to eat, but her enthusiasm in the evening hadn't waned.

"Carlo, it never ceases to amaze me how you perform. If you'd chosen show business, you'd have a wall full of Oscars."

"Timing, *innamorata.* It all has to do with timing."

"You had them eating your pasta out of your hand."

"I found it difficult," he confessed and stopped at the door to take her into his arms. "When I could think of nothing but coming back here tonight with you."

"Then you do deserve an Oscar. Every woman in the audience was certain you were thinking only of her."

"I did receive two interesting offers."

Her brow lifted. "Oh, really?"

Hopeful, he nuzzled her chin. "Are you jealous?"

She linked her fingers behind his neck. "I'm here and they're not."

"Such arrogance. I believe I still have one of the phone numbers in my pocket."

"Reach for it, Franconi, and I'll break your wrist."

He grinned at her. He liked the flare of aggression in a woman with skin the texture of rose petals. "Perhaps I'll just get my key then."

"A better idea." Amused, Juliet stood back as he opened the door. She stepped inside and stared.

The room was filled with roses. Hundreds of them in every color she'd ever imagined flowed out of baskets, tangled out of vases, spilled out of bowls. The room smelled like an English garden on a summer afternoon.

"Carlo, where did you get all these?"

"I ordered them."

She stopped as she leaned over to sniff at a bud. "Ordered them, for yourself?"

He plucked the bud out of its vase and handed it to her. "For you."

Overwhelmed, she stared around the room. "For me?"

"You should always have flowers." He kissed her wrist. "Roses suit Juliet best."

A single rose, a hundred roses, there was no in between with Carlo. Again, he moved her unbearably. "I don't know what to say."

"You like them."

"Like them? Yes, of course, I love them, but—"

"Then you have to say nothing. You promised to share a late supper and champagne." Taking her hand, he led her across the room to the table already set by the wide uncurtained window. A magnum of champagne was chilling in a silver bucket, white tapers were waiting to be lit. Carlo lifted a cover to show delicately broiled lobster tails. It was, Juliet thought, the most beautiful spot in the world.

"How did you manage to have all this here, waiting?"

"I told room service to have it here at ten." He pulled out her chair. "I, too, can keep a schedule, my love." When he'd seated her, Carlo lit the candles, then dimmed the lights so that the silver glinted. At another touch, music flowed out toward her.

Juliet ran her fingertip down the slim white column of a candle then looked at him when he joined her. He drew the cork on the champagne. As it frothed to the lip, he filled two glasses.

He'd make their last night special, she thought. It was so like him. Sweet, generous, romantic. When they parted ways, they'd each have something memorable to take with them. No regrets, Juliet thought again and smiled at him.

"Thank you."

"To happiness, Juliet. Yours and mine."

She touched her glass to his, watching him as she sipped. "You know, some women might suspect a seduction when they're dined with champagne and candlelight."

"Yes. Do you?"

She laughed and sipped again. "I'm counting on it."

God, she excited him, just watching her laugh, hearing her speak. He wondered if such a thing would mellow and settle after years of being together. How would it feel, he wondered, to wake comfortably every morning beside the woman you loved?

Sometimes, he thought, you would come together at dawn with mutual need and sleepy passion. Other times you would simply lie together, secure in the night's warmth. He'd always considered marriage sacred, almost mysterious. Now he thought it would be an adventure—one he intended to share with no one but Juliet.

"This is wonderful." Juliet let the buttery lobster dissolve on her tongue. "I've been completely spoiled."

Carlo filled her glass again. "Spoiled. How?"

"This champagne's a far cry from the little Reisling I splurge on from time to time. And the food." She took another bite of lobster and closed her eyes. "In three weeks my entire attitude toward food has changed. I'm going to end up fat and penniless supporting my habit."

"So, you've learned to relax and enjoy. Is it so bad?"

"If I continue to relax and enjoy I'm going to have to learn how to cook."

"I said I'd teach you."

"I managed the linguini," she reminded him as she drew out the last bite.

"One lesson only. It takes many years to learn properly."

"Then I guess I'll have to make do with the little boxes that say complete meal inside."

"Sacrilege, *caro,* now that your palate is educated." He touched her fingers across the table. "Juliet, I still want to teach you."

She felt her pulse skid, and though she concentrated, she couldn't level it. She tried to smile. "You'll have to write another cookbook. Next time you tour, you can show me how to make spaghetti." Ramble, she told herself. When you rambled, you couldn't think. "If you write one book a year, I should be able to handle it. When you come around this time next year, I could manage the next lesson. By then, maybe I'll have my own firm and you can hire me. After three bestsellers, you should think about a personal publicist."

"A personal publicist?" His fingers tightened on hers then released. "Perhaps you're right." He reached in his pocket and drew out an envelope. "I have something for you."

Juliet recognized the airline folder and took it with a frown. "Is there trouble on your return flight? I thought I'd..." She trailed off when she saw her own name on a departing flight for Rome.

"Come with me, Juliet." He waited until her gaze lifted to his. "Come home with me."

More time, she thought as she gripped the ticket. He was offering her more time. And more pain. It was time she accepted there'd be pain. She waited until she was certain she could control her voice, and her words. "I can't, Carlo. We both knew the tour would end."

"The tour, yes. But not us." He'd thought he'd feel confident, assured, even cheerful. He hadn't counted on desperation. "I want you with me, Juliet."

Very carefully, she set the ticket aside. It hurt, she discovered, to take her hand from it. "It's impossible."

"Nothing's impossible. We belong with each other."

She had to deflect the words, somehow. She had to pretend they didn't run deep inside her and swell until her heart was ready to burst. "Carlo, we both have obligations, and they're thousands of miles apart. On Monday, we'll both be back at work."

"That isn't something that must be," he corrected. "It's you and I who must be. If you need a few days to tidy your business here in New York, we'll wait. Next week, the week after, we fly to Rome."

"Tidy my business?" She rose and found her knees were shaking. "Do you hear what you're saying?"

He did, and didn't know what had happened to the words he'd planned. Demands were coming from him where he'd wanted to show her need and emotion. He was stumbling over himself where he'd always been surefooted. Even now, cursing himself, he couldn't find solid ground.

"I'm saying I want you with me." He stood and grabbed her arms. The candlelight flickered over two confused faces. "Schedules and plans mean nothing, don't you see? I love you."

She went stiff and cold, as though he'd slapped her. A hundred aches, a multitude of needs moved through her, and with them the knowledge that he'd said those words too many times to count to women he couldn't even remember.

"You won't use that on me, Carlo." Her voice wasn't strong, but he saw fury in her eyes. "I've stayed with you until now because you never insulted me with that."

"Insult?" Astonished, then enraged, he shook her. "Insult you by loving you?"

"By using a phrase that comes much too easily to a man like you and doesn't mean any more than the breath it takes to say it."

His fingers loosened slowly until he'd dropped her arms. "After this, after what we've had together, you'd throw yesterdays at me? You didn't come to me untouched, Juliet."

"We both know there's a difference. I hadn't made my success as a lover a career." She knew it was a filthy thing to say but thought only of defense. "I told you before how I felt about love, Carlo. I won't have it churning up my life and pulling me away from every goal I've ever set. You—you hand me a ticket and say come to Rome, then expect me to run off with you for a fling, leaving my work and my life behind until we've had our fill."

His eyes frosted. "I have knowledge of flings, Juliet, of where they begin and where they end. I was asking you to be my wife."

Stunned, she took a step back, again as if he'd struck her. His wife? She felt panic bubble hot in her throat. "No." It came out in a whisper, terrified. Juliet ran to the door and across the hall without looking back.

It took her three days before she'd gathered enough strength to go back to her office. It hadn't been difficult to convince her supervisor she was ill and needed a replacement for the last day of Carlo's tour. As it was, the first thing he told her when she returned to the office days later was that she belonged in bed.

She knew how she looked—pale, hollow-eyed. But she was determined to do as she'd once promised herself. Pick up the pieces and go on. She'd never do it huddled in her apartment staring at the walls.

"Deb, I want to start cleaning up the schedule for Lia Barrister's tour in August."

"You look like hell."

Juliet glanced up from her desk, already cluttered with schedules to be photocopied. "Thanks."

"If you want my advice, you'll move your vacation by a few weeks and get out of town. You need some sun, Juliet."

"I need a list of approved hotels in Albuquerque for the Barrister tour."

With a shrug, Deb gave up. "You'll have them. In the meantime, look over these clippings that just came in on Franconi." Looking up, she noted that Juliet had knocked her container of paper clips on the floor. "Coordination's the first thing to go."

"Let's have the clippings."

"Well, there's one I'm not sure how to deal with." Deb slipped a clipping out of the folder and frowned at it. "It's not one of ours, actually, but some French chef who's just starting a tour."

"LaBare?"

Impressed, Deb looked up. "Yeah. How'd you know?"

"Just a sick feeling."

"Anyway, Franconi's name was brought up in the interview because the reporter had done a feature on him. This LaBare made some—well, unpleasant comments."

Taking the clipping, Juliet read what her assistant had highlighted. "Cooking for peasants by a peasant," she read in a mumble. "Oil, starch and no substance…" There was more, but Juliet just lifted a brow. She hoped Summer's plan of revenge went perfectly. "We're better off ignoring this," she decided, and dropped the clipping in the trash. "If we passed it on to Carlo, he might challenge LaBare to a duel."

"Skewers at ten paces?"

Juliet merely sent her a cool look. "What else have you got?"

"There might be a problem with the Dallas feature," she said as she gave Juliet a folder. "The reporter got carried away and listed ten of the recipes straight out of the book."

Juliet's head flew back. "Did you say ten?"

"Count 'em. I imagine Franconi's going to blow when he sees them."

Juliet flipped through the clippings until she came to it. The feature was enthusiastic and flattering. The timid Ms. Tribly had used the angle of preparing an entire meal from antipasto to dessert. Carlo's recipes from *The Italian Way* were quoted verbatim. "What was she thinking of?" Juliet muttered. "She could've used one or two without making a ripple. But this…"

"Think Franconi's going to kick up a storm?"

"I think our Ms. Tribly's lucky she's a few thousand miles away. You'd better get me legal. If he wants to sue, we'll be better off having all the facts."

After nearly two hours on the phone, Juliet felt almost normal. If there was a hollowness, she told herself it was a skipped lunch—and breakfast. If she tended to miss whole phrases that were recited to her, she told herself it was hard to keep up with legalese.

They could sue, or put Ms. Tribly's neck in a sling, both of which would create a miserable mess when she had two other authors scheduled for Dallas that summer.

Carlo would have to be told, she reflected as she hung up. It wouldn't be possible, or at least ethical, to crumple up the clipping and pretend it didn't exist as she had with the one from LaBare. The problem was whether to let legal inform him, pass it off through his editor or bite the bullet and write him herself.

It wouldn't hurt to write him, she told herself as she toyed with her pen. She'd made her decision, said her piece and stepped off the carousel. They were both adults, both professionals. Dictating his name on a letter couldn't cause her any pain.

Thinking his name caused her pain.

Swearing, Juliet rose and paced to the window. He hadn't meant it. As she had consistently for days, Juliet went over and over their last evening together.

It was all romance to him. Just flowers and candlelight. He could get carried away with the moment and not suffer any consequences. I love you—such a simple phrase. Careless and calculating. He hadn't meant it the way it had to be meant.

Marriage? It was absurd. He'd slipped and slid his way out of marriage all of his adult life. He'd known exactly how she'd felt about it. That's why he'd said it, Juliet decided. He'd known it was safe and she'd never agree. She couldn't even think about marriage for years. There was her firm to think of. Her goals, her obligations.

Why couldn't she forget the way he'd made her laugh, the way he'd made her burn? Memories, sensations didn't fade even a little with the days that had passed. Somehow they gained in intensity, haunted her. Taunted her. Sometimes—too often—she'd remember just the way he'd looked as he'd taken her face in his hand.

She touched the little heart of gold and diamonds she hadn't been able to make herself put away. More time, she told herself. She just needed more time. Perhaps she'd have legal contact him after all.

"Juliet?"

Turning from the window, Juliet saw her assistant at the door. "Yes?"

"I rang you twice."

"I'm sorry."

"There's a delivery for you. Do you want them to bring it in here?"

An odd question, Juliet thought and returned to her desk. "Of course."

Deb opened the door wider. "In here."

A uniformed man wheeled a dolly into the room. Confused, Juliet stared at the wooden crate nearly as big as her desk. "Where do you want this, miss?"

"Ah—there. There's fine."

With an expert move, he drew the dolly free. "Just sign here." He held out a clipboard as Juliet continued to stare at the crate. "Have a nice day."

"Oh—yes, thank you." She was still staring at it when Deb came back in with a small crowbar.

"What'd you order?"

"Nothing."

"Come on, open it." Impatient, Deb handed her the crowbar. "I'm dying."

"I can't think what it might be." Slipping the crowbar under the lid, Juliet began to pry. "Unless my mother sent on my grandmother's china like she's been threatening for the last couple of years."

"This is big enough to hold a set for an army."

"Probably all packing," Juliet muttered as she put her back into it. When the lid came off, she began to push at the heaps of Styrofoam.

"Does your grandmother's china have a trunk?"

"A what?"

"A trunk." Unable to wait, Deb shoved through the styrofoam herself. "Good God, Juliet, it looks like an elephant."

Juliet saw the first foolish glitter and stopped thinking. "Help me get it out."

Between the two of them, they managed to lift the big, bulky piece of ceramic out of the crate and onto her desk. "That's the most ridiculous thing I've ever seen," Deb said when she caught her breath. "It's ugly, ostentatious and ridiculous."

"Yes," Juliet murmured, "I know."

"What kind of madman would send you an elephant?"

"Only one kind," Juliet said to herself and ran her hand lovingly down the trunk.

"My two-year-old could ride on it," Deb commented and spotted the card that had come out with the packing. "Here you are. Now you'll know who to press charges against."

She wouldn't take the card. Juliet told herself she wouldn't look at it. She'd simply pack the elephant back up and ship it away. No sensible woman became emotional about a useless piece of glass three feet high.

She took the card and ripped it open.

Don't forget.

She started to laugh. As the first tears fell, Deb stood beside her without a clue. "Juliet—are you all right?"

"No." She pressed her cheek against the elephant and kept laughing. "I've just lost my mind."

When she arrived in Rome, Juliet knew it was too late for sanity. She carried one bag which she'd packed in a frenzy. If it'd been lost en route, she wouldn't have been able to identify the contents. Practicality? She'd left it behind in New York. What happened next would determine whether she returned for it.

She gave the cab driver Carlo's address and settled

back for her first whirlwind ride through Rome. Perhaps she'd see it all before she went home. Perhaps she was home. Decisions had to be made, but she hoped she wouldn't make them alone.

She saw the fountains Carlo had spoken of. They rose and fell, never ending and full of dreams. On impulse she made the driver stop and wait while she dashed over to one she couldn't even name. With a wish, she flung in a coin. She watched it hit and fall to join thousands of other wishes. Some came true, she told herself. That gave her hope.

When the driver barreled up to the curb and jerked to a halt she began to fumble with bills. He took pity on her and counted out the fare himself. Because she was young and in love, he added only a moderate tip.

Not daring to let herself stop her forward progress, Juliet ran up to the door and knocked. The dozens of things she wanted to say, had planned to say, jumbled in her mind until she knew she'd never be able to guarantee what would come out first. But when the door opened, she was ready.

The woman was lovely, dark, curvy and young. Juliet felt the impetus slip away from her as she stared. So soon, was all she could think. He already had another woman in his home. For a moment, she thought only to turn and walk away as quickly as she could. Then her shoulders straightened and she met the other woman's eyes straight on.

"I've come to see Carlo."

The other woman hesitated only a moment, then smiled beautifully. "You're English."

Juliet inclined her head. She hadn't come so far, risked so much to turn tail and run. "American."

"Come in. I'm Angelina Tuchina."

"Juliet Trent."

The moment she offered her hand, it was gripped. "Ah, yes, Carlo spoke of you."

Juliet nearly laughed. "How like him."

"But he never said you would visit. Come this way. We're just having some tea. I missed him when he was in America, you see, so I've kept him home from the restaurant today to catch up."

It amazed her that she could find it amusing. It ran through her mind that Angelina, and many others, were going to be disappointed from now on. The only woman who was going to catch up with Carlo was herself.

When she stepped into the salon, amusement became surprise. Carlo sat in a high-backed satin chair, having an intense conversation with another female. This one sat on his lap and was no more than five.

"Carlo, you have company."

He glanced up, and the smile he'd used to charm the child on his lap vanished. So did every coherent thought in his mind. "Juliet."

"Here, let me take this." Angelina slipped Juliet's bag from her hand while she gave Carlo a speculative look. She'd never seen him dazed by a woman before. "Rosa, come say good morning to Signorina Trent. Rosa is my daughter."

Rosa slipped off Carlo's lap and, staring all the way, came to Juliet. "Good morning, Signorina Trent." Pleased with her English, she turned to her mother with a spate of Italian.

With a laugh, Angelina picked her up. "She says you have green eyes like the princess Carlo told her of. Carlo, aren't you going to ask Miss Trent to sit down?"

With a sigh, Angelina indicated a chair. "Please, be comfortable. You must forgive my brother, Miss Trent. Sometimes he loses himself in the stories he tells Rosa."

Brother? Juliet looked at Angelina and saw Carlo's warm, dark eyes. Over the quick elation, she wondered how many different ways you could feel like a fool.

"We must be on our way." Angelina walked over to kiss her still silent brother's cheek. As she did, she was already planning to drop by her mother's shop and relate the story of the American who'd made Carlo lose his voice. "I hope we meet again while you're in Rome, Miss Trent."

"Thank you." Juliet took her hand and met the smile, and all its implications, with an acknowledging nod. "I'm sure we will."

"We'll let ourselves out, Carlo. *Ciao.*"

He was still silent as Juliet began to wander around the room, stopping here to admire this, there to study that. Art of every culture was represented at its most opulent. It should've been overwhelming, museumlike. Instead it was friendly and lighthearted, just a bit vain and utterly suited to him.

"You told me I'd like your home," she said at length. "I do."

He managed to rise but not to go to her. He'd left part of himself back in New York, but he still had his pride. "You said you wouldn't come."

She moved one shoulder and decided it was best not to throw herself at his feet as she'd intended. "You know women, Franconi. They change their minds. You know me." She turned then and managed to face him. "I like to keep business in order."

"Business?"

Grateful she'd had the foresight, Juliet reached in her purse and drew out the Dallas clipping. "This is something you'll want to look over."

When she came no farther, he was forced to go over and take it from her. Her scent was there, as always. It reminded him of too much, too quickly. His voice was flat and brisk as he looked at her. "You came to Rome to bring me a piece of paper?"

"Perhaps you'd better look at it before we discuss anything else."

He kept his eyes on hers for a long, silent minute before he lowered them to the paper. "So, more clippings," he began, then stopped. "What's this?"

She felt her lips curve at the change of tone. "What I thought you'd want to see."

She thought she understood the names he called the unfortunate Ms. Tribly though they were all in fast, furious Italian. He said something about a knife in the back, balled the clipping up and heaved it in a scrubbed hearth across the room. Juliet noted, as a matter of interest, that his aim was perfect.

"What does she try to do?" he demanded.

"Her job. A bit too enthusiastically."

"Job? Is it her job to quote all my recipes? And wrong!" Incensed, he whirled around the room. "She has too much oregano in my veal."

"I'm afraid I didn't notice," Juliet murmured. "In any case, you're entitled to retribution."

"Retribution." He relished the word and made a circle of his hands. "I'll fly to Dallas and squeeze my retribution from her skinny throat."

"There's that, of course." Juliet pressed her lips together to keep the laughter in. How had she ever thought she'd convince herself she could do without him? "Or a legal suit. I've given it a lot of thought, however, and feel the best way might be a very firm letter of disapproval."

"Disapproval?" He spun back to her. "Do you simply disapprove of murder in your country? She overspiced my veal."

After clearing her throat, Juliet managed to soothe. "I understand, Carlo, but I believe it was an honest mistake all around. If you remember the interview, she was nervous and insecure. It appears to be you just overwhelmed her."

Muttering something nasty, he stuck his hands in his pockets. "I'll write to her myself."

"That might be just the right touch—if you let legal take a look at it first."

He scowled, then looked at her carefully from head to foot. She hadn't changed. He'd known she wouldn't. Somehow that fact comforted and distressed all at once. "You came to Rome to discuss lawsuits with me?"

She took her life in her hands. "I came to Rome," she said simply.

He wasn't sure he could go any closer without having to touch, and touching, take. The hurt hadn't faded. He wasn't certain it ever would. "Why?"

"Because I didn't forget." Since he wouldn't come to her, she went to him. "Because I couldn't forget, Carlo. You asked me to come and I was afraid. You said you loved me and I didn't believe you."

He curled his fingers to keep them still. "And now?"

"Now I'm still afraid. The moment I was alone, the moment I knew you'd gone, I had to stop pretending.

Even when I had to admit I was in love with you, I thought I could work around it. I thought I had to work around it."

"Juliet." He reached for her, but she stepped back quickly.

"I think you'd better wait until I finish. Please," she added when he only came closer.

"Then finish quickly. I need to hold you."

"Oh, Carlo." She closed her eyes and tried to hang on. "I want to believe I can have a life with you without giving up what I am, what I need to be. But you see, I love you so much I'm afraid I'd give up everything the moment you asked me."

"*Dio,* what a woman!" Because she wasn't certain if it was a compliment or an insult, Juliet remained silent as he took a quick turn around the room. "Don't you understand that I love you too much to ask? If you weren't who you are, I wouldn't be in love with you? If I love Juliet Trent, why would I want to change her into that Juliet Trent?"

"I don't know, Carlo. I just—"

"I was clumsy." When she lifted her hands, he caught them in his to quiet her. "The night I asked you to marry me, I was clumsy. There were things I wanted to say, ways I'd wanted to say them, but it was too important. What comes easily with every woman becomes impossible with the only woman."

"I didn't think you'd meant—"

"No." Before she could resist, he'd brought her hands to his lips. "I've thought back on what I said to you. You thought I was asking you to give up your job, your home, and come to Rome to live with me. I was asking less, and much more. I should have said—Juliet, you've become my life and without you, I'm only half of what I was. Share with me."

"Carlo, I want to." She shook her head and went into his arms. "I want to. I can start over, learn Italian. There must be a publisher in Rome who could use an American."

Drawing her back by the shoulders, he stared at her. "What are you talking about, starting over? You're starting your own firm. You told me."

"It doesn't matter. I can—"

"No." He took her more firmly. "It matters a great deal, to both of us. So you'll have your own firm one day in New York. Who knows better than I how successful you'll be? I can have a wife to brag about as much as I brag about myself."

"But you have your restaurant here."

"Yes. I think perhaps you'd consider having a branch of your public relations company in Rome. Learning Italian is an excellent decision. I'll teach you myself. Who better?"

"I don't understand you. How can we share our lives if I'm in New York and you're in Rome?"

He kissed her because it had been much too long. He drew her closer because she was willing to give something he'd never have asked. "I never told you my plans that night. I've been considering opening another restaurant. Franconi's in Rome is, of course, the best. Incomparable."

She found his mouth again, dismissing any plans but that. "Of course."

"So, a Franconi's in New York would be twice the best."

"In New York?" She tilted her head back just

enough to see him. "You're thinking of opening a restaurant in New York?"

"My lawyers are already looking for the right property. You see, Juliet, you wouldn't have escaped me for long."

"You were coming back."

"Once I could be certain I wouldn't murder you. We have our roots in two countries. We have our business in two countries. We'll have our lives in two countries."

Things were so simple. She'd forgotten his unending generosity. Now she remembered everything they'd already shared, thought of everything they'd yet to share. She blinked at tears. "I should've trusted you."

"And yourself, Juliet." He framed her face until his fingers slid into her hair. "*Dio*, how I've missed you. I want my ring on your finger, and yours on mine."

"How long does it take to get a license in Rome?"

Grinning, he whirled her in his arms. "I have connections. By the end of the week you'll be—what is it?—stuck with me."

"And you with me. Take me to bed, Carlo." She pressed against him, knowing she had to get still closer. "I want you to show me again what the rest of our lives will be like."

"I've thought of you, here, with me." He pressed his lips against her temple as he remembered the words she'd hurled at him on that last night. "Juliet." Troubled, he drew away, touching only her hands. "You know what I am, how I've lived. I can't take it back, nor would I if I could. There've been other women in my bed."

"Carlo." Her fingers tightened on his. "Perhaps I said foolish things once, but I'm not a fool. I don't want to be the first woman in your bed. I want to be the last. The only."

"Juliet, *mi amore,* from this moment there is only you."

She pressed his hand to her cheek. "Can you hear it?"

"What?"

"The carousel." Smiling, she held out her arms. "It's never stopped."

* * * * *